Multiple Family Housing

David Mackay

Multiple Family Housing

From Aggregation to Integration

Architectural Book Publishing Co. New York

Published 1977 in the U.S.A. by
Architectural Book Publishing Co., Inc.,
New York
All rights reserved
including the right of reproduction in whole
or in part in any form
Published simultaneously in Canada
by Saunders of Toronto, Ltd., Don Mills,
Ontario

© Copyright 1977 by Verlag Gerd Hatje,
Stuttgart

ISBN 8038–0164–5
Printed in Germany

Contents

Inhalt

Prologue

The purpose of this book is to provide a working manual for all those who are concerned about the quality of our domestic built environment. The major part of the book is an album containing examples of community housing from many parts of the world. Their selection was based upon two factors, the first being to cast the net throughout the world in the belief that today the problems of community housing are common to every culture, the second being to select the examples in such a way that we could learn something different from each one.

The critical method of presentation of the projects is based upon the number of dwellings, since the problems involved change considerably according to the size of the project. The cultural, social, and economic variables, though obviously important, are so erratic that the attempt to classify the projects according to any principle based upon these considerations was abandoned. However, when comparing one building with another, these factors must be borne in mind. Public and private housing involve the architect in completely different relationships with the client. Economic, cultural and climatic considerations also involve different approaches, but it is the thesis of this book that the typological problems of community housing and the creative possibilities of architecture are common to all.

What is meant by the term community housing? Negatively, it excludes homes that have been conceived as isolated units without any positive relationship with other homes. The individual mansion or house is obviously excluded, but so is the mere assembly of individual houses into one building. Just piling homes on top of each other does not convert them into community architecture. Certain relationships have to be added: between the dwellings themselves, between groups of dwellings and between these and the larger urban context. Community housing and its environment has been, and remains, one of the principal concerns of twentieth-century architecture.

Vorwort

Das vorliegende Buch soll all denen ein Arbeitsinstrument an die Hand geben, denen eine qualitative Verbesserung unserer Wohnumwelt am Herzen liegt.

Den Hauptteil des Buches nehmen Bildbeispiele von Mehrfamilienhäusern aus vielen Teilen der Welt ein. Die Auswahl der Beispiele erfolgte unter zwei Gesichtspunkten: Zum einen sollte der Rahmen weltweit gespannt werden, da die Probleme des Wohnungsbaus heute in allen Kulturen gleich geartet sind; zum anderen sollen wir aus jedem beschriebenen Projekt etwas Besonderes lernen können.

Für die Reihenfolge der Bauten war der zahlenmäßige Anteil der Wohnungen ausschlaggebend, denn die entstehenden Probleme hängen in starkem Maß von der Größe des Projekts ab. Kulturelle, soziale und ökonomische Einflüsse spielen selbstverständlich eine Rolle, sind jedoch so schwer zu fassen, daß sie nicht als Klassifikationsmittel dienen konnten. Beim Vergleich der Gebäude müssen sie freilich berücksichtigt werden. Öffentliche und private Bauvorhaben stellen den Architekten in völlig verschiedene Beziehungen zum Auftraggeber. Wirtschaftliche, kulturelle und klimatische Erwägungen führen ebenfalls zu unterschiedlichen Ansätzen. Wir gehen aber von der Voraussetzung aus, daß die typologischen Probleme des kollektiven Wohnens und die schöpferischen Möglichkeiten der Architektur bei allen Projekten in gleicher Weise gegeben sind.

Was ist mit dem Terminus ›kollektives Wohnen‹ gemeint? In negativer Abgrenzung schließt er jene Wohnungen aus, die als isolierte Einheiten ohne positive Beziehung zu anderen konzipiert wurden, also das Einfamilienhaus, ebenso aber die bloße Ansammlung von Einzelwohnungen in einem Gebäude, denn wenn man lediglich eine Wohnung auf die andere stellt, entsteht noch längst keine kollektive Architektur. Es müssen vielmehr bestimmte Beziehungen hinzutreten: Beziehungen zwischen den Wohnungen selbst, zwischen Gruppen von Wohnungen sowie zwischen diesen und dem größeren städtischen Kontext.

Bauten für kollektives Wohnen waren – und bleiben – eine der Hauptaufgaben der Architektur des zwanzigsten Jahrhunderts.

Introduction

The notion of a community spirit, as opposed to feudal paternalism, first developed in the public mind during the French Revolution. Its long drawn out education, forged upon the bitter fires of industrial and agricultural social strife and national wars, only came to maturity after the Second World War.

The English Romantics nurtured the idea in its infancy, protesting against the miseries of the Industrial Revolution. William Blake, Samuel Taylor Coleridge, and William Wordsworth awakened the consciousness to the evils of the industrial exploitation of the working class, first with hopes of more immediate results from the French Revolution, then, disenchanted, with praise of rural life and Utopia. There was some response from industrialists like Josiah Wedgwood for his workers in his factory Etruria at Hanley, but until the popular pamphlets of William Cobbett the workers never identified themselves as a class. To combat rising unemployment (due to rising population, itself the result of better sanitation, nourishment, and decreasing mortality, the ending of the Napoleonic wars, rapid mechanization of production and enclosure of public land), Robert Owen, a self-made man who began work as a shop assistant at the age of 10, started his own weaving business at 19 and at 28 in 1799 bought the spinning-mills of New Lanark on the upper Clyde in Scotland. It was he who had the original idea of creating an ideal physical environment for small communities of between 500 and 1500 but preferably 1000 (ill. 1). These 'villages of unity' were to be almost self-contained economic units needing $1/2 - 1 1/2$ acres of land per person. Each village was to be formed by a large square with one long dwelling (up to 4 stories high) down each side, three of the dwellings for families with children up to 3 years old, and the fourth for all the other children; in the centre of the square would be three public buildings, one for the communal restaurant and kitchens, and the other two for infant and primary schools with libraries and meeting-rooms for adults, as well as a lecture-

Einführung

Gemeinschaftsgeist im heutigen Sinn und im Gegensatz zum Paternalismus des Feudalismus bildete sich im Gefolge der Französischen Revolution. Langsam wuchs er im läuternden Feuer der sozialen Kämpfe in Industrie und Landwirtschaft und der Nationalkriege, gelangte aber erst nach dem Zweiten Weltkrieg zur Reife.

Seine Anfänge finden sich bei den englischen Romantikern, die gegen das Elend der industriellen Revolution aufbegehrten. William Blake, Samuel Taylor Coleridge und William Wordsworth weckten das Bewußtsein für die industrielle Ausbeutung der Arbeiterklasse, zuerst mit der Hoffnung auf sofortige Ergebnisse aus der Französischen Revolution, dann mit enttäuschter Verherrlichung des ländlichen Lebens und Utopias. Eine gewisse Reaktion zeigte sich bei Industriellen wie Josiah Wedgwood, der in seiner Fabrik Etruria in Hanley einiges für seine Arbeiter unternahm. Vor der Verbreitung der Aufrufe von William Cobbett fühlten sich die Arbeiter jedoch nicht als eigene Klasse. Mit seiner politischen Agitation für radikale Reformen wurde Cobbett zum einflußreichsten Führer der Arbeiterschaft.

In Anbetracht der steigenden Arbeitslosigkeit infolge des Bevölkerungszuwachses, der auf besseren sanitären Verhältnissen, besserer Ernährung, Abnahme der Sterblichkeit, Beendigung der Napoleonischen Kriege, rascher Mechanisierung der Produktion und Flurbereinigung beruhte, trug der Selfmademan Robert Owen, der mit 10 Jahren als Botenjunge zu arbeiten begann, mit 19 Jahren eine eigene Wirkerei gründete und mit 28 Jahren – im Jahr 1799 – die Spinnerei in New Lanark am oberen Clyde in Schottland erwarb, den neuen Gedanken vor, eine ideale Umwelt für kleine Gemeinschaften von 500 bis 1500, vorzugsweise aber 1000 Personen zu schaffen (Abb. 1). Diese Dörfer waren als fast autarke wirtschaftliche Einheiten mit einem Landbedarf von 0,2 bis 1 ha pro Person konzipiert. Ihr Aufbau unterlag einer strengen geo-

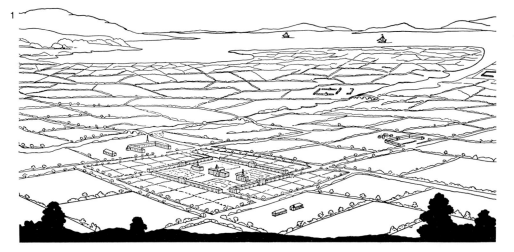

1. Robert Owen. Village of Unity. 1817.

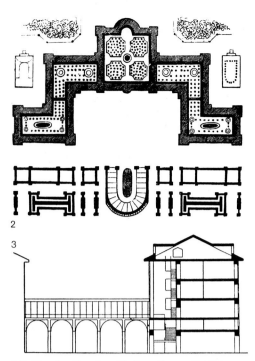

2

3

2,3. Charles Fourier. Phalanstère. 1829/30.

4,5. Jean Godin. Familistère. 1859-77.

4

5

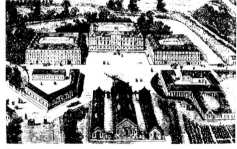

room and chapel. The dwellings themselves were to be arranged so that the sitting-rooms overlooked the community square and the bedrooms, on the quiet side, the gardens and country.

Although one must admit that Owen's Village of Unity has the air of a military barracks, complete with parade ground and messrooms, its break with street planning and its substitution of communal dwellings for individual urban rooms while maintaining the privacy of the perimeter gardens shows the clear understanding that Robert Owen had of human nature. His far-reaching ideas provoked interest and criticism, but he was unable to translate them into practice and eventually followed other Utopians to the land of hope: the New World of North America. He bought the village of Harmony from the German religious reformer Georg Rapp in Indiana in 1825, renaming it New Harmony; two years later, however, it failed for economic and human reasons. Owen returned to England, which after the shock of the Peterloo massacre in Manchester in 1819 had repealed the combination laws so that workers' associations could be more or less freely formed. Co-operative movements grew in strength, as did trade unions, but they were mainly concerned with economic conditions rather than Owen's principal concern for a proper community environment.

Small harmonious societies that cast aside moral inhibitions and competition between individuals or classes but respect the rights of others formed the basis of the philosophical and political system which Charles Fourier first published in 1808 and developed over the years. He rejected the small individual house as being unsociable and proposed communal accommodation in order to concentrate services and human relationships. Apart from detailed regulations which would control development, anticipating our building regulations today, his main contribution to community housing was his idea that a single building (like Le Corbusier's 'Unité') should be the basic city unit. This unit, or Phalanstère (ills. 2,3), was to house between 1,500 and 1,600 people in a 'regular' building signifying its rational order, articulated to reduce its scale. Pedestrian traffic was to be set on a first-floor street within a three-storey-high glass gallery which was common to all the individual apartments. Between buildings the street-galleries were to be connected by glass-enclosed bridges. The ground floor was left free for vehicles, community rooms and accommodation for the elderly and children. Fourier's formal model, however advanced his revolutionary thoughts, was limited by its adherence to the neo-classical palace of the aristocracy. His idea went no further forward than that the workers too should live in palaces.

In the United States, Fourier's ideas spread and more than forty communities were founded, the most famous being Brook Farms, West Roxbury, Massachusetts. In France his ideas

failed to take root until Jean Godin, who had an iron foundry at Guise, built a smaller modified version of the Phalanstère between 1859 and 1877, which he called the 'Familistère' (ills. 4,5). Instead of the street galleries the buildings consisted of dwellings built around a large glazed central court. The community services were accommodated in separate buildings. Up to the Second World War the buildings and the co-operative were still in use. The vision of a new world continued to inspire Utopian projects, such as Etienne Cabet's Icaria which precariously survived for 50 years, moving from Nauvoo, Illinois, to Corning, Iowa, with splinter groups in California. Many of the Utopians were religiously inspired, for example the Harmonists founded by Georg Rapp, or Amana, Bethel, Noyes, Bull, and of course the Mormons who founded Nauvoo in 1839 and Salt Lake City in 1847. Even more recently we find the kibbutz settlements in Israel which began at Degania in 1910 and now number over 200, housing some 80,000 people. But the most influential visionary of them all was Ebenezer Howard who, with his book *Tomorrow: a Peaceful Path to Real Reform,* first published in 1898 (re-issued in 1902 as *Garden Cities of Tomorrow),* rallied reformers to Arcadia with a proposal for a network of new towns housing 32,000 people each. Like most original thinkers who express themselves simply in diagrammatic form, Howard (ill. 6) was misinterpreted, with the result that many people now live happily in dormitory garden suburbs, safely independent of the formal responsibilities of architectural communities. The resulting destruction of the countryside and the strengthening of class divisions with the discrimination involved in speculative building and land values, may have improved the physical health of the individual, but the social, political and economic health of the community as a whole has undoubtedly suffered. This comfortable isolation has created indifference on the part of one half of the community for the problems of the other half.

Friedrich Engels, who in 1844 had described the condition of the English working class, and Karl Marx, whom Engels met in Paris the same year, rejected this social paternalism in favour of the participation of the working class itself in building its own future. They made clear their approach in the 'Communist Manifesto' of 1848. However, the right of the working class to determine its own environment still remains an unrealized vision. Meanwhile it was the paternal Utopian socialists, and other reformers, who began the actual experiments. The Reform Bill of 1832, championed by John Fielden to extend the franchise, the Factory Acts of 1833 and 1847, Edwin Chadwick's sanitary report 1842, followed by the Public Health Act 1848, and 1855 building regulations, reflected the growing awareness on the part of Disraeli's rich half of England that they had a 'duty' towards the poor half. The evangelical conscience was also awakened, as J. N. Tarn

metrischen Ordnung: Vier bis zu vier Stockwerke hohe Wohnhauszeilen (drei für Familien mit Kindern bis zu drei Jahren sowie für alleinstehende Erwachsene, die vierte für alle Kinder ab dem dritten Lebensjahr) sollten einen quadratischen Platz umschließen, auf dem sich drei öffentliche Gebäude erhoben hätten – eines für das Speiselokal und die Küchen der Gemeinschaft, die beiden anderen für Kindergarten, Primarschule, Lese- und Gemeinschaftsräume, Vortragssaal und Kirche. Die Wohnungen selbst waren so angelegt, daß die Wohnräume auf den Dorfplatz und die Schlafzimmer auf die Gärten und die Landschaft hinausgingen.

Owens ›Village of Unity‹ wirkt zwar fast wie eine Kaserne mit Paradeplatz und Messen, trotzdem zeugt die straßenlose Anlage, bei der der gemeinschaftliche Platz der Kommunikation dient und die am Außenrand angeordneten Gärten das Privatleben gewährleisten, von einem tiefgründigen Verständnis für das Wesen des Menschen.

Da Owen seine revolutionären Ideen, die sowohl Interesse als auch Kritik hervorriefen, nicht in die Praxis umsetzen konnte, folgte er schließlich anderen Utopisten ins Land der großen Hoffnungen, in die Neue Welt Nordamerikas. Im Jahr 1825 kaufte er dem deutschen Glaubensreformer Georg Rapp das Dorf Harmony in Indiana ab und nannte es New Harmony. Zwei Jahre später brach das Projekt wegen wirtschaftlicher und menschlicher Schwierigkeiten zusammen. Owen kehrte nach England zurück. Dort waren nach dem Schock des Peterloo-Massakers von 1819 in Manchester die Gesetze über Zusammenschlüsse und Verbände reformiert worden, so daß nun Arbeiterbünde mehr oder weniger frei gebildet werden konnten. Genossenschaftliche und gewerkschaftliche Bewegungen nahmen an Umfang zu, befaßten sich aber hauptsächlich mit wirtschaftlichen Fragen und kaum mit Owens Grundanliegen, einer für das Leben einer Gemeinschaft geeigneten Umwelt.

Kleine harmonische Gemeinschaften, die den Wettbewerb von einzelnen oder Klassen sowie auch jeglichen moralischen Zwang ablehnen und die Rechte des anderen anerkennen, lagen auch dem 1808 veröffentlichten und im Lauf der Jahre weiterentwickelten philosophischen und politischen System von Charles Fourier zugrunde. Das kleine Einfamilienhaus verwarf Fourier als unsozial. Dagegen verfocht er das Wohnen im Mehrfamilienhaus, um die Einrichtungen besser zu nutzen und menschlichen Kontakt zu fördern. Abgesehen von detaillierten baulichen Regelungen, mit denen er unsere heutigen Bauvorschriften vorwegnahm, lag sein wichtigster Beitrag zum kollektiven Wohnen in seiner Konzeption eines Großbauwerks ähnlich Le Corbusiers Unité als städtebaulicher Grundeinheit. Diese Einheit oder Phalanstère (Abb. 2, 3) sollte 1500 bis 1600 Menschen aufnehmen. In der Form war die Phalanstère

regelmäßig, um ihre rationale Ordnung zum Ausdruck zu bringen, aber unterteilt, um nicht durch ihre Größe zu erdrücken. Für den Fußgängerverkehr war eine Straße im ersten Geschoß vorgesehen, einbezogen in eine dreigeschossige Glasgalerie zur Erschließung der Wohnungen. Zwischen den Gebäuden sollten die Fußgängerstraßen durch verglaste Brücken verbunden werden. Das Erdgeschoß war Fahrzeugen, Gemeinschaftsräumen sowie Unterkünften für ältere Menschen und Kinder vorbehalten. Trotz seiner weitreichenden revolutionären Ideen im sozialen Bereich blieb Fourier im Formalen beim neoklassischen Adelspalast stehen. Er kam hier über die Forderung, daß auch die Arbeiter in Palästen wohnen sollten, nicht hinaus.

In den Vereinigten Staaten fanden Fouriers Gedanken schnell Verbreitung. Mehr als 40 Gemeinschaften wurden gegründet. Die berühmteste ist Brook Farms in West Roxbury, Massachusetts. In Frankreich faßten Fouriers Ideen erst Fuß, als Jean Godin, Eigentümer einer Eisengießerei in Guise, zwischen 1859 und 1877 eine kleinere, abgewandelte Version der Phalanstère baute, die er Familistère nannte (Abb. 4, 5). Statt der Glasgalerien findet man hier überdachte Höfe mit umlaufenden offenen Gängen und getrennte Gebäude für die Versorgungseinrichtungen. Die Genossenschaft bestand übrigens bis zum Zweiten Weltkrieg, auch wurden die Gebäude bis dahin in der alten Form genutzt.

Der Vision einer neuen Welt entsprangen auch weiterhin utopische Projekte wie etwa Etienne Cabets Icaria, das mit Mühe 50 Jahre überlebte, von Nauvoo, Illinois, nach Corning, Iowa, umsiedelte und Splittergruppen in Kalifornien gründete. Viele Utopisten waren religiös motiviert, zum Beispiel die von Georg Rapp begründete Gemeinschaft der Harmonisten, oder auch Amana, Bethel, Noyes, Bull und natürlich die Mormonen, die 1839 Nauvoo und 1847 Salt Lake City gründeten. Aus jüngerer Zeit seien die Kibbutz-Siedlungen in Israel genannt. Die erste entstand 1910 in Degania; heute sind es über 200 mit ungefähr 80 000 Menschen. Den größten Einfluß erzielte allerdings Ebenezer Howard, der mit seinem Buch *Tomorrow: a Peacefull Path to Real Reform*, das 1898 erstmals erschien und 1902 unter dem Titel *Garden Cities of Tomorrow* neu aufgelegt wurde, die Reformer um Arkadien scharte mit seinem Vorschlag eines ganzen Netzes neuer Städte, die jeweils 32 000 Menschen aufnehmen sollten. Wie die meisten eigenständigen Denker, die sich der Einfachheit halber in Diagrammform ausdrücken, wurde auch Howard (Abb. 6) vielfach falsch ausgelegt, und so leben heute viele Menschen glücklich in gartenreichen Schlafvorstädten, ohne sich für die Belange des Gemeinwesens verantwortlich zu fühlen. Die Folgen sind bekannt: Verwüstung der Landschaft, außerordentlich starke Segregation der verschiedenen Bevölkerungsschichten, exzessive Bau- und Grundstücksspekulation. Das mag zwar

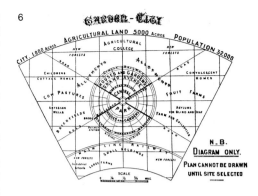

6. Ebenezer Howard. Garden City. 1898.
7,8. Henry Roberts. Model Houses for Families, Bloomsbury, London. 1850.
9. Henry Darbishire. Peabody building in Spitalfields. 1864.

6. Ebenezer Howard. Garden City. 1898.
7,8. Henry Roberts. Model Houses for Families, Bloomsbury, London. 1850.
9. Henry Darbishire. Peabody-Gebäude in Spitalfields. 1864.

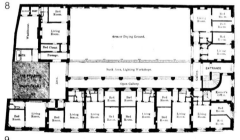

9

12

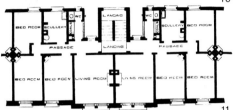

11

10,11. H. Macaulay. Competition entry for the Improved Industrial Dwellings Company. 1874.

12. Henry Darbishire. Columbia Square, Bethnal Green, London. 1859-62.

13. Saltaire, near Bradford. Founded in 1851.

14. Port Sunlight. Founded in 1887.

15. Bournville. Founded in 1895.

10,11. H. Macaulay. Wettbewerbsentwurf für die Improved Industrial Dwellings Company. 1874.

12. Henry Darbishire. Columbia Square, Bethnal Green, London. 1859-62.

13. Saltaire bei Bradford. Gegründet 1851.

14. Port Sunlight. Gegründet 1887.

15. Bournville. Gegründet 1895.

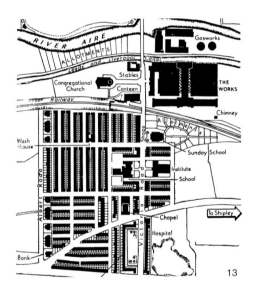

13

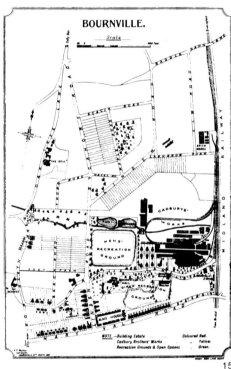

15

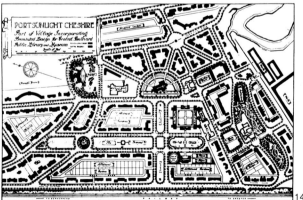

14

has pointed out in his book *Working-class Housing in 19th-century Britain,* which brought the architect Henry Roberts into national prominence under Lord Shaftesbury. Roberts designed several experimental communal houses, one of the most interesting being his Model Houses for families in Bloomsbury, London, in 1850, with its gallery access and through ventilation (ills. 7,8). Philanthropic organizations like the Peabody Trust, with its dull but well-managed buildings designed by Henry Darbishire (ill. 9), failed to meet the appalling housing conditions, mainly because of high rents and the relatively small amount of building work undertaken. Sidney Waterlow's Improved Industrial Dwellings Company tackled the city housing problem with efficiency (ills. 10,11), while Angela Burdett-Coutts, with Dickens' advice, her money, and Darbishire's gothic architecture, built Columbia Square, Bethnal Green (1859–62; ill. 12), four blocks around a communal court with community services and social rooms in the attic. Factory villages were also built, such as Saltaire near Bradford in 1851 (ill. 13), Port Sunlight in 1887 (ill. 14) and Bournville in 1895 (ill. 15). Apart from Liverpool, Frankfurt and Amsterdam, housing did not become a public problem until after the rude shock of the First World War.

Architects had hardly touched the problem of designing these buildings, except in works of criticism, such as those of Robert Kerr or Banister Fletcher, or as followers of the school of William Morris and Philip Webb, such as the L. C. C. Architects Department, until bourgeois clients allowed Victor Horta to apply his skill to the Hôtel Tassel (1893), Auguste Perret to 25a Rue Franklin (1902/03), Antoni Gaudí to the Casa Batlló (1905–07) and Casa Milá (1905–10).

These clients, of course, built for themselves or their likes, and were therefore isolated from the social problems of community housing. However, the importance of such bourgeois houses lies not only in their special architectural features and styling, but also in their historical role as the forerunners of a series of architectural models that were to replace the old aristocratic ones. In other words, the feudal cottage, the summer lodge, or neo-palace in the form of town terraces, were to be replaced by a new building type designed in scale and comfort to suit the needs of the bourgeoisie within the urban fabric.

Apart from the famous sinuous ironwork to the staircase hall, Horta's Hôtel Tassel (ill. 16) is notable for the free articulation and spatial sequence of the internal rooms, albeit symmetrical, which reflect a more informal life-style. The exposed metal structure contrasts with the English wall-paper patterns and thus indicates the new fashion towards progress and industry.

In contrast, Auguste Perret built his house in Rue Franklin (ills. 17,18) in reinforced concrete, assimilating the design to its rectangular framework with panel infill. The structure,

das Wohlbefinden einzelner nicht beeinträchtigt haben, schadete aber ohne Zweifel der sozialen, politischen und wirtschaftlichen Gesundheit der Gemeinschaft. Der Rückzug in die Privatheit führte zur Gleichgültigkeit der einen Hälfte der Gemeinschaft gegenüber den Problemen der anderen Hälfte.

Friedrich Engels, der 1844 die Zustände in der englischen Arbeiterschicht beschrieben hatte, und Karl Marx, mit dem er im gleichen Jahr in Paris zusammentraf, lehnten den gesellschaftlichen Paternalismus ab und kämpften für die Emanzipation der Arbeiterklasse zu einer mit Rechten ausgestatteten Schicht. Sie verdeutlichten ihren Ansatz 1848 mit dem ziemlich spontanen *Kommunistischen Manifest*. Das Recht der Arbeiterklasse, über die Gestalt ihrer Umwelt selbst zu bestimmen, blieb jedoch Vision. Es waren vielmehr die paternalistischen, utopistischen Sozialisten und andere Reformer, die hier zu experimentieren begannen.

Das Reformgesetz von 1832, das John Fielden zur Erweiterung der Bürgerrechte eingebracht hatte, die Fabrikgesetze von 1833 und 1847, Edwin Chadwicks Bericht von 1842 über die sanitären Verhältnisse und das darauffolgende Gesetz von 1848 über die öffentliche Gesundheitspflege sowie die Bauvorschriften von 1855 – sie alle sind Spiegelbild dessen, daß sich Disraelis reiche Hälfte der englischen Bevölkerung zunehmend ihrer ›Pflicht‹ gegenüber der armen Hälfte bewußt wurde. Auch das religiöse Gewissen wurde geweckt, wie J. N. Tarn in seinem Buch *Working-class Housing in 19th-century Britain* hervorhob; es rief unter Lord Shaftesbury den Architekten Henry Roberts auf den Plan. Roberts entwarf mehrere experimentelle Gemeinschaftsbauten, darunter auch die höchst interessanten Model Houses for Families mit Laubengangerschließung und Querlüftung in Bloomsbury/London aus dem Jahr 1850 (Abb. 7, 8). Philanthropische Zusammenschlüsse wie der Peabody Trust mit seinen reizlosen, aber gut verwalteten Gebäuden (Abb. 9), die von Henry Darbishire errichtet wurden, konnten die entsetzlichen Wohnverhältnisse nicht grundlegend ändern, da die Mieten zu hoch waren und das Bauvolumen relativ gering blieb. Sidney Waterlows Improved Industrial Dwellings Company machte sich mit Eifer an das städtische Wohnungsproblem (Abb. 10, 11), und Angela Burdett-Coutts baute mit Dickens' Ratschlägen, ihrem eigenen Geld und Darbishires gotischer Architektur Columbia Square in Bethnal Green (1859-62; Abb. 12), bestehend aus vier um einen gemeinschaftlichen Hof gescharten Blocks mit gemeinschaftlichen Versorgungseinrichtungen und Versammlungsräumen im Dachgeschoß. Auch Fabrikdörfer wurden gebaut, so Saltaire bei Bradford im Jahr 1851 (Abb. 13), Port Sunlight im Jahr 1887 (Abb. 14) und Bournville im Jahr 1895 (Abb. 15). Wenn man einmal von Liverpool und Amsterdam absieht, wurde das Wohnungselend jedoch erst nach den

16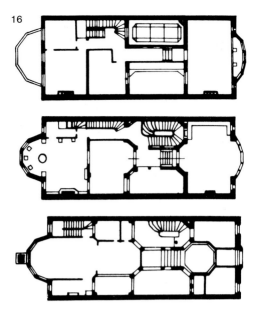

17

16. Victor Horta. Hôtel Tassel, Brussels. 1893.
17,18. Auguste Perret. House at 25a Rue Franklin, Paris. 1902/03.
19. Antoni Gaudí. Casa Batlló, Barcelona. 1905-07.
20,21. Antoni Gaudí. Casa Milá, Barcelona. 1905-10.

16. Victor Horta. Hôtel Tassel, Brüssel. 1893.
17,18. Auguste Perret. Haus in der Rue Franklin 25a, Paris. 1902/03.
19. Antoni Gaudí. Casa Batlló, Barcelona. 1905-07.
20,21. Antoni Gaudí. Casa Milá, Barcelona. 1905-10.

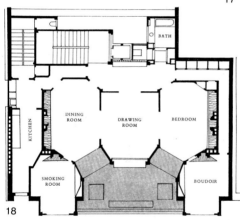
18

19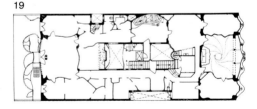

20

21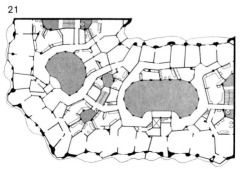

22

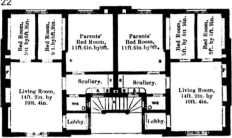

23

24

22,23. Henry Roberts. Model Houses for Four Families. 1851.
24. Edwin Lutyens. House at Munstead Wood near Godalming. 1896.
25,26. M.H. Baillie Scott. Terrace house. 1906.
27. Margarethenhöhe, Essen. Founded 1906.
28. Levittown, Pennsylvania. 1952-65.
29. Milton Keynes. Under construction. (Detail.)

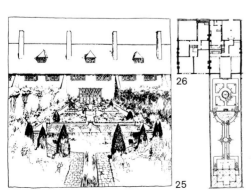

25

26

27

22,23. Henry Roberts. Model Houses for Four Families. 1851.
24. Edwin Lutyens. Haus in Munstead Wood bei Godalming. 1896.
25,26. M.H. Baillie Scott. Reihenhaus. 1906.
27. Margarethenhöhe, Essen. Gegründet 1906.
28. Levittown, Pennsylvania. 1952-65.
29. Milton Keynes. Im Bau. (Ausschnitt.)

28

29

however, was not exposed but sheathed in glazed tiles. The internal planning was freely articulated around a concave terrace again reflecting the needs of bourgeois social life. Servant spaces remained segregated and tortuous, unlike Frank Lloyd Wright's plans for a freer society in the northern United States, as in the Willitts house (Highland Park, Illinois; 1902), for example.

Antoni Gaudí flexed both muscle and mind in his remodelling of the Casa Batlló (ill. 19), making the most of the colourful spatial sequence of the staircase and lift up through the various floors. He brought the public face of street architecture into the communal patio of the vertical access. This he did with even more success in his steel-framed Casa Milá (ills. 20,21), where vehicles were absorbed into the bosom of the house with circular ramps and connecting patios. Not only did he realize that the steel frame gave extraordinary possibilities for free planning, different on each floor, but he rejected the economic discipline of the steel frame itself so that many a column rests upon a beam and spans vary at will. He also, perhaps for the first time, separated the lifts from the staircase, which released the hierarchy of rooms from the straightjacket of concentrated accesses in multi-storey buildings. Each dwelling became almost as free as a house standing in its own grounds, with servant entrances on one side, and the main entrances on the other.

Architecture's involvement in housing was mainly concerned with the picturesque in Arcadia, either in flight from the town with Henry Roberts (ills. 22,23), Norman Shaw, C.F. A. Voysey and Philip Webb, or in an attempt to exploit the vast open countryside of North America with Frank Lloyd Wright and McKim, Mead and White. But the real popular masters were Edwin Lutyens, who laid the solid foundations of English suburban picturesque with Munstead Wood (1896; ill. 24), Deanery Garden and other projects, and Baillie Scott who published *Houses and Gardens* in 1906 which contained a terrace house designed in the same English domestic vernacular (ills. 25,26). Raymond Unwin's design for Hampstead Garden Suburb in 1908 for Henriette Barnett applied Howard's Garden City concept to reality (Unwin's Letchworth competition design was built later) with buildings designed by Lutyens. The German Hermann Muthesius spent the years 1896–1903 studying this peculiarly English phenomenon, as a result of which he published *Das englische Haus,* which no doubt influenced Krupp in building his Margarethenhöhe district in Essen (1906; ill. 27).

In a way the Garden City concept was a release from the burdens of community planning, since it encouraged the excuse of 'getting away from it all', which culminated in the Tudor-Walters report in 1918 and 'Peacehaven' fit for the heroes of the First World War and finally Levittown, Pennsylvania 1952–65 (ill. 28), and Milton Keynes new town now under con-

Zerstörungen des Ersten Weltkrieges ein dringendes öffentliches Anliegen.

Die Architekten hatten sich noch kaum mit Fragen des Wohnungsbaus befaßt – Ausnahmen waren Kritiker wie Robert Kerr oder Banister Fletcher und das der Schule von William Morris und Philip Webb verpflichtete Bauamt des London County Council –, da vergaben bürgerliche Bauherren schon ihre Aufträge: an Victor Horta für das Hôtel Tassel (1893), an Auguste Perret für das Gebäude 25a in der Rue Franklin (1902/03), an Antoni Gaudí für die Casa Batlló (1905-07) und die Casa Milá (1905-10).

Diese Auftraggeber bauten natürlich für sich oder ihresgleichen; ihre Bauten waren daher esoterische Beispiele fernab vom gesellschaftlichen Problem des kollektiven Wohnens. Ihre Bedeutung liegt aber nicht nur in ihren besonderen architektonischen Qualitäten, sondern auch in ihrer Eigenschaft als Vorläufer einer Reihe neuer Bautypen, die an die Stelle der alten, von der Aristokratie bestimmten, traten. Mit anderen Worten: das Landhaus, die Sommervilla, der Neo-Palast in Form des luxuriösen Stadthauses wichen einem neuen Bautyp, der in Größe und Komfort auf die Bedürfnisse des städtischen Bürgertums zugeschnitten war.

Abgesehen von der berühmten Eisenornamentik im Treppenhaus ist Hortas Hôtel Tassel (Abb. 16) wegen der freien Gestaltung und Raumfolge der allerdings noch symmetrischen Innenräume, die eine größere Ungezwungenheit der Lebensweise widerspiegeln, bemerkenswert. Die überall zur Schau gestellten Metallkonstruktionen sind im übrigen – ebenso wie die an englische Tapeten erinnernden Muster auf den Wänden – ein Zeugnis der neuen Einstellung gegenüber Fortschritt und Industrie.

Auguste Perret verwendete bei seinem Haus in der Rue Franklin (Abb. 17, 18) ein Skelett aus Eisenbeton und füllte dieses mit Paneelen aus. Das Skelett selbst erhielt eine Verkleidung aus glasierten Ziegeln. Die Innenräume sind frei um eine konkave Terrasse angeordnet, wiederum Ausdruck der gesellschaftlichen Notwendigkeiten des bürgerlichen Lebens. Die Dienstbotenräume blieben abgesondert und unzulänglich – anders als bei Frank Lloyd Wright, dessen Architektur die freiere Gesellschaft der amerikanischen Nordstaaten spiegelt, so etwa beim Haus Willitts in Highland Park, Illinois (1902).

Bei seinem Umbau der Casa Batlló (Abb. 19) veränderte Antoni Gaudí Aussehen und Geist des Hauses vollkommen. Er holte aus dem eigenartigen Verlauf des Treppenhauses und des Aufzugs durch die verschiedenen Stockwerke das Beste heraus, indem er die Straßenfassade und damit den öffentlichen Raum in den zentralen Patio hineinzog. Noch größeren Erfolg erzielte er mit diesem Kunstgriff bei der Casa Milá (Abb. 20, 21); hier werden mit runden Rampen und Verbindungshöfen sogar Fahrzeuge ins Innere des Hauses geleitet.

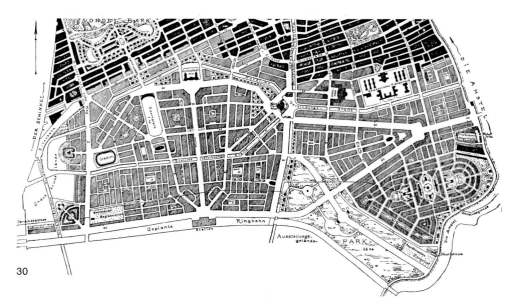

30

30. Hendrik Petrus Berlage. Amsterdam-Zuid. Plan of 1915.
31. Michel de Klerk. Henriette Ronner-Plein flats, Amsterdam-Zuid. 1920/21.
32. Michel de Klerk. Amstellaan flats, Amsterdam-Zuid. 1920-22.

30. Hendrik Petrus Berlage. Amsterdam-Zuid. Plan von 1915.
31. Michel de Klerk. Wohnbauten Henriette Ronner-Plein, Amsterdam-Zuid. 1920/21.
32. Michel de Klerk. Wohnbauten Amstellaan, Amsterdam-Zuid. 1920-22.

31

32

33

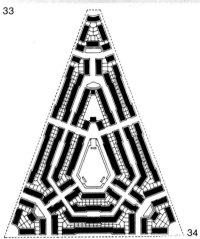

34

33.J.J.P. Oud. Stepped and staggered houses for Scheveningen. 1917.
34. J.J.P. Oud. Oud-Mathenesse district, Rotterdam. 1922.
35,36. J.J.P. Oud. Terrace houses, Hook of Holland. 1924.
37,38. J.J.P. Oud. Kiefhoek district, Rotterdam. 1925.

33. J.J.P. Oud. Terrassenhäuser für Scheveningen. 1917.
34. J.J.P. Oud. Wohnquartier Oud-Mathenesse, Rotterdam. 1922.
35,36. J.J.P. Oud. Reihenhäuser in Hoek van Holland. 1924.
37,38. J.J.P. Oud. Wohnquartier Kiefhoek, Rotterdam. 1925.

35

36

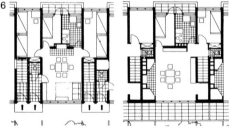

37

38

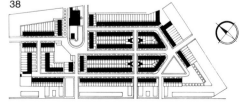

struction (ill. 29). Nevertheless, its picturesque human domesticity cannot be denied a part in the reality of that major architectural problem of solving mass housing for the individual as a member of the community. The solution must lie somewhere in between the suburban villa and the urban palace.

Hendrik Petrus Berlage's work must surely exemplify the very nature of architecture in community planning, particularly his scheme for Amsterdam-Zuid (ill. 30). He was commissioned by the city authorities to draw up a plan between two rivers which he did during the years 1902–07, amending it giving greater density before its final approval in 1915. His main concern was to continue the urban image of Amsterdam, incorporating the advantages of the Garden City not in the form and image of private property but with the use of public and semi-public parks and gardens. He used the simple geometric formula of city blocks 50 m wide by either 100 or 200 m long, with enclosed garden courts, to be treated as an architectural whole. The streets were wide enough to carry both vehicular and pedestrian traffic and to separate the different styles that would naturally occur throughout the time needed to build the district. The size of each block was adjusted to the size of the undertaking of a particular building co-operative, according to L. Benevolo in his *History of Modern Architecture*. The plan was formal, symmetrical and almost academic, but any rigidity in style was alleviated with a spicing of informalism introduced by the slight bending of the street system, which helped the plan reflect and adjust to the original twisting canal system of the seventeenth-century city. Berlage's design was so clear and practical that after the war Michel de Klerk (ills. 31, 32), Pieter Lodewigk Kramer, Hendrikus Theodorus Wijdeveld (flowers of the Amsterdam School) were able to remain faithful to the plan without sacrificing their own architecture. This is what we may term 'soft town-planning', just as we will later refer to 'soft architecture', quiet evolutionary building lacking the brilliance of the monumental.

Jacobus Johannes Pieter Oud adopted a position theoretically opposed to the Amsterdam School (the Wendingen Group) with the apparently more progressive De Stijl movement. This was immediately apparent in his project for stepped and staggered houses along the beach at Scheveningen (1917; ill. 33) which is broken up rather than unified. In his first attempts at town-planning Oud rather timidly followed Berlage's tradition, of which his plan for the triangular site 'Oud-Mathenesse' (1922; ill. 34) is the most typical in its symmetry and central enclosed public green. It was too near to the Garden City concept, with its single-storey cottages and private gardens, to be any advance upon Berlage. But Oud's twin-terrace houses at the Hook of Holland (1924; ills. 35, 36) are uncompromisingly modern, with rounded ends, cantilevered canopies, strip windows and walls rendered white; realism

Gaudí ging bis an die Grenzen der dem Stahl-
skelett innewohnenden außergewöhnlichen
Möglichkeiten freier Planung; ja, im Hinblick
auf die Wirtschaftlichkeit überschritt er diese
sogar, so daß manche Stütze auf einem Träger
ruht und die Spannweiten beliebig schwanken.
Er trennte auch –vielleicht erstmals – die Aufzüge vom Treppenhaus und befreite damit die
Raumdisposition von vielgeschossigen Bau-
werken aus der Zwangsjacke der konzentrier-
ten Zugänge. In der Casa Milá ist jede
Wohnung fast so frei wie ein Haus auf eigenem
Boden.

Die Rolle der Architektur im Wohnungsbau er-
schöpfte sich ansonsten größtenteils in der
arkadischen Pittoreske – bei Henry Roberts
(Abb. 22, 23), Norman Shaw, C.F.A. Voysey
oder Philip Webb als Stadtflucht, bei Frank
Lloyd Wright oder McKim, Mead and White
als Nutzung der weiten, freien Landschaft
Nordamerikas. Am bekanntesten und belieb-
testen wurden der mit Mun-
stead Wood (1896; Abb. 24), Deanery Garden
und anderen Arbeiten den festen Grundstein
zur englischen Vorortpittoreske legte, sowie
Baillie Scott, der in seinem 1906 erschienenen
Werk *Houses and Gardens* ein Reihenhaus im
gleichen, in England heimischen Stil beschrieb
(Abb. 25, 26). Raymond Unwin setzte mit
seinem Entwurf der Gartenvorstadt Hampstead (1908) für Henrietta Barnett die Gartenstadtkonzeption von Howard in die Wirklichkeit um (Unwins Wettbewerbsentwurf für
Letchworth wurde später gebaut); die Gebäude wurden von Edwin Lutyens entworfen.
Herman Muthesius weilte von 1896 bis 1903
eigens in England, um dieses landesspezifi-
sche Phänomen zu untersuchen; anschließend
veröffentlichte er das Werk *Das englische
Haus,* das zweifellos Krupp beim Bau der
Gartenvorstadt Margarethenhöhe in Essen
(1906; Abb. 27) anregte.

In gewisser Weise suchte die Gartenstadtkonzeption eine Entlastung von der Bürde der
Planung für die Gemeinschaft, ermutigte sie
doch zu der Ausflucht, ›allem entgehen zu
wollen‹, die im Tudor-Walters-Bericht von
1918 gipfelte und in ›Peacehaven‹, eingerich-
tet für die Helden des Ersten Weltkrieges,
sowie schließlich in Levittown, Pennsylvania
(1952-65; Abb. 28) und in der noch im Bau
befindlichen Stadt Milton Keynes (Abb. 29).
Dennoch darf ihrer pittoresken, menschlichen
Heimeligkeit eine Rolle in der Realität des
großen Bauproblems der Massenwohnung
für den einzelnen als Mitglied der Gemeinschaft nicht abgesprochen werden.
Hendrik Petrus Berlage lieferte mit seinem
Plan für Amsterdam-Zuid (Abb. 30) zweifellos
ein hervorragendes Beispiel für die Möglichkeiten der Architektur im Wohnungsbau. Der
Plan entstand zwischen 1902 und 1907 und
wurde durch eine Erhöhung der Dichte noch
weiter verbessert, bis er 1915 letztgültige
Billigung fand.
Da es Berlage darum ging, die Vorzüge der
Gartenstadt zum Tragen zu bringen, zugleich

39

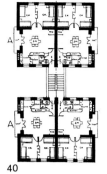
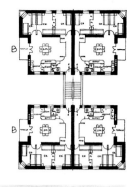
40

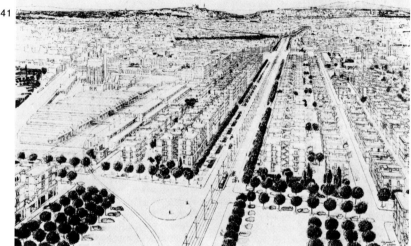
41

42

39. Tony Garnier. Cité Industrielle. 1901-04.
40, 41. Tony Garnier. Etats Unis district,
Lyons. 1920-35.
42. Antonio Sant'Elia. Staggered house. 1914.
43. Mario Chiattone. Block of flats. 1914.

39. Tony Garnier. Cité Industrielle. 1901-04.
40,41. Tony Garnier. Wohnquartier Etats Unis,
Lyon. 1920-35.
42. Antonio Sant'Elia. Terrassenhaus. 1914.
43. Mario Chiattone. Wohnblock. 1914.

43

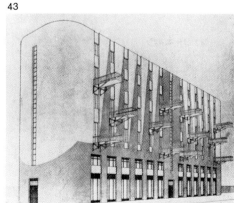

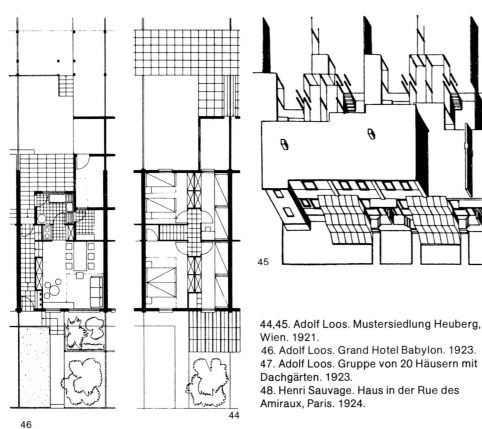

44,45. Adolf Loos. Mustersiedlung Heuberg, Wien. 1921.
46. Adolf Loos. Grand Hotel Babylon. 1923.
47. Adolf Loos. Gruppe von 20 Häusern mit Dachgärten. 1923.
48. Henri Sauvage. Haus in der Rue des Amiraux, Paris. 1924.

44,45. Adolf Loos. Heuberg district, Vienna. 1921.
46. Adolf Loos. Grand Hotel Babylon, 1923.
47. Adolf Loos. Group of 20 houses with roof gardens. 1923.
48. Henri Sauvage. House in Rue des Amiraux, Paris. 1924.

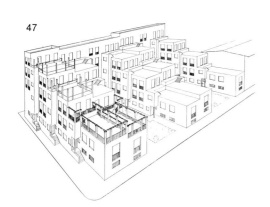

was introduced with brick dados and thresholds. The style imposed communal identity but at the same time was so vigorous that it set the buildings apart from their neighbours, a failing that Oud repeated in the Kiefhoek district in Rotterdam (1925; ills. 37,38). What is curious in the Hook of Holland terraced houses is the wide frontage given to each dwelling by the placing of one floor of dwellings upon another within a rather complicated structural system imposed by the entrance and staircases, which thus restricts the internal planning.

Tony Garnier was another anti-Garden City architect, well known for his plan of 1901–04 for a 'Cité Industrielle' (ill. 39), which was drawn with magisterial simplicity like Costa's Brasilia with its functions clearly separated. One quarter was actually built, the 'Etats Unis' district in Lyons between 1928 and 1935, based on Garnier's plan of 1920 (ills. 40,41). Originally the buildings were four or five stories high, with dwellings designed in groups of two or four per staircase, so that each city block contained a line of buildings with a lineal park for pedestrians in between, alternating with fast traffic. Unfortunately the economy of the plan put the bedrooms on the outer sides of the buildings, facing the road, with the living area on the inside overlooking the neighbours. Opposed to both the Garden City architecture for the individual and the soft architecture of Berlage and to some extent Garnier, were the designs of Antonio Sant'Elia (ill. 42) and Mario Chiattone (ill. 43) and the radical communal super-blocks of the Socialist administration in Vienna which decided in 1923 to build 25,000 dwellings, a target later raised to 60,000. Influenced by Berlage's city blocks for the Amsterdam Co-operatives the Vienna municipal authorities decided in favour of the super-block which fitted in administratively with their social-development plan. One architect the authorities did not call upon was Adolf Loos, whose architectural style was too daring for them, even though he had been municipal architect from 1920–22 and tackled the design of workers' housing with vigour and complete identification. For Loos the problem of the workers' house was pre-eminent amongst the problems of a new society completely identified with the purpose of modern architecture. One of his most prominent designs in the field of housing is the Heuberg estate (1921; ills. 44, 45) only part of which was built according to his intentions. The axonometric drawing suggests a system building, while the cascade of glass covering the winter garden reminds one of James Stirling's later buildings. His plans for the Hotel Babylon (1923; ill. 46) again used the stepped profile of his 'set-back' houses, but showed haste and lack of discipline, unlike his group of twenty houses on the Côte d'Azur (ill. 47) designed in the same year, where the roofs of each lower house become a succession of terraces and gardens. He was always anxious to recover this 'lost' space for chil-

jedoch das Amsterdamer Stadtbild weiterzuführen, ersetzte er das eigene Haus durch Wohnblocks und öffentliche sowie halböffentliche Parks und Gärten. Er bediente sich der einfachen geometrischen Formel von Blocks mit 50 m Breite und 100 oder 200 m Länge, die zusammen mit gärtnerisch gestalteten Innenhöfen als bauliches Ganzes anzusehen sind. Die Straßen sind breit genug, um sowohl Fahrzeug- als auch Fußgängerverkehr aufzunehmen; sie trennen zudem die verschiedenen Baustile, die sich, wie vorauszusehen war, während der langen Zeit, die zur Erbauung des ganzen Bezirks benötigt wurde, ergaben. Wie L. Benevolo in seinem Werk *Geschichte der Architektur des 19. und 20. Jahrhunderts* schildert, wurde die Größe der Blocks dem Umfang der den einzelnen Baugenossenschaften anvertrauten Bereiche entsprechend gewählt. Der Plan wirkt auf den ersten Blick starr, symmetrisch und akademisch, nur gemildert durch den Hauch von Zwanglosigkeit, der sich aus der leichten Krümmung des Straßensystems ergab. Diese beruhte darauf, daß das Layout an das aus dem 17. Jahrhundert stammende Kanalsystem angeglichen werden mußte. Es spricht für Berlages Entwurf, daß Michel De Klerk (Abb. 31, 32), Pieter Lodewik Kramer und Hendrikus Theodorus Wijdeveld, die Spitzen der Amsterdamer Schule, nach dem Krieg daran festhalten konnten, ohne ihre eigene Architektur aufzugeben. Parallel zur sogenannten wandlungsfähigen Architektur – einer zurückhaltenden, auf Evolution gerichteten Bauweise, die auf die Brillanz des Monumentalen verzichtet – können wir hier mit gutem Recht von wandlungsfähiger Stadtplanung sprechen.

Jacobus Johannes Pieter Oud nahm als Vertreter der zweifellos progressiveren De-Stijl-Bewegung eine Position ein, die theoretisch der Amsterdamer Schule (der Wendingen-Gruppe) entgegengesetzt ist. Dies zeigte sich sofort bei seinem Projekt einer Gruppe von abgetreppten und versetzten Häusern am Strand von Scheveningen (1917; Abb. 33), die ziemlich aufgelöst wirkt. Bei seinen ersten Versuchen in der Stadtplanung folgte Oud jedoch schüchtern der Tradition Berlages. Typisch dafür ist sein Plan für die dreieckige Anlage Oud-Mathenesse (1922; Abb. 34) mit ihrer Symmetrie und ihrem zentralen, umschlossenen öffentlichen Grünplatz. Diese Anlage kam mit ihren eingeschossigen Häusern und Privatgärten gefährlich nahe an die Gartenstadtkonzeption heran und war deshalb Berlage gegenüber kein Fortschritt. Ouds Reihenhäuser in Hoek van Holland (1924; Abb. 35, 36) sind kompromißlos modern mit ihren abgerundeten Ecken, dem vorkragenden Sonnenschutz, den schmalen, streifenartigen Fenstern und den weißen Wänden; eine Spur Tradition zeigt sich lediglich in dem Ziegelmauerwerk der kleinen Vorhöfe und der Brüstungen der dahinter liegenden Fenster. Dieser Stil war Ausdruck des Anspruchs auf soziale Gleichheit, doch zugleich war er so eindringlich, daß er die Bauten von den angrenzenden Häusern isolierte. Diesen Fehler machte Oud auch beim Kiefhoek-Bezirk in Rotterdam (1925; Abb. 37, 38). Auffallend an den Reihenhäusern in Hoek van Holland sind die breiten Fronten der geschoßweise übereinanderliegenden Wohnungen. Sie sind zurückzuführen auf die gewählte Erschließung, die im übrigen mit dem komplizierten räumlichen System, das sie zur Folge hatte, die Grundrißdisposition in unangenehmer Weise einschränkte.

Ein weiterer gegen die Gartenstadtkonzeption eingestellter Architekt war Tony Garnier. Berühmt wurde er durch seinen Plan für eine Cité Industrielle (1901–04; Abb. 39), der wie Costas Brasilia mit autoritärer Einfachheit aufgestellt ist und die Funktionen eindeutig trennt. 1928 bis 1935 wurde nach einem Plan von ihm aus dem Jahr 1920 das Viertel Etats Unis in Lyon gebaut (Abb. 40, 41). Die ursprünglich vier oder fünf Stockwerke hohen Häuser wurden in Gruppen zu vier oder zwei pro Treppenhaus angeordnet; zwischen den aneinandergereihten Blocks zieht sich eine gerade Grünanlage für Fußgänger, der motorisierte Verkehr fließt seitlich vorbei. Unglücklicherweise liegen aus wirtschaftlichen Gründen die Schlafzimmer an der Außenseite der Häuser, während die Wohnräume mit Blick zu den Nachbarn nach innen orientiert sind. Einen starken Gegensatz zur Gartenstadtarchitektur, die vom einzelnen ausging, und zur angepaßten Architektur von Berlage und in gewissem Maß auch von Garnier bildeten die Entwürfe von Antonio Sant'Elia (Abb. 42) und Mario Chiattone (Abb. 43) sowie die radikal kollektivistischen Superblocks der sozialistischen Stadtverwaltung in Wien, die im Jahr 1923 den Bau von 25000 Wohnungen beschloß und die Anzahl später auf 60000 erhöhte.

Für den Superblock, der verwaltungsmäßig zu ihrem Sozialentwicklungsplan paßte, entschieden sich die Wiener Behörden unter dem Einfluß von Berlages Stadtblocks für die Amsterdamer Genossenschaften. Allerdings zogen sie Adolf Loos, dessen architektonische Sprache beunruhigend gewagt war, nicht heran, obgleich er von 1920 bis 1922 Stadtbaumeister war und die Planung von Arbeiterwohnungen mit Energie und vollem Einsatz anging. Für Loos war das Problem der Arbeiterwohnung unter allen Problemen einer neuen Gesellschaft am vordringlichsten und entsprach voll und ganz dem Zweck der modernen Architektur. Eine seiner besten Arbeiten auf dem Gebiet des Wohnungsbaus ist die Heuberg-Siedlung (1921; Abb. 44, 45), die aber nur teilweise nach seinen Vorstellungen gebaut wurde. Die axonometrische Zeichnung läßt an einen Systembau denken, und die Glaskaskade über dem Wintergarten erinnert an Stirlings spätere Bauwerke. In seinen Plänen für das Hotel Babylon (1923; Abb. 46) taucht die abgetreppte Fassade wieder auf, doch zeigt sich hier eine gewisse Hast und ein

49

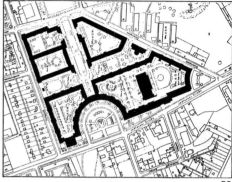

50

49,50. Hubert Grassner. Karl-Seitz-Hof, Vienna. Start of construction 1926.
51,52. Karl Ehn. Karl-Marx-Hof, Vienna. Start of construction 1927.

49,50. Hubert Grassner. Karl-Seitz-Hof, Wien. Baubeginn 1926.
51,52. Karl Ehn. Karl-Marx-Hof, Wien. Baubeginn 1927.

51

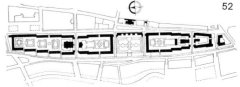

52

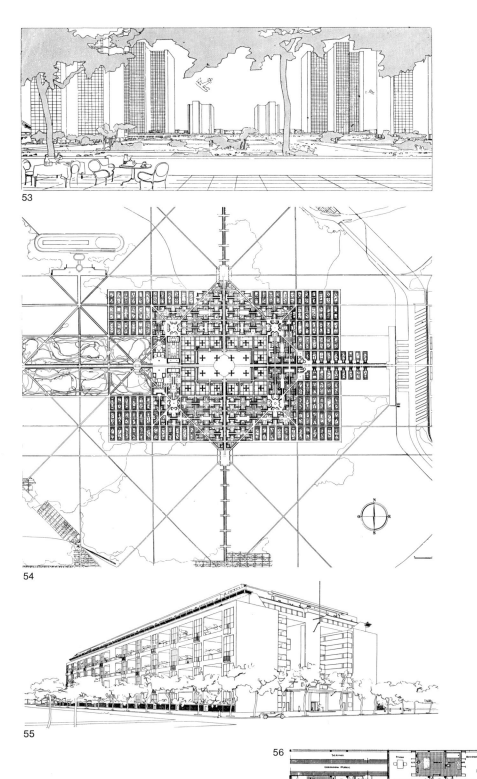

53

54

55

56

53,54. Le Corbusier. Ville contemporaine
de 3 millions d'habitants. 1922.
55,56. Le Corbusier. Immeuble-Villas. 1922.

dren's play areas, etc. Loos' strong individualism, his failings as a leader and his inability to transmit his pesonal experience to others brought to an end his employment with the Vienna authorities, and he moved to Paris. Here Henri Sauvage designed a super-block with a step-back façade in Rue des Amiraux in 1924, enclosing a swimming pool (ill. 48). So it was without Loos that Vienna built its super-blocks, the Karl-Seitz-Hof by Hubert Grassner (1926; ills. 49,50) based on a six-storey semi-circular crescent with 1,173 dwellings, and the Karl-Marx-Hof by Karl Ehn (1927; ills. 51,52), five and seven storeys high and double-banked alongside an internal series of public parks 1 km long. These workers' citadels became Communist strongholds against the Nazis and had to be reduced by shelling by the army during the Fascist take-over in 1934. The Vienna achievements attracted attention elsewhere, in Leeds for example where the newly elected Labour council built a 938-dwelling, seven-storey super-block called Quarry Hill designed by R.A.H. Livett (1934–38).

Le Corbusier, both visionary and artist, was the poet of modern architecture. In the twenties with his review *L'Esprit nouveau,* produced together with his friend, the painter Ozenfant, and his books, *Vers une architecture, L'Art décoratif d'aujourd'hui* and *Urbanisme,* he together with Walter Gropius, almost alone carried the banner of modern architecture to its final victory. Gropius through his teaching rather than his questionable architecture and Le Corbusier through his stark propaganda and poetic creations that flounced even his own rules made an undoubted impact on architecture. Community housing was no exception. Apart from working on the problems of the mass-produced house – Dom-ino houses (1914), Monol houses (1919) and the Citrohan houses (1920–22) – Le Corbusier prepared plans for 'une ville contemporaine de 3 millions d'habitants' in 1922 (ills. 53,54). The building elements were all based on the super-block: cruciform towers in the centre, six-storey lineal blocks around the centre, and 'immeuble-villas' (ills. 55,56) on the outside. The overall plan was academic and symmetrical. Lc Corbusier was a sort of latter-day Haussmann as far as town-planning was concerned, for if his proposals are to be taken seriously they must be judged immature, failing to offer any bridge between planning and the reality of architecture. Guideposts they are, however, for their simple brilliance, and they serve as models (albeit Utopian ones) for communal housing. A literal application of his ideas with the resulting unfortunate social as well as aesthetic consequences, can be seen in the Stuyvesant Town in New York. Le Corbusier's 'Unités' (ills. 57,58), huge blocks to be built in public parks, destroyed the urban freedom of the individual – each block was a prison, without the scale of time and place related to the little natural accidents

Mangel an Entwurfsdisziplin. Im gleichen Jahr entwarf Loos eine Gruppe von 20 Häusern an der Côte d'Azur (Abb. 47), bei denen die abgetreppten Dächer eine Folge von Terrassen und Gärten bilden. Loos war von starkem Individualismus geprägt. Führereigenschaften gingen ihm ab; er war nicht fähig, seine persönlichen Erfahrungen anderer mitzuteilen. Daher trat er aus den Diensten der Wiener Stadtverwaltung aus und zog nach Paris. Dort errichtete Henri Sauvage in der Rue des Amiraux einen Superblock mit rückwärts gestufter Fassade und innerem Schwimmbad (1924; Abb. 48).

Wien baute also ohne Loos seine Superblocks, den Karl-Seitz-Hof (1926; Abb. 49, 50), der von Hubert Grassner geplant wurde und sechs im Halbkreis angeordnete Geschosse mit 1173 Wohnungen umfaßt, und den Karl-Marx-Hof von Karl Ehn (1927; Abb. 51, 52), der fünf und sieben Geschosse hoch ist und sich beiderseits eines 1 km langen öffentlichen Parks hinzieht. Diese Arbeiterzitadellen wurden zu kommunistischen Bollwerken gegen die Nationalsozialisten. Bei der faschistischen Machtergreifung im Jahr 1934 wurden sie mit Granaten beschossen, bis sie den Widerstand aufgaben. Diese Wiener Großbauten erregten überall Aufsehen, so auch in Leeds, wo der kurz zuvor gewählte Labour-Stadtrat den von R.A.H. Livett entworfenen, siebengeschossigen Superblock Quarry Hill mit 938 Wohnungen erbaute (1934-38).

In Le Corbusier, Visionär und Künstler zugleich, fand die moderne Architektur ihre höchste poetische Kraft. Mit seiner Zeitschrift *L'Esprit nouveau,* die er zusammen mit seinem Freund, dem Maler Ozenfant, herausgab, sowie mit seinen Büchern *Vers une architecture, L'Art décoratif d'aujourd'hui* und *Urbanisme* führte er – wenn man einmal von Walter Gropius absieht – in den zwanziger Jahren praktisch allein die moderne Architektur zum endgültigen Sieg. Der Einfluß auf die Architektur, den Gropius mehr als Lehrer als mit seiner fragwürdigen Architektur und Le Corbusier mit seiner unermüdlichen Propaganda und seinen sogar die eigenen Regeln überschreitenden poetischen Schöpfungen ausübten, ist gar nicht hoch genug einzuschätzen. Der Wohnungsbau bildete keine Ausnahme. Abgesehen von der Arbeit an den Problemen des massengefertigten Hauses – Dom-ino-Häuser (1914), Monol-Haus (1920) und Citrohan-Häuser (1920-22) –, befaßte sich Le Corbusier im Jahr 1922 mit den Plänen zu einer ›zeitgenössischen Stadt mit drei Millionen Einwohnern‹ (Abb. 53, 54). Alle Bauelemente gingen auf den Superblock zurück: kreuzförmige Türme im Kern, sechsgeschossige Linearblocks um den Kern herum, ›Immeuble-Villas‹ (Abb. 55, 56) an der Außenseite. Der Gesamtplan ist akademisch und symmetrisch. Was die Stadtplanung betrifft, war Le Corbusier eine Art Haussmann-Nachfahre; wenn man seine Vorschläge ernst nehmen wollte, müßte man sie unreif nennen und beanstan-

57

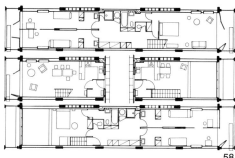

58

57,58. Le Corbusier. Unité d'habitation at Marseilles. 1947-52.
59. L.C.C. Roehampton, London. 1952-55.
60. Walter Gropius. Törten district, Dessau. 1926.
61. Ludwig Mies van der Rohe (general plan). Weissenhof district, Stuttgart. 1927.
62. Ernst May. Römerstadt, Frankfurt-am-Main. 1925-30.
63,64. Walter Gropius. Dammerstock district, Karlsruhe. 1928.

59

57,58. Le Corbusier. Unité d'habitation in Marseille. 1947-52.
59. L.C.C. Roehampton, London. 1952-55.
60. Walter Gropius. Siedlung Törten, Dessau. 1926.
61. Ludwig Mies van der Rohe (Gesamtplan). Weißenhofsiedlung, Stuttgart. 1927.
62. Ernst May. Römerstadt, Frankfurt a.M. 1925-30.
63,64. Walter Gropius. Siedlung Dammerstock, Karlsruhe. 1928.

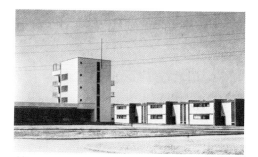

60

61

62

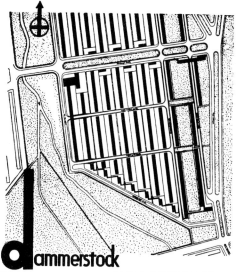

dammerstock

63

64

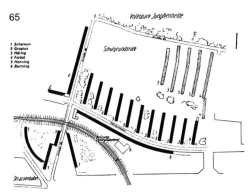

65,66,67,68. Walter Gropius (Gesamtleitung). Siemensstadt, Berlin. 1930. – Die einzelnen Bauten stammen von Scharoun (66), Gropius (67), Häring (68), Forbat, Henning und Bartning.
69. Bruno Taut und Martin Wagner. Großsiedlung Britz, Berlin. 1925-31.
70. Ginzburg und Milinis. Haus für Angestellte des Kommissariats für Finanzen. 1928.
71. Giuseppe Terragni. Apartmenthaus in Como. 1929.

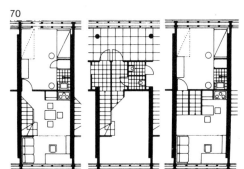

65,66,67,68. Walter Gropius (overall design) Siemensstadt, Berlin 1930. – The different buildings were designed by Scharoun (66), Gropius (67), Häring (68), Forbat, Henning and Bartning.
69. Bruno Taut and Martin Wagner. Housing estate at Britz, Berlin. 1925-31.
70. Ginzburg and Milinis. House for employees of the Commissariat of Finances. 1928.
71. Giuseppe Terragni. Apartment house in Como. 1929.

of nature. These super-blocks failed for two basic reasons, the first being the absence of public parkland – its scaling down in Roehampton (1952–55; ill. 59) is mean – and the second that only Le Corbusier himself worked out a suitable architectural style.

It was a seeking after the romantic that bedevilled so many of the long low housing developments in Germany after the First World War. Aware that monotony had to be tempered to humanize buildings, the only recourse was to turn to arbitrary academic layouts, after the fashion of Berlage, many of which were surprisingly successful thanks to good design and low density.

The Törten district in Dessau (ill. 60) set the prismatic style with neat detailing in 1926, but this was swiftly followed by Ludwig Mies van der Rohe's scuptural grouping of the Weissenhofsiedlung in Stuttgart in 1927 (ill. 61), where the cream of European talent exercised its skill. This was an exhibition to test both the architects and the public. Its success later aroused the wrath of Hitler who stygmatized it as unworthy of the Aryan race. Ernst May, a disciple of Raymond Unwin, began the huge development of Frankfurt (1925–30; ill 62) while in Karlsruhe Walter Gropius drew a strictly rational' layout for the Dammerstock district (1928; ills. 63,64). Only the advent of the curving railway line and collaborators in Hans Scharoun, Hugo Häring, and Otto Bartning, made Gropius' Siemensstadt district in Berlin (ills. 65,66,67,68) more notable than the others. The earlier Britz (1925–31; ill. 69) and Zehlendorf districts (1926–31) by Bruno Taut still reflected the Vienna super-block design although the dwellings were only three stories high.

In Russia a six-storey, long gallery-access block was designed by Ginzburg and Milinis in 1928 (ill. 70), where the duplex (two-storey) apartment had to be introduced to prevent the bedrooms being overlooked from the gallery. Ginzburg also designed with others an extraordinary 'communal house' called Narkomfin (1928/29) for 198 families, with school, clubs and restaurant.

In Italy, Giuseppe Terragni built a five-storey apartment house in Como in 1929 (ill. 71). That the communal dwelling house had now taken its place as the main typological element in twentieth-century architecture may best be demonstrated by the care that Terragni took over the corners of his building. Not only did he combine two megaforms, the cube and the cylinder, he also maintained the repetitive scale of the minor elements, such as the windows, and at the same time varied the volume with recesses and projections, contrasting with the surface to create drama. As a result of this variation he succeeded in holding the composition together, bringing down the overall scale of the building as regards its height, and bringing up the scale from a collection of apartments to an architectural whole. Arne Jacobsen introduced another model with

den, daß sie keine Brücke über den Abgrund zwischen der Theorie und der Realität des Bauens schlagen. Schon allein wegen ihrer Brillanz waren sie aber Wegweiser, und sie dienen als (wenn auch utopische) Modelle für kollektives Wohnen. Eine plangetreue Verwirklichung mit ihren katastrophalen sozialen und ästhetischen Folgen zeigt beispielhaft die Stuyvesant Town in New York.

Le Corbusiers Unités (Abb. 57, 58), riesige Blocks in öffentlichen Parks, schmälern die Freiheit des einzelnen in der Stadt. Jeder Block ist ein Gefängnis; es fehlen die Dimensionen von Zeit und Ort, die Gegebenheiten der Natur. Aus zwei weiteren Gründen waren die Superblocks ein Mißerfolg: Zum einen war der öffentliche Park nicht vorhanden – in Roehampton (1952-55; Abb. 59) wurde er allzu stark beschnitten –; zum anderen war Le Corbusier der einzige, der einen passenden Architekturstil entwickelte.

Sehnsucht nach Romantik prägte viele nach dem Ersten Weltkrieg in Deutschland entstandene Flachbausiedlungen. Man war bestrebt, die Monotonie aufzulockern, um den menschlichen Maßstab zu retten, und als einziger Ausweg boten sich willkürliche, akademische Gruppierungen im Stil von Berlage an. Wegen ihres guten Entwurfs und der geringen Bebauungsdichte erzielten diese Siedlungen jedoch zu einem Teil einen überraschenden Erfolg.

Die Siedlung Törten in Dessau von 1926 (Abb. 60) wies mit ihrer sauberen Detaillierung dem prismatischen Stil den Weg, und rasch darauf folgte Ludwig Mies van der Rohe mit der skulptural gruppierten Weißenhofsiedlung in Stuttgart (1927; Abb. 61), die den Spitzentalenten Europas Gelegenheit gab, ihr Geschick zu beweisen. Es handelte sich hier um eine Ausstellung, bei der nicht nur die Architekten eine Prüfung zu bestehen hatten, sondern ebenso die Öffentlichkeit.

Durch ihren großen Erfolg zog die Weißenhofsiedlung später Hitlers Zorn auf sich; er bezeichnete sie als der arischen Rasse unwürdig. Architektur ist, wenn sie gut ist, immer ein Politikum. Wenn sie schlecht ist, natürlich ebenfalls. Ernst May, Schüler von Raymond Unwin, begann mit der umfassenden Entwicklung Frankfurts (1925-30; Abb. 62), während Walter Gropius in Karlsruhe einen streng ›rationalen‹ Plan für die Siedlung Dammerstock schuf (1928; Abb. 63, 64). Nur die Einbeziehung der gekrümmten Eisenbahngleise und die Mitarbeit von Hans Scharoun, Hugo Häring und Otto Bartning ließen die Siemensstadt von Walter Gropius (Abb. 65, 66, 67, 68) unter anderen Siedlungen herausragen. Die früher entstandenen Großsiedlungen in Britz (1925-31; Abb. 69) und in Zehlendorf (1926-31) von Bruno Taut spiegelten noch den Wiener Superblock wider, wenn auch die Wohnhäuser nur drei Geschosse hoch waren.

1928 entwarfen Ginzburg und Milinis in Rußland einen sechsgeschossigen Laubengangblock mit Duplexwohnungen, das heißt mit

73

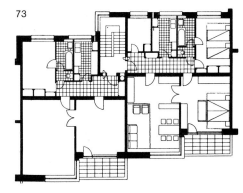

74

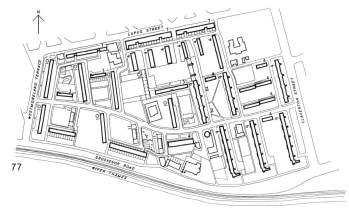

75

72,73. Arne Jacobsen, Bellavista housing estate, Copenhagen. 1934.
74. Clarence Stein. Radburn, New Jersey. 1928.
75. Yuba City, California.
76,77. Powell & Moya. Churchill Gardens, Pimlico, London. 1951.

76

72,73. Arne Jacobsen. Wohnanlage Bellavista, Kopenhagen. 1934.
74. Clarence Stein. Radburn, New Jersey. 1928.
75. Yuba City, Kalifornien.
76,77. Powell & Moya. Churchill Gardens, Pimlico, London. 1951.

77

78

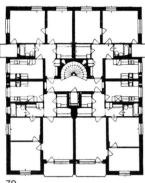

79

82

78,79. Ancker, Gate und Lindegren. Wohnquartier Torsviks, Lidingo, Stockholm.
1943-46.
80,81. Mario Ridolfi, Ludovico Quaroni und
Mario Fiorentino. Wohnquartier INA-Casa
Tiburtino, Rom.
82. Auguste Perret. Avenue Foch, Le Havre.
83,84. Denys Lasdun. Wohnblock in Bethnal
Green, London. 1958.

78,79. Ancker, Gate and Lindegren. Torsviks
district, Lidingo, Stockholm. 1943-46.
80,81. Mario Ridolfi, Ludovico Quaroni and
Mario Fiorentino. INA-Casa Tiburtino district,
Rome.
82. Auguste Perret. Avenue Foch, Le Havre.
83,84. Denys Lasdun. Cluster towers in
Bethnal Green, London. 1958.

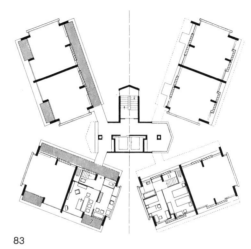

83

80

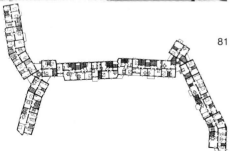

81

84

his Bellavista housing just north of Copenhagen (1934; ills. 72,73), bending his block
in a horseshoe fashion around a communal
garden, and also staggering the dwellings in
plan so that each would have a view of the sea.
This housing group became the ideal post-war
model for many thousands of resorts along
the coast, often badly copied and much higher,
but even so far superior to the succession of
blocks at right-angles to the shore.
In North America, with so much space, and as
a reaction to the compact European settle-
ment, communal housing hardly existed
except for the very poor or very rich, for both
of whom such housing was conceived as little
independent boxes piled on top of each other.
One of the few exceptions was the clustering
of individual dwellings according to Ebenezer
Howard's Garden City model, developed by
Clarence Stein for Radburn on the outskirts of
New York in 1928 (ill. 74), or rationally assembled for agricultural villages such as Yuba City,
California (ill. 75).
The Second World War brought about a pro-
found change in the structure of society
throughout the world. The six years of war with
its terrible sacrifice – the result of the foolish
mistakes of a decadent European leadership –
demanded change. Nationalist frontiers
meant nothing to the conscripts who had shed
blood on foreign soil, and the guilt of a tragi-
cally misled Germany engendered an enormous will for fraternity and renewal. 'Never
again' was the common catchword, and while
new leaders sought to build a united Europe
popular feeling impelled individual govern-
ments to spread the national inheritance of
wealth and resources more evenly throughout
society. The socialist welfare state was introduced at various stages of development de-
pending on the characteristics of each country.
The ideal new society was to become a reality.
Ex-service men flooded the universities and
technical colleges, demanding a new pragmatic application for these ideals. Professors
and teachers climbed down from their academic stools to tackle the realities of the problems that faced them.
The sharing of suffering welded the community
together and the speculator was at first given
little opportunity to return. New planning laws
were introduced and an enormous housing
programme was embarked upon. Architecture
without a social content no longer interested
architects. In a way architecture suffered a
period of mediocre design with 'a peoples'
architecture' symbolized by the Festival of
Britain (1951) and the projects begun soon
after: Lansbury neighbourhood in London's
East End, Churchill Gardens in Pimlico (ills. 76,
77) and the Alton Estate in Roehampton. Swe-
dish architecture set the fashion for romantic
estate layouts with the Torsviks district at
Lidingo, Stockholm, by Ancker, Gate and
Lindegren (1943–46; ills. 78,79). In Italy the
romance of the historical model influenced the
better-quality developments like the famous

Wohnungen, deren Zimmer sich über zwei Stockwerke verteilen, damit man von der Galerie aus nicht in die Schlafzimmer hineinschauen kann (Abb. 70). Zusammen mit anderen entwarf Ginzburg auch das außergewöhnliche ›Kollektivhaus‹ Narkomfin (1918-29) für 198 Familien mit Schule, Clubräumen und Restaurant zum gemeinschaftlichen Leben.

Aus dem italienischen Bereich muß vor allem das im Jahr 1929 in Como entstandene fünfgeschossige Wohnhaus von Giuseppe Terragni erwähnt werden (Abb. 71). Daß der Wohnblock eines der wichtigsten typologischen Elemente der Architektur des 20. Jahrhunderts darstellt, zeigt sich nicht zuletzt an der formalen Sorgfalt, die Terragni bei seinem Bauwerk walten ließ. Der Bau lebt davon, daß zwei Großformen, der Kubus und der Zylinder, kombiniert sind, doch wurden dabei die vielfach wiederholten kleineren Elemente, zum Beispiel die Fenster, nicht außer acht gelassen. Das Volumen des Bauwerks ist durch vor- und zurückspringende Teile aufgelöst, um die Fassaden zu gliedern und den Bau in seiner Gesamtheit überschaubar werden zu lassen. Die Höhe wird somit optisch aufgeschlüsselt, der Eindruck aufeinandergestellter Wohnungen tritt zurück zugunsten der Wirkung eines baulichen Ganzen, das sich harmonisch in die Stadt einfügt.

Ein anderes Modell führte Arne Jacobsen 1934 mit der Wohnanlage Bellavista nördlich von Kopenhagen vor (Abb. 72, 73). Sie zieht sich in Hufeisenform um einen gemeinschaftlichen Garten; die Wohnungen sind im Grundriß gegeneinander versetzt, so daß alle Seeblick genießen. Diese Anlage wurde nach dem Krieg zum Vorbild von vielen tausend Feriensiedlungen am Wasser. Oft wurde sie einfach kopiert; oft kamen auch noch einige Stockwerke hinzu, aber selbst dann blieb der Vorteil gegenüber aneinandergereihten, rechtwinklig zum Strand stehenden Blocks.

In Nordamerika, wo Platz genug vorhanden ist und die Häuser nicht so gedrängt beieinanderstehen wie in Europa, kannte man das Problem des kollektiven Wohnens außer bei den sehr Armen und den sehr Reichen kaum, und in beiden Fällen wurden kleine, unabhängige Einheiten aufeinandergestapelt. Die wenigen Ausnahmen waren die Gruppen von Einzelhäusern im Stil von Ebenezer Howards Gartenstadt, wie sie Clarence Stein 1928 für Radburn an der Peripherie von New York entwickelte (Abb. 74), oder die streng rational konzipierten landwirtschaftlichen Siedlungen wie Yuba City, Kalifornien (Abb. 75).

Der Zweite Weltkrieg verursachte auf der ganzen Welt einen tiefen gesellschaftlichen Strukturwandel. Auf die sechs Kriegsjahre mit ihren entsetzlichen Opfern, herbeigeführt durch die törichten Fehler einer dekadenten Führung in Europa, mußte eine Veränderung folgen. Nationalgrenzen bedeuteten den Soldaten, die auf ›fremdem‹ Boden ihr Leben eingesetzt hatten, nichts mehr, und aus der Schuld des tragisch irregeführten Deutsch-

85

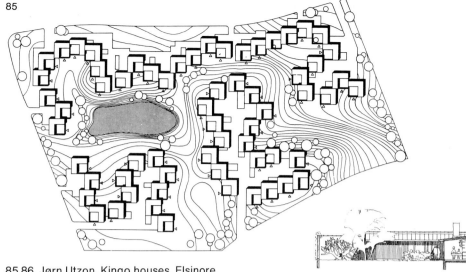

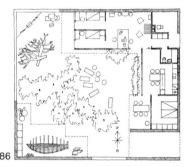

85,86. Jørn Utzon. Kingo houses, Elsinore. 1958/59.
87. Arne Jacobsen. Terrace houses at Klampenborg near Copenhagen. 1950-55.
88. R. Llewelyn Davies and John Weeks. Village housing in Rushbrooke, Suffolk. 1957.

85,86. Jørn Utzon. Kingo-Häuser, Helsingør. 1958/59.
87. Arne Jacobsen. Reihenhäuser in Klampenborg bei Kopenhagen. 1950-55.
88. R. Llewelyn Davies und John Weeks. Dorfhäuser in Rushbrooke, Suffolk. 1957.

86

87

88

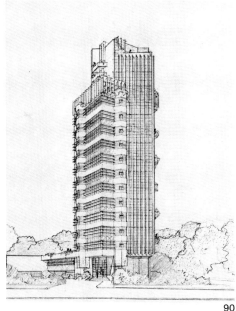
89
90

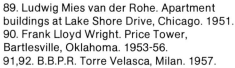

89. Ludwig Mies van der Rohe. Apartment
buildings at Lake Shore Drive, Chicago. 1951.
90. Frank Lloyd Wright. Price Tower,
Bartlesville, Oklahoma. 1953-56.
91,92. B.B.P.R. Torre Velasca, Milan. 1957.

89. Ludwig Mies van der Rohe. Apartmenthäuser am Lake Shore Drive, Chicago. 1951.
90. Frank Lloyd Wright. Price Tower,
Bartlesville, Oklahoma. 1953-56.
91,92. B.B.P.R. Torre Velasca, Mailand. 1957.

91
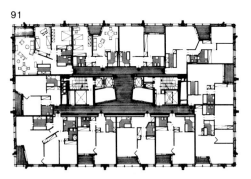

92

INA-Casa Tiburtino district in Rome by Mario
Ridolfi, Ludovico Quaroni and Mario Fiorentino (ills. 80,81). In France, Auguste Perret's
formal planning for Le Havre (ill. 82) symbolized the rational Gallic approach that decayed
into the 'grands ensembles', later to spread
round all the important cities. Denmark developed a highly sophisticated system of prefabricated buildings – low, quiet and very domestic – as well as the most advanced social
planning of all with strict laws enforcing mixed
development and variety of dwelling sizes.
Pedestrian streets were rediscovered at
Coventry and Lijnbaan Rotterdam, which
greatly influenced other housing developments throughout Europe. The traffic-free
court or street was the basis of all the commu-
nity-orientated housing groups. 'Group' and
'cluster' became architectural adjectives and
nouns essential in design for housing districts,
from Denys Lasdun's cluster towers in Bethnal
Green (1958; ills. 83,84) to Jørn Utzon's Kingo
houses in Elsinore (1958/59; ills. 85,86). The
farmyard rural image, reaching back to
Howard's Garden City, was given a new life by
Arne Jacobsen's terrace housing at Klampenborg near Copenhagen (1950–55; ill. 87), and
Llewelyn Davies' and John Week's Rushbrooke
village housing (1957; ill. 88). Landmarks such
as Mies van der Rohe's apartments at Lake
Shore Drive (1951; ill. 89) and Frank Lloyd
Wright's Price Tower (1953–56; ill. 90) made
little impression upon community housing.
However, Le Corbusier's 'Unités' at Marseilles
produced thousands of copies devoid of architectural and social merit, while B.B.P.R.'s
'Torre Velasca' (1957; ills. 91,92) caused a
resounding crisis in contemporary modern
architecture itself. Doubt and self-questioning
replaced the mood of optimism which had
produced the too-easy solutions of the first
post-war period. This crisis was made clear by
the 'jumble-sale' of styles offered at the Berlin
Interbau (1957), where only a building of extraordinary beauty designed by Alvar Aalto (ills.
93,94,95) suggested a style which might combine the social, technical and architectural
elements of community housing for the first
time since the early struggles in the nineteenth
century. Unfortunately Aalto's effort was
restricted in this case to only one building, so
that the more complex problem of relating
larger groups was not tackled.
The proper lines for a typology of community
housing are now beginning to emerge. First,
there is the growing awareness that community housing is not simply a means to ease the
capitalist's conscience towards his workforce
but is also a popular response to the reality of
life in a society that struggles towards equality
without infringement of liberties. Secondly,
the environment is now recognized as a positive element in the forging of this new society.
Thirdly, man 'cannot live by bread alone' and
needs a poetic stimulus to spark his imagination and to foster his desire for social contact,
and it is to this that architecture must respond.

land erwuchs ein ungeheurer Wille zur Brüderlichkeit und Erneuerung. ›Nie wieder!‹ war überall die Losung, und während eine neue Führung sich bemühte, ein vereinigtes Europa zu schmieden, sahen sich die Regierungen auf allgemeines Drängen veranlaßt, nach einer gleichmäßigeren Verteilung des nationalen Erbes an Reichtum und Gütern zu streben. Der soziale Wohlfahrtsstaat prägte sich je nach den Merkmalen der einzelnen Länder mehr oder weniger stark aus. Die ideale neue Gesellschaft sollte Realität werden. Entlassene Soldaten strömten in die Universitäten und Technischen Hochschulen und verlangten nach einer neuen pragmatischen Anwendung dieses Ideals. Professoren und Lehrer stiegen vom akademischen Podium herab und griffen die Realitäten der vor ihnen liegenden Probleme an.

Das geteilte Leid schweißte die Gemeinschaft zusammen, und der gerissene Spekulant hatte zuerst wenig Gelegenheit zur Rückkehr. Neue Planungsgesetze wurden erlassen und riesige Wohnbauprogramme in Angriff genommen. Architektur ohne soziale Inhalte interessierte die Architekten nicht mehr. In gewisser Weise erlebte die Architektur eine Periode mittelmäßiger formaler Qualität. Diese ›Volksarchitektur‹ fand beispielhaften Ausdruck im ›Festival of Britain‹ (1951) sowie in der Lansbury-Siedlung im Londoner East End, in den Churchill Gardens in Pimlico (Abb. 76, 77) und in der Alton-Siedlung in Roehampton, die alle kurz darauf entstanden. Mit der 1943-46 entstandenen Torsviks-Siedlung in Lidingo, Stockholm, von Ancker, Gate und Lindegren (Abb. 78, 79) wurde Schweden zum Mentor des romantischen Stils im Siedlungsbau. In Italien führte die romantische Anlehnung an historische Vorbilder zu qualitätsmäßig besseren Ergebnissen, so bei der berühmten Anlage INA-Casa Tiburtino in Rom von Mario Ridolfi, Ludovico Quaroni und Mario Fiorentino (Abb. 80, 81). In Frankreich stand Auguste Perrets streng formale Planung für Le Havre (Abb. 82) symbolhaft für den rationalen Ansatz der Gallier, der aber bald in die ›Grandsensembles‹, wie sie in allen Großstädten aus dem Boden schossen, entartete. Dänemark erarbeitete ein hochentwickeltes Fertigbausystem für flache, ruhige und sehr heimelige Häuser. Das Gefühl für soziale Verantwortung ist hier am weitesten entwickelt, strenge Gesetze erzwingen eine gemischte Bebauung und Abwechslung in den Wohnhausgrößen. Einen starken Einfluß auf die Entwicklung des europäischen Wohnbaus übten die Fußgängerstraßen aus, die in Coventry und in der Lijnbaan in Rotterdam ihre Wiederentdeckung erlebten. So wurden verkehrsfreie Hof- oder Straßenbereiche die Grundlage jeder gemeinschaftsorientierten Planung. Gruppierung und Ballung, dies waren nun die Hauptmittel der architektonischen Artikulation im Wohnungsbau, angefangen bei Denys Lasduns Türmen in Bethnal Green (1958; Abb. 83, 84), bis zu Jørn Utzons Kingo-Häusern in Helsingør (1958/

59; Abb. 85, 86). Das Bild vom Leben auf dem Lande, seit Howards Gartenstadt lebendig, erhielt einen neuen Ausdruck in Arne Jacobsens Reihenhäusern in Klampenborg bei Kopenhagen (1950-55; Abb. 87) sowie auch mit den Dorfhäusern in Rushbrooke von Llewelyn Davies und John Weeks (1957; Abb. 88). Bauten wie Ludwig Mies van der Rohes Apartmenthäuser am Lake Shore Drive (1951; Abb. 89) oder auch Frank Lloyd Wrights Price Tower (1953-56; Abb. 90) beeinflußten den Wohnungsbau kaum. Le Corbusiers Unité in Marseille dagegen wurde zahllose Male nachgeahmt, dabei jedoch ihres architektonischen und sozialen Inhalts beraubt. Mit dem Torre Velasca von B.B.P.R. (1957; Abb. 91, 92) begann eine umfassende Krise in der modernen Architektur. Zweifel und Selbstbezichtigungen wurden angesichts der zu einfachen Lösungen, die in der frühen Nachkriegszeit geboten wurden, laut. Besonders deutlich zeigte sich die Krise bei der Interbau-Ausstellung von 1957 in Berlin, wo nur Aalto ein Bauwerk von außerordentlicher Schönheit schuf (Abb. 93, 94, 95). Es ließ einen Stil erahnen, der die sozialen, technischen und architektonischen Inhalte des Wohnungsbaus erstmals seit den frühen Bemühungen im 19. Jahrhundert in sich vereint. Leider beschränkte sich in diesem Fall Aaltos Beitrag auf ein einziges Gebäude, so daß das kompliziertere Problem der Verbindung mehrerer Bauten nicht behandelt wurde.

Folgende Faktoren sind heute in erster Linie für den Wohnungsbau bestimmend: zum ersten das erwachende Bewußtsein für die soziale Realität des Problems, und zwar nicht einfach als Wandel in der moralischen Einstellung des Kapitalisten gegenüber dem Arbeiter, sondern als allgemeine Reaktion auf die Realität des Lebens in einer Gesellschaft, die der Gleichheit zustrebt, ohne die Freiheit einzuschränken; zum zweiten die Anerkennung der Umwelt als Element, das bei der Entwicklung dieser neuen Gesellschaft in Betracht gezogen werden muß; zum dritten die Erkenntnis, daß der Mensch ›nicht vom Brot allein‹ lebt, sondern daß er ästhetische Anreize zur Beflügelung seiner Phantasie und soziale Kontakte braucht. Diese Forderungen zu erfüllen, ist Aufgabe der Architektur.

93

94

93,94,95. Alvar Aalto. Apartment block in the Hansaviertel, Berlin. 1957.

93,94,95. Alvar Aalto. Wohngebäude im Hansaviertel, Berlin. 1957.

95

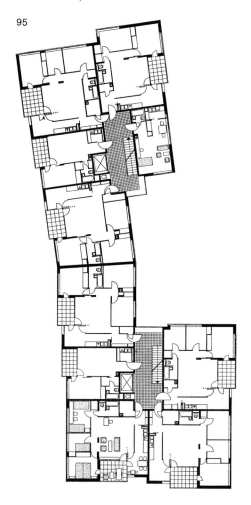

25

Row Houses in Bergwald-Siedlung, Karlsruhe, Germany. 1965–67
Architect: Heinz Mohl

These houses are included here, not only for their undoubted architectural quality, which we will discuss later, but because they lie somewhere within that ambiguous frontier zone between the individual house and the community housing group. Six individual houses in a row (ills. 1, 2) maintain their individuality with separate entrances (ill. 3) and a certain amount of privacy, but share in common the internal organization of the available space, unity of materials and an overall external relationship with each other so that the six units read as a single architectural concept. In a way these community houses are more individual than the 'individual' house itself: through identity with the whole group, each is freed from the necessity of public self-expression.

The internal spatial structure of the houses – their split-level plans on three levels (ill. 4) – allows for full privacy and independence in the study-bedrooms with direct external access from the garden, and a casual privacy for the 'den' or hobby-room and playroom (ill. 7), which leaves the more formal 'parlour' (ill. 6) and dining-room (ill. 5) free for the communal activities of the family. Entertaining can be carried out in public or in relative privacy, thus ensuring a major freedom within the family itself.

Architecture helps human relationships not only with thoughtful planning but also with beautiful design. Beauty is more subjective, but if delight is obtained through the careful balance of stimulation with relaxation the people involved are more sensitive and creative. Stimulation is provided within these houses by half-disclosed views, glass screens, split-levels and a flowing transparency that suggests interest around the corner (ill. 5). There is a sort of gothic mystery about each house. But any 'artful' sublimity is avoided with the use of ordinary, 'poor', domestic materials like clinker-tile floors, lime sandstone bricks and wooden ceilings, materials which induce a sense of confidence and security. The play and counter-play of such elements elevates these ordinary buildings to the level of architecture itself.

The exterior is not quite so successful because the ordinariness has been jazzed up with the uncomfortable romantic timber cladding of the hobby-room and playroom storey, which sits awkwardly next to the lime sandstone blocks (ill. 3).

Reihenhäuser in der Bergwald-Siedlung, Karlsruhe. 1965-67
Architekt: Heinz Mohl

Wir beschreiben diese Häuser hier nicht nur wegen ihrer unzweifelhaften architektonischen Qualitäten, auf die wir später zu sprechen kommen, sondern auch, weil sie im schwierigen Grenzbereich zwischen dem Einfamilienhaus und der Wohnhausgruppe angesiedelt sind. Sechs einzelne Häuser in einer Reihe (Abb. 1, 2) behalten ihre Individualität mit getrennten Eingängen (Abb. 3) und einem gewissen Maß an Abgeschlossenheit, haben aber die innere Raumstruktur, das Baumaterial und die äußere Erscheinung gemeinsam, so daß sie wie ein einziges Gebäude wirken. Diese Reihenhäuser sind gewissermaßen individueller als das Einfamilienhaus selbst, denn die Identität mit der Gesamtheit befreit sie von der Notwendigkeit, ihr Eigenwesen zur Schau zu stellen.

Durch die Verteilung der Räume auf drei gegeneinander versetzte Geschosse (Abb. 4) gewährleisten die Häuser völlige Abgeschlossenheit und Unabhängigkeit in den Arbeits- und Schlafzimmern, die unmittelbar vom Garten aus zugänglich sind, und eine gewisse Abgeschlossenheit des Spiel- und Hobbyraums (Abb. 7). Dadurch bleiben der etwas formalere ›Gesellschaftsraum‹ (Abb. 6) und das Eßzimmer (Abb. 5) frei für die Gemein-

samkeiten der Familie. Geselligkeit kann in größerem Kreis oder in relativer Abgeschiedenheit stattfinden, so daß innerhalb der Familie selbst viel Freiheit besteht.

Die Architektur fördert aber die menschlichen Beziehungen nicht nur mit durchdachter Funktionsplanung, sondern ebenso mit schönen Formen. Schönheit ist ein subjektiver Begriff. Entsteht sie aber durch sorgfältige Ausgewogenheit zwischen Anregung und Erholung, so werden Empfindungsvermögen und Kreativität der Bewohner gesteigert. Die Anregung beruht in diesen Häusern auf halb erschlossenen Ausblicken, Glaswänden, Zwischengeschossen und einer fließenden Transparenz, die gleich um die nächste Ecke etwas Interessantes vermuten läßt (Abb. 5). Eine Art von gotischem Mysterium durchdringt das Haus. Allerdings ist jede ›kunstvolle‹ Sublimität vermieden, denn zur Verwendung kamen ganz gewöhnliche, ›unscheinbare‹ Baumaterialien wie Klinker als Fußbodenbelag, Kalksandsteine als Mauerwerk sowie Holz als Deckenverkleidung. Sie wirken als das, was sie sind: vertraute Materialien, die das Gefühl der Zuverlässigkeit und Sicherheit erwecken. Mit dem Wechselspiel dieser Elemente beweisen diese schlichten Häuser ihre Zugehörigkeit zum Reich der Architektur.

Nicht sehr geglückt ist das Äußere. Hier wurde die Schlichtheit mit der aufdringlich romantischen Holzverkleidung des Hobby- und Spielzimmers aufgeputzt, die sich neben dem Kalksandstein-Mauerwerk fehl am Platz ausnimmt (Abb. 3).

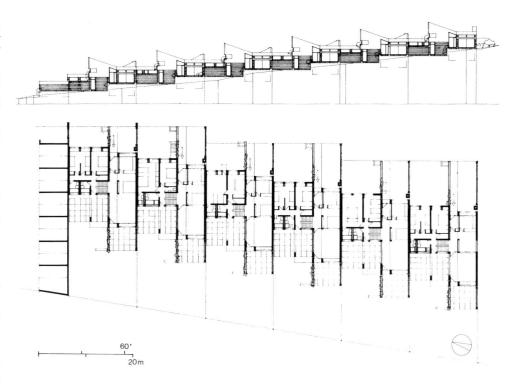

1. General view from the west.
2. Site plan and sectional view.
3. The entrance front of a house.

1. Gesamtansicht von Westen.
2. Lageplan und Ansicht.
3. Eingangsseite eines Hauses.

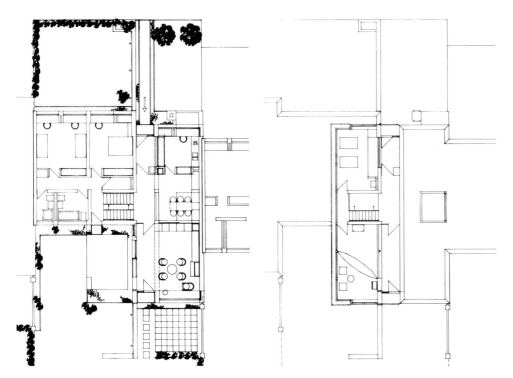

4. Ground plans of a house.
5. View of the dining-space and entrance from the living-room.
6. View of the living-room from the playroom.
7. View of the playroom from the living-room.

4. Grundrisse eines Hauses.
5. Blick vom Wohnraum auf den Eßplatz und den Eingang.
6. Blick vom Spielraum auf den Wohnraum.
7. Blick vom Wohnraum auf den Spielraum.

**Hillside Terrace, Daikanyama, Tokyo.
1967–69 (first phase)**
Architect: Fumihiko Maki (assistant: Masahiro Ono)

Fumihiko Maki's Hillside Terrace on the slopes of Shibuya to the west of Tokyo in a quiet residential neighbourhood shows an unusual tenderness in the handling of movement and place.

The first phase along a narrow site with a street front of 200 m to the north-east consists of two buildings (ills. 1, 2). The lower one on the corner is a complex broken cube with a small corner 'plaza' and contains a glazed porch giving on to the street, and a higher lineal building with a raised balcony walkway parallel to the pavement with an open-access gallery above to the four duplex apartments. The corner buildings contain shops, offices and two flats, one a very large one, the other a smaller one to the south-west. The lineal building has a restaurant below street level, a beauty parlour above and four maisonettes on the top floors. The architects emphasize[1] that the design was developed along two axes. One runs parallel to the street from the corner 'plaza' through the inside-outside glazed porch and up along the lineal building regulating height differences and mediating 'between the building interior and the outside world' (ill. 7). The other axis breaks off from the plaza to run through the shops and down into a sunken garden behind the building to the south-west and therefore acts as an internal community street that will eventually link all the phases together.

However, the most interesting architectural feature is the doubling of the pavement area (ill. 3), a redundant exercise, but which serves to create a mediating space between the building and the initial walkway. This both protects the building from passers-by and prepares the visitor for his entrance to or exit from the building, rather in the manner of a forecourt. The decision to enter or leave has essentially been taken before actually entering or leaving. This lineal forecourt follows the level of the building rather than the pavement which leads to the duplex flats; it too becomes part of the street, open and safe, busy and human.

The buildings are low because of the building regulations, but the articulation of the cubic massing and the decision to divide the development into separate buildings has allowed this new complex to merge into the existing small residential 'grain' of the neighbourhood. Certain styling elements retain some of the mannerisms picked up by Maki from J.L. Sert (he both studied under Sert at Harvard and worked in his office): the sculptural gimmick of a deeply moulded façade on the duplex reminds one of Sert's Boston University, while the protruding symmetrical chamfered ventilators and lightheads, timid imitations of the Maeght Foundation, are the most obvious frills (ill. 2). The north-west wall canterlevers out over the duplex gallery because of the imposed composition of the north-east façade rather than for any other reason. The aesthetic quality of the architecture might well have been enhanced if more attention had been paid to eliminating these mannerisms.

Hillside Terrace, Daikanyama, Tokio. Erster Bauabschnitt. 1967–69
Architekt: Fumihiko Maki (Assistent: Masahiro Ono)

Fumihiko Makis Hillside Terrace in einer ruhigen Wohngegend von Shibuya westlich von Tokio zeugt von ungewöhnlicher Behutsamkeit im Umgang mit Bewegung und Ort.
Der erste Bauabschnitt liegt auf einem schmalen Gelände mit einer Straßenfront im Nordosten und besteht aus zwei Gebäuden (Abb. 1, 2). Das tiefer gelegene an der Ecke ist ein komplizierter, unterbrochener Kubus mit einer kleinen Eckplaza; seine verglaste Vorhalle geht auf die Straße hinaus. Das höher gelegene ist ein gestreckter Bau mit einem erhöhten Fußgängerdeck parallel zum Bürgersteig und einer oberen Galerie, die Zugang zu den Wohnungen gewährt. Im Eckbau sind Läden, Büros und zwei Wohnungen untergebracht; die eine Wohnung ist sehr groß, die andere etwas kleiner und nach Südwesten gelegen. In dem gestreckten Bau befinden sich ein Restaurant unter und ein Schönheitssalon über der Straßenebene sowie vier Maisonettes in den oberen Geschossen. Die Architekten heben hervor [1], daß die Baugruppe an zwei Achsen ausgerichtet wurde. Die eine verläuft parallel zur Straße von der Eckplaza durch die verglaste Vorhalle und aufwärts an dem gestreckten Bau entlang; sie gleicht Höhenunterschiede aus und vermittelt ›zwischen dem Gebäudeinneren und der Außenwelt‹ (Abb. 7). Die andere Achse zweigt von der Plaza ab und zieht sich in südwestlicher Richtung durch die Läden hinunter in einen vertieften Garten hinter dem Gebäude; sie fungiert als innerer Erschließungsweg und wird später alle Bauabschnitte verbinden und eine Beziehung zwischen ihnen herstellen. Das interessanteste architektonische Detail ist die Verdoppelung des Gehwegs (Abb. 3). Der erhöhte Fußweg ist eigentlich ein überzähliges Element, das jedoch einen zwischen Haus und Straße vermittelnden Raum schafft. Das Haus ist vor neugierigen Blicken der Passanten geschützt, während Besucher wie durch einen Vorhof auf das Betreten oder Verlassen der Anlage vorbereitet werden. Den Entschluß, ein Anwesen zu betreten oder zu verlassen, faßt man ja schon, ehe man sich tatsächlich dazu anschickt. Dieser lineare Vorhof ist einmal Teil des Gebäudes wie die Galerie vor den Wohnungen; er ist aber zugleich auch Teil der Straße, zugänglich und sicher, belebt und von menschlicher Atmosphäre durchdrungen.
Auf Grund der Bauvorschriften mußten die Häuser niedrig gehalten werden, aber mit der Gliederung der kubischen Masse und der Aufteilung in getrennte Gebäude hat man es verstanden, den neuen Komplex in die bestehende kleinteilige Bebauungsstruktur einzupassen. In manchen Stilelementen zeigt sich eine gewisse Manieriertheit, die Maki von J. L. Sert übernommen hat (er studierte

1. Aerial view of the building group.
2. General view from the north.
3. The pedestrian deck in front of the
west wing which serves as a mediating space
between the building and the pavement.

1. Blick von oben auf die Gruppe.
2. Gesamtansicht von Norden.
3. Der erhöhte Fußweg vor dem westlichen
Flügel, der einen zwischen Haus und Straße
vermittelnden Raum schafft.

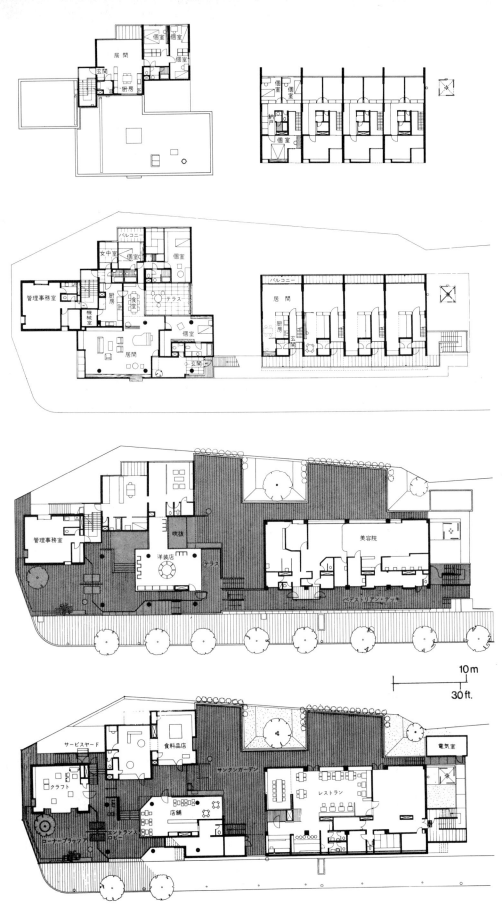

bei ihm an der Harvard University und arbei-
tete auch in seinem Büro). Der skulpturale
Formalismus der tief gefurchten Fassade vor
den Maisonettes erinnert an die Bostoner
Universitätsbauten von Sert, und die symmetrisch angeordneten Oberlicht- und Lüf-
tungsaufbauten müssen als schüchterne
Nachbildungen der Oberlichter auf dem Gebäude der Fondation Maeght angesehen
werden (Abb. 2). Die über die Galerie aus-
kragende Nordwestwand scheint eher von der
funktional gerechtfertigten Form der Nordost-
fassade als von der realen Situation bedingt
zu sein. Die Qualität der Architektur wäre
sicher deutlicher hervorgetreten, wenn darauf geachtet worden wäre, ohne diese
Manierismen auszukommen.

4. Ground plans (basement, street level,
1st floor, 2nd floor). The two lower floors
contain shops, offices, a restaurant and a
beauty parlour.
5,6. One of the duplex flats in the west wing.
7. View of the central garden terrace.

4. Grundrisse (Untergeschoß, Straßen-
geschoß, 1. Obergeschoß, 2. Obergeschoß).
Die beiden unteren Geschosse enthalten
Läden, Büros, ein Restaurant sowie einen
Schönheitssalon.
5,6. Eine der Duplexwohnungen im
westlichen Flügel.
7. Blick auf die zentrale Gartenterrasse.

10 m
30 ft.

Row Houses in Genterstrasse, Munich. 1968–72

Architect: Otto Steidle (assistants: Ralph and Doris Thut)

One's first impression upon encountering this group of houses in the midst of a suburb of nondescript semi-detacheds is of delight and excitement. Delight because of the obvious care that has been taken in designing all the parts equally well, excitement because of the infinite complexity of the structures which makes one want to find out what all the fuss is about (ill. 1). The strength and weakness of the architecture of these six houses and architects' offices lies in the very care taken over each element and the complexity of the whole. First, we must consider the ideology that motivated the experiment. The social one concerning use was to increase the shared community facilities to the maximum limit, which in practice meant without over-straining the existing family structure or challenging the property rights of those involved.

These shared facilities eventually consisted of a common constructional and aesthetic building capable of allowing each unit to express the prevailing community spirit, a common garden lawn between the houses and the street, a covered porch for meetings, play and parties, a small swimming-pool, and finally a public footpath which runs through the building from the street to the pedestrian lane behind. The lane will connect with a second phase to be built later. From the point of view of function the Dutch architect Habraken's ideas on support structures (i.e., supplying the essential organs of a house to which each and everyone can add on to as they like)[2] have been developed and used during the course of the design; rather optimistically the possibility of both internal and external change in the future has been provided for.

The other basic ideological premise was that these houses should show how the social requirements – allowing in the design for self-expression and changes in function – could be satisfied by industrialized mass-housing. The factory-like product image was deliberately sought after in spite of the expense and redundancy involved. The metal staircases, with their open grill treads and wire-mesh hand-rail infills, are straight from the engineers' catalogue for staircases suitable for machinery inspection and access (ill. 2). The dominant horizontal theme of the enclosing infill panels of the façade is an echo of the 'streamline efficiency' of the thirties. The 'adjustable' complex of major and minor beams within the overall pre-cast concrete frame structure with repetitive corbels enables the client to support floor slabs wherever he wants reasonably to place them, although the result is to give the whole building a 'meccano-set' feeling.

As for the distribution of the houses, the complex arrangements for extension and multiple access mean that one has to enter either through the kitchen or across the front window of one's neighbour's house. In the larger houses there is no direct access to the garden from the main living-room. There has been no attempt to accommodate the individual's freedom within the family by providing a separate access to the children's area. The open planning also conflicts with privacy (ill. 5).

These criticisms, however, arise more from the natural inexperience of the architect with an experimental building than from bad architecture. The beauty and poetry of the place make this tiny group of houses an exceptional architectural achievement and are a pointer to the way community housing may one day free people to live in their own kind of homes without removing from them the responsibility of being members of a larger community.

1. General view of the south-west side.
2. North-east side. The metal staircases seem to be taken straight out of a catalogue for machinery inspection walkways.

Reihenhäuser in der Genterstraße, München. 1968-72

Architekt: Otto Steidle (Assistenten: Ralph und Doris Thut)

Die erste Reaktion angesichts dieser zwischen ziemlich unauffälligen Vorstadt-Doppelhäusern gelegenen Häusergruppe ist freudige Überraschung und Aufregung: freudige Überraschung, weil sichtlich große Sorgfalt darauf verwendet wurde, allen Teilen harmonische Proportionen zu geben, und Aufregung wegen der ungeheuren strukturellen Komplexität der Gesamterscheinung, die neugieriges Interesse am Sinn des Ganzen weckt (Abb. 1). Gerade in dieser Sorgfalt im Detail und Komplexität im Gesamten liegen Stärken und Schwächen der Architektur bei diesen sechs Häusern.

Zuerst muß man sich die Ideologie vor Augen führen, die dem Experiment zugrunde liegt. Der gesellschaftliche, die Nutzung betreffende Gedanke war der, daß ein Höchstmaß an Gemeinsamkeit erreicht werden sollte, ohne jedoch dadurch die Realitäten der gegebenen Familienstrukturen und individuellen Besitzrechte zu beeinträchtigen.

Das Ergebnis dieses Gedankens war ein gemeinsamer konstruktiver und ästhetischer Rahmen für die einzelnen Einheiten, in dem die Identifizierung des einzelnen mit der Gemeinschaft zum Ausdruck kommt, ein gemeinsamer Rasen zwischen den Häusern und der Straße, eine überdachte Vorhalle für Zusammenkünfte, Spiel und Geselligkeit, ein kleines Schwimmbad und schließlich ein öffentlicher Fußweg, der von der Straße durch die Anlage zu der dahinter liegenden Fußgängerstraße führt und die Verbindung zum geplanten zweiten Bauabschnitt herstellen wird. Im Hinblick auf die Nutzung wurden die Gedanken des holländischen Architekten Habraken über Tragwerke (das heißt, über die Bereitstellung der wesentlichen Teile eines Gebäudes, auf denen jeder beliebig aufbauen kann) [2] schon in den Entwurfsprozeß hineingenommen, um – ziemlich optimistisch – für künftige Veränderungen im Inneren und Äußeren vorzusorgen.

Die andere grundlegende ideologische Zielvorstellung lag darin, mit diesen Häusern den Beweis zu erbringen, daß im industrialisierten Massenwohnungsbau sowohl gesellschaftlich wünschenswerte individuelle Ausdrucksweisen als auch durch Nutzungswandel notwendig werdende bauliche Veränderungen möglich sind. Das Aussehen eines Fabrikerzeugnisses wurde absichtlich gewählt, obwohl man nicht an Kosten und Details sparte. Die metallenen Treppen mit den offenen Gitterstufen und dem mit Maschendraht ausge-

1. Gesamtansicht der Südwestseite.
2. Nordostseite. Die metallenen Treppen scheinen geradewegs aus einem Katalog für Kontrollstege von Maschinenanlagen zu stammen.

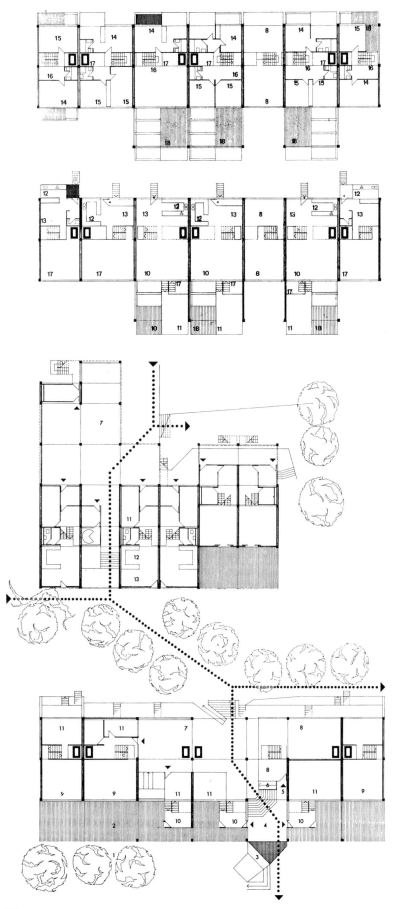

fachten Geländer scheinen geradewegs aus einem technischen Katalog für Kontrollstege von Maschinenanlagen zu stammen (Abb. 2). Die vorherrschende horizontale Linie der Fassadenelemente erinnert an die Stromlinieneffizienz der dreißiger Jahre. Das vorgefertigte Betonskelett mit den in gleichmäßigen Abständen angebrachten Konsolen für die ganz nach Wunsch des Benutzers anzuordnenden Bodenträger verleiht der Anlage etwas von einem Stabilbaukasten.

Die Plazierung der Häuser und die komplizierten Vorrichtungen für spätere Erweiterung und Mehrfachzugang bringen es mit sich, daß man entweder durch die Küche oder aber vor den Wohnraumfenstern des Nachbarn eintreten muß. In den größeren Häusern hat der Wohnraum keinen direkten Ausgang in den Garten. Man sucht auch vergeblich nach einem getrennten Eingang zu den Kinderzimmern und vermißt die Vorsorge für die Freiheit des einzelnen innerhalb der Familie. Die offene Planung läßt keine Privatsphäre zu (Abb. 5).

Diese offensichtlichen Fehler beruhen jedoch mehr auf der natürlichen Unausgereiftheit eines Versuchsbaus als auf schlechter Architektur. Die kleine Häusergruppe ist vielmehr in ihrer Schönheit und Poesie eine außergewöhnliche architektonische Leistung und ein Hinweis darauf, wie der Wohnungsbau eines Tages den Menschen ermöglichen kann, in einem ihnen gemäßen Haus zu wohnen und mit einer kulturdurchdrungenen Technologie zu leben, die die Freiheit des einzelnen mit seiner Verantwortung für andere als Mitglied einer größeren Gemeinschaft verbindet.

3. Ground plans (ground floor with planned 2nd phase, 1st floor, 2nd floor). Key: 1 open area, 2 garden, 3 swimming-pool court, 4 dwelling entrance, 5 office entrance, 6 swimming-pool access, 7 open entrance area, 8 office, 9 living-room, 10 'glass case', 11 side room, 12 kitchen, 13 dining-area, 14 parents' bedroom, 15 children's bedroom, 16 gallery, 17 void, 18 terrace.
4. Office.
5. Living area of a dwelling unit.

3. Grundrisse (Erdgeschoß mit geplantem 2. Bauabschnitt, 1. Obergeschoß, 2. Obergeschoß). Legende: 1 Grünfläche, 2 Garten, 3 Lichthof des Schwimmbads, 4 Wohnungseingang, 5 Büroeingang, 6 Zugang zum Schwimmbad, 7 offener Eingangsbereich, 8 Büro, 9 Wohnraum, 10 ›Glaskasten‹, 11 Nebenraum, 12 Küche, 13 Eßbereich, 14 Elternzimmer, 15 Kinderzimmer, 16 Galerie, 17 Luftraum, 18 Terrasse.
4. Büro.
5. Wohnbereich einer Wohneinheit.

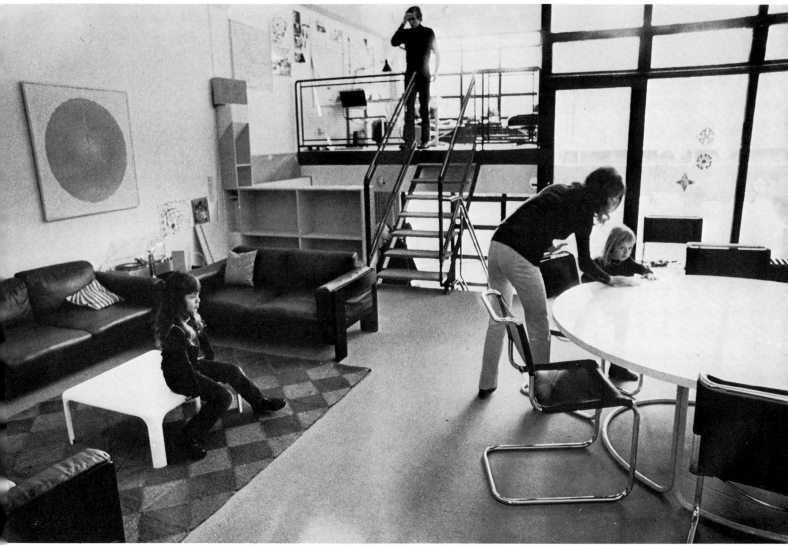

Multi-Purpose Building, Rotonda dei Mille, Bergamo, Italy. 1969–70

Architects: Guiseppe Gambirasio, Giorgio Zenoni, Baran Ciagà, Walter Barbero

The building, for an insurance company, contains parking areas and a cinema below ground, shops at street level, a floor of offices with more parking above, reached by a spiral ramp (ill. 1), another floor of offices, and then split-level flats arranged on either side of a central passage (entrance on one side, study or office on the other side which connect internally over the public passage). The flats are large and are obviously meant for the professional class – architects and lawyers. Keeping to a strict Bauhaus moral of functional expression the architects have divided the different uses physically into separate bodies but unlike the pioneers of the thirties the architects have forced the functional expression into the section (ills. 2, 3).

We should point out that the building being considered is only half the complete project. The L-shaped complex should have been completed by another arm to form two sides of the gardens of a public square. The arm that now seems unlikely to be built would have given both a major architectural character to the square and, with its passages, completed the pedestrian walk through to the lively neo-classic city centre of the Piazza Matteotti (ill. 4). The uncompromising moral attitude of the architects in designing a building that expresses both its functions and its epoch has not led them to deny the pre-existing character and form of the neighbourhood. They have had to resolve the design integrity of a multi-purpose building with the need to harmonize with the circular Rotonda dei Mille, the sloping Via Piccini, the gardens of the public square in Via Crispi Francesco to the south-east, and the pitched tiled roofs of the whole neighbourhood. The last point is all important not only as regards the pitching of the roofs themselves but also as regards the scale of each roof, since the historic medieval city (Città Alta) towers above its nineteenth century brother (Città Piana) in no uncertain manner. The roofscape in the new design had to be carefully composed so as not to make a crude intrusion into the city skyline. This problem has been conveniently solved by placing the living units on the upper floors and giving each its own form with a broken roof that reduces the scale of the building at sky-level (ill. 7).

The concave façade of the Rotonda dei Mille is maintained by the horizontal wafer image of the building, but the concave form is accentuated by giving a tighter concave to the upper layer of offices so that the façades converge at one corner and separate at the other (ill. 8). The rather brutal concrete gable walls of the flats above reject the concave form altogether, being at rightangles to the main structure of the building itself. Surprisingly this gives the building a strong finish which produces the same effect as a cornice, such as on the building next to it. However, a romantic effect is created by the two opposing half cylinders of glass with the anti-solar glass fins attached which 'turn' the gable at its extreme point without touching like the index fingers of God and Adam in Michelangelo's famous 'Creation of Man' in the Sistine Chapel (ill. 8). The detailing of the façade elements, staircase, and other public spaces is of streamlined thirties' technical efficiency, a welcome contrast to the Italian realist 'neo-liberty' of the fifties and sixties.

However, the most controversial aspect of the building lies in its somewhat brutal expression of its functions. The design emphasizes the complexity of the building's mixed use, but of course does not allow for changes in function in the future. Whether this is a positive or negative approach is really the most fundamental question that this building asks. This expression of its service to the complex requirements of the community, home life, work, shopping, amusement, and so on is what makes this building interesting enough to include in this book on community housing. It attacks the notion that neighbourhoods and buildings can be neatly classified into the houses or offices, factories or commercial areas which make such colourful quilt patches on the town planners' drawings. Life is made of richer mingling relationships which are in reality constantly confused and overlapping.

1. The spiral ramp to the parking deck.
2,3. General views of the buildings.
4. Site plan.

1. Die Spiralrampe zum Parkdeck.
2,3. Gesamtansichten des Gebäudes.
4. Lageplan.

Mehrzweckgebäude an der Rotonda dei Mille, Bergamo, Italien. 1969-70

Architekten: Giuseppe Gambirasio, Giorgio Zenoni, Baran Ciagà, Walter Barbero

Der von einer Versicherungsgesellschaft errichtete Bau enthält unter der Erde eine Kaufhaus-Tiefgarage und ein Kino, auf der Straßenebene Läden, im ersten Obergeschoß Büros, im zweiten, offenen Obergeschoß Autoabstellplätze, zu denen eine Spiralrampe hinaufführt, (Abb. 1), im dritten Obergeschoß wiederum Büros und ganz oben beiderseits eines Mittelgangs Wohnungen mit versetzten Geschossen, die sich über den Gang hinziehen (Eingang auf der einen, Arbeitszimmer oder Büro auf der anderen Seite mit innerer Verbindung oberhalb des Mittelgangs). Die Wohnungen sind groß und offensichtlich auf Benutzer wie Architekten und Rechtsanwälte zugeschnitten. Die Erbauer des Gebäudes hielten sich an die strenge Bauhaus-Moral des funktionellen Expressionismus und brachten die verschiedenen Nutzungen in getrennten Bauteilen unter, aber im Gegensatz zu den Pionieren der dreißiger Jahre ließen sie die verschiedenen Funktionen auch formal zum Ausdruck kommen (Abb. 2, 3).

Man sollte nicht vergessen, daß das Bauwerk nur die Hälfte des ganzen Projekts darstellt. Ein Flügel des L-förmigen Gebäudekomplexes, der einen begrünten öffentlichen Platz auf zwei Seiten abschließen soll, harrt noch der Realisierung. Der zweite Flügel, um dessen Verwirklichungschancen es heute schlecht steht, würde dem Platz einen eindrucksvollen architektonischen Charakter verleihen und mit seinen Passagen zugleich das Fußgängerwegenetz durch das lebhafte neoklassische Stadtzentrum von Bergamo ergänzen (Abb. 4). Das kompromißlose Pflichtgefühl der Architekten beim Entwurf eines Gebäudes, das sowohl seinen Funktionen wie auch seiner Epoche Ausdruck gibt, verführte sie nicht dazu, die charakterlichen und formalen Gegebenheiten der Umgebung abzuleugnen. Sie paarten die entwurfliche Integrität eines Vielzweckgebäudes mit korrektem urbanem Verhalten, das die Kreisform der Rotonda dei Mille, die Hanglage der Via Piccini, die Gartenanlagen auf dem öffentlichen Platz an der Via Crispi Francesco im Südosten und die steilen Ziegeldächer der ganzen Nachbarschaft berücksichtigt. Der letzte Punkt ist besonders wichtig, nicht nur wegen der Steildächer selbst, sondern auch wegen des ihnen zugrunde liegenden Maßstabs, ragt doch die historische mittelalterliche Stadt (Città Alta) in unmißverständlicher Weise über ihre aus dem 19. Jahrhundert stammende jüngere Schwester (Città Piana) hinaus. Die Dachgestaltung war wesentlich, damit hier im Zentrum der Stadt kein Bruch entstand. Die Lösung bestand darin, die Wohneinheiten in den oberen Geschossen anzusiedeln und stark aufzugliedern. So entstand ein vielfach unterbrochenes Dach, das die Größe des Gebäudes

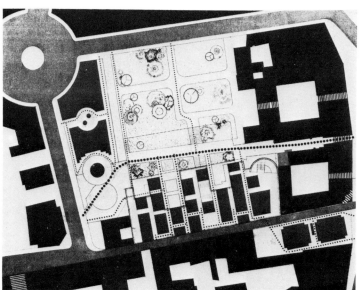

in der oberen Zone optisch herunterspielt (Abb. 7).

Die runden Platzwände der Rotonda dei Mille wurden in den horizontalen Bändern des Gebäudes aufgenommen. Die konkave Form wird dadurch gesteigert, daß die Krümmungen der Bürogeschoßfassaden sowohl zueinander als auch zur Krümmung des Platzraumes nicht parallel verlaufen (Abb. 8). Die ziemlich rohen Betongiebelwände der oberen Wohnungen folgen der konkaven Form nicht, sondern sind orthogonal zur Hauptrichtung des rektangulären Gebäudes angeordnet. Dies gibt dem Gebäude einen erstaunlich strengen Abschluß, wie er sonst von Gesimsen bewirkt wird (zum Beispiel an dem benachbarten Gebäude). Ein Hauch von Romantik liegt über den zwei entgegengesetzten gläsernen Halbzylindern mit den daran befestigten gläsernen Sonnenschutzlamellen, die den Giebel an seinem äußersten Punkt ›drehen‹, ohne sich zu berühren – wie die Zeigefinger Gottes und Adams auf Michelangelos berühmtem Gemälde ›Die Erschaffung des Menschen‹ in der Sixtinischen Kapelle (Abb. 8).

Die Einzelheiten der Fassade, des Treppenhauses und anderer öffentlicher Räume folgen der Stromlinieneffizienz der dreißiger Jahre und stehen damit in einem begrüßenswerten Gegensatz zu der italienischen ›Neo-Libertät‹ der fünfziger und sechziger Jahre.

Am umstrittensten ist zweifellos die fast brutale Zurschaustellung der Funktionen des Gebäudes. Sie unterstreicht die Komplexität der gemischten Nutzung, erlaubt aber natürlich keine künftigen Veränderungen. Ob dies positiv oder negativ zu werten sei, ist die Grundfrage, die das Gebäude aufwirft. Gerade die Zurschaustellung seiner Dienstfunktion für die vielfachen Anforderungen der Gemeinschaft – Privatleben, Arbeit, Einkaufen, Vergnügungen usw. – qualifiziert dieses Bauwerk für die Aufnahme in ein Buch über kollektives Wohnen. Es erschüttert die Vorstellung von säuberlich nach Wohnbauten, Büros, Fabriken, Läden usw. getrennten Stadtvierteln und Baukomplexen, die auf den Zeichnungen der Stadtplaner so schöne farbige Flickmuster ergeben. Das Leben besteht dagegen aus vielseitig ineinandergreifenden Beziehungen, die sich in Wirklichkeit ständig verwirren und überlagern.

5,6. Detailed views.
7. View over the upper floors of the building towards the Città Alta.
8. North side of the building.
9. Passage between the street and the public square behind the building.

5,6. Detailansichten.
7. Blick über die oberen Geschosse des Gebäudes auf die Città Alta.
8. Nordseite des Gebäudes.
9. Passage zwischen der Straße und dem öffentlichen Platz hinter dem Gebäude.

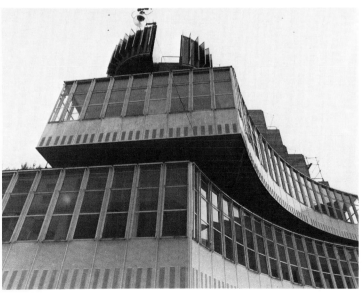

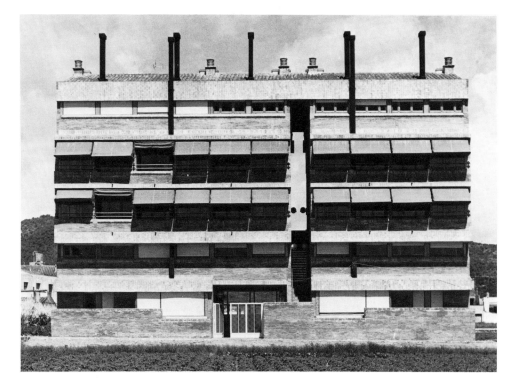

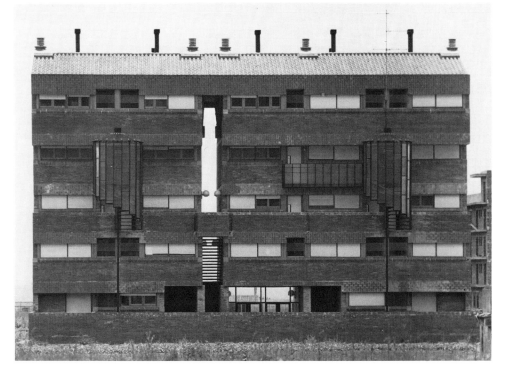

Housing for Teachers in Pineda, Spain. 1967–69

Architects: Josep Martorell, Oriol Bohigas, David Mackay

Thresholds are miraculous. Birth and death, the slipping in and out of sleep with the wonder of each day born anew – these experiences are echoed every time we pass the threshold from inside to outside or from outside to inside. If we have lost this sense of wonder of the threshold, and with it the sense of mystery, adventure and of the unknown, we have surely lost a part of life.

The threshold was the principle architectural theme in the design of this small building with twelve dwellings for teachers at a nearby school. Independence, essential for those who have just spent the day working together, had to be balanced against isolation. Private, ground-level houses sharing a common court would have been the best solution, but the small site available permitted only a multi-storey building. Nevertheless many of the characteristics of the ground-level dwelling were kept, such as the immediate contact with the outside weather and views upon opening the front door, which itself gives on to a common deck (ill. 5) that replaces the shared court access, or in historical terms the atrium. At street level a porch under the building provides the first filter, welcoming and sheltering the visitor who is enticed to enter by the view of the garden and fountain beyond. However, the zig-zag alley staircase that leads from this porch up to the street deck above (ills. 1, 2) suggests a more private area up and beyond. The duplex flats have been inverted with bedrooms either above or below (ill. 6) so that ten of the twelve dwellings share this common balcony deck. This deck rises through two floors so that the upper dwellings are spatially incorporated within this area. The accesses have been designed as lightly as possible so that they are not visually isolated. Each door is recessed within a small alcove to increase the threshold area, and then once the door is opened three options are available for the dweller. The visitor can be kept within the threshold so that he is neither in nor out, or can be shown immediately into an adjoining parlour or study next to the entrance hall, or in the case of a more generous welcome can be invited right into the family hearth.

Architecturally too, the building allows an almost classical ordering on a public scale beyond the additive grouping of individual dwellings, with duplex dwellings giving a larger scaled 'order' resting upon the ground-floor base.

1. South side of the building.
2. North side of the building.
3. View of the deck on the north side.

1. Südseite des Gebäudes.
2. Nordseite des Gebäudes.
3. Blick auf das Deck an der Nordseite.

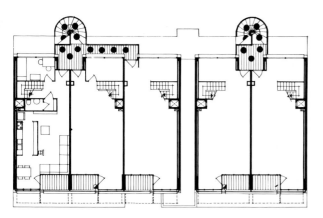

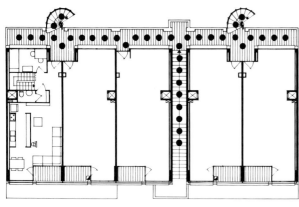

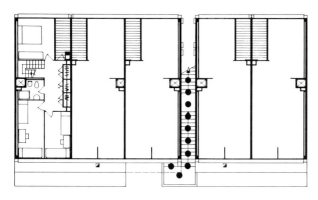

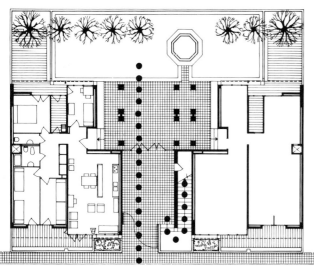

Lehrerhaus in Pineda, Spanien. 1967-69
Architekten: Josep Martorell, Oriol Bohigas,
David Mackay

Schwellen haben etwas von einem Wunder
an sich. Geburt und Tod, Einschlafen und Auf-
wachen und das Staunen über jeden neuen
Tag klingen in uns an, wenn wir über Schwellen treten, von innen nach außen oder von
außen nach innen. Wenn uns dieses Gespür
für das Wunder der Schwelle und damit das
Gefühl für das Geheimnisvolle des Abenteuer-
lichen und Unbekannten abhanden gekom-
men ist, haben wir ohne Zweifel einen Bereich
des Lebens eingebüßt.
Die Schwelle war das architektonische Haupt-
thema beim Entwurf dieses Gebäudes mit 12
Wohnungen für Lehrer der nahe gelegenen
Schule. Unabhängigkeit, die wesentlich ist für
alle, die den ganzen Tag mit anderen zusam-
menarbeiten, mußte gegen Isolierung ausge-
wogen werden. Eingeschossige Privathäuser
mit gemeinsamem Hof hätten wohl die beste
Lösung ergeben, aber das kleine Baugelände
zwang zu einem mehrgeschossigen Gebäude.
Allerdings konnten viele Merkmale des ein-
stöckigen Hauses beibehalten werden, so der
unmittelbare Kontakt mit Wetter und Ausblick
beim Öffnen der Haustür, die auf ein gemein-
sames Deck hinausgeht (Abb. 5). Dieses er-
setzt den gemeinsamen Hofzugang oder –
historisch ausgedrückt – das Atrium. Auf
Straßenebene betritt der Besucher eine Vorhalle unter dem Haus, von wo sein Blick auf den
jenseits gelegenen Garten und Brunnen
weitergeleitet wird. Die langgezogene Treppe,
die von hier zum Deck hinaufführt (Abb. 1, 2),
läßt oben eine privatere Sphäre erwarten. Die
Duplexwohnungen sind jeweils gegeneinander verkehrt; die Schlafräume liegen entweder im oberen oder im unteren Geschoß
(Abb. 6). Zehn der zwölf Wohnungen teilen
das gemeinsame Balkondeck. Das Deck zieht
sich über zwei Geschosse, so daß die oberen
Wohnungen räumlich in dieses einbezogen
sind. Die Zugänge wurden möglichst unauf-
fällig gestaltet, damit sie optisch nicht isoliert
wirken. Die einzelnen Türen sind in einen
kleinen Alkoven zurückgesetzt; der Schwellenbereich wird dadurch größer. Ist die Tür
einmal aufgegangen, so stehen dem Bewohner drei Möglichkeiten offen. Er kann den
Besucher im Schwellenbereich abfertigen, so
daß der Gast sich weder ausgestoßen noch
eingeladen fühlt; er kann ihn gleich in den
angrenzenden Salon oder Arbeitsraum neben
dem Eingang führen; er kann ihn aber auch,
wenn er ihm einen großherzigen Empfang be-
reiten will, sofort ins Zentrum der Familie ge-
leiten.
Architektonisch zeigt das Gebäude durch die
oberhalb der Erdgeschoßbasis größere Dimensionen erzeugenden Duplexwohnungen
eine fast klassische Ordnung mit einer städtischen Maßstäblichkeit, die jenseits der addi-
tiven Reihung einzelner Wohnungen liegt.

4. Ground plans (ground floor, 1st, 2nd and
3rd floors).
5. The deck.
6. Schematic section through the building.
7. One of the two staircases leading from
the deck to the 3rd floor.

4. Grundrisse (Erdgeschoß, 1., 2. und
3. Obergeschoß).
5. Das Deck.
6. Schemaschnitt durch das Gebäude.
7. Eine der beiden Treppen, die vom Deck
in das 3. Obergeschoß führen.

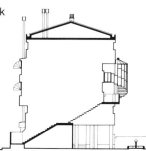

The Cloisters, Cincinnati, Ohio, 1967–70
Architects: Hardy Holzman Pfeiffer Associates

The project was designed for the high-income market and built on the southern slope of Mount Adams with panoramic views over the Ohio river and Kentucky countryside beyond (ills. 1, 3). 'An essential prerequisite of the project was to insure that each living unit had unobstructed access to this view.' This is how the architects described their brief.

Because of the slope, the architects divided the group into two parts. The upper one comprises a horizontal L-shaped set of 7 dwellings (known as Typical A Units) bent around a flat parking and garage court leading off Hatch St. which serves as the communal entrance area; the lower one consists of a stepped L-shaped set of 9 dwellings (Typical B Units) set at 45° to the higher set to optimize the views without interfering with the dwellings above. At the junction of the two sets a special dwelling was designed for a specific client.

The architects describe these different sets in the following terms:

'The Typical A Units are provided with 'view grabbers' (angular bay window projections) which take maximum advantage of the views as well as alter the configuration of an otherwise rectangular living environment. To provide variety and give each unit an individual character, every other Typical Unit plan is reversed, and the view grabbers occur in different places on each unit. In addition, the 'grabber' roofs of adjacent units pitch in opposite directions and the balconies overhead are placed in different locations, thus altering the space below.

'The Typical B units, because of their orientation on the site, have no view grabber, but the balconies above are used to provide a variety in the living area below. In these units all the sleeping facilities are in a straight forward manner on the lower level while all the living and entertaining spaces were left open above'. Even with the help of this description the building is a little difficult to understand. That this was a formal intention, the architects leave one in no doubt; they had designed a repetitive unit, and since this was a style normally associated with economy housing (in the eyes of future buyers) they did their best to disguise the fact. And they have done it very well, making the building fit in successfully with the scale of the village above it. The 'view grabbers' set at 45° are at rightangles to the lower set of dwellings so that there is a continuity along the façades of both sets.

Without doubt, the group reads well as a whole and in relation to the neighbourhood. There are, however, several weaknesses that mar the promising quality of the architecture. The first is the lack of any positive use of the triangular space between the two L-shaped sets. The attempt to bring the natural surface of the hill up under the lower set into this space

has not been a success. It is not at all clear why the lower set was tilted at 45°, so that more than half the dwellings face away from the sun, if it was not intended to do something with this court. Another drawback to the design is its inexplicable failure to catch the sun in the living areas of the four north-orientated dwellings in the upper A set. With so much tilting of the roofs one wonder why the architects paid so little attention to this point. The windows, with their frames painted black, were obviously carefully, if not consistently, designed, and their composition was obviously meant to be read as such (ill. 2), but it appears that they were mainly drawn in two dimensions since there are some very awkward corners which do not turn very well, and judging from the interior photographs very strange, if not ugly, effects are obtained (ill. 6). The rather obsessive use of the dramatic diagonal that cuts through most of the dwellings is a little overplayed for such small spaces, although, as has been pointed out before, it becomes an essential catalytic element in the façade.

1. General view.
2,3. Detailed views.

The Cloisters, Cincinnati, Ohio. 1967-70
Architekten: Hardy Holzman Pfeiffer Associates

Die für den gehobenen Markt bestimmte Gebäudegruppe liegt am Südhang des Mount Adams mit Rundblick über den Ohio und die jenseits gelegene Landschaft Kentuckys (Abb. 1, 3). ›Eine wesentliche Entwurfsvorgabe war, daß jede Wohneinheit in den ungehinderten Genuß dieses Blicks kommt.‹ So die Architekten in ihrer Entwurfserläuterung.
Wegen der Hanglage wurde die Häusergruppe unterteilt. Oben befindet sich eine horizontale L-förmige Gruppe von 7 Wohnhäusern (A-Einheiten); sie stehen um einen ebenen Park- und Garagenhof, der auf die Hatch Street mündet und als gemeinsamer Eingangsbereich dient. Unten liegt eine abgetreppte L-förmige Gruppe von 9 Wohnhäusern (B-Einheiten); sie ist um 45° gegen die obere Gruppe abgewinkelt, um optimalen Ausblick zu gewährleisten und eine gegenseitige Sichtbehinderung der oberen und unteren Häuser zu vermeiden. Den Berührungspunkt der beiden Gruppen bildet ein besonderes Haus für einen besonderen Auftraggeber.
Die Architekten beschreiben die Häusergruppen wie folgt: ›Die A-Einheiten sind mit 'Sicht-

1. Gesamtansicht.
2,3. Detailansichten.

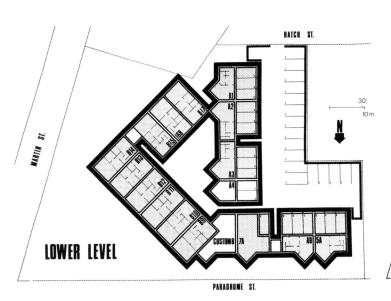

LOWER LEVEL

MARTIN ST.

30'
10 m

N

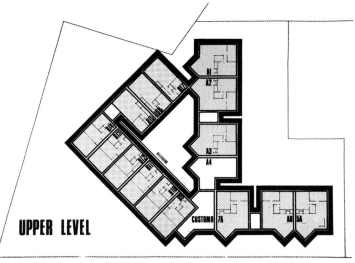

UPPER LEVEL

PARADROME ST.

UNIT A

GARAGE

SLEEP

1

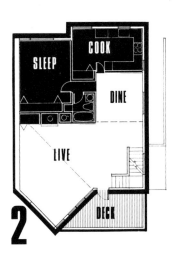

SLEEP

COOK

DINE

LIVE

DECK

2

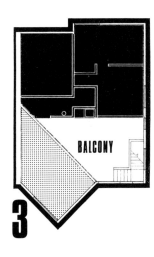

BALCONY

3

UNIT B

SLEEP

SLEEP

1

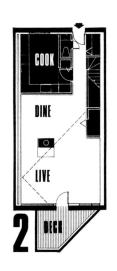

COOK

DINE

LIVE

DECK

2

BALCONY

3

fängern' (vorgezogenen Eckfenstern) ausgestattet, die eine optimale Aussicht bieten und
zugleich die sonst rechteckige Wohnland-
schaft gestaltlich aufbrechen. Um Abwechslung zu schaffen und jeder Einheit individuellen Charakter zu verleihen, wurde der
Grundriß jeder zweiten Einheit umgekehrt, so
daß sich die Sichtfänger jeweils an anderer
Stelle finden. Außerdem wurden die Sicht-
fängerdächer der benachbarten Einheiten in
entgegengesetzter Richtung und die Balkone
darüber in unterschiedlicher Weise angeordnet, um den Raum darunter abzuwandeln.
Die B-Einheiten haben wegen ihrer Ausrich-
tung im Gelände keine Sichtfänger, aber die
oberen Balkone sorgen für Abwechslung in
den Wohnräumen darunter. Bei diesen Einheiten sind alle Schlafräume auf der unteren
Ebene angesiedelt, während die offenen
Wohn- und Unterhaltungsräume oben angeordnet sind.‹

Selbst mit Hilfe dieser Beschreibung lassen sich die Gebäude nicht leicht verstehen. Darüber, daß dies Absicht war, lassen die Architekten keinen Zweifel offen. Sie hatten eine wiederholbare Einheit gewählt, und da dies (in den Augen zukünftiger Käufer) ein Merkmal des Billigwohnungsbaus ist, taten sie ihr möglichstes, um die Wiederholung zu verschleiern. Das ist ihnen zweifellos gelungen. Die Anlage fügt sich gut in den Maßstab des darüber gelegenen Dorfes ein. Die unter 45° angeordneten ›Sichtfänger‹ liegen orthogonal zu der tieferen Gruppe von Wohnungen, so daß sich eine Kontinuität in den Fassaden beider Gruppen ergibt.

Zweifellos macht die Gruppe als Ganzes und in Beziehung zur Nachbarschaft einen guten Eindruck. Die vielversprechende Qualität der Architektur wird jedoch durch einige Schwächen geschmälert, so zum Beispiel durch das Fehlen irgendeiner architektonischen oder städtebaulichen Bestimmung für den dreieckigen Raum zwischen den beiden L-förmigen Gruppen. Der Versuch, die natürliche Hanggestalt unter der tieferen Gruppe in diesen Raum zu ziehen, ist fehlgeschlagen. Unverständlich bleibt auch, warum die untere Gruppe um 45° gedreht wurde und somit mehr als die Hälfte der Häuser von der Sonne abgewandt ist, wenn nicht beabsichtigt war, aus diesem Hof irgend etwas zu machen. Weiterhin ist nicht erklärlich, daß keine Vorsorge getroffen wurde, um die Wohnbereiche der vier nach Norden liegenden Wohnhäuser der oberen A-Gruppe zu besonnen. Angesichts so vieler Dachschrägen fragt man sich, warum die Architekten diesen Punkt außer acht ließen. Die Fenster mit den schwarz gestrichenen Rahmen wurden offenbar mit großer Sorgfalt und Logik entworfen, und ihre Anordnung sollte zweifellos als Komposition gelesen werden (Abb. 2), aber anscheinend liegt ihnen eine zweidimensionale Konzeption zugrunde, denn es gibt einige sehr ungeschickt wirkende Ecken und – nach Innenaufnahmen zu urteilen – auch sonst einige merkwürdige, ja häßliche Stellen (Abb. 6). Die in ihrer Häufigkeit zwanghaft anmutende Diagonale, die die meisten Wohnungen durchschneidet, ist für so kleine Räume übertrieben, wenn sie auch, wie bereits erwähnt, an der Fassade als wesentlicher Katalysator wirkt.

4. Overall plans of the lower and upper level of the group.
5. Ground plans of the A and B Units.
6,7. Living area on the 3rd and 2nd level of an A Unit.

4. Übersichtspläne der unteren und der oberen Ebene der Anlage.
5. Grundrisse der A- und B-Einheiten.
6,7. Wohnbereich auf der 3. und 2. Ebene einer A-Einheit.

Housing in Bonanova, Spain. 1970–73
Architects: Josep Martorell, Oriol Bohigas, David Mackay

'Architects, sculptors, painters, we must all return to the crafts!' was Gropius' slogan in 1919. Gropius taught us that the machine was in reality just another craft that the artist has to master and so put to an end to the craft versus industry controversy within the Werkbund. The concept of the Bauhaus was at first essentially medieval and obviously owed a lot to the theories of nineteenth-century critics like Violett-le-Duc, William Morris, and especially John Ruskin. Ruskin's open philosophy of art was woven around his 'Seven Lamps of Architecture' – Sacrifice, Truth, Power, Beauty, Life, Memory, and Obedience – which really set the moral tone for whole generations of architects.

Naturally the group of dwellings shown here was not designed with Ruskin's rulings and suggestions in mind; for these very reasons it will be interesting to test the validity of Ruskin today.

One of the essential differences between buildings and architecture, according to Ruskin, is the uselessness of the latter. By that he meant that architecture cannot arise from mere material necessity of function, comfort and economy. The unnecessary feature must be added, be it through decoration, or through labour with the effort and sacrifice of offering the most costly in order to honour the spirit of mankind. Costly not so much in the sense of luxury but in the hours of work necessary for good and honest workmanship employed in the service of beauty. There are details in the Bonanova building the delicacy of which, as Ruskin points out, 'will not be seen nor loved by one beholder of ten thousand ... it is not the emotion of admiration, but the act of adoration: not the gift, but the giving'. Here we could point out as an example the colour, size, and laying of the brickwork, its unity with the flow of burnt ceramic out over the gardens and up and down the steps (ills. 6, 7, 8).

One cannot ban morals from architecture, and certainly there are few architects nowadays who would deny the ethical content of their work. Ruskin's Lamp of Truth held that deceit was a moral delinquency that violated the very nature of architecture: Buildings should not look more expensive than they are – nothing could be closer to the moral spine of the modern movement. In the Bonanova buildings the aim was to provide comfortable dwellings within a reasonably economic budget. Simple and ordinary materials were used which do not conceal their purpose. The entrance is an almost flagrant disregard of property which overemphasizes the poverty of the architectural means, but this is immediately compensated for by a complex succession of communal open-air vestibules which display the real wealth in what has been conserved of the old garden, with its chestnut and lime trees.

With the 'Lamp of Power' Ruskin revalues the monumental aspect of architecture. The monumental aspect is not only achieved by 'size and weight', but, as Ruskin remarks, 'the Power of architecture may be said to depend on the quantitiy (whether measured in space or intenseness) of its shadow .... Let him design with the sense of cold and heat upon him; the first necessity is that the quantities of shade or light ... shall be thrown into masses, either of something like equal weight, or else large masses of the one relieved with small of the other. ... No design that is divided at all, and yet not divided into masses, can ever be of the smallest value ....'

In the Bonanova buildings the two L-shaped masses are maintained within the tight brown brick skin that wraps around the edges with rounded bricks, and the balcony window slits are merged into the surface with lace metal railings and brown paint and brown plastic blinds (ill. 2). Every effort has been made to play down their importance so that in effect they become dull unobtrusive elements within the major mass of the building. The shadows have been chopped out violently with slashes of metal and glass and with organ-like chimney tubes that multiply from bottom to top.

Decoration was the most tangible evidence of beauty for Ruskin. His first major law is that one should not 'decorate things belonging to purposes of active and occupied life. Wherever you can rest, there decorate; where rest is forbidden, so is beauty' (beauty in Ruskin's sense meaning decoration). What also interests us here in relation to the Bonanova building is Ruskin's observation 'that natural colour never follows form, but is arranged on an entirely separate system'. The colour of the Bonanova building does follow the form, but in a negative way so as to reduce its impact to a minimum. The window frames, blinds and balcony railings are all submerged in various hues of brown into the brick skin. In contrast, the repetitive white living-room balconies stand out as focal points in the composition; it is here that colour has been introduced in its own right and following its own separate system. The multiple chimneys are coloured from the garden in dark green to the sky in light yellow. The large sky-blue chimney shaft and the yellow gates mark the entrance emphasizing an arbitrary addition to the main architectural system.

In his 'Lamp of Life' Ruskin has come as close as anyone to a definition of a living architecture, impatient, struggling towards 'something unattained'. It contains a 'certain neglect or contempt of refinement in execution, or, at all events, a visible subordination of execution to conception'. This audacity, together with a frankness towards imitation of other designs, distinguishes the living architecture from the dead, the uncomfortable from the comfortable the progressive from the perfect. With this in mind it is appropriate to quote the art critic Alexandre Cirici on the Bonanova buildings:

'The greatest interest of the group lies in the interior space. What seems to be most significant, in a world that everyday is more private, is the character that it takes of a public space. It has things that the street has. Like the old streets that have alleys under the English mediaeval city houses. One has the sensation that one should find children playing street games as in a poor district . . .'

Back to Ruskin: 'There are two duties respecting national architecture . . . the first, to render the architecture of the day, historical; and, the second, to preserve, as the most precious of inheritances, that of past ages.' The 'Lamp of Memory' is for Ruskin a sign of true perfection. When dwellings are designed and built beyond immediate requirements then we will achieve a true domestic architecture that will form part of the history of the civilization that built it.

Ruskin's final lamp, the 'Lamp of Obedience', is perhaps the most provocative of all, for he suggests that Liberty is a wolf in false clothing, the result of anarchy. Freedom, on the other hand, according to Ruskin is only obtainable when Law is respected, or obeyed. Although we may not have achieved a recognized school of architecture within the modern movement we do realize that each building demands its own laws if order is to be imposed upon chaos. Does Ruskin matter? The answer is surely yes. On the one hand, the battle of the styles is still with us. Micro-planning or functional architecture with each piece responding to its use is in reality no different from the neo-gothic freedom of organic growth. Macro-planning, with flexible multi-use space served by all the latest technological gimmicks, is very close to the neo-classic container. Ruskin saw the errors and advantages of both. For architecture as a whole Ruskin is essential, because his strong Protestant biblical faith led him to pragmatic socialism[3] and made him one of the spiritual fathers of the modern movement.

1. The access from the street.
2,3. The court.
4. A detail showing the chimney tubes that multiply from bottom to top.

1. Zugang von der Straße.
2,3. Der Hof.
4. Detailansicht mit den sich von unten nach oben vermehrenden Kaminen.

Wohngebäude in Bonanova, Spanien. 1970-73
Architekten: Josep Martorell, Oriol Bohigas,
David Mackay

›Architekten Bildhauer, Maler – wir müssen
alle zum Handwerk zurück!‹ lautete Gropius'
Motto im Jahr 1919. Gropius lehrte uns, daß
die Maschine in Wirklichkeit nur ein anderes
Handwerkszeug ist, das der Künstler be-
herrschen muß. Damit beendete er im Werkbund die Kontroverse zwischen Handwerk
und Industrie. Der Bauhausgedanke war im
wesentlichen vom Mittelalter bestimmt. Viel
verdankte er den Theorien von Kritikern des
19. Jahrhunderts wie Viollet-le-Duc, William
Morris und besonders John Ruskin. Ruskins
offene Kunstphilosophie, die sich um seine
›Sieben Lampen der Architektur‹ (Opferbe-
reitschaft, Wahrhaftigkeit, Macht, Schönheit,
Leben, Gedächtnis und Gehorsam) rankte,
gab für ganze Generationen von Architekten
den moralischen Ton an.
Die hier gezeigte Gruppe von Wohnbauten
wurde natürlich nicht nach Ruskins Regeln
und Vorstellungen entworfen, doch gerade
deshalb ist es interessant, Ruskins heutige
Gültigkeit daran zu messen.
Einer der wesentlichen Unterschiede zwischen normalem Bauen und Architektur ist
nach Ruskin die Nutzlosigkeit der letzteren.
Damit wollte er sagen, daß Architektur nicht
aus den rein materiellen Notwendigkeiten der
Funktion, des Komforts und der Wirtschaftlichkeit entstehen kann. Das Unnötige muß
dazutreten, sei es als Dekor oder als etwas
anderes höchst Kostspieliges zur Ehre des
Menschengeistes. Unter Kostspieligkeit wird
hier weniger der Luxus im engeren Sinn als
der Aufwand an guter, ehrlicher Arbeit im
Dienst der Schönheit verstanden. Der Bona-
nova-Bau enthält Details, deren Feinheit, wie
Ruskin sagt, ›nicht einem von zehntausend
Betrachtern auffallen oder zusagen wird . . .
es geht nicht um das Gefühl der Bewunderung,
sondern um die Tat der Verehrung, nicht um
die Gabe, sondern um das Geben.‹ Als Beispiel hierfür möchten wir Farbe, Maßstab und
Fügung des Mauerwerks nennen, seine Einheit mit der Flut keramischer Platten über die
Gärten hin und die Stufen hinauf und hinunter
(Abb. 6, 7, 8).
Die Moral läßt sich aus der Architektur nicht
verbannen, und es gibt sicher heute wenige
Architekten, die den ethischen Gehalt ihrer
Arbeit ableugnen würden. Im Sinne von Ruskins Lampe der Wahrhaftigkeit ist Falschheit
ein moralisches Vergehen gegen das Wesen
der Architektur: Gebäude sollten nicht teurer
aussehen, als sie sind; es dürfen also mit anderen Worten falscher Produktion und unrichti-
gem Konsum keine Zugeständnisse gemacht
werden. Nichts steht der moralischen Prämis-
se der modernen Bewegung näher. Das Pro-
gramm für die Bonanova-Gebäude sah bequeme Wohnungen zu erschwinglichen Preisen vor. Es wurden einfache, gewöhnliche
Materialien verwendet, die ihren Zweck nicht

verschleiern. Der Eingang ist eine geradezu
bodenlose Mißachtung des Eigentums und
hebt die Bescheidenheit der baulichen Mittel
fast übermäßig hervor. Dies wird aber sofort
kompensiert durch die komplexe Aufeinanderfolge gemeinschaftlicher Freiluftvesti-
büle, die, indem sie offenbaren, was von dem
alten Garten mit seinen Kastanien und Linden
gerettet werden konnte, wirklichen Reichtum
bezeugen.
Mit der Lampe der Macht läßt Ruskin den
Monumentalaspekt der Architektur wieder zu
seinem Recht kommen. Monumentalität entsteht nicht nur durch ›Größe und Gewicht‹.
Ruskin vermerkt: ›Die Macht der Architektur
kann als von der Menge ihres Schattens (ob
in Raum oder Intensität gemessen) abhängig
angesehen werden . . . Der Architekt soll beim
Entwerfen Kälte und Hitze mitempfinden; . . .
zuallererst ist es notwendig, daß die Mengen
von Schatten oder Licht . . . in Massen umge-
setzt werden, entweder in Massen von glei-
chem Gewicht oder in große Massen durch-
setzt mit kleinen Massen . . . Kein überhaupt
gegliederter Bau, der nicht in verschiedene
Massen aufgeteilt ist, kann je auch nur den
geringsten Wert haben . . .‹ Bei den Bonanova-
Gebäuden werden die beiden L-förmigen
Massen von der festen, braunen Ziegelsteinhaut, die sich mit Rundziegeln um die Ecken
zieht, zusammengehalten. Die schlitzartigen
Balkonfenster verschmelzen mit der Fläche
durch die Engmaschigkeit des metallenen
Gittergeländers, den braunen Anstrich und die
braunen Kunststoffjalousien (Abb. 2). Es
wurde keine Mühe gescheut, um ihre Bedeutung herunterzuspielen, und sie sind tatsächlich ganz unauffällige Elemente innerhalb
der Gebäudemasse. Eine starke und in dieser
Form gewollte Schattenwirkung ergeben die
durchlaufenden Schneisen aus Metall und
Glas sowie die sich von unten nach oben vermehrenden orgelpfeifenartigen Kamine.
Dekor war für Ruskin der greifbarste Beweis
für Schönheit. Sein erstes Hauptgesetz lautete: ›Dinge, die Zwecken des aktiven und ge-
schäftigen Lebens angehören, sollte man
nicht verzieren. Wo man ausruht, soll man
auch Dekor anbringen; wo Ruhe untersagt ist,
ist es Schönheit auch‹ (Schönheit in der Rus-
kinschen Gleichsetzung mit Dekor). Im Blick
auf die Bonanova-Gebäude interessiert auch
die folgende Bemerkung Ruskins: ›Die natürliche Farbe folgt nie der Form, sie wird vielmehr nach einem völlig anderen System angeordnet.‹ Bei dem Bonanova-Gebäude folgt
die Farbe der Form, aber in negativer Weise,
indem sie deren Wirkung stark reduziert. Die
Fensterrahmen, die Jalousien, die Balkonge-
länder fügen sich mit ihren verschiedenen
Brauntönen in die Ziegelsteinhaut ein. Dagegen stehen die sich wiederholenden weißen
Wohnzimmerbalkone als Brennpunkte in der
Komposition; hier wurde die Farbe als eigenständiges Element verwendet, das einem
eigenen, getrennten System folgt. Die Farb-
skala der Kaminbündel reicht von Dunkelgrün

im Gartenbereich bis zu Hellgelb im Bereich
der oberen Geschosse. Der große himmel-
blaue Kaminschacht und die gelben Tore mar-
kieren den Eingang und stellen ein gewolltes
Zusatzelement innerhalb des architektonischen Gesamtrahmens dar.
Mit seiner Lampe des Lebens gelingt Ruskin
wie kaum einem die Definition einer lebendigen Architektur, die sich ungeduldig auf
›etwas noch nicht Erreichtes‹ zukämpft. ›Sie
enthält eine gewisse Vernachlässigung oder
Mißachtung der Raffinesse bei der Ausführung oder jedenfalls eine sichtbare Unter-
ordnung der Ausführung unter die Konzeption.‹ Diese Kühnheit im Verein mit der Frei-
zügigkeit gegenüber der Nachahmung anderer Entwürfe unterscheidet die lebendige
von der toten, die unbequeme von der be-
quem gewordenen, die progressive von der
perfekten Architektur. Wir möchten hier das

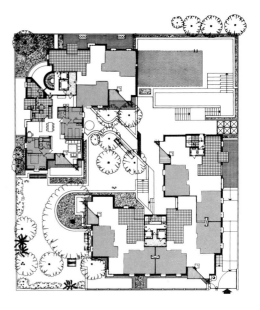

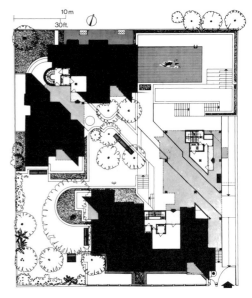

Urteil des Kunstkritikers Alexandre Cirici über die Bonanova-Gebäude zitieren: ›Am interessantesten an der Gruppe ist der Raum zwischen den Häusern. Höchst bedeutsam ist wohl in einer Welt, die täglich privater wird, der ihm eigene öffentliche Charakter. Der Raum hat Dinge, die auch die Straße hat. Wie die alten Straßen mit ihren Durchgängen unter den englischen Stadthäusern des Mittelalters. Man kann sich vorstellen, hier Kinder bei Straßenspielen wie in einem Armenviertel anzutreffen. . .‹

Zurück zu Ruskin: ›Hinsichtlich einer nationalen Architektur gibt es zwei Pflichten . . . die erste ist die Wahrung des historischen Bezugs in der zeitgenössischen Architektur; die zweite Pflicht ist die Wahrung der Architektur vergangener Epochen als des kostbarsten Erbes.‹ Mit der Lampe des Gedächtnisses verbindet sich für Ruskin wahre Vollkommenheit. Wenn Wohnhäuser über die unmittelbaren Erfordernisse hinaus entworfen und gebaut werden, dann erzielen wir eine wahrhaft häusliche Architektur, die die Geschichte der Kultur, die sie hervorgebracht hat, nachzeichnet.

Ruskins letzte Lampe, die Lampe des Gehorsams, provoziert vielleicht am meisten, wird hier doch die Ansicht verfochten, Ungebundenheit sei der Wolf im Schafskleid, das eitle Ergebnis hochmütiger Anarchie. Freiheit besteht nach Ruskin nur dort, wo das Gesetz respektiert oder befolgt wird. Wenn wir auch vielleicht keine allgemein anerkannte Architekturschule innerhalb der modernen Bewegung ins Leben gerufen haben, ist uns doch klar, daß jedes Bauwerk seine eigenen Gesetze verlangt, wenn Ordnung ins Chaos gebracht werden soll.

Ist Ruskin heute noch relevant? Die Frage ist zweifellos zu bejahen. Einmal geht der Richtungskampf auch bei uns noch weiter. Mikroplanung oder funktionelle Architektur, bei der jedes Detail seinem Verwendungszweck entspricht, unterscheidet sich in Wirklichkeit keineswegs von der neugotischen Freiheit des organischen Wachstums; Makroplanung mit flexiblem Vielzweckraum und den jüngsten technischen Errungenschaften kommt dem neoklassischen Großbehälter sehr nahe. Ruskin erkannte Mängel und Vorzüge beider Methoden. Für die Architektur in ihrer Gesamtheit ist Ruskin insofern wichtig, als er durch seinen unerschütterlichen evangelischen Bibelglauben zu einem pragmatischen Sozialismus kam [3] und somit einer der geistigen Väter der modernen Bewegung wurde.

5. Ground plans (ground floor, typical upper floor).
6,7,8. Different views of the court.

5. Grundrisse (Erdgeschoß, typisches Obergeschoß).
6,7,8. Verschiedene Hofansichten.

Housing in Trafalgar Road, Greenwich, London. 1963–68
Architect: James Gowan; structural engineer: Stephen Revesz

If the title of this book had to be justified by only one example, then this small formal quadrangle of four-storey maisonettes would qualify as perhaps the best way to explain it. It is relativley easy to define architecture in words, but when it comes to the crucial choice between declaring that this building is architecture and that is not we have to use feeling as well as intellect. We all know that architecture must contain 'firmness, commodity and delight', we also know that it must be authentic (true) in solving the right problems, and we know too that it must tell us something about the cultural, social and economic problems of the moment that it is built. We also know that an architectural solution goes beyond the consumer article and in the final analysis assumes the character of a monument. Architects build monuments, not monumental buildings – which have very different and unfortunate connotations – otherwise they would not work so hard for their profession. James Gowan is one of these who tries to build monuments, and in Trafalgar Road he has succeeded. The success is due to the fact that he has set out to solve a series of problems: (1) to build with economy; (2) to design for privacy, with optional small neighbourhood belongingness both within the new building itself and in relation to the adjoining neighbours; (3) to give meaning by communication, to express through the style, with its proportions, rhythm, and details, the aesthetic preoccupations of the time.

Working within the limits of maximum cost control and minimum floor sizes the architect has little choice but to spend money available on the necessary things. Careful design has produced a sheltered internal communal court that protects the inhabitants from the chilly breeze which sweeps across from the adjoining Thames in winter (ills. 1, 5). It has also given private gardens to the ground-floor dwellings and small private balconies to those who live above. The corridor access is expressive and at times wasteful (in the staggered block) but does avoid the sociological and psychological problems of lonely staircases going up to pairs of flats. The balcony, or passage, access does have the real advantage that people still feel that they live in a house; when they open their front door it is to the sun, wind and rain, not to the no-man's-land of a municipal staircase.

The court itself is skilfully planned with the southern building staggered to run parallel to the adjoining railway cutting. This oblique façade immediately complicates the simple quadrangle personalizing its character (ill. 3). The effect is heightened by one 'front' façade on the north, with its protective lawn in front of the living-rooms, and three 'back' access façades facing east, west and south. Perhaps one of the most observant decisions of the architect was to leave the courtyard open at one corner, which helps avoid any feeling of isolation from the world outside (ill. 6).

Trafalgar Road is not a monument in the sense of those 'monuments' which we usually assume should be knocked down. The difference lies in its democratic relationship to its inhabitants and the surrounding buildings. It is even difficult to recognize and to find amongst its neighbours. This unobtrusiveness is a quality which cultured people appreciate today – it is a sign of respect and education, the main characteristics of a democratic way of life.

More telling than all this, however, is the quality that derives from the building's attempt to recover the best stylistic features of the beginning of the modern movement in architecture when simple materials were also the main ones used. Dudok and the Amsterdam School are recalled in the brick detailing, the horizontally divided casements and the use of the corner window. The modern movement is now mature enough not to have to *invent* new forms (which in the end become an exhausting fad) when we have an enormous vocabulary at our disposal to be *developed*. Trafalgar Road is a lesson in what our new architectural monuments could be about.

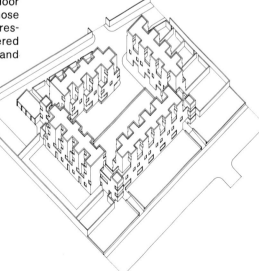

Wohnbauten in der Trafalgar Road, Greenwich, London. 1963-68
Architekt: James Gowan; Statiker: Stephen Revesz

Müßte man den Titel dieses Buches durch ein einziges Beispiel rechtfertigen, so fände man kaum ein geeigneteres als dieses kleine strenge Viereck viergeschossiger Maisonettehäuser. Architektur läßt sich unschwer mit Worten definieren, aber wenn es darum geht, die Bezeichnung Architektur einem Bauwerk beizulegen und einem anderen abzusprechen, müssen wir außer dem Intellekt auch das Gefühl sprechen lassen. Wir wissen, daß ein Gebäude, soll es der Architektur zugerechnet werden können, ›Festigkeit, Zweckmäßigkeit und Freude‹ ausstrahlen muß, daß es insofern authentisch (wahr) sein muß, als es die richtigen Probleme löst, und daß es uns etwas über die kulturellen, gesellschaftlichen und wirtschaftlichen Zustände zur Zeit seines Entstehens offenbaren muß. Wir wissen auch, daß ein architektonisches Werk mehr ist als ein Gebrauchsartikel und letzten Endes Monumentcharakter annimmt. Die Architekten bauen Monumente, nicht monumentale Gebäude mit dem ganz anderen und vielleicht abstoßenden Beiklang des Begriffs, sonst würden sie nicht so eifrig forschen und streben. James Gowan gehört zu denen, die Monumente zu bauen versuchen, und in der Trafalgar Road ist es ihm gelungen. Sein Erfolg beruht darauf, daß er sich um verschiedene Zielvorstellungen bemühte: 1. sparsam zu bauen; 2. Abgeschlossenheit und zugleich wahlfreie Nachbarschaftlichkeit innerhalb des neuen Komplexes selbst wie auch gegenüber den angrenzenden Häusern zu gewährleisten; 3. erkennbaren Sinn zu stiften und mit den Stilmitteln Proportion, Rhythmus und Detail die ästhetischen Anliegen der Zeit zum Ausdruck zu bringen.

Der Architekt, der in den Begrenzungen maximaler Kostenkontrolle und minimaler Raumgrößen arbeitet, muß zwangsläufig das verfügbare Geld für die notwendigsten Dinge verwenden. Eine sorgfältige Planung ergab einen gemeinsamen, geschützten Innenhof, den im Winter die kühle Brise von der nahen Themse nicht erreicht (Abb. 1, 5). Die Wohnungen im Erdgeschoß haben kleine Gärten, die oberen Wohnungen kleine Balkone. Die Erschließung über Laubengänge ist eindrucksvoll und gelegentlich auch kostspielig (bei dem gestaffelten Block), aber sie vermeidet die soziologisch und psychologisch anfechtbaren Treppenhäuser, die jeweils zu Wohnungspaaren hinaufführen. Sie bietet den Vorteil, daß die Leute das Gefühl haben, in einem eigenen Haus zu wohnen, und daß sie nicht einem unpersönlichen, städtischen Treppenhaus, sondern Sonne, Wind und Regen ihre Wohnungstür öffnen.

Der Hof ist sehr geschickt angelegt; das südliche, abgetreppte Gebäude verläuft parallel zu der angrenzenden Eisenbahntrasse. Die

Schräge läßt das einfache Rechteck komplizierter erscheinen und verleiht ihm Charakter (Abb. 3). Diese Wirkung wird noch dadurch gesteigert, daß auf der Nordseite die ›Frontfassade‹ nach außen gekehrt ist – ein schützender Rasen befindet sich vor den Wohnräumen –, auf der Ost-, West- und Südseite dagegen die ›Rückfassade‹ mit den Zugängen. Einer der bemerkenswertesten Kunstgriffe des Architekten bestand darin, den Hof in einer Ecke offen zu lassen; somit kann nicht das Gefühl völliger Absonderung von der Außenwelt aufkommen (Abb. 6).

Trafalgar Road ist ein Monument. Es unterscheidet sich dadurch von den Monumenten, die wir lieber abreißen würden, daß es in einer demokratischen Beziehung zu Bewohnern und Nachbarschaft steht. Die Einpassung geht so weit, daß es unter den Nachbargebäuden nur schwer auszumachen ist. Unauffälligkeit ist eine Eigenschaft, die von gebildeten Leuten heute überhaupt sehr geschätzt wird als ein Zeichen der Achtung und des Selbstwertbewußtseins, also der Hauptmerkmale eines demokratischen Lebens.

Deutlich spürbar geht von dem Bauwerk in seinem ästhetischen Anliegen, die besten stilistischen Elemente aus den Anfängen der modernen Architekturbewegung wieder aufzunehmen, aus der Zeit also, da ebenfalls überwiegend einfache Materialien verwendet wurden, eine besondere Kultiviertheit aus. An Dudok und die Amsterdamer Schule erinnern die Ziegelsteinwände, die horizontale Fenstergliederung und die Eckfenster. Die moderne Bewegung ist jetzt soweit ausgereift, daß sie es nicht nötig hat, neue Formen zu *erfinden* (die schließlich nur noch wie angestrengte Grillen wirken), da sie über ein ungeheures Vokabular verfügt, das sie *weiterentwickeln* kann. Trafalgar Road ist beispielhaft dafür, wie unsere neuen baulichen Monumente aussehen könnten.

1. Isometric view of the complex.
2. The north wing.
3. The staggered south wing.

1. Isometrie der Anlage.
2. Der nördliche Flügel.
3. Der gestaffelte südliche Flügel.

SECTION A   ELEVATION   SECTION B

2BR MAISONETTE

3BR MAISONETTE

3RD FLOOR   2ND FLOOR   1ST FLOOR   GROUND FLOOR

FEET

2BR MAISONETTE   3BR MAISONETTE

SECTION C   ELEVATION   SECTION D

2BR MAISONETTE

O.P. 1BR

O.P. 1BR

3RD FLOOR   2ND FLOOR   1ST FLOOR   GROUND FLOOR

2BR MAISONETTE   O.P. 1BM FLAT   O.P. 1BR FLAT

10 m

30 ft.

4. Ground plans and sections (above: the west wing; below: the east wing).
5. The west wing.
6. View along the west wing.
7. Passage between the south and the east wing.

4. Grundrisse und Schnitte (oben westlicher, unten östlicher Flügel).
5. Der westliche Flügel.
6. Blick entlang dem westlichen Flügel.
7. Durchgang zwischen dem südlichen und dem östlichen Flügel.

**Rainpark Housing, Brügg, Switzerland.
1968–70**
Architects: Atelier 5 (head of project: A. du Fresne and A. Pini)

The building group at Rainpark is a refreshing reminder that the vocabulary of the thirties, the fifties and the sixties is still a valid language for the creative architecture of today. This basic vocabulary is found first in the use of a seven-storey block connected to two groups of row houses (ill. 5). We find it again in the use of reinforced exposed concrete, glass walls and flat roofs. But, of course, this heroic basic vocabulary does not lead on to poetic creation. What it does ensure is that a discipline is imposed which makes no concessions to easy historicism and popular folklore. Comfortable and conservative solutions usually avoid the problems.

Here, the basic problem was to root a high density (economically feasible) building group (29 m² per person or 120 people to the acre) into a low density suburban setting without disturbing the existing character or what Kevin Lynch calls the 'grain'; a further problem was to adapt the design to a site plan previously proposed and approved by the local authorities. The neighbours were not to be upset, starting a dangerous emigration that would create decay and change the character of the district, nor was the new group of buildings to be without a genuine personality which in turn would contribute positively to the social and aesthetic interest of the area.

The architects solved these primary problems by placing one row house in front nearer the road, with another row behind and above up the slope of the hill, and the block beyond. However, they have been careful to keep the roof below the tree-line which acts as a splendid backcloth to the stage (ill. 2). It is a stage in the traditional sense of a show because this building group does have a 'front' and a 'back' as the photographs demonstrate.

The row houses all have gardens, balconies and back-yards. These are well planted, and with grass on the roof, their scale is skilfully brought down to that of the neighbouring villas. The main pedestrian alley (ill. 3) runs through the middle on an axis that is broken at the centre, which forms a small semi-public square where the children gather and from where the drivers and passengers enter the garage below (ill. 11).

The tall block at the back lies in a semi-public park that flows up and around part of the building from the public right-of-way running along the northern end of the site (ills. 1, 11). This building, an obvious grandchild of Le Corbusier, shows a rich independence of its heritage, in that the module of the structure does not necessarily coincide with the divisions of the dwellings.

The buildings were never intended to provide housing for workers, as the high land values made it imperative to design more spacious

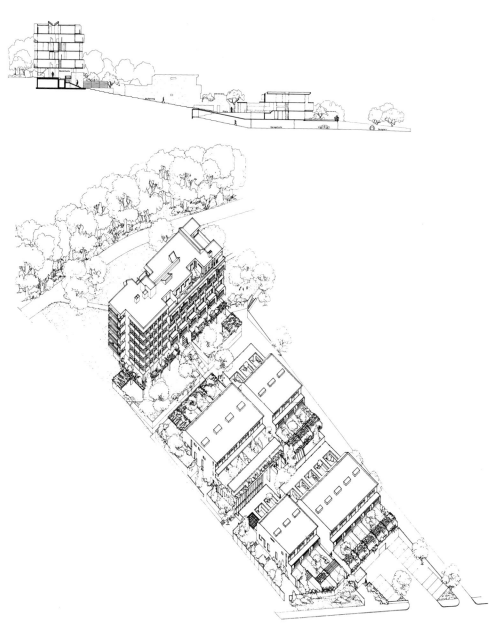

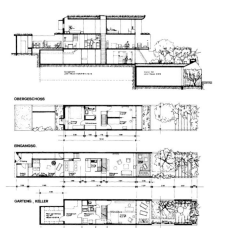

1. North side of the seven-storey block.
2. South side of the seven-storey block.
3. View of the main pedestrian alley.
4. Section.
5. Isometric view of the building group.
6. Plans of a row house.
7. Plans of the seven-storey block.

1. Nordseite des siebengeschossigen Blocks.
2. Südseite des siebengeschossigen Blocks.
3. Blick in den Hauptfußweg.
4. Schnitt.
5. Isometrie der Anlage.
6. Pläne eines Reihenhauses.
7. Pläne des siebengeschossigen Blocks.

and therefore more expensive dwellings; but this does not invalidate the design as an example to be followed since the lesson lies in the care that has been taken in its conception. Rainpark goes a long way to prove that the mere fact that a building is a multi-storey slab does not prevent its being creatively and pleasantly designed. It also seems to be an agreeable place to live in, and as yet there are no signs that anybody has moved from the neighbouring villas.

It is a building group that has mastered all three areas of community relationship. First of all, it fits well into a suburban landscape (through scale, detail and proportion) so that the 'we-and-they' distance has been reduced to a minimum. Secondly, the group maintains sufficient personality, or character, to help the inhabitants identify with the place and share the pleasures and problems of living together there. This character is achieved not only by modernity but also by a skilful mellowing of radicalism with the use of an internal alley along a broken-axis and the gentle curve of the cornice, for example. On a practical level the visual unity is reinforced by the shared garage and central path access forming an internal street and semi-public porch and lawn. Thirdly, sufficient privacy for each family is vouched for. In the row houses, this has been achieved by the deep walled front and back gardens; it has also been achieved in the multi-storey block with the really deep terraces, making them into outdoor living areas with plant balconies separating them from their neighbours (ill. 13). The deep through living-rooms, with light and air from north and south, and the kitchen in the middle, provide alternative privacy within the 'public' living-space of the family itself. This is further accentuated by the bedrooms being on a different floor in the row houses and the duplex flats.

8. View of the building group from the west.
9. View along the western boundary.
10. Northern access to the seven-storey block.
11. Main pedestrian alley.
12. Living-room in the seven-storey block.
13. Living-room in a row house.

8. Blick von Westen auf die Gruppe.
9. Blick entlang der Westgrenze.
10. Nordzugang zum siebengeschossigen Block.
11. Hauptfußweg.
12. Wohnraum im siebengeschossigen Block.
13. Wohnraum in einem Reihenhaus.

**Überbauung Rainpark, Brügg, Schweiz.
1968-70**
Architekten: Atelier 5 (Sachbearbeiter: A.du Fresne und A. Pini)

Die Überbauung Rainpark erinnert erneut daran, daß das Vokabular der dreißiger, fünfziger und sechziger Jahre nach wie vor Gültigkeit besitzt, daß es einen Hauch von Poesie hervorzubringen vermag und das Wohnen zu einem schönen Erlebnis werden lassen kann. Die Anwendung jenes Vokabulars zeigt sich vor allem in der Kombination eines siebengeschossigen Blocks mit Gruppen von Reihenhäusern (Abb. 5), dann aber auch in der Verwendung von nicht verputztem Stahlbeton, Glaswänden und Flachdächern. Das klassische Vokabular allein ist aber noch keine Garantie für eine poetische Schöpfung; es erlegt einem jedoch eine Disziplin auf, die keine Zugeständnisse an einen leichten Historizismus oder eine farbige Folklore duldet. Bequeme konformistische Lösungen gehen gewöhnlich an den Problemen vorbei.
Hier bestand das Grundproblem darin, eine hochverdichtete (wirtschaftlich tragbare) Überbauung (29 m² Gesamtfläche/Person oder 345 Personen/ha) in einem locker besiedelten vorstädtischen Rahmen zu verwurzeln, ohne den bestehenden Charakter – oder das, was Kevin Lynch das ›Korn‹ nennt – zu stören. Der Entwurf mußte außerdem auf einen Überbauungsplan, der vorher von den dortigen Behörden ausgearbeitet und gebilligt worden war, zugeschnitten werden. Die Nachbarn durften nicht verärgert werden, weil es sonst zu einer gefährlichen Flucht hätte kommen können, die zu Verfall und Veränderung des Charakters der Gegend geführt hätte. Die neue Gebäudegruppe sollte aber auch eine eigene Persönlichkeit besitzen und somit zum sozialen und ästhetischen Reiz des Gebiets beitragen.
Die Architekten lösten diese Primärprobleme damit, daß sie die Reihenhäuser in zwei hintereinander liegenden Riegeln vorn bei der Straund den Block im hinteren, am höchsten gelegenen Bereich des Grundstücks plazierten. Sie achteten aber darauf, daß die Dachkante nicht über den Wald, der wie ein prachtvoller Bühnenprospekt wirkt, hinausragt (Abb. 2). Es handelt sich hier übrigens um eine Bühne im traditionellen Sinn, denn sie hat einen ›Vordergrund‹ und einen ›Hintergrund‹, wie aus den Fotos ersichtlich ist.
Alle Reihenhäuser haben Gärten, Balkone und Eingangshöfe. Durch die grasbewachsenen Dächer und die großzügige Bepflanzung erscheinen sie nicht größer als die angrenzenden Villen. Der Hauptfußweg (Abb. 3) geht durch die Mitte des Grundstücks entlang einer im Zentrum geknickten Achse. An der Knickstelle ist ein kleiner, halböffentlicher Platz entstanden, auf dem die Kinder spielen und von dem aus die Autofahrer die darunter gelegene Garage betreten (Abb. 11).
Der hohe Block im Hintergrund liegt an einem halböffentlichen Park, der sich von dem öffentlichen Weg im Norden des Geländes halb um den Komplex herumzieht (Abb. 1, 11). Das Gebäude, offensichtlich ein Enkelkind von Le Corbusier, beweist doch große Unabhängigkeit von seinem Erbe, da der Konstruktionsmodul nicht unbedingt mit den Wohnungsunterteilungen zusammentrifft.
Die Siedlung erhebt nicht den Anspruch, für Arbeiter gebaut zu sein, denn die hohen Grundstückspreise erzwangen geräumigere und deshalb teurere Wohnungen, doch dadurch wird sie in ihrer Eigenschaft als nachahmenswertes Beispiel nicht beeinträchtigt, denn die Lektion, die sie erteilt, liegt in der Sorgfalt der Planung. Die Rainpark-Siedlung kann als Beweis dafür gelten, daß die Wahl einer mehrgeschossigen Scheibe eine kreative, befriedigende Lösung nicht unmöglich macht. Offenbar ist das Wohnen in der Siedlung angenehm, und bis jetzt gibt es noch keine Anzeichen dafür, daß jemand aus den benachbarten Villen ausziehen will.

Die Gebäudegruppe hat alle drei Bereiche kollektiver Beziehungen gemeistert. Zum ersten paßt sie sich gebührlich in die Vorstadtlandschaft ein (nach Maßstab, Detail und Proportion), so daß der Abstand zwischen ›uns und den andern‹ kaum spürbar ist. Zum zweiten hat die Gruppe soviel Charakter, daß sich die Bewohner, die die Annehmlichkeiten und Probleme des Zusammenlebens teilen, mit ihr identifizieren können. Dieser Charakter wird nicht durch schiere Modernität erzielt, sondern durch eine, die einen allzu radikalen Bruch mit der Tradition durch pittoreske Sanftheit zu vermeiden sucht, zum Beispiel in Form der Abknickung des Fußwegs oder der sanften Schwellung des Gesimses. Im Praktischen wird die optische Identifizierung durch die Gemeinschaftsgarage ergänzt wie auch durch den zentralen, eine innere Straße bildenden Zugang und den halböffentlichen zentralen Platz. Zum dritten ist für eine ausreichende Sicherung des familiären Privatraums gesorgt: bei den Reihenhäusern durch die von hohen Wänden umgebenen vorderen und hinteren Gärten, bei dem siebengeschossigen Block durch die sehr tiefen, vom Nachbarn durch Grünbarrieren abgeschirmten Terrassen, die als echte Frei-Wohnräume anzusehen sind (Abb. 13). Die tiefen, durchgehenden Wohnräume mit Licht und Luft von Norden und Süden und der Küche in der Mitte gestatten auch Rückzugsmöglichkeiten innerhalb des ›öffentlichen‹ Bereichs der Familie. Der innerfamiliäre Aspekt der Sicherung der Privatsphäre fand ferner darin seine Berücksichtigung, daß den Schlafräumen sowohl in den Reihenhäusern als auch in den Duplexwohnungen ein eigenes Geschoß zugewiesen wurde.

Terraced Houses in Umiken, Switzerland. 1963–71

Architect: Hans Scherer

'By persons resident in the country, and attached to rural objects, many places will be found unnamed or of unknown names, where little incidents must have occurred, or feelings been experienced, which will have given to such places a private and peculiar interest.'[4]

This phrase taken from William Wordsworth's short introductory note to seven of his poems on the naming of places suggests the life-line that links man to the world around him. The joys and sorrows of life are recalled by the places where these experiences occurred. Such places are given positive or negative values by each individual according to the incident or feeling that once occurred.

But even if Wordsworth was a countryman and wrote mainly of rural places and people we can learn from him the value of memories generally, which are equally important – perhaps even mor so – in cities. Yet nowadays we seem to have less time in cities to dwell upon memories of places. It is perhaps for this reason that we have a wealth of literature and art on rural life, both sophisticated and rustic, which tends to create a subconscious need within us for everything rural so that we can search in peace for past times and places. In an ever more impersonal and technological world we seem to strive for sanity in rural or simulated rural surroundings. An extreme and absurd caricature would have us equate city with evil and country with good. The success of man in adapting and cultivating God's architecture in the country is matched by his failure to cultivate Man's architecture in the city. For this reason many reject the attempt to cultivate the city and flee to rural surroundings. The excessive reproduction of the country in the town is a flight from the problems that face urban civilization.

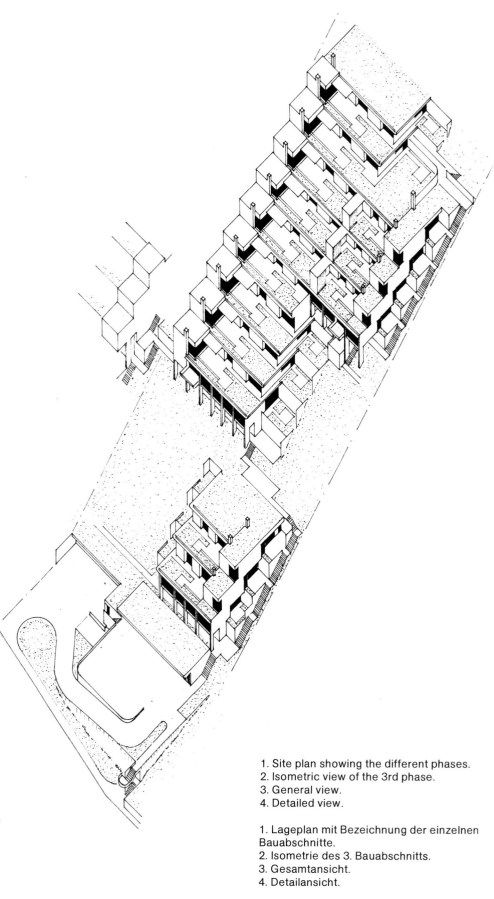

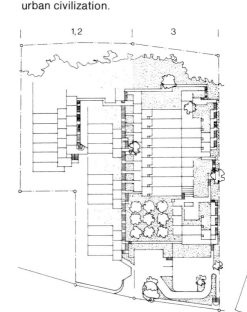

1. Site plan showing the different phases.
2. Isometric view of the 3rd phase.
3. General view.
4. Detailed view.

1. Lageplan mit Bezeichnung der einzelnen Bauabschnitte.
2. Isometrie des 3. Bauabschnitts.
3. Gesamtansicht.
4. Detailansicht.

With this in mind, the terraced housing at Umiken may be judged the result of a compromise between the rural and urban values of civilized living. It both succeeds and fails.

What in fact has been done is to urbanize the frontier between the rural hillside and the traditional villa-and-garden suburban edge of the growing town of Brugg. The urbanization of the hillside has been so carefully planned, with stepped gardens and roof-top 'fields', that the architectural statement as a whole has been lost under shrubs (ills. 3, 4). The effort to provide private places in a relatively dense group of dwellings has been skilfully handled, but the device is overplayed, creating a back-garden culture run wild. Any casual relationship between an individual and his neighbour has to take place on an appalling slope 250 steps long which forms the central spine of the hill. The three transversal alleys running through the four lines of stepped houses from the lift-stops have not been exploited as a positive design element which might have encouraged the formation of a lively urban balcony and a pleasant communal space.

If the objective was to create an architectural feature, such as a tower, then these sociological considerations could have been admitted, for at least the dwellers would have lived in one identifiable place, in *that* building, even if it shrieks. But here, the architecture is proposed as a model to be extended, and herein lies its weakness and failure. The architects' arguments in favour of extended hillside housing as against towers in the valley for the Klingrau development project have not been substantiated in Brugg. The reasons are clear enough: 1) There is a limit in terrace housing to the steepness of the slope that can be admitted if the depth of the development is considerable; 2) if not incorporated within a normal street system the development becomes dangerously similar to a ghetto; 3) the urban architectural form must be readable for the proper identification of the individual dwelling so that half the Garden City concept is not lost in an uncontrolled jumble of back-garden allotments; and 4) a direct street-level access, or its substitute the lift, is an indispensable precondition for comfortable living, especially for the old, the very young and the physically handicapped.

Terrace housing is an interesting type of architecture since it provides both the views which can be obtained from multi-storey buildings and the gardens of the individual house, but its typological limitations must be taken into account in any large-scale development.

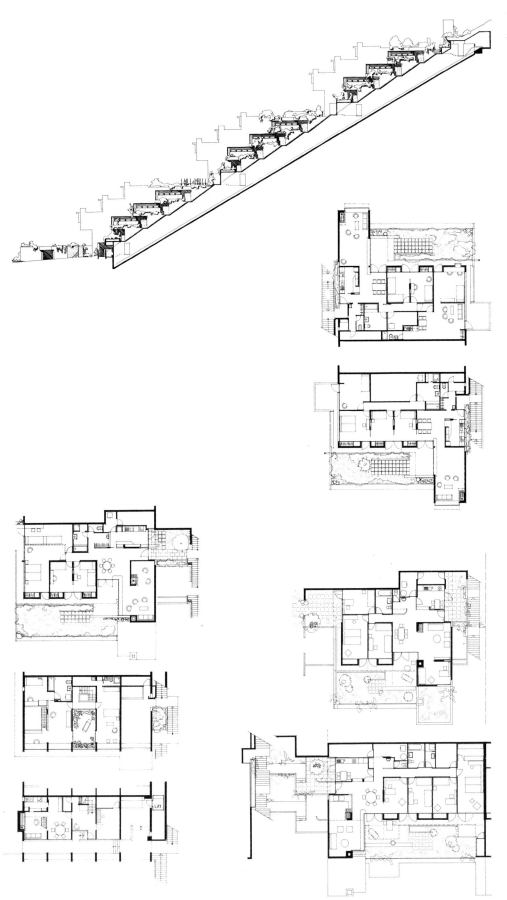

Terrassensiedlung in Umiken, Schweiz. 1963-71
Architekt: Hans Scherer

›Menschen, die auf dem Lande wohnen und an ländlichen Dingen hängen, werden viele Orte ohne Namen oder mit unbekannten Namen finden, wo sich kleine Ereignisse zugetragen haben oder Gefühle empfunden wurden, die diesen Orten ein privates, eigenständiges Interesse verliehen haben.‹[4]

Dieser Satz aus William Wordsworths kurzer Einleitung zu sieben seiner Gedichte über Ortsnamen verweist auf das Verwachsensein des Menschen mit seiner Umwelt. Freuden und Leiden des Lebens werden von den Orten, an denen sie sich ereigneten, ins Gedächtnis gerufen. Die Orte werden je nach dem damaligen Ereignis oder Gefühl vom einzelnen mit positivem oder negativem Wert belegt.

Obwohl Wordsworth ein Landmensch war und hauptsächlich über ländliche Orte und Menschen schrieb, können wir von ihm ganz allgemein den Wert der Erinnerung des Menschen an Schauplätze von Geschehnissen erfahren, und zwar nicht nur auf dem Land, sondern fast mehr noch in Städten. Nur scheinen wir Stadtmenschen heute weniger Zeit auf die Erinnerung an Orte verwenden zu können. Vielleicht entstand aus diesem Grund eine umfangreiche, sowohl hochgezüchtete als auch rustikale Literatur und Kunst über das Landleben mit der Tendenz, eine Unterströmung zu schaffen, die uns auf der Suche nach Zeit und Orten, an denen wir die Erinnerung pflegen können, allem Ländlichen zutreibt. In einer immer unpersönlicheren technisierten Welt streben wir nach Natürlichkeit in ländlicher oder nachgeahmt ländlicher Umgebung. Obwohl die Karikatur, die die Stadt mit dem Bösen und das Land mit dem Guten gleichsetzt, zu weit geht, ist es doch so, daß dem Erfolg des Menschen bei der Nutzung und Pflege der gegebenen Natur ein beklagenswerter Mißerfolg bei der Kultivation der von ihm selbst geschaffenen städtischen Welt gegenübersteht. Deshalb geben viele den Versuch auf, die Stadt zu verbessern, und nehmen, wenn sie sich eine angenehme Umgebung schaffen wollen, Zuflucht bei ländlichen Vorbildern. Mit der Nachahmung des Landes in der Stadt weicht man aber den Problemen unserer städtischen Zivilisation aus.

Im Hinblick darauf sind die Terrassenhäuser in Umiken als Ergebnis eines Kompromisses zwischen den ländlichen und städtischen Werten kultivierten Wohnens zu beurteilen. Sie sind voller Erfolge und Fehlschläge.

Faktisch wurde das Grenzgebiet zwischen dem ländlichen Hügel und dem bestehenden gartenreichen Villenvorort der wachsenden Stadt Brugg verstädtert. Mit den Gärten und ›Feldern‹ auf den abgetreppten Dächern wurde die Urbanisation des Hügels jedoch so vorsichtig betrieben, daß die architektonische Aussage als Ganzes sozusagen im Buschwerk verlorenging (Abb. 3, 4). Bei dem Einsatz von

Naturelementen zur Sicherung der Privatsphäre in einer relativ dichten Häusergruppe waltete zwar großes Geschick, aber die Bemühung war übertrieben, und es entstand eine Hausgartenkultur, die jegliches Maß überschreitet. Will ein Bewohner mit einem Nachbarn irgendeine Beziehung anknüpfen, so muß dies auf der abschreckenden, 250 Stufen hohen zentralen Erschließungstreppe geschehen. Die drei Querverbindungen, die von den Aufzughaltepunkten aus durch die vier Terrassenhäuserzeilen führen, wurden nicht als positives Entwurfselement genutzt. Als belebte Balkone hätten sie hübsche Gemeinschaftsplätze abgegeben.

Wäre die Zielvorstellung ein architektonisches Objekt – wie zum Beispiel ein Turm – gewesen, so hätte man diese soziologischen Überlegungen beiseite lassen können, denn die Bewohner lebten wenigstens an einem identifizierbaren Ort, in einem bestimmten Gebäude, auch wenn sich dieses von der Umgebung unschön abheben würde. Hier beansprucht aber die Architektur, ein erweiterungsfähiges Modell zu bieten, und darin liegt ihre Schwäche und ihr Versagen. Die Argumente des Architekten zugunsten einer ausgedehnten Hügelsiedlung im Gegensatz zu den Türmen im Tal beim Klingnau-Projekt wurden in Brugg nicht untermauert. Die Gründe liegen klar zutage: 1. Terrassenanlagen sind bei größerer Höhe nur bis zu einer bestimmten Hangneigung zumutbar. 2. Wenn die Siedlung nicht in ein normales Straßensystem einbezogen ist, kommt sie einem Ghetto gefährlich nahe. 3. Die städtebauliche Form muß erkennbar sein, damit die Einzelwohnung identifizierbar ist und nicht die Hälfte der ›Gartenstadt‹-Konzeption in einem Wirrwarr von Kleingärten untergeht. 4. Ein direkter Zugang auf Straßenebene oder statt dessen ein Aufzug ist unerläßlich für bequemes Wohnen, vor allem im Gedanken an ältere Menschen, Kinder und Behinderte.

Terrassensiedlungen sind interessante Versuche, denn sie vereinen die freie Sicht, die bei mehrgeschossigen Gebäuden erzielt wird, mit den Gärten des einzelnen Hauses; sollen sie aber in großem Maßstab gebaut werden, so ist sorgfältig auf die typologischen Grenzen zu achten.

5. Section through the oblique lift.
6. Ground plans (above: 1st phase; below left: 2nd phase; below right: 3rd phase).
7,8,9. Detailed views.

5. Schnitt durch den Schräglift.
6. Grundrisse (oben 1. Bauabschnitt, links unten 2. Bauabschnitt, rechts unten 3. Bauabschnitt).
7,8,9. Detailansichten.

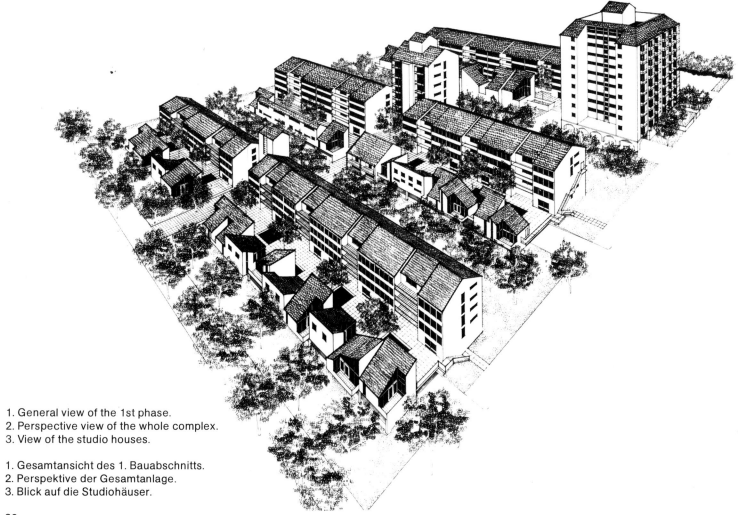

1. General view of the 1st phase.
2. Perspective view of the whole complex.
3. View of the studio houses.

1. Gesamtansicht des 1. Bauabschnitts.
2. Perspektive der Gesamtanlage.
3. Blick auf die Studiohäuser.

Housing in Carlton, Australia. 1967–70
Architects: Graham Shaw, Denton and Corker

Any community housing group in Australia at present must be classified as 'pioneer building', since the great majority of Australians are living in 'Levittown' bungalows with garden and garage. Even though the Australian subcontinent has immense territorial possibilities for a suburban Los Angeles-type expansion, the metropolitan growth of cities like Melbourne (population 2 million with a density of 10 per acre or 25 per hectare), Sydney and Canberra have begun to show signs that this 'Broadacre' way of life is not universally desired. Perhaps, as in that other former European colony, the United States, the settler's first reaction from the compact medieval city was an innate desire for rural privacy with freedom and independence: Arcadia rather than Utopia. Unrestrained by a pre-existing historical context, the new urban centres normally adhere to strictly commercial standards which tend to exclude conscientious civic responsibility. The results are usually oppressive and, after work, everyone is only too glad to get away. The idea of drifting back to the centre to escape social isolation and save commuting time evolved some years ago. What is new is the growing recognition that rebuilding must go hand in hand with a designed environment if the quality of life is to be preserved within this inner urban location.

The Carlton Cross Street housing built by the university co-operative gave an opportunity to provide an architectural response to this problem of a designed environment. Here outdoor spaces were to be created, where people could meet casually and so foster a sense of community. The architects also tried to fit the buildings into the physical grain of old Carlton with its short one- and two-storey terraces built between the 1840s and 1860s. The existing urban texture is varied, yet unified with the use of common building materials and ornamental cast-iron ballustrades on the verandas and balcony fronts. The rhythm of the 5 m and 6 m frontages of these terraced houses has been picked up by the architects and used to modulate the new buildings. The complete group will eventually consist of two tower blocks and ten terraces, five high five low, running uphill north-east to south-west with pedestrian streets between them (ill. 2). These pedestrian streets are raised up over the ground-floor parking and are therefore un-fortunately weakly linked with the existing pavement system.

The architects have also tried to imitate the undulating profiles of the old buildings in the neighbourhood which resulted from independent developments, and the effect is rather forced and fussy (ill. 1). Like Thamesmead New Town in London, this Camillo Sitte approach to design apes spontaneity with contrivance. Another mischievous consequence of this false spontaneity is found in the lower studio houses, some of which have been turned round to face the sunless south. Admittedly this juxtaposition helps to enclose the pedestrian street but comfort should not have been sacrificed to such an extent for the sake of the design.

These aesthetic criticisms should not detract from the pioneering spirit of the design. This is further displayed by the use of three-bay structural elements for each pair of dwellings which has enabled the architects to combine a great range of accommodation. This was to encourage a mixed community to develop: roughly fifty per cent of the dwellings are for families with children.

Wohnhausgruppe in Carlton, Australien. 1967-70

Architekten: Grahame Shaw, Denton and Corker

Jede Mehrfamilienhausgruppe in Australien muß heute als ›Pionierbau‹ bezeichnet werden, denn die allermeisten Australier wohnen in ›Levittown‹ Bungalows mit Garten und Garage. Obgleich der australische Subkontinent fast unbegrenztes Gelände für eine Vorstadterweiterung in der Art von Los Angeles besitzt, zeigt doch das Städtewachstum von Großstädten wie Melbourne (2 Millionen Einwohner bei einer Bevölkerungsdichte von 25 Personen pro Hektar), Sydney und Canberra, daß dieses weitläufige Wohnen nicht überall erwünscht ist. Wie in jener anderen einstigen Kolonie Europas, den Vereinig-

ten Staaten, war vielleicht die erste Reaktion der Siedler auf die dichtgedrängte mittelalterliche Stadt ein großes Verlangen nach ländlicher Abgeschiedenheit mit Freiheit und Unabhängigkeit: Arkadien und nicht Utopia. Ungehindert von einem vorgegebenen geschichtlichen Zusammenhang wurden die Stadtzentren gewöhnlich nach rein kommerziellen Maßstäben gebaut, die häufig eine bewußte Bürgerverantwortung ausschließen. Das Ergebnis ist meist bedrückend, und nach der Arbeit ist jedermann froh, wenn er sich schnell davonmachen kann. Schon seit einigen Jahren zeigt sich nun der Trend, wieder ins Zentrum zurückzukehren, um der Vereinzelung und dem zeitraubenden Pendlerdasein zu entgehen. Jetzt kommt die Einsicht hinzu, daß die neue Bautätigkeit mit einer Pflege der gesamten Umwelt Hand in Hand

gehen muß, wenn die Lebensqualität in diesen innerstädtischen Bereichen gewahrt werden soll.

Die von der Universitätsgenossenschaft erbaute Siedlung Carlton Cross Street bot Gelegenheit, das Problem der Umweltpflege architektonisch zu lösen. In diesem besonderen Fall ging es darum, Freilufträume zu schaffen, in denen sich die Menschen zwanglos treffen können, so daß ihr Gemeinschaftsgefühl gestärkt wird. Die Architekten bemühten sich zudem, den Komplex an den Charakter des alten Carlton mit seinen schmalen, ein- und zweigeschossigen Reihenhäusern aus der Zeit zwischen den vierziger und sechziger Jahren des vorigen Jahrhunderts anzupassen. Das vorhandene städtebauliche Erscheinungsbild ist abwechslungsreich und doch einheitlich durch das gleiche Baumaterial und

die gleichen gußeisernen Zierbalustraden an Veranden und Balkonen. Die Architekten griffen den Rhythmus der 5 und 6 m betragenden Frontlängen der Reihenhäuser auf, um den Modul der neuen Gebäude danach auszurichten. Der Gesamtplan umfaßt zwei Türme und zehn Zeilenbauten – fünf hoch, fünf flach –, die sich von Nordosten nach Südwesten einen Hang hinaufziehen und Fußgängerwege zwischen sich freilassen (Abb. 2). Diese Fußwege liegen über dem im Erdgeschoß befindlichen Parkplatz und sind daher leider nur ungenügend mit dem vorhandenen Bürgersteigsystem verbunden.

Die Architekten legten Wert darauf, das lebendige Profil der alten umstehenden Häuser, das sich aus unabhängigem Bauen ergeben hatte, nachzuahmen. Das Ergebnis ist, daß die Gruppe in ihrer formalen Erscheinung ziemlich krampfhaft und wirr wirkt (Abb. 1). Wie bei dem neuen Viertel Thamesmead in London wurde auch hier nach Camillo-Sitte-Manier Spontaneität mit einem unangebrachten Aufwand an Phantasie nachgeahmt. Eine weitere schlimme Folge dieser falschen Spontaneität findet sich bei den niedrigeren Studiohäusern, die teilweise nach Süden orientiert und so von der Sonne abgewendet sind. Zwar dient dies der lebendigen Begrenzung der Fußgängerstraßen, aber ein Erfordernis so grundlegender Art wie die Besonnung hätte nicht in solchem Maß einem ästhetischen Belang geopfert werden dürfen.

Die ästhetische Kritik schmälert allerdings nicht den sozialen Pionierwert, den die Architekten mit dieser Gebäudegruppe verwirklicht haben. Er zeigt sich bis ins Detail: So erlaubte der dreiachsige Aufbau der höheren Zeilenbauten, eine große Anzahl verschiedener Wohnungstypen anzubieten (Abb. 4). Zudem ist etwa die Hälfte aller Wohnungen für Familien mit Kindern ausgelegt, so daß auch von daher ein Anreiz zur Entwicklung einer gemischten Gemeinschaft gegeben ist.

4. Plans of the four-storey terraces and the studio houses. The use of three-bay structural elements for the four-storey terraces has enabled the architects to provide a great range of accommodation.
5,6. Deck between the four-storey terraces and the studio houses. Here, the residents can meet casually and thus develop a sense of community.

4. Pläne der viergeschossigen Zeilenbauten und der Studiohäuser. Der dreiachsige Aufbau der Zeilenbauten erlaubte es, eine große Anzahl verschiedener Wohnungstypen anzubieten.
5,6. Deck zwischen den viergeschossigen Zeilenbauten und den Studiohäusern. Hier können sich die Bewohner zwanglos treffen und so ein Zusammengehörigkeitsgefühl entwickeln.

Co-operative Housing in Via Meera, Milan. 1962–71

Architects: Vittorio Gregotti, Lodovico Meneghetti and Giotto Stoppino

'The relations of the cooperative group with the planners were lengthy and difficult. The nature of the cooperative enterprise (stipulating divided property) entailed the fragmentation of the cooperative effort into so many individual requirements that the unity of the overall composition was almost compromised. Moreover, it had already been hobbled by the subdivision of the site into lots which, in keeping with the building code, ruled out the construction of one new building. The results are three integrated blocks of equal weight in which the basic formal scheme springs from the reversal of normal compositional practice: instead of being grouped at the same level and then reproduced on similar floors, the various flats are freely overlapped within a reinforced concrete structure standing on seven vertical supporting structures. This adds up to a highly individual façade which unifies the blocks in context over-looking the street.'[5]

The last sentence in this quotation from an article by Meneghetti is true but misleading. The building group, which reads as a single construction, stands in sharp contrast to the neighbouring speculative workers housing (ill. 1). The result of having the right building in the wrong place is that the group plays the role of the individual monument. Instead of relating to the neighbourhood, the neighbourhood is required to relate to it.

Leaving aside this dissociation from the neighbourhood, symbolized by a neat high metal fence, and the extraordinary internal planning of the dwellings, no doubt due to the freedom given to each individual owner, our criticism is best concentrated on the morphology of the façade and volume of the three blocks.

The façade gives a singular architectural lesson in the use of a megascale to reduce the apparent height of the building and to relate one building to the other, lessening the differences between each floor and building. As can be seen from the photographs, the two upper floors containing the larger dwellings read as an enormous cornice nearly one-third the total height of the building (ills. 3, 6, 7). This cornice, or in classical terms, architrave, is supported by thin vertical columns to the ground, which are in fact dark concrete fins that support the whole structure. The base is similarly marked off, behind the columns, from the rest of the building by the recessed third floor which has a gallery. At the same time this recess echoes in a minor key the major composition by articulating the lower floors with each other.

The composition is ultimately unified by the repetitive narrow concrete panels which give a modular order to the various window openings. The sculptural flourish to the top of the staircase and lift tower shows that art is still a very valid aspect of architecture (ill. 7).

1. General view. The result of having the right building in the wrong place is that the group plays the unfortunate role of the individual monument.
2,3. Detailed views.

1. Gesamtansicht. Der merkwürdige Charakter eines richtigen Gebäudes, das aber am falschen Platz steht, zwingt die Gruppe in die unbeabsichtigte Rolle des individuellen Monuments.
2,3. Detailansichten.

Genossenschaftliche Wohnhausgruppe in der Via Meera, Mailand. 1962-71

Architekten: Vittorio Gregotti, Lodovico Meneghetti, Giotto Stoppino

›Die Unterhandlungen zwischen der genossenschaftlichen Gruppe und den Planern waren langwierig und schwierig. Dem Wesen des genossenschaftlichen Unternehmens zufolge, das geteiltes Eigentum voraussetzt, mußte die genossenschaftliche Bemühung in so viele einzelne Erfordernisse aufgesplittert werden, daß die Einheit der Gesamtkomposition kaum mehr gewahrt werden konnte. Sie war auch schon durch die Unterteilung des Geländes in Einzelbauplätze beeinträchtigt worden; den Vorschriften gemäß war damit die Errichtung eines einzigen neuen Gebäudes unmöglich. Das Ergebnis sind drei integrierte Blocks gleicher Gewichtigkeit, bei denen das formale Grundschema aus der Umkehrung der normalen Kompositionspraxis erwächst: Die verschiedenen Wohnungen sind nicht auf einer Ebene nebeneinandergereiht und dann geschoßweise wiederholt, sondern in freier Überlagerung innerhalb eines Stahlbetonskeletts mit sieben Ebenen angeordnet. So entstanden sehr individuelle Fassaden, die die Blocks mit dem Straßenraum zusammenschließen.‹[5]

Der letzte Satz des obigen Zitats aus einem Artikel von Meneghetti ist richtig, aber irreführend. Die Baugruppe, die wie ein einziger Komplex wirkt, steht in großem Gegensatz zu den umliegenden öffentlich geförderten Arbeiterwohnblocks (Abb. 1). Der merkwürdige Charakter eines richtigen Gebäudes, das aber am falschen Platz steht, zwingt die Gruppe in die unbeabsichtigte Rolle des individuellen Monuments. Statt sich mit der Nachbarschaft zu arrangieren, verlangt der Komplex Anpassung von seiten der Nachbarschaft. Dies ist eine der positiven Aufgaben der Architektur in der städtischen Ökologie.

Wenn man von dieser Abgerücktheit gegenüber der Nachbarschaft, versinnbildlicht durch einen sauberen, hohen Metallzaun, und von der ungewöhnlichen räumlichen Disposition im Inneren, die zweifellos auf die ›Freiheit‹ des einzelnen Eigentümers zurückzuführen ist, absieht, konzentriert man seine Kritik wohl am besten auf die Morphologie der Fassaden und das Volumen der drei Blocks. Die Fassaden enthalten mit ihrem Megamaßstab, der die Gesamthöhe optisch verringert und die Gebäude jenseits der Abwandlungen, die durch die unterschiedliche Gestaltung der einzelnen Geschosse und Häuser entstehen, miteinander in Verbindung setzt, eine einzigartige architektonische Lektion. Die Fotos zeigen, daß sich die zwei oberen Geschosse mit den größeren Wohnungen wie ein riesiges Gesims ausnehmen, das fast ein Drittel der Gesamthöhe besetzt (Abb. 3, 6, 7). Dieses Gesims – in klassischer Ausdrucksweise ein Architrav – ruht auf schmalen Stützen aus dunklem Beton, die das ganze Bauwerk tragen.

Ebenso markiert sich hinter den Stützen eine vom übrigen Gebäude abgesetzte Basis, und zwar dadurch, daß das dritte Geschoß zurückspringt, um einer Galerie Platz zu machen. Der Rücksprung wiederholt zugleich in kleinerem Maß die Gesamtkonzeption, indem er die unteren Geschosse auch in sich artikuliert. Zusammengebunden wird die Komposition ferner durch die sich wiederholenden schmalen Betonpaneele, die die unterschiedlichen Fensteröffnungen in eine Modulordnung setzen. Zu guter Letzt beweisen auch die skulptural gestalteten Köpfe der Treppen- und Aufzugstürme, daß die Kunst bis heute noch ein gültiger Aspekt der Architektur geblieben ist (Abb. 7).

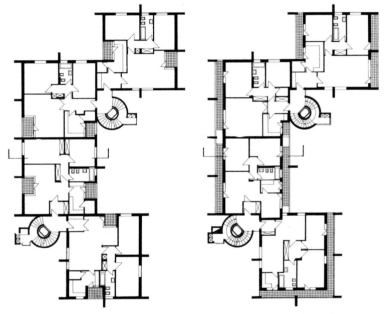

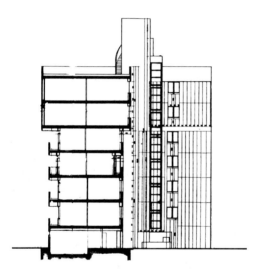

4. Model.
5. Ground plans and section.
6,7. The skilful use of a megascale:
the façade reduces the apparent height of the group and helps relate one building to the other, lessening the differences between each floor and each building.

4. Modell.
5. Grundrisse und Schnitt.
6,7. Mit ihrem Megamaßstab verringern die Fassaden die Gesamthöhe und setzen die Gebäude jenseits der Abwandlungen, die durch die unterschiedliche Gestaltung der einzelnen Geschosse und Häuser entstehen, miteinander in Beziehung.

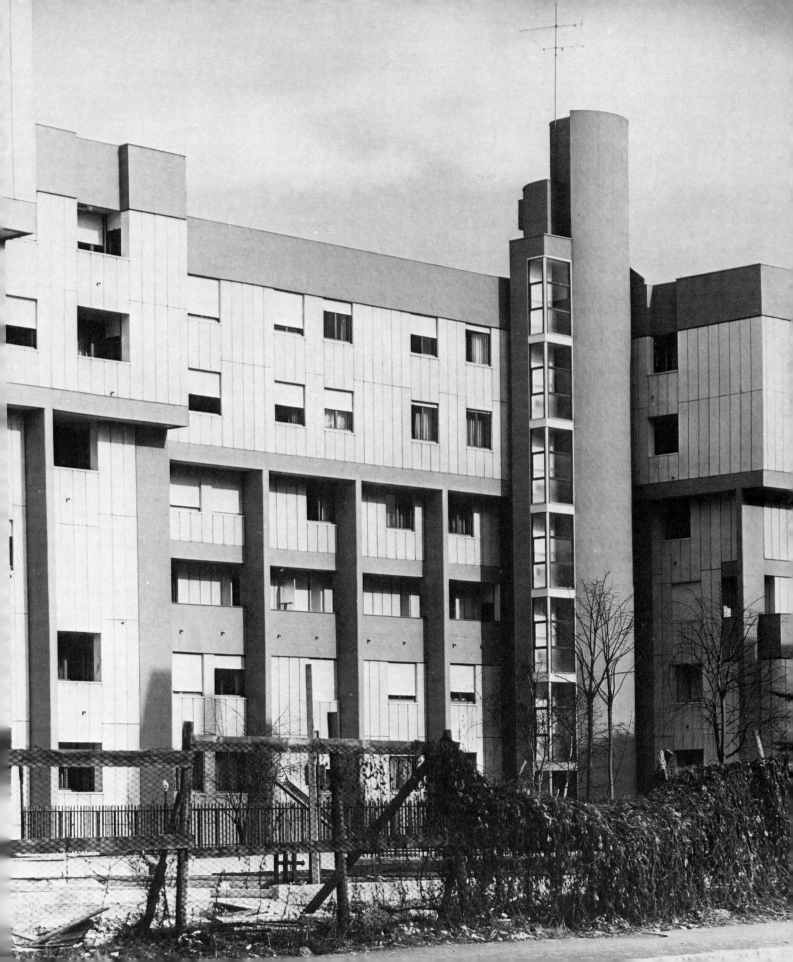

1. General view from the south-west.
2. Site plan.
3. North side of the 'lean-to'.
4. Section.
5. West side of the 'lean-to'.

1. Gesamtansicht von Südosten.
2. Lageplan.
3. Nordseite des Terrassenhauses.
4. Schnitt.
5. Westseite des Terrassenhauses.

Housing in Tapachstrasse, Stuttgart. 1965–70
Architects: Faller + Schröder (head of project: Reinhold Layer)

The fact that the architects were not given the opportunity to design the neighbourhood according to their competition entry but were only allowed to build a 'prototype', means that the architectural effort was confined to the actual working-out and result of the single building itself, rather than its relationship to its surroundings.

On the south side, the single-storey 'patio' houses and the terraces of the 'lean-to' merge into one another, making the whole group easy on the eye (ill. 1). The north and street elevation duplicates the street functions, with an enormous first-floor terrace for walking, entering and parking shelter, which is less successful (ill. 3). It is so obviously a design that suggests a more extensive urban treatment that it seems ridiculous and out of proportion in a single building. However, there is one very important lesson to be learned from the open decks of the Stuttgart 'lean-to'. The great psychological advantage of the open design is that there is absolutely no feeling of being in a ghetto, no danger of being isolated from the protective vigilance of the passer-by (ill. 9). By contrast, a walk through the under-decks of 'Barrio Gaudi' in Reus, or through the deserted gangways of Patrick Hodgkinson's development on the Foundling Estate in London is a lonely Kafkaesque experience which is distinctly unpleasant.

If the building is described as severe, that is because of the intellectual discipline evident throughout the design. Its beauty lies in both its honesty and its architectural rhythm. If we analyse the section we see that, in the 'lean-to', it is the same dwelling that is set over the lower one, not, as in other cases, a succession of smaller flats (ill. 4). Of course, the major showpiece of the building are the terraces (ills. 7, 10,

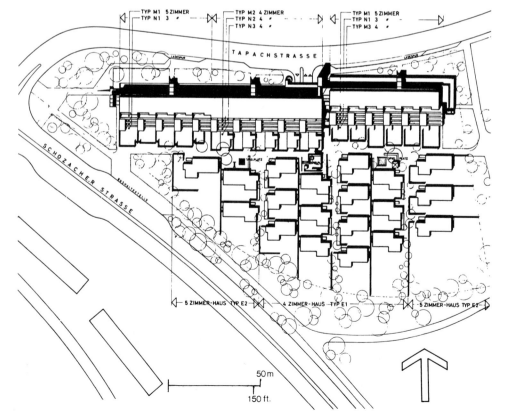

TYP M1 5 ZIMMER
TYP N1 3 "
TYP M2 4 ZIMMER
TYP N2 4 "
TYP N3 4 "
TYP M1 5 ZIMMER
TYP N1 3 "
TYP M3 4 "

TAPACHSTRASSE

SCHOZACHER STRASSE

5 ZIMMER-HAUS TYP E2   4 ZIMMER-HAUS TYP E1   5 ZIMMER-HAUS TYP E2

50 m
150 ft.

11). Nobody can deny the extent to which these have enhanced the living conditions in the flats, each of which really becomes a house and garden in the air.

There is one weakness in the design that should be commented on. That is the lack of any clear structural image among the nineteen single-storey houses. They present a confused frontage to anyone walking at ground level trying to identify the individual houses and the relationship between them. If the layout of these houses had followed, albeit at a different scale, the rhythm initiated by the 'lean-to' building, not only would the internal structure have been better, the relationship between the buildings would have been stronger too.

The metrical movement of the south façade is set up by the alternate succession of solid inclined planes and voids represented by the recessed terraces. A variation upon the same theme is introduced within the central third of the building by a slight lengthening of the voids to accommodate a larger dwelling. This is immediately reflected in the different shape of the ground-floor dwelling and the top-floor duplex. After the richness of this movement there is a moment of silence introduced by a space that cuts through the building and a set-back of the third and last section of the work. Finally, the elements of the composition are sufficiently robust in detail that they allow of free interpretation by the occupiers. Sunshades and washing actually add to the whole effect.

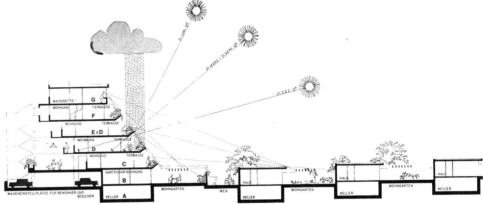

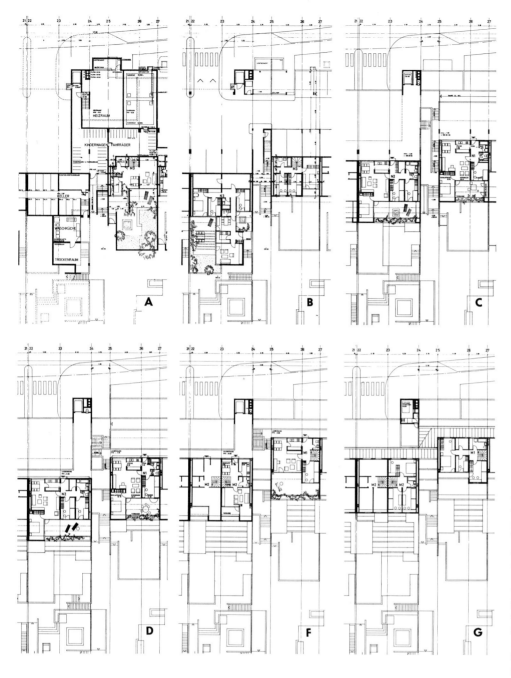

A B C

D F G

Wohnanlage in der Tapachstraße, Stuttgart. 1965-70

Architekten: Faller + Schröder (Projektleiter: Reinhold Layer)

Die Architekten erhielten leider nicht Gelegenheit, einen größeren Bereich ihrem Wettbewerbsentwurf entsprechend zu gestalten; sie durften lediglich einen ›Prototyp‹ bauen, so daß das architektonische Bemühen darauf beschränkt bleiben mußte, eine Einzelanlage in sich stimmig zu machen, statt einen größeren Zusammenhang herzustellen.

Auf der Südseite gibt es ein gutes Zusammenspiel zwischen den eingeschossigen Gartenhofhäusern und den Terrassen des zurückgelehnten Hauptbaus (Abb. 1). Die zur Straße orientierte Nordseite dagegen bietet mit der im ersten Stock gelegenen Wandel- und Zugangsterrasse, die auch die Autoabstellplätze überdacht, eine Aufdoppelung der Straßenfunktion, die dagegen wenig geglückt wirkt (Abb. 3). Dieser Entwurfsaspekt verlangt so offenkundig eine ausgedehntere städtebauliche Verwirklichung, daß er bei einer einzigen Anlage lächerlich und unproportioniert erscheint. Die offenen Decks des Terrassenhauses indes halten eine wichtige Lektion bereit. Ihr großer psychologischer Vorzug liegt darin, daß sie nach der Straße offen sind, so daß kein Ghettogefühl entstehen kann und die Bewohner auch der beschützenden Wachsamkeit der Vorübergehenden nicht entzogen sind (Abb. 9). Im Gegensatz dazu ist der Wandel durch die Unterdecks des ›Barrio Gaudí‹ in Reus oder durch die verlassenen Gänge von Patrick Hodgkinsons doppelt terrassiertem Bau in London ein bedrückendes kafkaeskes Erlebnis.

Wenn die Anlage als nüchtern bezeichnet wird, so beruht dies auf der intellektuellen Disziplin, die sich in jedem Detail zeigt. Ihre Schönheit liegt in ihrer Ehrlichkeit und ihrem architektonischen Rhythmus. Betrachten wir den Schnitt, so erkennen wir, daß im Hauptbau jeweils gleiche Wohnungen übereinandergestellt wurden, daß es sich also nicht wie in anderen Fällen um eine Folge immer kleiner werdender Wohnungen handelt. Am auffälligsten sind natürlich die Terrassen (Abb. 7, 10, 11). Niemand wird sich dem Reiz des Lebens in diesen Wohnungen, die tatsächlich Häusern mit Gärten gleichen, entziehen können.

Auf eine Schwäche des Entwurfs sollte noch hingewiesen werden: auf das Fehlen eines klaren Strukturbildes bei den 19 eingeschossigen Häusern. Wer zwischen den Häusern umhergeht, erhält einen verworrenen Eindruck, da weder ihre Identität noch ihre gegenseitige Beziehung deutlich hervortritt. Wäre die Anlage dieser Häuser, wenn auch vielleicht in anderem Maßstab, dem von den Terrassen vorgegebenen Rhythmus gefolgt, so hätten sie nicht nur eine bessere innere Struktur erhalten, sondern wären auch in ihrer Beziehung zu den mehrgeschossigen Gebäuden noch glaubwürdiger geworden.

6. Ground plans of part of the 'lean-to' (the letters here refer to the letters in ill. 4).

7. View over the terraces. As the photograph shows, one cannot look into the terraces from above.

8. View through the patio houses towards the 'lean-to'.

9. The walking and access deck of the 'lean-to'.

10. The elements of the composition are sufficiently robust to allow of free interpretation by the occupiers.

11. Terrace of a four-room flat.

6. Grundrisse aus dem Terrassenhaus (die Buchstaben beziehen sich auf die Buchstaben in Abb. 4).

7. Blick über die Terrassen. Wie das Bild zeigt, können die Terrassen von oben nicht eingesehen werden.

8. Blick durch die Gartenhofhäuser auf das Terrassenhaus.

9. Wandel- und Zugangsdeck des Terrassenhauses.

10. Die Elemente der Komposition sind kräftig genug, um eine persönliche Gestaltung durch die Bewohner zuzulassen.

11. Terrasse einer 4-Zimmer-Wohnung.

Die metrische Bewegung der Südfassade des Hauptbaus ergibt sich aus der Aufeinanderfolge der massiven geneigten Flächen und der Hohlräume der zurückgesetzten Terrassen. Eine Variation dieses Themas findet sich im mittleren Drittel des Gebäudes: Hier sind die Hohlräume wegen größerer Wohnungen etwas breiter. Weitergeführt wird diese Variation in der unterschiedlichen Form der Erdgeschoßwohnungen und der Duplexwohnungen im obersten Geschoß. Auf die Reichhaltigkeit dieser Bewegung folgt ein Augenblick der Ruhe, hervorgebracht durch einen Einschnitt, der durch den Bau hindurchläuft, und einen Rücksprung des dritten und letzten Abschnitts.

Zweifellos sind die Elemente der Komposition kräftig genug, um eine freie Interpretation seitens der Bewohner zuzulassen. Sonnenschirme und flatternde Wäsche auf der Leine wirken hier keineswegs fehl am Platz.

My aunt Mary (somewhere in her seventies) said that she would like to live here. Although she had an apartment in northern Sydney overlooking Port Jackson Bay, the advantages of being only fifteen minutes from the centre in a place with friends around and in such nice surroundings, made St John's Village extraordinarily appealing to her. It is a pity, she added, that St John's Village is an exception; there should be more places to live in like that. In planning accommodation for the young and old architects have tried to come to terms with the conflicting requirements of community life and independence. Regarding children, bedrooms tend to be designed as bedsitting-rooms, places both for sleeping and living (studying and entertaining), even with independent outside entrances in some advanced projects. The older generation too require this sort of accommodation, but, since their mobility is more restricted than children and teenagers, they need to be near others of their own age. Until now, this has been solved by the creation of institutions for the aged. But the residential institution conjures up in the mind ghetto-like homes where society places the ill, the poor, the orphaned and the elderly. Socially-minded architects have tried to break away from this straitjacket. They have either merged the institution into the general housing scheme – which is what the 'Lillington Street' architects did in London – or they have 'domes-

ticated' and individualized it as in St John's Village. This happy balance between individualization and institutionalization was achieved in Sydney by the grouping and arrangement of the bedsitting-rooms first in pairs around common halls, then in six sets around a common courtyard (ill. 3). The courtyard, which is a subtle link with the world outside, acts as a large open-air entrance hall, since each set of buildings is entered through it (ill. 2).
Except for the unit of the main entrance each house has two floors. The two bedsitting-rooms on each floor share a bathroom and kitchen (with double cooking units); married couples take two rooms. The unit at the main entrance has a third floor, accommodating the wardens' flats, an office and a common lounge.
I would like to call this architecture 'soft'. By this adjective I mean anti-heroic. Something very similar to the Venturis' 'ordinary architecture', but different from Venturis' cultural loft, in that it is in line with the social mission of modern architecture for a new world. It conducts modern architecture along the lines of a quiet revolution. It is revolutionary because it is a new architectural response to a new way of life; it is soft, because it recognizes history – the context of a seventy-year-old brick-and-tile neighbourhood – and softens the architecture to merge and blend into it (ill. 1). It is also architecture, perhaps even with a capital 'A' although many architects seem afraid of it.

Meine schon in den Siebzigern stehende Tante Mary sagte, hier würde sie gern wohnen. Obgleich sie eine Wohnung im Norden Sydneys mit Blick auf die Port Jackson Bay hat, erschien ihr St John's Village außerordentlich verlockend, weil man nur eine Viertelstunde vom Zentrum entfernt ist und weil man inmitten von Freunden und in so hübscher Umgebung wohnt. Sie meinte, es sei schade, daß St John's Village eine Ausnahme ist; es sollte mehr solche Wohnstätten geben.
Bei der Planung von Wohnraum für Jugendliche und alte Leute stehen die Architekten vor der schwierigen Aufgabe, die widerstreitenden Erfordernisse des Gemeinschaftslebens und der Privatsphäre zu vereinbaren. Die Schlafzimmer der Jungen sind meist auch zum Wohnen, Lernen und Spielen ausgelegt; bei einigen weit fortgeschrittenen Projekten sind sie sogar mit eigenem Eingang versehen. Auch die älteren Menschen verlangen nach dieser Art des Wohnens, aber da sie nicht mehr so mobil sind wie Kinder und Jugendliche, müssen sie ihren Altersgenossen näher sein. Bis jetzt hat man dieses Problem mit Heimen zu lösen versucht. Mit dem Begriff Heim verbindet sich jedoch die Vorstellung von ghettoähnlichen Räumen, in die die Gesellschaft ihre Kranken, Armen, Waisen und Alten abschiebt. Sozial eingestellte Architekten versuchen, dieses Klischee zu durchbrechen. Sie beziehen das Altenheim in die allgemeine Wohn-

anlage mit ein – so die ›Lillington-Street‹-
Architekten in London –, oder sie domesti-
zieren und individualisieren es, wie es mit dem
St John's Village geschehen ist. Der geglückte
Ausgleich zwischen Individuum und Institution
erfolgte dadurch, daß die paarweise zusam-
mengefaßten Wohnschlafräume zum einen
gemeinsame Hallen, zum anderen einen gemeinsamen Hof umschließen (Abb. 3). Der
Hof, ein subtiles Bindeglied zur Außenwelt,
fungiert als große, offene Eingangshalle, da
man alle Häuserkomplexe von hier aus betritt
(Abb. 2).

1. View of the group from the street.
2. The central courtyard.
3. Site plan. Key: 1 main gate, 2 access
cluster, 3 typical cluster, 4 entry, 5 bed-
sitting-room, 6 bathroom, 7 kitchen,
8 courtyard, 9 parking, 10 church, 11 rectory,
12 park gate, 13 laundry.

1. Blick von der Straße auf die Gruppe.
2. Der zentrale Hof.
3. Lageplan. Legende: 1 Hauptzugang,
2 Zugangseinheit, 3 Normaleinheit,
4 Vorraum, 5 Wohnschlafraum, 6 Bad,
7 Küche, 8 Hofraum, 9 Parkplatz, 10 Kirche,
11 Pfarrhaus, 12 Parktor, 13 Wäscherei.

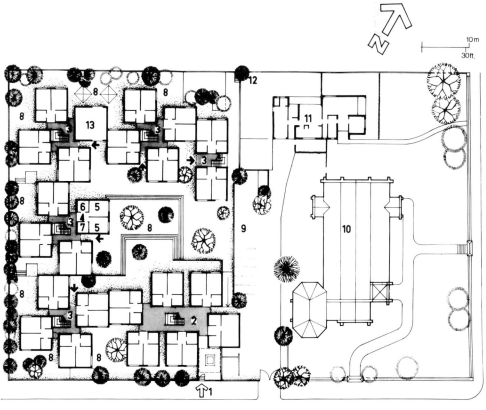

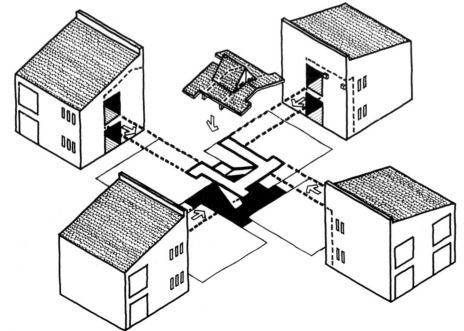

4. The central courtyard.
5. Ground plan of a pair of bed-sitting-rooms.
6. Schematic drawing of a cluster.
7. Perimeter courtyard.

4. Der zentrale Hof.
5. Grundriß eines Wohnschlafraumpaares.
6. Schemazeichnung einer Einheit.
7. Äußerer Hofraum.

Mit Ausnahme der Einheit am Hauptzugang sind die Häuser zweigeschossig. Die beiden Wohnschlafräume auf jedem Stockwerk teilen sich jeweils Bad und Küche (mit zweifachen Kochgelegenheiten). Ehepaare wohnen in zwei Zimmern. Die Einheit am Hauptzugang hat einen dritten Stock und enthält die Wohnung des Heimleiters, das Büro und einen Gemeinschaftsraum.

Ich möchte diese Architektur ›leise‹ nennen. Ich will damit sagen, daß sie antiheroisch ist. Sie kommt der ›gewöhnlichen‹ Architektur der Venturis sehr nahe, unterscheidet sich von dieser jedoch dadurch, daß ihr deren Bildungsdünkel fehlt, daß sie mit der sozialen Mission der modernen Architektur in einer neuen Welt übereinstimmt. Sie führt die moderne Architektur auf den Weg einer stillen Revolution. Sie ist revolutionär, weil sie eine neue architektonische Reaktion auf eine neue Lebensweise ist; sie ist leise, weil sie die Geschichte anerkennt – den 70 Jahre alten nachbarschaftlichen Kontext von Ziegelmauerwerk und Ziegeldächern – und die neuen Bauten darin aufgehen läßt (Abb. 1). Auch das ist Architektur, vielleicht sogar große Architektur, obwohl viele Architekten sich vor ihr zu fürchten scheinen.

Torres Blancas, Madrid. 1961–68
Architect: Francisco Javier Saenz de Oiza

Only a very cultured, vain client, with the economic means at his disposal, could actually have commissioned the right architect to build this Utopian monument. Only a society such as that found in Spain today would have allowed it. Saenz de Oiza has used the opportunity given him to create a catalyst of all the Utopian desires current in the modern movement to provide houses and gardens in the air. The effort, and the experience, was eminently worth while as these dreams have been understood and translated into reality.

It is ironic that Saenz de Oiza was commissioned to design the building without a site; eventually an incongruous resting place was found just off the motorway from the Madrid airport, amongst shabby working-class buildings which emphasize its triumphant monumental isolation (ill. 2).

A tall massive original building is by definition monumental because it permanently stands apart. It does not fit into the environment, it changes it. Monuments, or monumental buildings, are the symbolic landmarks of civilization, they go beyond the ordinary, and no matter how socially conscious we may be, we must also recognize that out of our hard-working routine lives we need images of possible objectives. Monuments to the dead may remind us of the eternal values of the past, but monuments to the living may remind us of our hopes for the future. This building is an organic monument. Organic because its plan has grown out geometrically around the centre in a series of L-shaped dwelling units symmetrically placed to catch the sun (ills. 1, 3). Organic because the northern dwelling unit breaks the geometrical rhythm in response to its otherwise unfavourable position. Organic because its structure has been moulded according to the convenience of the internal plan of the dwelling; it is an irregular impure structure of columns and loadbearing walls which also satisfies the requirements of wind stiffening. It is also organic in the choice of circular forms that always relate to each other irrespective of size. It is organic because it exploits the natural mechanical and structural properties of reinforced concrete. Finally it is organic because it is a building decorated with wooden blinds and shutters and windows, and with terrace upon terrace of luxuriously growing plants, which makes the building look like an enormous hanging garden behind which are hidden the dwellings (ills. 5, 6). It is as though Frank Lloyd Wright's Broadcare City had been turned up on its end.

The 21 floors of dwellings have been designed to absorb basically 3 different sizes of apartments: 48 small apartments, (8 to a floor – 7th, 8th, 9th, 19th, 20th and 21st), 16 very large duplex dwellings (4 to a floor – 4th, 5th, 10th and 11th) and 44 one-floor dwellings (4 to a floor – on the remaining floors).

There are two independent vertical routes of access, one for the owners, the other for the servants and goods. The service access is always at a different level from the main entrance (except for the six floors containing the small apartments). The independent accesses appear at every third floor (2nd, 5th, 8th, 11th, 14th and 17th). The main entrances are to the other floors either directly or via one flight of stairs. (This last point is a weakness, because 32 flat owners have to climb up or down a flight of stairs to answer the front door: all for the sake of not meeting the servants.)

However, apart from this perhaps over-ingenious double system of access, the really spectacular element in these dwellings is the enormous number of sheltered terraces that create a genuine sensation of being in the open as in a garden. Only the noise from the motorway disturbs the rural effect.

The 22nd floor contains services, the 23rd floor a private club belonging to the owner, and the 24th a public restaurant which also serves hot meals direct to each apartment below by means of a food lift. The terrace contains a sun deck and swimming-pool for the inhabitants.

The connection between the ground and the tower is beautifully handled: the terraced gardens sink gradually towards the entrance, thus creating the illusion that the building grows out of the ground. Underneath is an underground garage. The rest of the site remains to be developed, probably by another architect.

1. Saenz de Oiza has used the opportunity given him to create a catalyst of all the Utopian desires current in the modern movement in architecture to provide houses and gardens in the air.

Torres Blancas, Madrid. 1961-68
Architekt: Francisco Javier Saenz de Oiza

Nur der Ambition eines hochgebildeten Auftraggebers mit den entsprechenden finanziellen Mitteln konnte es gelingen, den richtigen Architekten für dieses utopische Monument zu finden. Nur eine Gesellschaft wie die heutige Gesellschaft Spaniens ist bereit, dieses zu dulden. Saenz de Oiza nutzte die ihm gebotene Chance eines Katalysators für die in der modernen Architektur umgehenden utopischen Sehnsüchte nach Häusern und Gärten in der Luft. Der Erfolg rechtfertigte die Mühe, die er darauf wandte, diese Träume zu erfassen und Wirklichkeit werden zu lassen. Als Saenz de Oiza beauftragt wurde, das Gebäude zu entwerfen, hatte man kurioserweise noch kein Baugelände. Erst später fand man neben der Straße zum Madrider Flughafen einen wenig passenden Platz zwischen schäbigen Arbeitersiedlungen, die die sieghafte Monumentalität des Bauwerks noch hervorheben (Abb. 2).

Ein hoher, massiver, in sich geschlossener Bau ist zwangsläufig monumental, weil er immer für sich steht. Er paßt sich nicht an die Umgebung an, er verändert sie. Monumente oder monumentale Bauten sind die symbolischen Marksteine der Zivilisation, sie reichen über das Gewöhnliche hinaus, und so sozialbewußt wir auch sein mögen, müssen wir doch zugeben, daß wir im Zwang unserer Arbeitsroutine Abbilder möglicher Ziele brauchen. Monumente des Todes erinnern uns an die bleibenden Werte der Vergangenheit, Monumente des Lebens können uns unsere Zukunftshoffnungen zum Bewußtsein bringen. Der Bau ist ein organisches Monument. Er ist organisch, weil die gleichmäßig angeordneten, L-förmigen Wohneinheiten aus dem Zentrum heraus der Sonne entgegenwachsen (Abb. 1, 3). Organisch ist er auch, weil die nördliche Wohneinheit wegen ihrer sonst ungünstigen Lage den gleichmäßigen Rhythmus unterbricht. Weiterhin ist er organisch, weil das konstruktive Gefüge der Disposition der Wohnungsgrundrisse angepaßt wurde und entsprechend unregelmäßig und uneinheitlich ist; die Lasten werden einmal von Stützen, einmal von Wänden, die zugleich die Windkräfte aufnehmen, abgetragen. Ebenfalls organisch ist er durch die Wahl runder, unabhängig von ihrer Größe aufeinander bezogener Formen. Organisch muß auch die Nutzung der mechanischen und konstruktiven Eigenschaften des Stahlbetons genannt werden. Schließlich ist der Bau organisch, weil er mit Jalousien, Läden und Fenstern aus Holz ausgestattet ist und sich auf allen Terrassen üppige Pflanzen finden, so daß man einen riesigen hängenden Garten vor sich zu haben meint, hinter dem sich die Wohnungen verbergen (Abb. 5, 6). Es ist, als sei Frank Lloyd Wrights Broadacre City senkrecht gestellt worden.

Die 21 Wohngeschosse wurden so ausgelegt, daß sie Wohnungen in drei verschiedenen Grundgrößen aufnehmen: 48 kleine Apartments (8 je Geschoß im 7., 8., 9., 19., 20. und 21. Stock), 16 sehr große Duplexwohnungen (4 je Doppelgeschoß im 4. und 5. sowie im 10. und 11. Stock) und 44 Eingeschoßwohnungen (4 je Geschoß in den übrigen Stockwerken). Der eine der beiden voneinander unabhängigen senkrechten Verkehrsstränge dient den Eigentümern, der andere wird von der Dienerschaft und für Waren benutzt. Die Lieferanteneingänge befinden sich nicht auf der Ebene der Hauptwohnungseingänge (ausgenommen bei den sechs Geschossen mit den kleinen Apartments). Die unabhängigen Zugänge befinden sich in jedem dritten Stockwerk (im 2., 5., 8., 11., 14. und 17. Stock), die Haupteingänge liegen auf den anderen Geschossen und sind entweder direkt oder über eine Treppe zugänglich. (Das letztere wirkt sich insofern ungünstig aus, als 32 Wohnungseigentümer erst eine Treppe hinauf- oder hinuntergehen müssen, wenn sie ihre Haustür aufmachen wollen, und das alles nur, um nicht den Dienstboten zu begegnen.)

Es ist zu fragen, ob dieses Doppelsystem von Zugängen nicht übertrieben sinnreich geriet. Wirklich aufregend an diesen Wohnungen ist jedoch die ungeheure Zahl überdachter Terrassen, die den Eindruck vermitteln, man befinde sich im Freien wie in einem Garten. Nur der Verkehrslärm stört die ländliche Wirkung. Im 22. Geschoß sind technische Einrichtungen untergebracht, im 23. Geschoß liegt ein privater Club, der dem Besitzer gehört, das 24. Geschoß beherbergt ein öffentliches Restaurant, das über einen Speisenaufzug warme Mahlzeiten direkt in die einzelnen Wohnungen liefert. Auf der Dachterrasse findet sich ein Sonnendeck und ein Schwimmbad für die Bewohner.

Die Verbindung zwischen Boden und Turm ist sehr schön gelöst. Terrassierte Gartenanlagen neigen sich dem Eingang zu, so daß man meint, der Bau wachse aus der Erde heraus. Darunter befindet sich eine Tiefgarage. Das übrige Gelände muß noch gestaltet werden – wahrscheinlich von einem anderen Architekten.

1. Saenz de Oiza nutzte die ihm gebotene Chance eines Katalysators für die in der modernen Architektur umgehenden utopischen Sehnsüchte nach Häusern und Gärten in der Luft.

2. General view of the tower.
3. View of the façade.
4. Ground plans of the two-storey apartments (above: the bedrooms; below: the living-rooms). Key: 1 central area, 2 terrace or balcony, 3 service area, 4 lift.
5,6. One of the terraces.

2. Gesamtansicht des Turms.
3. Blick entlang der Fassade.
4. Grundrisse der zweigeschossigen Wohnungen (oben Schlafgeschoß, unten Wohngeschoß). Legende: 1 innerer Bereich, 2 Terrasse bzw. Balkon, 3 Servicezone, 4 Lift.
5,6. Eine der Terrassen.

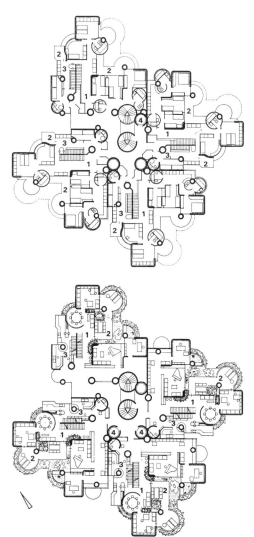

Spring Pond Apartments, Painted Post, New York. 1966–68
Architect: Louis Sauer

First of all take a pond, a large five-acre artificial pond, with a small island for a club and swimming-pool. This will establish a centre of interest which will help link the different buildings. Then draw a loop road around the pond. So that the project can be built in stages arrange small subsidiary loops in three groups, connecting rectangular carports set out at rightangles north-south or east-west. This will set up a geometrical pattern to counterbalance the irregular contour of the artificial lake. Now link the carports with irregular, picturesque U-groups with houses, so that they overlook common green areas. To do this we must study how the houses can be put together with components (ill. 2).

Firstly we must divide the given units – 1, 2 and 3 bedroom units – into two different classes: flats and houses (or duplexes). This leaves us with six different types. We will call these 1F (1-bedroom flat), 2F (2-bedroom flat) and 3F (3-bedroom flat); and 1D (1-bedroom duplex) 2D (2-bedroom duplex) and 3D (3-bedroom duplex) (ill. 4).

Secondly we design each unit on a 14" structural module (determined by the customary rules of timber construction) with a constant 140" span.

Thirdly we simplify the planning by having only one entrance, with the kitchen right next to it. All other rooms must lead off this entrance hall (in the duplex using the staircase) which makes for good independent use of all rooms. The only black sheep in the family is the 1-bedroom duplex which is more like a studio flat than anything else.

The fourth rule, so that we can join the units together, is to eliminate all window openings in the side walls. Again the 1-bedroom duplex is the one exception to the rule.

The fifth rule is to begin making up the components, like putting one flat on top of another, or one duplex on top of a flat – the maximum height being three floors.

The sixth rule is that one must put the components together to form a group. The 3-bedroom flat used on the ground floor is the best component to use when turning a corner.

Since the rules have been invented with skill and understanding, one would expect the final composition to be of the same standard. Judging from the photographs, it is more than that (ills. 3, 5, 6, 7, 8). The proportions, the detailing and unifying 14" visible module give an almost severe unity to this otherwise picturesque grouping. It is only where the brick walls are exposed that the composition becomes somewhat folksy.

Oddly enough North Americans, who are otherwise intensely social, have until now preferred individual houses. Louis Sauer has therefore broken new ground with his design for Spring Pond, which is so skilfully thought out that it meets the home-dweller's basic need to be private and public at the same time. His groups are not so small that you are forced to share everything with your neighbour nor so large that you fail to share anything of real meaning. Twelve to sixteen seems to be about the average group. The larger three groups are on a 30-40-unit basis. All the dwellings have some sort of private outdoor space, and all are entered off a common green where one can sit around and relax with friends and neighbours. Possibly the same sociological result could have been obtained with bad architecture, but I doubt it. The quiet dignity of the buildings, brought about not only by the light touch of a pencil, but also by the rational logic of its assembly, makes the common area civic as well.

1. Site plan.
2. Scheme of how the basic units can be put together into components and buildings.
3. View of a building group.
4. Ground plans of the different dwelling types.

1. Lageplan.
2. Schema der Zusammenstellung der Grundeinheiten zu Komponenten und Gebäuden.
3. Blick auf eine Baugruppe.
4. Grundrisse der verschiedenen Wohntypen.

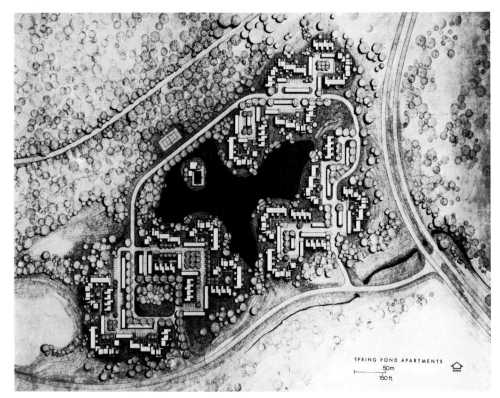

SPRING POND APARTMENTS
50m
150 ft.
NORTH

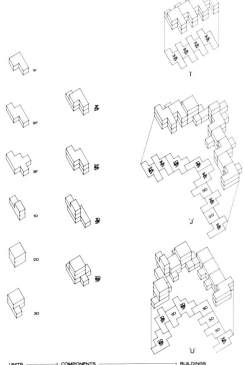

UNITS ⟶ COMPONENTS ⟶ BUILDINGS

1F First Floor

2F First Floor

3F First Floor

1D Second Floor

2D Second Floor

3D Second Floor

1D First Floor

2D First Floor

3D First Floor

Spring Pond Apartments, Painted Post, New York. 1966-68
Architekt: Louis Sauer

Zuallererst braucht man einen See, einen 2 ha großen künstlichen See mit einem Inselchen für Clubgebäude und Schwimmbad. So erhält man ein Zentrum, das eine starke Verbindung zwischen den Gebäuden schafft. Außen herum führt man eine Straßenschleife.

In drei Gruppen, damit das Projekt in Stufen gebaut werden kann, legt man kleinere Nebenschleifen zur Verbindung mit rechteckigen, oktogonal nord-südlich oder ost-westlich ausgerichteten Parkplätzen an und erzielt damit ein geometrisches Muster, das in Kontrast zu dem unregelmäßigen Umriß des künstlichen Sees steht.

Nun werden die Parkplätze mit unregelmäßigen, pittoresken, U-förmigen Häusergruppen verbunden, die auf gemeinsame Grünflächen gehen – doch zuvor muß untersucht werden, wie sich die Häuser als addierbare Einheiten realisieren lassen (Abb. 2).

Zum ersten werden die gegebenen Einheiten – mit 1, 2 und 3 Schlafzimmern – in Normalwohnungen und Häuser (oder Duplexwohnungen) unterteilt. Damit sind sechs verschiedene Grundtypen vorhanden. Wir wollen sie 1F (1-Schlafzimmer-Normalwohnung), 2F (2-Schlafzimmer-Normalwohnung), 3F (3-Schlafzimmer-Normalwohnung) und 1D (1-Schlafzimmer-Duplex), 2D (2-Schlafzimmer-Duplex) und 3D (3-Schlafzimmer-Duplex) nennen (Abb. 4).

Zum zweiten wird jede Einheit auf einem Konstruktionsmodul von 35,6 cm aufgebaut (nach den herkömmlichen Regeln der Fachwerkkonstruktion), als konstante Spannweite wird ein Maß von 3,56 m gewählt.

Zum dritten wird die Planung insofern vereinfacht, als man nur einen Eingang vorsieht; die Küche muß gleich daran anschließen. Auch alle anderen Räume gehen von der Eingangsdiele ab (bei den Duplexwohnungen vom Trep-

penhaus), so daß sie unabhängig genutzt werden können. Das ›schwarze Schaf‹ in der Familie ist die 1-Schlafzimmer-Duplexwohnung, die eher einem Studio gleicht.

Zum vierten müssen, damit die Einheiten zusammengepaßt werden können, die Fensteröffnungen an den Seitenwänden wegfallen. Wieder ist die 1-Schlafzimmer-Duplexwohnung die Ausnahme, die die Regel bestätigt.

Zum fünften werden die Einheiten endlich zusammengepaßt. Man setzt eine Normalwohnung auf die andere oder eine Duplexwohnung auf eine Normalwohnung. Die Maximalhöhe beträgt drei Geschosse.

Zum sechsten werden die Einheiten so addiert, daß sie eine Gruppe bilden. Die 3-Schlafzimmer-Normalwohnung im Erdgeschoß eignet sich am besten für Gebäudeecken.

Da diese Regeln mit großem Geschick und Verständnis aufgestellt wurden, ist man darauf gefaßt, daß die endgültige Anlage diesem Standard entspricht. Den Fotos nach zu urteilen, geht sie sogar darüber hinaus (Abb. 3, 5, 6, 7, 8). Die Proportionen, die Details und der sichtbare Modul von 35,6 cm verleihen der ansonsten pittoresken Gruppe eine fast strenge Einheitlichkeit. Nur dort, wo die Ziegelmauern zutage treten, wird die Komposition ein bißchen volkstümlicher.

Merkwürdigerweise bevorzugten die sonst so geselligen Nordamerikaner bisher das Einfamilienhaus. Louis Sauer hat mit seinem gefälligen Entwurf für Spring Pond Neuland er-

schlossen, weil der Doppelwunsch des Be-
wohners nach Privatheit und Öffentlichkeit
architektonisch gekonnt erfüllt wurde. Die
Häusergruppen sind nicht so klein, daß man
gezwungen wäre, alles mit den Nachbarn zu
teilen; sie sind aber auch nicht so groß, daß
man überhaupt nichts Wichtiges gemeinsam
hätte. Die Gruppen bestehen im Durchschnitt
aus 12 bis 16 Einheiten. Die drei größeren
Gruppen bauen auf 30-30-40 Einheiten auf.
Alle Wohnungen haben den gleichen privaten
Platz im Freien, alle liegen an einer gemeinsamen Grünfläche, auf der man mit Freunden
und Nachbarn sitzen und plaudern kann.
Wahrscheinlich wäre das gleiche soziologische Ergebnis mit schlechter Architektur nicht
erzielt worden: Die ruhige Würde der Gebäude, die nicht nur von einem leichten Bleistift-
strich, sondern auch von der Logik des Zu-
sammenbaus herrührt, verleiht dem gemeinschaftlichen Bereich überhaupt erst den spe-
zifisch öffentlichen Charakter.

5,6,7,8. Detailed views. The proportions,
the detailing and the visible 14" module give
an almost severe unity to this otherwise
picturesque grouping.

5,6,7,8. Detailansichten. Die Proportionen,
die Details und der sichtbare Modul von
35,5 cm verleihen der ansonsten pittoresken
Gruppierung eine fast strenge Einheitlichkeit.

The Sakura-dai Village, and its neighbour, the Sakura-dai Court Village, grew from a suburban development plan by Kiyonori Kitutake, for whom Uchii used to work. This plan was sponsored by a private Tokyo commuter express railway company to stimulate population concentrations in the areas it serves.

Uchii explained with clear realism how he adapted and formed his ideas on what are the problems and purposes of group housing[6]: 'Earlier the image of the project was one of a secluded suburban housing area linked with town by means of express trains, but this picture began to fade as the areas surrounding the 4,500 hectares of the site began to go up for sale in small parcels and as, consequently, dense groups of smaller residential buildings began rapidly to appear. Under such circumstances it became dubious that the secluded-housing approach would work in such highly subdivided circumstances. Furthermore, when we began work, a road network, based on a land apportionment plan, was almost complete, private land districts were undergoing subdivision, public facilities had achieved a degree of uniformity, a reservoir and other public lands had been established to the effect that our work, becoming extremely difficult, took on the coloration of redevelopment rather than of initial planning.

'Our final image, therefore, took the forms of creating a concentration of natural vital energies, adjusting the merits of this concentration to regional development requirements and by providing stimulus in one location, creating a better living environment.'

The Sakura-dai Court Village (ills. 1—6) consists of three parallel buildings on the west side of a hill. Two of these buildings, to the south, are set one above the other with pedestrian access along the upper east side, and are regular two-storey buildings. Dwellings consist of 45° L-shaped units displaced one above the other, thus giving a rich configuration to what would otherwise be a rather dull layout. The three buildings are linked by narrow alleys (ill. 4) that meet and cross each other at the centre of the site. This is where the main entrance steps are located; the centre is further emphasized by the tall water tower that, visible from afar, acts as a signpost for this hillside community. These narrow alleyways appear to be very successful in creating a feeling of intimacy and of being in a small commune. From a distance the general massing of the group reads like a Mediterranean village, adapted to the natural contour and unified somewhat romantically around the church tower (ill. 3).

Although Sakura-dai Court Village is an obvious step in the right direction in the otherwise chaotic housing development in Japan, it is curious that the Court Village lacks just what

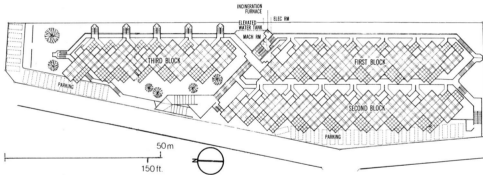

its name boasts – a court! Narrow paths do make sure that the neighbours meet, perhaps even by walking into each other, but they also reduce public space, which needs looking after, to a minimum. The space left over after planning, to use Leslie Ginsburg's phrase[7], runs over the rest of the site and under the forest of pillars beneath the buildings where rain and vegetation will never reach. It would have been better perhaps to fill in the under-carriage.

The fact that the steps are the only approach to the dwellings creates difficulties for young and old as well as for rubbish removal and even moving furniture in and out of the house. Another doubtful point is the architects' decision to make people enter the building from the upper eastern side of the buildings. Would it not have been better to increase the population of the central pedestrian alley by making it serve both the upper and lower buildings? This would have meant more steps, but would have been a compromise which would have lessened the segregation between the three buildings.

1. Aerial view. In the foreground Sakura-dai Court Village, in the background, Sakura-dai Village.
2. Site plan of Sakura-dai Court Village.
3. West side of Sakura-dai Court Village.
4. Alley within Sakura-dai Court Village.
5. View of Sakura-dai Court Village from the north.
6. Ground plans and sections of Sakura-dai Court Village.

1. Luftbild der Gesamtanlage. Vorn das Sakura-dai Court Village, hinten das Sakura-dai Village.
2. Lageplan des Sakura-dai Court Village.
3. Westseite des Sakura-dai Court Village.
4. Fußweg im Sakura-dai Court Village.
5. Blick von Norden auf das Sakura-dai Court Village.
6. Grundrisse und Schnitte zum Sakura-dai Court Village.

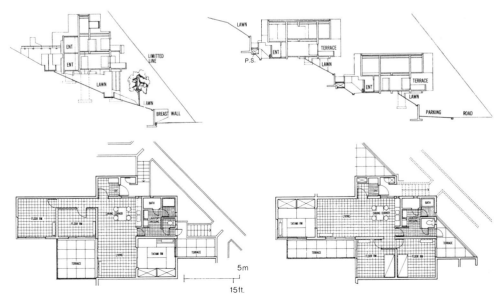

5m

15ft.

Sakura-dai Court Village und Sakura-dai Village, Yokohama, Japan. 1967-70
Architekten: Shozo Uchii and Associates

Das Sakura-dai Village und das benachbarte Sakura-dai Court Village fußen auf einem vorstädtischen Bebauungsplan von Kiyonori Kitutake, für den Uchii lange Zeit tätig war. Dieser Plan wurde initiiert von einer privaten, in Tokio ansässigen Eisenbahngesellschaft für Pendlerverkehr, um einen Anreiz für Bevölkerungskonzentrationen in den bedienten Gebieten zu geben.

Mit ungeschminktem Realismus beschreibt Uchii, wie er seine Vorstellungen an die Probleme und Zwecke des Siedlungsbaus anpaßte [6]:

›Zuerst bestand die Idee einer in sich geschlossenen vorstädtischen Wohngegend, die durch Eilzugverkehr mit der Stadt verbunden ist, aber dieses Bild verblaßte, als die Grundstücke um den 4,5 ha großen Bauplatz herum in kleinen Parzellen verkauft wurden und infolgedessen gedrängte Gruppen von kleineren Wohnhäusern rasch aus dem Boden schossen. Es erhob sich die Frage, ob unter diesen Umständen eine in sich geschlossene Wohnsiedlung überhaupt noch sinnvoll sei. Als wir anfingen, war das Straßennetz, das dem Plan der Landzuteilung folgte, fast fertiggestellt, private Landbereiche wurden weiter aufgeteilt, öffentliche Bauten hatten schon eine gewisse Form angenommen, ein Reservoir und andere öffentliche Einrichtungen waren bereits gebaut, und so wurde unsere

In Sakura-dai Village (ills. 7–10) this segregation between buildings has been eased by the use of a 'semidetached' model, which permits a cross-penetration of the buildings (ill. 9). The site bounded by public roads on three sides allows easy and natural access to the four buildings. The interior space has been given a slight undulation in plan since it was originally projected as the first part of a linear park that was to lead to the railway station itself. This undulating plan, plus the rather steep slope of the gardens, and the major architectural scale given by the protruding upper floor which acts as a giant cornice to the lower buildings and the vertical gaps of the staircases, all combine to give an urban scale to this collection of 124 flats (ill. 7).

The shops along a colonnade in the ground floor of the two western blocks are a marked improvement on the earlier Court Village design because they link the buildings and the street without any isolating space left over in between. It must be remembered that we are dealing with 124 dwellings here and not the 40 of the Court Village which could not support so many shops. Nevertheless, a colonnade for car parking, for example, could have been used in the Court Village scheme.

7. The inner area of Sakura-dai Village.
8. Site plan of Sakura-dai Village.
9. Ground plans and section of Sakura-dai Village.
10. West side of Sakura-dai Village with colonnade.

7. Zwischenraum im Sakura-dai Village.
8. Lageplan des Sakura-dai Village.
9. Grundrisse und Schnitt zum Sakura-dai Village.
10. Westseite des Sakura-dai Village mit Kolonnade.

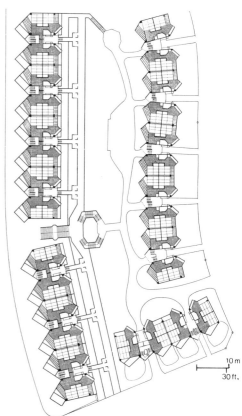

10 m
30 ft.

Arbeit außerordentlich schwierig und glich eher einer Sanierung als einer Neuplanung. Unser endgültiges Projekt setzte sich daher zum Ziel, eine Konzentration natürlicher Lebensenergien herbeizuführen, die Vorteile dieser Konzentration an die regionalen Entwicklungserfordernisse anzupassen und durch einen punktuellen Stimulus mitzuhelfen, eine bessere Wohnumwelt zu schaffen.‹

Das Sakura-dai Court Village (Abb. 1-6) besteht aus drei parallel angeordneten Gebäudereihen, die die Westseite eines Hügels einnehmen. Die beiden südlichen Gebäude liegen übereinander, die Erschließung erfolgt von der oberen Ostseite. Insgesamt haben wir es mit regelmäßigen, zweigeschossigen Bauten zu tun. Dadurch, daß die L-förmigen Wohnungen um 45° abgewinkelt und gegeneinander versetzt wurden, erfuhr das sonst ziemlich langweilige Spekulationsobjekt jedoch eine starke gestalterische Bereicherung. Die drei Gebäude sind durch schmale Wege verbunden (Abb. 4), die sich im Mittelpunkt des Geländes treffen und kreuzen. Hier befindet sich die Hauptzugangstreppe. Der Mittelpunkt wird noch betont durch den hohen Wasserturm, für die Hügelgemeinschaft ein schon von weitem sichtbares Wegzeichen. Offenbar tragen die schmalen Wege in hohem Maß dazu bei, daß ein Gefühl der Intimität und des Eintritts in eine kleine Gemeinde entsteht. Aus der Ferne wirkt die Gruppe wie ein mittelalterliches Dorf, eingebettet in die natürliche Umwelt und dicht zusammengedrängt um den Kirchturm (Abb. 3).

Wenngleich das Sakura-dai Court Village offenkundig in der sonst chaotischen Wohnhausentwicklung in Japan ein Schritt in die richtige Richtung ist, fehlt ihm merkwürdigerweise gerade das, was sein Name in Anspruch nimmt: ein Hof. Die schmalen Wege gewährleisten zwar, daß die Bewohner miteinander in Kontakt kommen und einander vielleicht sogar anrempeln, aber sie beschränken auch den öffentlichen Raum, der gepflegt werden müßte. Der Platz, den die Planung übrigläßt, geht – um Leslie Ginsburg zu zitieren [7] – über die Restflächen des Grundstücks und den Raum zwischen dem Wald von Stützen unter den Gebäuden, wo nie Regen und Pflanzen hinkommen, nicht hinaus. Es wäre vielleicht besser gewesen, man hätte den Unterbau aufgefüllt.

Die Stufen als einziger Zugang zu den Wohnungen bringen Schwierigkeiten für Kinder und ältere Menschen, aber auch für die Müllabfuhr und für den Möbeltransport beim Einzug und Auszug. Weiterhin ist anfechtbar, daß jedes Haus an der oberen Ostseite betreten wird. Wäre es nicht sinnvoll gewesen, den Verkehr auf dem mittleren Fußweg zu steigern und ihn die oberen und unteren Gebäude bedienen zu lassen? Das hätte zwar noch mehr Stufen bedeutet, aber eine derartige Kompromißlösung hätte den Eindruck der Absonderung zwischen den drei Gebäuden abgeschwächt.

Beim Sakura-dai Village (Abb. 7-10) wurde diese Absonderung zwischen den Gebäuden gemildert, da man ein ›Doppelhaus‹-Modell verwendete, das tiefe Quereinschnitte in den Baukörpern erlaubt (Abb. 9). Das Gelände wird auf drei Seiten von öffentlichen Straßen begrenzt, so daß die vier Gebäude leicht und natürlich zugänglich sind. Der Zwischenraum wurde im Grundriß leicht gewellt, weil er ursprünglich als erster Teil eines zur Eisenbahnstation hinführenden linearen Parks gedacht war. Die gewellte Raumumfassung, die ziemlich abschüssigen Grünflächen, der kräftige architektonische Maßstab, erzeugt durch die vorstehenden oberen Geschosse, die wie ein riesiges Gesims aussehen, die senkrechten Einschnitte der Treppenhäuser – das alles wirkt zusammen, um dieser Ansammlung von 124 Wohnungen städtischen Charakter zu verleihen (Abb. 7).

Die Läden entlang einer durchgehenden Kolonnade im Erdgeschoß der beiden westlichen Blocks sind ein bedeutender Vorzug gegenüber dem Court Village, da hiermit eine direkte Verbindung zwischen den Gebäuden und der Straße entsteht und dazwischen kein zu Vereinzelung führender Raum übrigbleibt. Allerdings geht es hier um 124 Wohnungen und nicht nur um 40 wie im Court Village, das nicht so viele Läden braucht; hier hätte eine Kolonnade jedoch zum Beispiel als Parkplatz genutzt werden können.

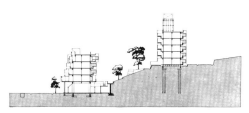

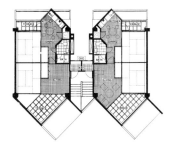

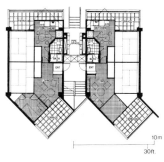

10m
30ft.

Suvikumpu, Tapiola, Finland. 1961–69
Architects: Reima Pietilä and Raili Paatelainen

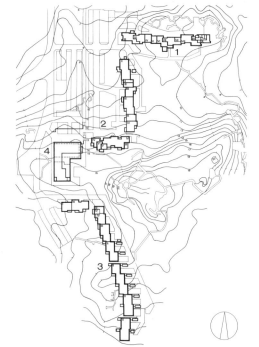

At Suvikumpu the romantic echo of Frank Lloyd Wright is omnipresent. That the search for an architectural expression should find a home in Wright is not surprising, for Wright stressed the horizontal in his architecture and town planning, and Finland is nothing if not horizontal. This land of a thousand lakes, with coniferous and deciduous forests slipped in between, and the pink rock always breaking the earth's surface in city and country alike, is regulated by two horizons: the land- and lake-line and the tree-line. Finland's sensitive architects are even conscious of their buildings when they approach the tree-line or break above it.

The Suvikumpu flats glide through the forest up the gentle slope of a hill (ill. 2). It is an architecture dedicated to the landscape, with dark and light façades lending irregular splashes of colour to the stepped string of buildings that mingle with the same irregular game of the forest (ill. 1). Surface colour is a controlled aesthetic pattern applied to the whole project rather than merely as a detail. We have slight variations of green paint over boarded surfaces and horizontal shuttering of the exposed concrete along the upper floor which occasionally drops down to the ground around the enclosed terraces to join the plinth in a similar game. The white wall in between is punctured with small groups of windows with variable lintel heights, so that the small scale of the individual rooms is subservient to the major composition of the façade (ill.3).This technique is an apparent violation of the rational and functional code, but upon reflection the major architectural problem of large building groups is their relationship with both the individual and the community. The buildings here serve both. So this aesthetic freedom, based on a keen sensibility of the natural surroundings, is not only romantic, but in a way rational. Romance, if true, cannot be banished from architecture.

The urban distribution of the lineal buildings themselves skilfully breaks out of the enclosed space as the only natural outside space that creates a community feeling amongst the inhabitants. L-shaped, or Z-shaped buildings

that turn outwards can also be related to each other as Pietilä and Paatelainen clearly demonstrate. A walk around the buildings shows a clear but soft relationship between the flats themselves and between them and the forest (ills. 6, 8). The individual is not only identifiable in his home but with his particular staircase, and with the group as a whole.

1,3,4. Detailed views.
2. Site plan. Key: 1,2,3 housing, 4 centre. The Roman numerals indicate the number of floors.

1,3,4. Detailansichten.
2. Lageplan. Legende: 1,2,3 Wohngebäude, 4 Zentrum. Die römischen Ziffern geben die Anzahl der Stockwerke an.

5. Ground plans of different dwelling types (from top to bottom: top floor in the seven-storey part of section 1, typical floor in the five- to seven-storey part of section 1, typical floor in the four- to five-storey part of section 2, ground floor in the two-storey part of section 2).
6,7,8. Detailed views.

5. Grundrisse verschiedener Wohnungstypen (von oben nach unten: Dachgeschoß im siebengeschossigen Teil von Abschnitt 1, Normalgeschoß im fünf- bis siebengeschossigen Teil von Abschnitt 1, Normalgeschoß im vier- bis fünfgeschossigen Teil von Abschnitt 2, Erdgeschoß im zweigeschossigen Teil von Abschnitt 2).
6,7,8. Detailansichten.

Suvikumpu, Tapiola, Finnland. 1961-69
Architekten: Reima Pietilä und Raili Paatelainen

In Suvikumpu ist das romantische Echo Frank Lloyd Wrights überall gegenwärtig. Daß die Suche nach architektonischem Ausdruck Wright beherrschte, ist nicht Neues; Wright betonte die Horizontale sowohl in seinen Einzelbauten als auch in seinen städtebaulichen Arbeiten, und Finnland ist nichts ohne die Horizontale. Das Land der tausend Seen, mit den endlosen Nadel- und Laubwäldern, in die diese gebettet sind, und dem rosafarbenen Fels, der in Stadt und Land die Erdkrume durchbricht, kennt zwei Horizonte: den Land- und Seenhorizont sowie den Baumhorizont. Die feinfühligen finnischen Architekten sind sich bewußt, wann sie mit ihren Gebäuden an den Baumhorizont heranreichen oder darüber hinausgehen können.
Die Suvikumpu-Siedlung zieht sich über einen sanften, bewaldeten Hang (Abb. 2). Die Architektur steht ganz im Dienst der Landschaft; die abwechselnd dunkel und hell gehaltenen Fassaden setzen unregelmäßige Farbtupfer auf die gestaffelten Häuser, die das Licht- und Schattenspiel des Waldes nachvollziehen (Abb. 1). Farbe ist hier nicht eine Funktion des Details, sondern ein bewußtes ästhetisches Mittel, das die gesamte Anlage beherrscht. In den oberen Geschossen finden wir an den Holzverschalungen und dem horizontal geriffelten Beton Abstufungen von Grün, das gelegentlich um die Terrassen herum bis zum Sockel herunterreicht. In die dazwischen liegenden weißen Wände sind Fenstergruppen mit verschiedenen Sturzhöhen eingestreut, so daß der kleine Maßstab des einzelnen Raumelements im Dienst der Fassadenkomposition steht (Abb. 3). Diese Technik ist eine offenkundige Verletzung des rationalen und funktionalen Gesetzes, aber bei genauerem Überlegen ist doch das bauliche Hauptproblem bei großen Baukomplexen ihre Identität für den einzelnen und die Gemeinschaft. Bei diesen Häusern ist das Problem gelöst. Die ästhetische Freiheit, die sich auf großem Verständnis für die natürliche Umwelt gründet, ist also nicht nur romantisch, sondern in gewisser Weise auch rational. Wahrhaftige Romantik läßt sich nicht aus der Architektur verbannen.
Die Häuser sind so geschickt angeordnet, daß wie bei einem geschlossenen Außenraum ein hohes Maß an Gemeinschaftsgefühl unter den Bewohnern möglich ist. L-förmige oder Z-förmige Gebäude mit der Fassade nach außen können auch aufeinander bezogen werden, wie Pietilä und Paatelainen bewiesen haben. Bei einem Gang um die Häuser herum erkennt man die unaufdringliche Verwandtschaft zwischen den einzelnen Wohnungen sowie zwischen ihnen und dem Wald (Abb. 6, 8). Der einzelne kann sich nicht nur mit seinem Heim, sondern auch mit seinem Treppenhaus und mit der Gruppe als ganzer identifizieren.

10m
30ft.

Oriental Masonic Gardens, New Haven, Connecticut. 1968 – 71
Architect: Paul Rudolph; structural engineer: Paul Gugliotta

Looking somewhat like a trailer parking lot (ill. 2) these twelve-foot-wide modules with curved plywood roofs turn out in fact to be precisely that. They are entirely prefabricated (ill. 5). The roof elements were made in Hartford, while the production and assembly of the other parts took place in Maryland.
Rudolph arranged the modules in groups of four on a pinwheel plan, each dwelling being L-shaped, with day-rooms on the ground floor, bedrooms on the upper floor at rightangles to porches or carports underneath (ills. 4, 7). In this way each dwelling turns its back on its neighbour and overlooks its own private court, which is lightly fenced in. The modules literally grow longer to accommodate from two to five bedrooms. The groups are strung out in a continuous chain, forming a series of U-courts over the gently sloping site. Access is based on the Radburn principle of no through-traffic. In an apparent gesture to unify the whole, Rudolph has run the plywood vaults all in the same direction, perpendicular to the slope. Besides giving a restless air to the whole group it has complicated the structure, increased the costs and provided clerestory lighting that must be difficult to control. The original drawings by Rudolph show slightly more complex details like the hooded windows and curved staircases whichwere obviously simplified for economic reasons (ill. 3). But it is a pity that the more solid garden walls shown in the perspective were not built. It would make everyone feel that next morning the trailers would still be there.

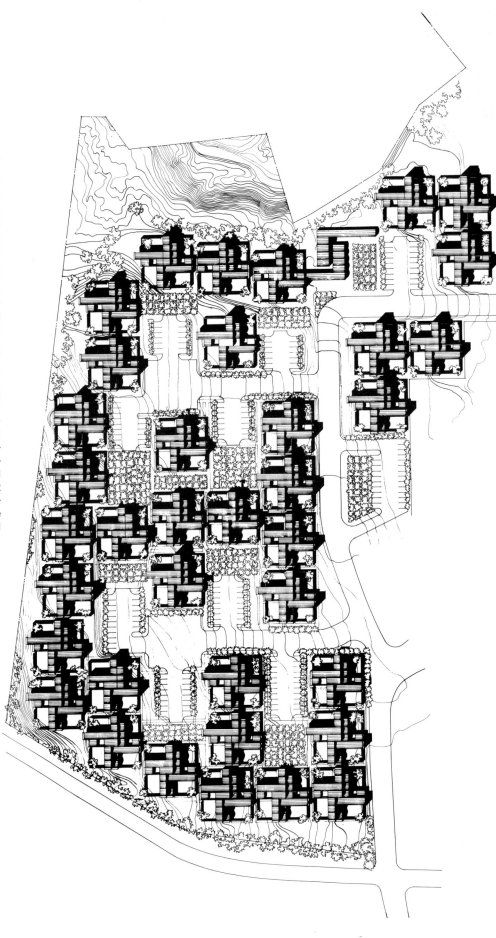

1. Site plan.
2. General view.
3. Perspective view of the original plan with hooded windows, curved staircases and more solid garden walls.

1. Lageplan.
2. Blick über die Siedlung.
3. Perspektive der ursprünglichen Planung mit Haubenfenstern, gekrümmten Treppen-häusern und festeren Gartenmauern.

Oriental Masonic Gardens, New Haven, Connecticut. 1968-71
Architekt: Paul Rudolph; Statiker: Paul Gugliotta

Angesichts der 3,65 m breiten, mit gewölbten Sperrholzelementen überdachten Hauseinheiten glaubt man sich in eine Trailerkolonie versetzt (Abb. 2). In Wirklichkeit sind die Einheiten auch nichts anderes als Trailer, die im übrigen vollständig vorgefertigt wurden (Abb. 5). Die Dachelemente entstanden in Hartford; die übrigen Teile wurden in Maryland hergestellt, wo auch die Montage erfolgte.

Rudolph baute die Einheiten zu windmühlenflügelartigen Gruppen mit jeweils vier zweigeschossigen Wohnungen zusammen, wobei sich die Aufenthaltsräume im Erdgeschoß befinden und die Schlafzimmer im L-förmigen Obergeschoß, das neben dem Erdgeschoßflügel einer überdachten Terrasse bzw. einem Wageneinstellplatz unter sich Raum gibt (Abb. 4, 7). Jede Wohnung steht mit der Rückfront zum Nachbarn und richtet die Vorderseite auf einen eigenen Hof, der leicht eingezäunt ist. Die Einheiten sind unterschiedlich lang, um zwischen zwei und fünf Schlafzimmer aufzunehmen. Die Vierergruppen ziehen sich, eine Reihe von U-förmigen Höfen bildend, in einer kontinuierlichen Kette über das sanft geneigte Grundstück. Der Zugang beruht auf dem Radburn-Prinzip der Sackstraße. In dem offenkundigen Bemühen, das Ganze zu einer Einheit zusammenzuziehen, ließ Rudolph die Sperrholzkuppeln allesamt in der gleichen Richtung senkrecht zum Hang verlaufen. Das verlieh der ganzen Anlage ein unruhiges Aussehen, führte zu einer komplizierteren Konstruktion und erhöhte damit die Kosten. Rudolphs Originalzeichnungen enthalten einige kompliziertere Details, zum Beispiel Haubenfenster und gekrümmte Treppenhäuser, die offenbar aus wirtschaftlichen Gründen fallengelassen wurden (Abb. 3). Bedauerlich ist, daß die auf dem perspektivischen Plan eingezeichneten festeren Gartenmauern nicht gebaut wurden. Sie hätten zweifellos die Bewohner in der Sicherheit bestärkt, daß die Wohnwagen am andern Morgen noch an ihrem Platz stehen.

4. Ground plans of a unit.
5. Test assembly.
6,7. Detailed views.

4. Grundrisse einer Einheit.
5. Testmontage.
6,7. Detailansichten.

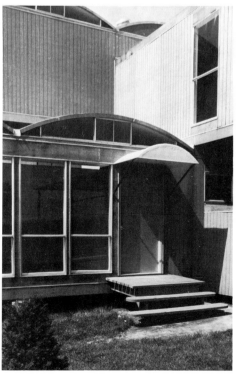

Habitat '67, Montreal. 1964–67

Architects: Moshe Safdie and David, Barott, Boulva; structural consultant: A. E. Kommendant; structural engineers: Monti, Lefebvre, Lavoie, Nadon & Associates

Like the Sydney Opera House, Habitat is one of those architectural white elephants that make life worth living. Both Utzon and Safdie may one day be considered martyrs of the modern movement in architecture, who personally suffered ridicule in pursuit of the beautiful and fell as a result of the redundant functionality of their works. It is even more ironic that Safdie defended his vision of a proper home life based on the economy and function of an essentially Utopian project. It would be unfair to quote from his naive book *Beyond Habitat,* as it is too transparent, honest and conceited. Flushed with the publicity accorded modern superstars, his conceit is not surprising; it is in a way the secret of his success and the reason for his downfall. But now, after the years, Habitat can be valued for the impetus it gave many housing projects around the world. Prefabrication need no longer be associated with dullness though on close analysis it is obvious that at the outset, Safdie had very little idea of the discipline any system of pre-

fabrication demanded. But no matter, he did change public opinion. He also showed the way for a sort of low-rise density as a compromise between the block and the suburban house, though here again Habitat is deceptively high. Finally, he fought for the dwelling that contained an outside living area. The battle has not yet been won, but his contribution has probably been decisive. One day building codes may well include this provision just as nowadays they insist on a kitchen and bathroom.
Since the building was built for experimental and exhibition purposes, and since the original project for 1,000 dwellings was cut to a mere 158, a detailed criticism would serve little purpose.
It is obvious that for any prefabricated system to be comparable to traditional methods the initial capital costs need to be absorbed by the production of at least 500–1000 units. It should also be obvious that the larger and more complete the unit, the more rigid and imposing must be the system. Safdie's only way out was to design 15 different home mo-,dules, which unnecessarily complicated and increased the cost of the system itself. The heavy reinforcement and post-tensioning cables complicated matters even further. The access to the flats is by no means simple, and

many dwellings have no lift-stop at the same level.
Although Moshe Safdie dislikes the thought that the visual arts are a significant part of our culture it is in the end the visual effect of Habitat that has been its most significant contribution to the architecture of community housing.

1. General view.
2. The aerial view reveals the formal rigour of the overall design.

Habitat '67, Montreal. 1964-67

Architekten: Moshe Safdie und David, Barott, Boulva; Konstruktionsberater: A.E. Kommendant; Statiker: Monti, Lefebvre, Lavoie, Nadon & Associates

Wie das Opernhaus in Sydney ist auch Habitat einer jener weißen Elefanten der Architektur, die das Leben lebenswert machen. Nicht nur Utzon, auch Safdie könnte eines Tages als Märtyrer der modernen Architekturbewegung gelten, der dem Spott anheimfiel, weil er das Schöne wollte und über die überflüssige Funktionalität seiner Werke stolperte. Die Ironie wollte es zudem, daß Safdie seine Vision eines angemessenen häuslichen Lebens auf die Wirtschaftlichkeit und Funktionalität eines ganz und gar utopischen Projektes stützte. Es wäre ungerecht, zum Beweis seiner Naivität sein Buch *Beyond Habitat* heranzuziehen, denn es ist dafür zu durchsichtig, aufrichtig und selbstgefällig. Da ihm die Publicity eines modernen Superstars zuteil wurde, überrascht sein Dünkel nicht; er ist in gewisser Weise das Geheimnis seines Erfolges und der Grund für seinen Sturz. Jetzt aber, im Abstand einiger Jahre, ist Habitat wegen des Anstoßes, den es vielen Wohnbauprojekten auf der ganzen Welt gab, der Würdigung wert. Vorferti-

gung braucht nicht mehr mit Langweiligkeit gleichgesetzt zu werden, wenn man auch bei näherem Hinsehen erkennt, daß Safdie zu Beginn kaum eine Ahnung von der Disziplin hatte, die jedes Vorfertigungssystem verlangt. Aber wie dem auch sei – er änderte die öffentliche Meinung, und er wies auch den Weg für eine niedrige Kompaktbauweise als Kompromiß zwischen Block und Vorstadthaus, wenn auch Habitat zu hoch wirkt. Schließlich kämpfte er um die Wohnung mit einem Wohnbereich im Freien. Die Schlacht ist noch nicht gewonnen, aber sein Beitrag war wahrscheinlich entscheidend. Künftige Bauvorschriften könnten durchaus dieses Element fordern, gerade wie die heutigen Regeln auf Küche und Badezimmer bestehen.

Da es sich um einen Versuchsbau für Ausstellungszwecke handelt und die tausend Wohnungen des ursprünglichen Projekts auf lediglich 158 zusammengestrichen wurden, ist eine ins einzelne gehende Kritik nicht angebracht.

Es ist bekannt, daß die Investitionskosten für ein Vorfertigungssystem zur Amortisierung mindestens 500 bis 1000 Einheiten erfordern; erst dann läßt sich das System mit traditionellen Methoden vergleichen. Bekannt sollte auch sein, daß das System um so starrer und

beherrschender sein muß, je größer und vollständiger die Einheit wird. Safdies Ausweg bestand darin, 15 verschiedene Wohnungsmoduln anzubieten, was das System unnötig komplizierte und verteuerte. Die schweren Bewehrungs- und Nachspannseile machten die Dinge noch schwieriger. Die Erschließung ist ebenfalls alles andere als einfach, und für viele Wohnungen ist kein Aufzugshalt auf gleicher Ebene vorgesehen.

Obwohl Moshe Safdie die Ansicht, daß die bildende Kunst ein bedeutsamer Teil unserer Kultur sei, nicht teilt, war es letzten Endes der visuelle Effekt von Habitat, der dessen wichtigsten Beitrag zur Architektur des Wohnungsbaus darstellte.

1. Gesamtansicht.
2. Die Luftaufnahme enthüllt die formale Strenge der Gesamtanlage.

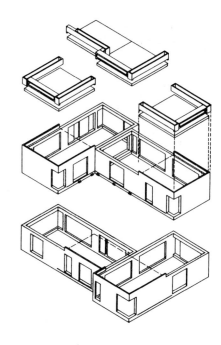

3. The complex under construction.
4. Section.
5. Schematic drawing of a unit.
6. One of the pedestrian streets.
7. Detailed view.
8. The bathrooms were entirely prefabricated.
9. Living-room and terrace of a unit.

3. Die Siedlung während der Montage.
4. Schnitt.
5. Schema einer Wohneinheit.
6. Eine der Fußgängerstraßen.
7. Detailansicht.
8. Die Badezimmer wurden vollständig vorgefertigt.
9. Wohnraum und Terrasse einer Wohneinheit.

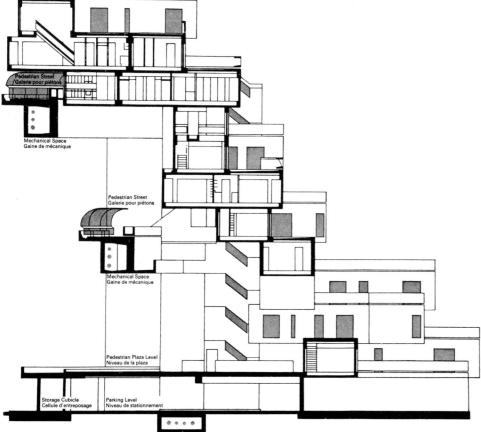

Pedestrian Street
Galerie pour piétons

Mechanical Space
Gaine de mécanique

Pedestrian Street
Galerie pour piétons

Mechanical Space
Gaine de mécanique

Pedestrian Plaza Level
Niveau de la plaza

Storage Cubicle
Cellule d'entreposage

Parking Level
Niveau de stationnement

1. North side of the west building.
2. Site plan and section.
3. View of the east building over the Blackwater tunnel approach.
4. The west building from the south.
5. View of the east building over the inner open area.

1. Nordseite des westlichen Gebäudes.
2. Lageplan und Gesamtschnitt.
3. Blick über die Zufahrt des Blackwatertunnels auf das östliche Gebäude.
4. Das westliche Gebäude von Süden.
5. Blick über den inneren Freiraum auf das östliche Gebäude.

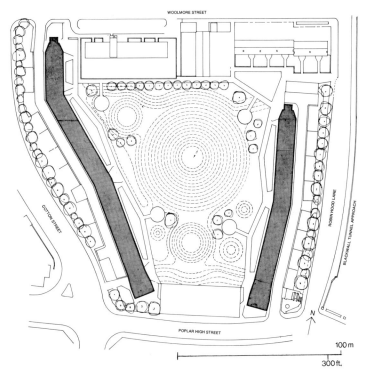

Architects: Alison and Peter Smithson
(assistants: C.H. Woodward and K.E. Baker)

Robin Hood Gardens consists of two parallel lineal corridor-access buildings, which enclose and protect a wide open area (the gardens) from the rest of the neighbourhood (ill. 2). The south side of the gardens is cut off from the road by a sunken hard-surface ball-game pit, and the north side runs into a jumble of left-over tenement buildings (ill. 1).

The idea of a high-level corridor street (ill. 9) has been a latent element in the Smithsons' theory of community housing for a long while. Here they have wisely used it facing out towards the neighbourhood to assist the visual integration of the buildings. Split-level flats have been avoided whilst keeping the duplex (either up or down from the access deck), and the working kitchen has been placed on the same level as the entrance, overlooking the 'private' gardens between the buildings so that mothers can watch both the front door and children playing below. The inner family sanctum with its TV and bedrooms is kept at a different level. One interesting pragmatic point is the rejection of the rationalist solution, which would orient all the buildings towards the south side, in favour of a symmetrical solution that leaves the majority of the bedrooms facing the quieter inner garden court and the living-rooms facing either east or west to the outer world. The reason for this was the need to insulate the bedrooms from the noise of road traffic in Blackwater tunnel and traffic going to the docks along Cotton Street to the west.

However, if noise was such a problem, why did the architects make the shorter Blackwater tunnel building higher so that it contains 110 dwellings as against 104 in the Cotton Street building? The 3-metre high 'acoustic wall' is insufficient for the upper floors – this at least was my own experience from the top deck. No doubt the technical reduction in noise level from 70–75 dBA to 50 dBA has been helped by the protruding vertical mullions, sills and absorbent window lintels, but the Cotton Street traffic is negligible compared with that on the Blackwater tunnel approach urban motorway, and the higher building surely would have been better here.

The group as a whole is very restful to the eye. The meandering buildings follow the natural boundaries of the site, arousing curiosity in their façades hidden from the street, and declaring their complete length to the enclosed court inside. To enjoy the space all at once one must go to the top of the higher earth mound in the centre of the gardens (ill. 5).

What is not so pleasant is to take a lift to one of the access decks. There is no architectural link with these decks. They have been designed as though one was always meant to be on them, to look down (psychologically as well) on the neighbourhood, but never to arrive or leave it. The deck actually narrows to dis-

courage you at the northern end, and to the south it appears to get lost. The lift lobbies and lifts are sordid in the extreme, contrasting in an extraordinary way with the otherwise sensitively detailed deck. The result is that these lift lobbies are really blind alleys ideal for vandalism if not robbery and rape.

One wonders why the architects did not group the lifts together thus giving the occupiers a greater choice of lifts (especially when one is out of order), and above all increasing the casual contacts between neighbours and fostering a community spirit. The caretaker could then control the ground-floor entrance better, while the lobbies would be larger and, with the increased movement of people coming and going, or waiting, would no longer be lonely places. This may seem a rather irrelevant criticism, but having spent ten years living in a corridor-access flat I can assure the reader of the importance of lift and lobby as a transitional element between the street (public) and the deck (semi-public) and they should be architecturally treated as such.

The same problem arises with the connection of the interior gardens to the surrounding streets. There is no clear access, but this may be deliberate in order to make the gardens private for the residents. However, if this is so there is a curious lack of incentive for the residents to use the gardens, since the paths and play areas are rigidly defined around the perimeter by 'rules' established in a printed 'householders manual' – a little totalitarian, to say the least. One concludes that the park is to be looked at from above and nothing more.

As for the aesthetics of the façades, one should note the conflict between the intellectual desire for order, with the minimum number of repetitive elements (wall-to-wall windows and applied double T-columns to the façade) and the artistic desire for expression (syncopated rhythm of the major applied columns to express the division between individual homes, and the cranked buildings to avoid monotony and vibrate the space between the two blocks). This conflict has not been successfully resolved, because the repetition of the windows becomes a dominating feature that presents a very dull monotonous façade especially when viewed perpendicularly across the gardens from another block.

To compare these buildings with Georgian terraces as Peter Eisenman does[8], may be justified by the intellectual aims of the authors, but the minor elements used are, in general, too poor for a real comparison to be justified. However, the larger urban image which has been achieved certainly does seem to give an indication of the future form community housing may take.

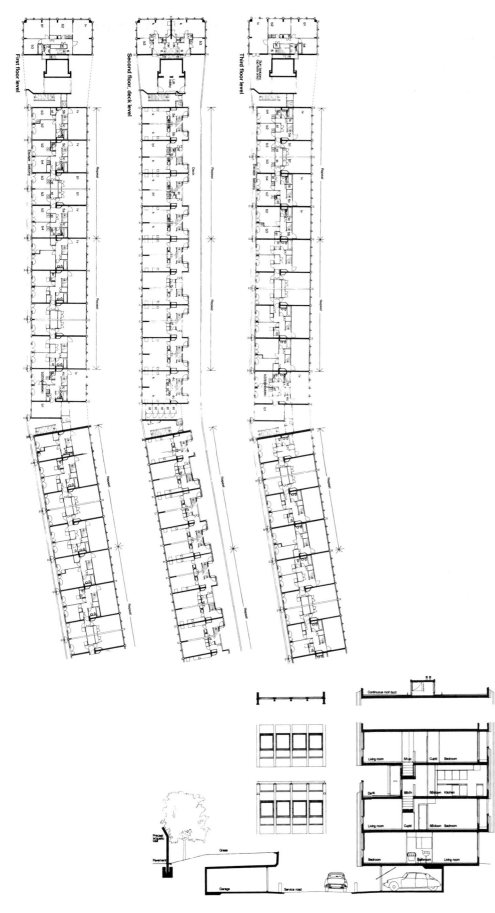

First floor level

Second floor, deck level

Third floor level

Robin Hood Gardens, London. 1966-72
Architekten: Alison und Peter Smithson (Mitarbeiter: C.H. Woodward und K.E. Baker)

Die Anlage Robin Hood Gardens umfaßt zwei parallele, lineare, über Außenkorridore zugängliche Gebäude, die einen großen Freiraum (die Gärten) von der Nachbarschaft abschließen und abschirmen (Abb. 2). Zwischen der Südseite des Grünbereichs und der Straße liegt ein vertiefter Sportplatz mit Hartbelag, die Nordseite läuft in ein Gewirr übriggebliebener Mietshäuser aus (Abb. 1).

Die Vorstellung von einer erhöhten Korridorstraße (Abb. 9) war schon lange ein latentes Element in der Theorie der Smithsons über kollektives Wohnen. Hier plazierten sie die Straße klugerweise zur Nachbarschaft hin, um die optische Integration der Gebäude zu steigern. Halbgeschosse wurden vermieden, dafür gibt es Duplexwohnungen (sie reichen vom Zugangsdeck aus entweder aufwärts oder abwärts); die Küche liegt stets auf der Ebene des Eingangs mit Blick auf die ›private‹ Grünanlage zwischen den Gebäuden, so daß die Mütter sowohl die Wohnungstür als auch die unten spielenden Kinder im Auge behalten können. Das Familienwohnzimmer mit Fernseher und die Schlafzimmer liegen abseits auf der anderen Ebene. In pragmatischer Hinsicht ist interessant, daß die rationalistische Lösung einer Orientierung aller Gebäude nach Süden zugunsten einer symmetrischen Lösung verworfen wurde, nach der die meisten Schlafzimmer auf den ruhigen inneren Gartenhof und die Wohnzimmer entweder östlich oder westlich nach außen gerichtet sind. Der Grund dafür war der Wunsch, die Schlafzimmer vor dem Verkehrslärm vom Blackwater-Tunnel und von der Cotton Street im Westen, auf der der Verkehr zu den Docks abgewickelt wird, zu schützen.

Wenn aber die Lärmbelästigung ein so großes Problem war, erhebt sich die Frage, warum die Architekten das kürzere Blackwater-Tunnel-Gebäude höher machten, so daß es 110 Wohnungen beherbergt im Gegensatz zu den 104 Wohnungen des Cotton-Street-Gebäudes. Die 3 m hohe ›Lärmschutzwand‹ reicht für die oberen Geschosse nicht aus; wenigstens gewann ich selbst diesen Eindruck auf dem obersten Deck. Zwar konnte der Lärmpegel von 70 bis 75 dBA auf 50 dBA reduziert werden, unter anderem auch durch die vorspringenden Längssprossen, die Gesimse und die schallschluckenden Fensterstürze, aber der Verkehr in der Cotton Street ist geringfügig im Vergleich zu dem auf dem Zubringer zum Blackwater-Tunnel, und zweifellos wäre es besser gewesen, das höhere Gebäude dort hinzustellen.

Die Gruppe als ganze ist für das Auge sehr erholsam. Die in sich gebogenen Bauten folgen den natürlichen Grenzen des Geländes. Von der Straße aus wecken die um die Ecke führenden Fassaden die Neugier, und in dem inneren Freiraum lassen sie ihre volle Länge erkennen.

Um das Ganze auf einmal zu sehen, muß man auf den höheren Erdhügel in der Mitte der Grünanlige hinaufsteigen (Abb. 5).

Weniger erfreulich ist es, mit dem Aufzug auf eines der Zugangsdecks hinaufzufahren. Zu diesen Decks besteht keine architektonische Verbindung. Sie wurden so gestaltet, als solle man sich dort stets aufhalten und auf die Nachbarschaft hinuntersehen (auch im übertragenen Sinn), aber nicht dort anlangen oder von dort weggehen. Am Nordende wird das Deck so schmal, daß es entmutigend wirkt, und am Südende scheint es sich irgendwo zu verlieren. Die Aufzugsvorplätze und Aufzüge sind abgrundtief häßlich und fallen gegenüber dem sonst sorgsam detaillierten Deck stark ab. Die Aufzugsvorplätze gleichen düsteren Sackgassen, die zur Verunreinigung, wenn nicht gar zu heimtückischen Überfällen geradezu einzuladen scheinen.

Man muß sich fragen, warum die Architekten die Aufzüge nicht zusammengefaßt haben. Die Bewohner hätten dann eine größere Auswahl (besonders, wenn ein Aufzug defekt ist), und vor allem hätten die zufälligen Kontakte unter den Nachbarn zugenommen, so daß der Gemeinschaftsgeist gefördert würde. Hinzu kommt, daß der Hausverwalter den Eingang im Erdgeschoß besser überwachen könnte und die Aufzugsvorplätze größer wären und nicht so einsam, da ein ständiges Kommen und Gehen stattfände.

Diese Kritik mag vielleicht unerheblich erscheinen; ich selbst wohnte aber 10 Jahre in einem Haus mit äußerem Korridorzugang und kann bezeugen, wie wichtig die Aufzüge als Übergangselement zwischen der Öffentlichkeit (der Straße) und dem (halböffentlichen) Deck sind. Sie sollten auch baulich so behandelt werden.

Das gleiche Problem stellt sich in der Beziehung zwischen der Grünanlage und den umgebenden Straßen. Es ist kein deutlich erkennbarer Zugang vorhanden, aber das mag Absicht sein, damit die Grünanlage für die Bewohner wirklich privat wird. Sollte dies zutreffen, so fehlt es jedoch seltsamerweise an einem Nutzungsanreiz, denn die Wege und Spielplätze in der Runde sind eng begrenzt und unterliegen autoritären Vorschriften, festgehalten in einer gedruckten Hausordnung. Daraus muß man schließen, daß die Grünanlage zu nichts anderem dient, als von oben betrachtet zu werden.

Im Hinblick auf die Ästhetik der Gebäudefassaden ist der Konflikt hervorzuheben zwischen dem intellektuellen Ordnungsstreben, aus dem eine minimale Zahl sich wiederholender Elemente (von Wand zu Wand reichende Verglasung und aufgesetzte Doppel-T-Sprossen) resultierte, und dem künstlerischen Verlangen nach Ausdruck (Synkopenrhythmus der größeren Sprossen zur Betonung der Wohnungsgrenzen, Krümmung der Gebäude, um der Monotonie zu entgehen und den Raum zwischen den beiden Blocks zu gliedern). Dieser Konflikt wurde nicht zufriedenstellend

gelöst, denn die gleichmäßige Reihung der Fensterelemente wird zum vorherrschenden Merkmal; die Folge ist, daß die Fassade langweilig und monoton wirkt, besonders wenn man über die Grünanlage hinweg von einem Block auf den andern schaut.

Diese Bauwerke mit der Architektur einer georgianischen Terrasse zu vergleichen, wie es Peter Eisenman tut [8], mag durch die intellektuelle Bemühung der Architekten und das Gesamtergebnis gerechtfertigt sein, doch die Details sind im allgemeinen zu anspruchslos, um einen echten Vergleich zu gestatten. Städtebaulich ist die Anlage jedoch zweifellos ein Hinweis auf die Form, die der Wohnungsbau in Zukunft annehmen könnte.

6. Ground plans (1st, 2nd and 3rd floors).
7. Section.
8. Detail of one building.
9. Deck in the west building.

6. Grundrisse (1., 2. und 3. Obergeschoß).
7. Schnitt.
8. Detailansicht eines Gebäudes.
9. Deck im westlichen Gebäude.

1. General view from the north-east.
2. Site plan.
3. The central court at Hellebo.
4. The access road at Hellebo.
5. View of Hellebo from the south-east.

1. Gesamtansicht von Nordosten.
2. Lageplan.
3. Der zentrale Hof von Hellebo.
4. Die Zugangsstraße von Hellebo.
5. Blick von Südosten auf Hellebo.

**Hellebo and Birkebo, Elsinore, Denmark.
1963–71**
Architects: Halldor Gunnløgsson and Jorn Nielsen

This almost completely self-contained housing group excels architecturally in its ordered hierarchy and its clear formal unity. But this excellence is gained precisely because of the narrowness of its purpose, which is the care of elderly people in quiet surroundings. The buildings are formal and very beautiful – even more than photographs can show, although the feeling of an institution is latently present. The almost complete absence of families and young children remove at a stroke all the advantages and necessary inconveniences of village life. This is of course a sociological problem that may be peculiar to the Danish way of life. With so much emphasis in Denmark on community areas, facilities and services for children, with play areas all over the place so that one is almost continuously falling into sand-pits or avoiding swinging rubber lorry tires, or leaping out of cycle paths that run through everything, even sometimes at first or second floor level, it is not surprising that the elderly may choose to get away from it all. However, one feels that the two institutes, Birkebo nursing home and social centre, and Hellebo service apartments, are a step in the wrong direction in that they create even more

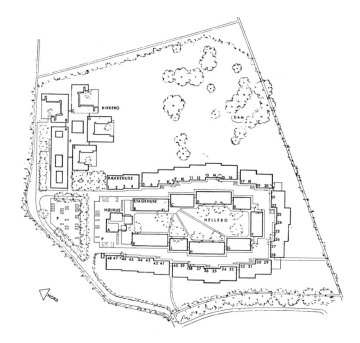

social divisions. The problem lies more in the field of urban planning than architecture, for if this institute lay more to the centre of Helsingør like its medieval counterpart, the brick Carmelite monastery, then this group would contribute to community life as a whole, rather than detract from it. Given the problem and the site, the architects could have offered a less formal architectural solution and even perhaps persuaded the clients to plan a mixed community which would have avoided this rather awesome step towards death. Instead they have seized upon the inhabitants' desire for quietness to emphasize the necropolistic character of the buildings. This they have done with extraordinary ability, producing a superb formality and a clear sense of place. The Hellebo group consists of a nine-storey tower and two parallel U-shaped chains of lower buildings (ill. 1), with one- or two-storey houses forming the outer chain (ill. 5) and four-storey houses forming the inner one (ill. 4).

The inner chain encloses a silent green that captures the contemplative nature of a cloister garden (ill. 3). This central space which many an architect would have designed as a communal outside room to stimulate casual relations has been rejected as such. Instead, the architects have preferred to turn the surrounding dwellings outwards, so that the living-rooms and terraces have a view of the country.

By the skilful use of levels the inner green is one floor higher than the access road. Garages are slipped under the flats of the four-storey houses on one side and carports and fenced-in 'patio' gardens in front of the one- or two-storey houses on the other, which also possess terraces and face outwards towards the country. The access road looping round between the two chains of houses is the natural meeting place of the inhabitants as they arrive and leave by car or walk across to the restaurant. Unfortunately the motor vehicle, with its associated garage doors, oil spots and disordered parking, dominates the aesthetic quality of this area and kills any desire people may have to linger here.

The Birkebo group has individual bedrooms arranged in four units, with open courts which are in turn related to a central court. It is a far more successful formal and social achievement (ill. 8). The key social and service building, which serves both the nursing-home and flats, is stretched out on the north-west side to link the heart of the nursing-home with the main entrance square in front of the tower. The relationship between nursing-home and the flats is sensitively handled: both are used to form a common entrance square, marked by the tower and smaller inlets off the main square at the entrances to the loop road on either side of the tower and the entrance to the nursing-home. This last one is the actual physical spatial link between the two institutes that at the same time articulates the space between the entrance and the large green beyond to the north-east.

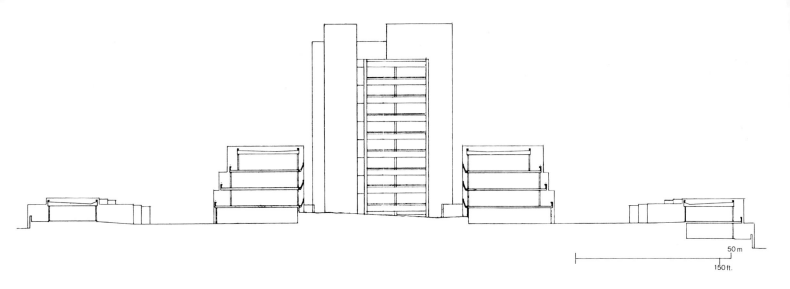

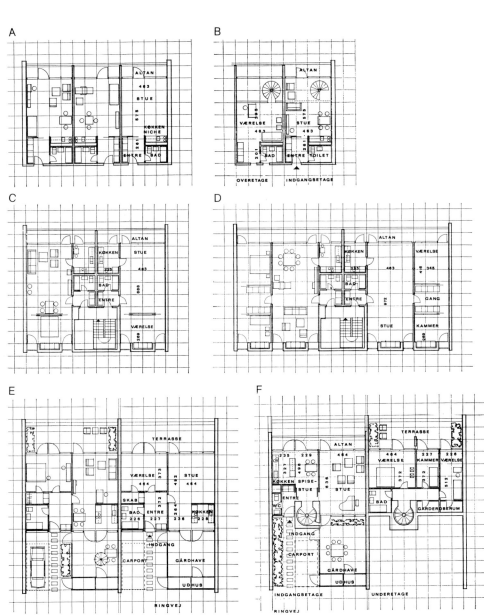

Hellebo und Birkebo, Helsingør, Dänemark. 1963-71

Architekten: Halldor Gunnløgsson und Jorn Nielsen

Diese beinahe ganz in sich abgeschlossene Häusergruppe besticht architektonisch durch ihre beherrschte, geordnete Hierarchie und ihre klare formale Einheitlichkeit. Dieser Vorzug ergab sich allerdings aus der Beengtheit des Verwendungszwecks, der Pflege älterer Menschen in stiller, abgelegener Gegend. Die formal strengen Gebäude sind von großer Schönheit – die Fotos geben davon nur ein unvollkommenes Bild –, aber die Atmosphäre eines Pflegeheims ist überall latent präsent. Da fast keine Familien mit Kindern hier wohnen, sind mit einem Schlag alle Vorteile und unvermeidlichen Nachteile des Dorflebens weggewischt. Möglicherweise haben wir es hier mit einer Reaktion auf die Besonderheiten der dänischen Lebensweise zu tun. In Dänemark wird ein überdurchschnittlich großer Wert auf gemeinschaftliche Bereiche mit Einrichtungen für Kinder gelegt, überall stößt man auf Kinderspielplätze und muß dauernd Sandkästen, schaukelnden alten Autoreifen oder flitzenden Fahrrädern aus dem Weg gehen (gelegentlich sogar auf dem ersten oder zweiten Geschoß), so daß es verständlich ist, wenn ältere Menschen danach streben, dem allem zu entgehen. Trotzdem drängt sich der Eindruck auf, daß die beiden Baugruppen – das Pflegeheim und gesellschaftliche Zentrum Birkebo sowie das Wohnheim Hellebo – einen Schritt in die falsche Richtung gehen, indem sie die gesellschaftliche Segregation auf die Spitze treiben. Das Problem liegt eher im stadtplanerischen als im architektonischen Bereich; denn wenn die Heime näher beim Zentrum von Helsingør lägen – so wie ihr mittelalterliches Gegenstück, der Ziegelbau des Karmeliterklosters –, würden sie das Gemeinschaftsleben als Ganzes bereichern und nicht aufsplittern, wie sie es jetzt tun. Aber

selbst angesichts dieser Probleme und des Baugeländes hätten die Architekten eine weniger formale bauliche Lösung anbieten und vielleicht sogar die Auftraggeber überreden können, für eine gemischte Gemeinschaft zu bauen, womit dieser ziemlich furchterregende Schritt auf den Tod vermieden worden wäre. Statt dessen gaben sie dem Ruhebedürfnis der Bewohner voll nach und unterstrichen den Nekropolencharakter der Anlage. Das freilich vollbrachten sie mit außergewöhnlichem Geschick. Die beiden Baugruppen sind von einer prachtvollen formalen Wirkung und vermitteln ein klares Ortsgefühl.

Die Hellebo-Gruppe besteht aus einem zehngeschossigen Turm und zwei parallel verlaufenden, U-förmigen Ketten niedrigerer Gebäude (Abb. 1). Die äußere Kette umfaßt ein- oder zweigeschossige Häuser (Abb. 5), die innere Kette viergeschossige Häuser (Abb. 4). Die letztere umschließt einen stillen Grünplatz, der in seiner kontemplativen Atmosphäre einem Klostergarten gleicht (Abb. 3). Dieser zentrale Raum, den so mancher Architekt als gemeinschaftlichen Außenbereich zur Förderung sozialer Kontakte gestaltet hätte, wurde nicht für diesen Zweck genutzt. Statt dessen zogen es die Architekten vor, die umgebenden Wohnungen nach außen zu orientieren und deren Wohnräume und Terrassen auf das Land hinausgehen zu lassen.

Durch die geschickte Einrichtung verschiedener Ebenen liegt der zentrale Grünplatz ein Geschoß höher als die Zugangsstraße, deren eine Seite von den unter die Wohnungen der viergeschossigen Häuser geschobenen Garagen gesäumt wird, während an der anderen Seite offene Parkplätze und die eingezäunten Vorgärten der ein- oder zweigeschossigen Häuser liegen. Auch diese sind mit ihren Terrassen dem offenen Land zugewandt. Die Zugangsstraße, die sich wie eine Schlinge durch die beiden Häuserketten zieht, ist der natürliche Treffpunkt der Bewohner, wenn sie mit dem Auto ankommen oder abfahren und wenn

sie zum Restaurant hinübergehen. Unglücklicherweise übertönt das Auto mit allem, was es nach sich zieht – Garagentüren, Öllachen, unordentliches Parken –, die ästhetische Qualität des Ortes und tötet somit jedes Verlangen, sich hier müßig aufzuhalten.

Der Form und gesellschaftlichen Forderung nach weitaus besser geglückt ist die Birkebo-Gruppe (Abb. 8). Die einzelnen Schlafräume bilden vier Baueinheiten mit offenen Höfen, die ihrerseits einen zentralen Hof einschließen. Das soziale und verwaltungsmäßige Schlüsselgebäude für das Pflegeheim wie für die Wohnungen liegt an der Nordwestseite und verbindet den Kern des Pflegeheims mit dessen Haupteingang.

Pflegeheim und Wohnheim sind mit Gefühl zueinander in Beziehung gesetzt. Sie bilden zusammen einen vom Turm beherrschten großen gemeinsamen Eingangsplatz, begleitet von buchtenartigen kleineren Plätzen vor den Mündungen der Schleifenstraße beiderseits des Turms und vor dem Eingang zum Pflegeheim. Der letztere ist das bauliche Bindeglied zwischen den beiden Heimen und artikuliert zugleich den Raum zwischen dem Zugang und der großen, jenseits nach Nordosten gelegenen Grünfläche.

6. Section through Hellebo.
7. Ground plans of different dwelling types in the Hellebo group (A block A, 1st-9th level; B block A, 9th and 10th level; C blocks C,F,G,H,K; D blocks B,D,E,J; E houses 1-4, 29-48; F houses 5-28).
8. View of block C at Birkebo.
9. Ground plan of Birkebo.

6. Schnitt durch Hellebo.
7. Grundrisse verschiedener Wohnungstypen in der Hellebo-Gruppe (A Block A, 1.-9. Geschoß; B Block A, 9.u.10. Geschoß; C Blocks C,F,G,H,K; D Blocks B,D,E,J; E Häuser 1-4, 29-48; F Häuser 5-28).
8. Blick auf Block C von Birkebo.
9. Grundriß von Birkebo.

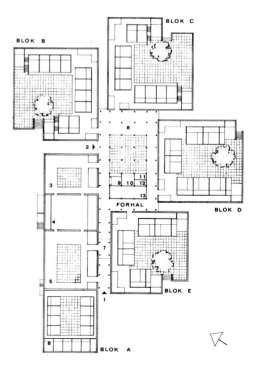

Santa Agueda Vacation Community, Benicasim, Spain. 1965–67 (first phase)

Architects: Josep Martorell, Oriol Bohigas, David Mackay

There were five a-priori design objectives for this project:
– to design a minimum number of different dwellings types, adjusted to the needs of a vacation community, and to assemble these elements in such a way that the conflicting requirements for privacy, views and communal life did not override each other;
– to absorb the car parking within the building fabric;
– to provoke social communication by assembling the dwellings along a spine of pedestrian promenades and a variety of courts;
– to design the urban neighbourhood in scale with the spatial and time sequences of the family on holiday, simultaneously providing for privacy, silence, natural surroundings and human contacts and communications;
– to ensure that the personality of the urban neighbourhood was the sum of each family unit, and that the individuality of the units was not lost in the merging of each unit in a greater personality.

The master plan provides for 306 dwellings with either sea or mountain views, each one related to the whole through a staggered continuity of semi-enclosed open spaces (ill. 3). The height of the buildings increases with distance from the sea, thus avoiding a brusque change of scale near the shore. There are basically three horse-shoe open spaces. The major one forms a park open to the shore with a large swimming-pool and tunnel to the beach under the public road; the central one is open to the sports area to the north and contains the cultural and commercial services; and finally the western horse-shoe facing the mountains and partially enclosed by the taller buildings is more urban in character, although it too contains a small swimming-pool.

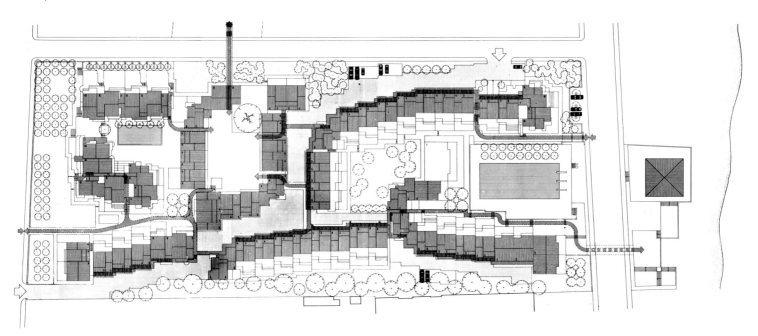

Access and internal communications are provided on two distinct levels, the lower one for cars and parking and the upper one for pedestrians only which connects each dwelling with the centre, and with the beach.

There are two types of dwellings: the first, normal holiday living units in three variations according to size (ills. 5, 6), the second, reduced economy units.

The three variations of the first unit form a set related in section on three distinct levels. The lowest level accommodates a 70-square-metre unit plus car parking for the complete set. The middle level accommodates an 83-square-metre unit plus the pedestrian communication deck. The upper level accommodates a 110-square-metre duplex. The dwellings themselves have two components, a larger, open multi-level activity space (eating, talking, entertaining, playing), and a smaller rigidly enclosed compartment group (sleeping, washing, thinking).

The Benicasim group was probably too violent a protest against the functional-capitalist rape of the Mediterranean shore. In order to protest against the sham architecture of Miami-style blocks perpendicular to the shore to provide the all-over advertised 'view-of-the-sea', the Benicasim building seems to have opted out in a mimic 'architecture without architects' approach. In the long run, and when the scheme is finally completed, it may well be seen as just another sham unit in the forefront of the tourist onslaught upon the Mediterranean. Instead of putting tourists in little boxes they are put into a little village (ill. 1), the only difference being a question of scale. Although the detailing of the buildings is uncompromisingly 'modern', the break-up of the building volume into smaller units assembled in a picturesque way is perhaps too romantic. The result is a motley collection of decorated bicycle sheds that are rather nice to live in (ills. 3, 4).

1. General view.
2. Site plan of the whole complex.
3,4. Detailed views.

1. Gesamtansicht.
2. Lageplan der Gesamtanlage.
3,4. Detailansichten.

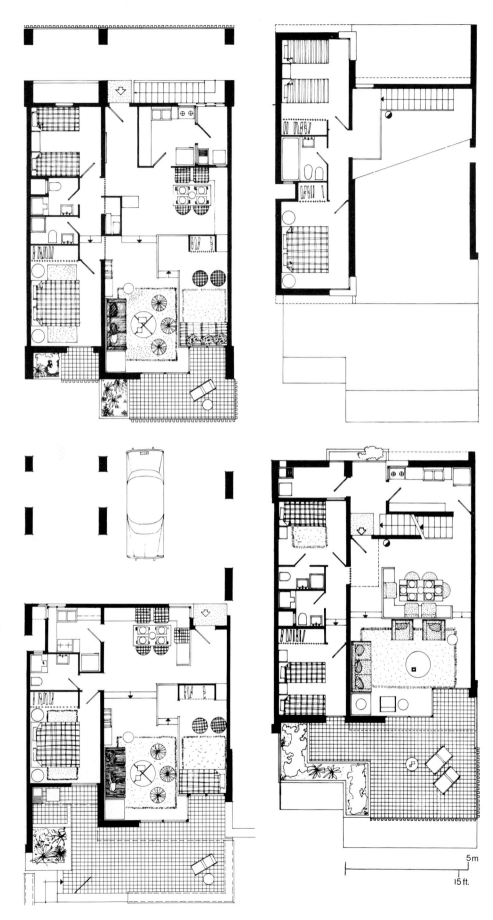

**Feriensiedlung Santa Agueda, Benicasim,
Spanien. Erster Bauabschnitt. 1965-67**
Architekten: Josep Martorell, Oriol Bohigas,
David Mackay

Dem Entwurf der Anlage lagen fünf Zielvorstellungen zugrunde:
– Einschränkung der Zahl der Wohnungstypen
auf ein Minimum entsprechend den reduzier-
ten Bedürfnissen einer Feriengemeinschaft;
Anordnung dieser Typen in der Weise, daß die
widerstreitenden Forderungen Privatsphäre,
Ausblick und Gemeinschaftsleben möglichst
gleichmäßig erfüllt werden;
– Integration der Parkplätze in die Anlage;
– Förderung gesellschaftlicher Kontakte
durch Anordnung der Wohnungen entlang
einem Netzwerk von Fußwegen und vielfälti-
gen Höfen;
– Abstimmung der Nachbarschaftseinheit auf
die räumliche und zeitliche Abfolge des Ur-
laubslebens der Familie, also Vorsorge für Un-
gestörtheit, Ruhe, natürliche Umwelt und
menschliche Kommunikation;
– Sicherstellung, daß die Persönlichkeit der
Anlage sich aus der Summe der einzelnen
Familieneinheiten ergibt, daß der Eigenwert
der einzelnen Einheit nicht durch das Aufgehen in einem größeren Zusammenhang
verlorengeht.
Der Gesamtplan sieht 306 Wohnungen vor,
die entweder See- oder Bergblick haben und
durch kontinuierlich gestaffelte, halbum-
schlossene offene Räume in das Ganze einge-
bunden sind (Abb. 2). Mit zunehmender Entfernung vom Meer werden die Gebäude höher;
auf diese Weise wird ein schroffer Wechsel
des Maßstabs in Ufernähe vermieden. Vorgesehen sind drei hufeisenförmige offene
Räume. Der größte bildet einen zum Ufer offenen Park mit großem Schwimmbad und
Durchgang unter der öffentlichen Straße zum
Strand. Der mittlere ist nach Norden offen mit
Blick auf die Sportplätze. An ihm liegen Einrichtungen für kulturelle Veranstaltungen und
Läden. Das westliche Hufeisen schließlich
blickt auf das Gebirge. Da es von den höheren
Gebäuden umschlossen wird, ist es seinem
Charakter nach städtischer. Es beherbergt
ein kleines Schwimmbad.
Zugänge und innere Verbindungswege befinden sich auf zwei unterschiedlichen Ebenen; die tiefere ist zur Anfahrt und zum Parken
bestimmt, die obere, die die einzelnen Wohnungen mit dem Zentrum und mit dem Strand
verbindet, ist ausschließlich dem Fußgänger
vorbehalten.
Die Wohnungen zerfallen in zwei Typen: nor-
male Ferienwohnungen in drei verschiedenen
Größen (Abb. 5, 6) und kleinere Spareinheiten.
Die drei Varianten der normalen Ferienwoh-
nung liegen auf drei Ebenen übereinander.
Die unterste Ebene beherbergt eine Einheit
mit 70 m^2 Grundfläche sowie Parkplätze für
die ganze Gruppe. Auf der mittleren Ebene
liegt eine Einheit mit 83 m^2 Grundfläche und
das Fußgängerdeck. Auf der oberen Ebene

befindet sich eine Duplexwohnung mit 110 m² Grundfläche. Die Wohnungen selbst sind in zwei Bereiche gegliedert, in einen größeren, verschiedene Niveaus bildenden Aktivitätsbereich (Essen, Unterhaltung, Geselligkeit, Spiel) sowie in einen kleineren, starr umschlossenen Rückzugsbereich (Schlafen, Baden, Nachdenken).

Die Anlage in Benicasim war vielleicht ein zu heftiger Protest gegen die funktionell-kapitalistische Eroberung der Mittelmeerstrände. In der Auflehnung gegen die Scheinarchitektur der Blocks im Miami-Stil, die wie zur Parade senkrecht zum Strand aufmarschieren, um den über alles geschätzten ›Meerblick‹ zu gewähren, scheint Benicasim sich dafür entschieden zu haben, so etwas wie eine ›Architektur ohne Architekten‹ anzusteuern. Auf die Dauer wird die vollständig realisierte Anlage vielleicht lediglich als eine weitere Scheinlösung an der vordersten Front der touristischen Eroberung des Mittelmeers beurteilt werden. Statt die Touristen in kleine Kisten zu stecken, pferchte man sie in ein kleines Dorf (Abb. 1), wobei der einzige Unterschied im Maßstab liegt. Im Detail sind die Gebäude unzweifelhaft ›modern‹, aber die Aufspaltung der Gebäudemasse in kleinere, pittoresk zusammengesetzte Einheiten ist vielleicht zu romantisch. So entstand eine buntscheckige Ansammlung aufgeputzter Fahrradschuppen, in denen sich gleichwohl recht gut wohnen läßt (Abb. 3,4).

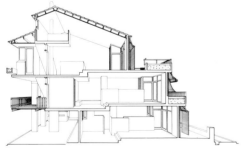

5. Ground plans of the three dwelling types in the three-storey part of the 1st phase.
6. Section through the three-storey part of the 1st phase.
7,8,9. Detailed views.

5. Grundrisse der drei Wohnungstypen im dreigeschossigen Teil des 1. Bauabschnitts.
6. Schnitt durch den dreigeschossigen Teil des 1. Bauabschnitts.
7,8,9. Detailansichten.

Housing in Meckenheim, Germany. Since 1965
Architects: Joachim and Margot Schürmann
(assistants: Hans-Georg Waechter, Walter
von Lom, Henning Drinhausen, Wilfried Eus-
kirchen, Johanna Seeger, Margitta Modelsee,
Eckehard Zielhofer and Helmut Brieler)

The housing estate Meckenheim-Süd forms
part of a future new town that will link the
villages of Meckenheim and Merl together.
Geographically the estate is stuck insecurely
on to the southern end of Meckenheim and
separated from its future brothers in the new
town by a stream and a ribbon park.

Its tenuous relationship with the existing
village is accentuated by their being effectively
connected only by a single entrance at a petrol
filling station, an impromptu symbol of the new
way of life (ill. 1). This road then enters the
estate and forms a mundane loop to enable
the bus to turn at the end of its route. The trau-
matic effect of this almost casual administrative
decision is a lost battle between one order,
transport, and another, the dwellings, with odd
pieces of land left over in between. The primary
internal structure of the estate consists of the
simple relationship at rightangles of all the
buildings and a timid, but real, merging of the
low and high dwellings. Architecturally, however, the different levels of sensitivity in the
design of these two types of dwelling (for the
low buildings separate architects were
engaged) strikes an odd note of discord
throughout the estate.

On the other hand the scale of the village of
Meckenheim is not lost – the density must be
about right – and it feels pleasant to live in.
The secret, I am convinced, lies in the sheer
architectural quality of the long multi-storey
strip buildings designed by the Schürmanns.
They have never wavered from the rectang-
ularity of the master plan but avoided parallel
blocks by staggering them so that they ease
the connection between one place and another
and relate to the loop road (ill. 2). Each of the
separate buildings responds to its neighbour
to form a common space that in turn is not
quite limited to itself but gently overflows into
the next, and so on. In spite of sometimes
reaching eight floors in height the overall effect
is horizontal and continuous, which gives a
restful and protective feeling to the open
spaces. One is reminded of the comfortableness
of finding a table by a wall or in a corner in a
restaurant – open places need this 'cosy'
element of protection if they are to be pleasant.
After the destruction of the street this humane
feature seemed to be lost but at Meckenheim
there is an indication that it is being recovered.
What are the architectural qualities of the multi-
storey strip buildings? Simplicity and unity of
materials, repetition of recognizable elements
juxtaposed so that the point of boredom is
never reached, the overtensioning of form by
the horizontal galleries and strip windows,
borrowed perhaps from Alvar Aalto, the do-
minance of mass over void and finally the

ambiguity between the classical discipline of
style and the romantic staggering of the buildings both in plan and section.

However, if we can acclaim the youthful brilliance of this design, we must also point out its
immaturity. The ruthless formal control of the
volume and façade has led to some incongruous situations that are not architecturally
valid. For example, the three-storey building
in block 2 has five duplex dwellings on the
ground floor and a staircase plus corridor
access to three flats on the third, which results

in a disproportionate amount of space being
given to the access to these flats (ill. 4).
Why does the Meckenheim estate seem to
have a magic quality of liveliness that attracts
people, that children will remember with pleas-
ure? Firstly, high density has not meant high
buildings dwarfing people, secondly, the continuous façades enclose and protect the
inhabitants, and lastly, the architectural character, albeit 1930 revival with an anti-rational
and romantic massing, gives the whole estate
a strong personality.

Wohnbebauung in Meckenheim. Seit 1965
Architekten: Joachim und Margot Schürmann
(Mitarbeiter: Hans-Georg Waechter, Walter
von Lom, Henning Drinhausen, Wilfried Eus-
kirchen, Johanna Seeger, Margitta Modelsee,
Eckehard Zielhofer und Helmut Brieler)

Diese Wohnbebauung ist Teil einer künftigen
neuen Stadt, die die Orte Meckenheim und
Merl verbinden wird. Geographisch liegt das
Wohngebiet am Südende von Meckenheim
und ist von seinen zukünftigen Nachbarn
durch einen Bach und Grünflächen getrennt.
Seine schwache Beziehung zum bestehenden
Ort wird dadurch hervorgehoben, daß nur ein
einziger Übergang vorhanden ist, markiert
durch eine Tankstelle – zufälliges Symbol der
neuen Lebensweise (Abb. 1). Diese Straße
führt dann in die Wohnsiedlung hinein und bildet eine großzügige Schleife, den Endpunkt
der Buslinie. Diese fast beiläufige verwaltungsmäßige Anordnung vermittelt den traumati-

schen Eindruck einer verlorenen Schlacht
zwischen den beiden Ordnungen Verkehr und
Wohnen, die ganz zufällige Restflächen zwischen sich übrigließen. Die innere Primär-
struktur des Wohngebiets beruht auf einer einfachen orthogonalen Beziehung zwischen
allen Gebäuden und einer zaghaften, aber
echten Mischung niedriger und hoher Häuser.
Architektonisch führte die unterschiedliche
Entwurfshaltung, die in den beiden Gebäude-
typen zum Ausdruck kommt – für die niedrigen
Häuser wurden andere Architekten verpflich-
tet –, allerdings zu einem überall spürbaren
Mißklang.
Andererseits ist aber der Maßstab des alten
Ortes Meckenheim nicht verlorengegangen
– die Bebauungsdichte muß etwa richtig sein –,
und man hat das Gefühl, daß es angenehm ist,
dort zu wohnen.
Das Geheimnis liegt wohl in der architektonischen Reinheit der von den Schürmanns entworfenen langen, mehrgeschossigen Streifen-

1. Site plan.
2. Model without the low-rise houses built
by other architects.
3. View of the south group.

1. Lageplan.
2. Modell ohne die von anderen Architekten
erbauten niedrigen Häuser.
3. Blick auf die südliche Gruppe.

bauten (Abb. 3). Die Architekten sind von der orthogonalen Richtung des Gesamtplans nirgendwo abgewichen; sie vermieden aber parallele Blocks, indem sie die Bauten staffelten, so daß der Zusammenhang zwischen den einzelnen Räumen deutlicher wird und eine Beziehung zur Schleifenstraße entsteht (Abb. 2). Jedes Haus bildet mit seinem Nachbarn einen gemeinsamen Platz, der wiederum nicht ganz in sich geschlossen ist, sondern sanft in den nächsten übergeht. Obwohl gelegentlich acht Geschosse auftreten, ist die Gesamtwirkung horizontal und kontinuierlich. Dies verleiht den offenen Plätzen eine erholsame, beschützende Atmosphäre. Man fühlt sich erleichtert, wie wenn man in einem Restaurant einen Tisch an der Wand oder einen Ecktisch findet – offene Plätze brauchen dieses ›gemütliche‹ Element des Behütetseins, wenn sie befriedigen sollen. Nach der Zerstörung der Straße schien dieses menschliche Element verloren; in Meckenheim jedoch findet man Anzeichen dafür, daß man es wiederentdeckt.

Die baulichen Charakteristika der mehrgeschossigen Streifenbauten sind Einfachheit und Einheitlichkeit in den Materialien, Wiederholung erkennbarer Elemente, die so nebeneinandergestellt sind, daß sie nicht langweilig wirken, Überdehnung der Form durch die vielleicht von Alvar Aalto übernommenen horizontalen Galerien und Streifenfenster, Übergewicht der Masse gegenüber dem Leerraum und schließlich der Zwiespalt zwischen der klassischen Stildisziplin und der romantischen Staffelung der Gebäude im Grundriß und Schnitt.

Wenn wir die jugendliche Brillanz dieses Entwurfs bewundern, müssen wir auch auf seine Unreife hinweisen. Die unbarmherzige formale Kontrolle der Massen und Fassaden führte zu einigen architektonisch nicht schlüssigen Situationen. So hat der dreigeschossige Block 2 fünf Duplexwohnungen in den beiden unteren Geschossen sowie drei Geschoßwohnungen im dritten Stock, der durch Treppenhaus und Laubengang erschlossen wird, womit dem Zugang zu diesen Wohnungen übermäßig viel Platz eingeräumt ist.

Warum ist das Wohngebiet Meckenheim-Süd ein Ort, der Lebendigkeit atmet, zu dem die Leute sich zugehörig fühlen, der als Kinderheimat in guter Erinnerung steht? Grund dafür ist zum einen die Dichte, die keine den Menschen einschüchternden hohen Bauten gestattete, zum anderen die umschließende und schützende Funktion der kontinuierlichen Fassaden und schließlich der architektonische Charakter, der zwar mit der antirationalen und romantischen Massierung einen Rückgriff auf die dreißiger Jahre darstellt, aber doch der ganzen Siedlung Persönlichkeit verleiht.

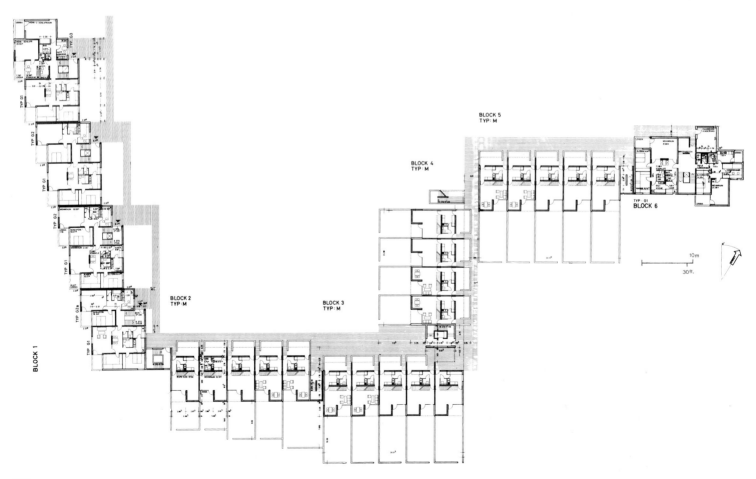

4. Ground plan of the south group.
5,6,7,8. Detailed views.

4. Grundriß der südlichen Gruppe.
5,6,7,8. Detailansichten.

Twin Parks Northeast, Bronx, New York. 1969–73

Architects: Richard Meier & Associates

The Twin Parks area of the Bronx shows the now classical symptoms of what is known as urban decay – the numbers of the poor are increasing and previous middle-class residents of the area are moving elsewhere. In 1966 the city authorities decided to create about 800 new dwellings here. Their initial plans met the opposition of various community groups: Catholic and Protestant pastors leading the Twin Parks Association (TPA) which included Jews, whites, blacks and Puerto Ricans, and an 'advocacy' architects' group, Jonathan Barnett, Giovanni Pasanella, Jacqueline Robertson, Richard Weinstein and Myles Weintraub, working under the Housing and Development Administration (HDA). Difficulties in finding finance and maintaining sponsorship forced TPA to hand over the development to the UDC but the TPA and other organizations managed to retain an advisory role and to select the architects.

The site for Twin Parks Northeast is roughly L-shaped, covering three city blocks in an irregular street grid that called for a base of twin rightangles for the buildings if they were to 'fit in'. Meier designed one building for each of the three city blocks, shaped so that it would squeeze in between the existing tenement buildings and relate to them and the street grid, as well as relate to the other buildings and give some recognizable continuity of form to the whole group (ill. 3). Grote Street, which formerly separated the building on the southern city block from the rest, was blocked off by the creation of a large 'plaza' which was meant to act as a forum or public concourse for the neighbourhood (ills. 1, 2, 4). The street actually forms the boundary between the Italo-Americans and the blacks in the community, so that it became a teenage battleground on a few hot summer nights. Even these occasional outbreaks of violence show the success of the place as a meeting place. However, a mis-reading of Oscar Newman's *Defensible Space,* in the form of fortress design, would only have been a retrograde step back to the ghetto.

As Kenneth Frampton has pointed out[9], Meier has based his model on the received tradition of 19th- and 20th-century architecture. The isolated set-back blocks from Le Corbusier's Radiant City as an anti-street element is paradoxically mixed with the romantic urban sequences analysed and proposed by Camillo Sitte, no doubt as an attempt to 'fit in' to the existing neighbourhood context. The heights of the buildings have been kept to the neighbourhood run of seven floors except for the diagonally opposed ends which are accentuated with sixteen-storey towers, 'much in the same way as the English Georgian terrace did', comments Frampton, 'through modulating an assembly of related parts that refer to a larger entity'. Undoubtedly, from the point of view of

an urban layout and fit, Meier has produced a brilliant solution, not only in relating everything together but in his use of difficult elements, like angled blocks forming corners, that most architects try to avoid.

The other remarkable feature of Twin Parks Northeast is the 19th-century factory façade that has been made to absorb all the dwellings (ill. 5). This almost cardboard container effect brings an extraordinary unity to the three buildings in spite of the different massing. The regular rhythm of horizontal, over-scaled casement windows achieves order without boredom through the skilful introduction of two details. The first is the living-room window, which has one of its panes replaced by a smaller opening separate from the window (ill. 4) to accommodate an optional air-conditioning unit (this opening is so positioned that the hasty eye would miss this 'accident' at first). Secondly, in the upper part of the window there is an opening-out casement with frosted glass which reflects the light, or sun, to produce an irregular and everchanging ripple of light over the building's surface. When this casement is open a narrow panel of sliding windows for night ventilation is revealed, introducing yet another amazing detail.

The brick-faced façade is taken straight down to the ground to form thick pillars framing open porches which connect the adjoining streets with the 'plaza' and other courts (ill. 6).

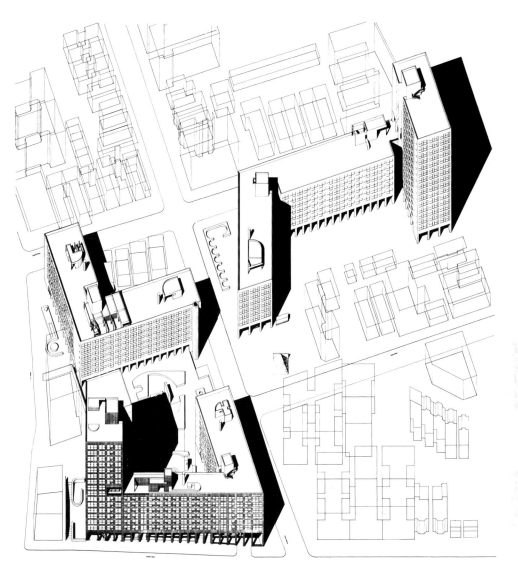

1,2. The 'plaza' between the two west blocks.
3. Isometric view of the whole complex.
4. The almost cardboard-container effect gives the three buildings an extraordinary unity in spite of the different massing.

1,2. Die Plaza zwischen den beiden westlichen Blocks.
3. Isometrie der Gesamtanlage.
4. Die pappkartonmäßige Wirkung verleiht den drei Gebäuden trotz der unterschiedlichen Volumen eine außergewöhnliche Einheitlichkeit.

Das Twin-Parks-Gebiet in der Bronx zeigt die heute schon klassischen Symptome städtischen Verfalls: die Zahl der Armen wird immer größer, während die bisherigen mittelständischen Bewohner des Gebiets sich andere Wohnstätten suchen. 1966 beschlossen die Stadtbehörden, hier etwa 800 neue Wohnungen zu schaffen. Ihre anfänglichen Pläne stießen auf den Widerstand verschiedener Vereinigungen, so der von katholischen und evangelischen Pfarrern angeführten Twin Parks Association (TPA), die Juden, Weiße, Schwarze und Puertoricaner umfaßt, und einer als ›advocacy planners‹ wirkenden Architektengruppe – Jonathan Barnett, Giovanni Pasanella, Jacquelin Robertson, Richard Weinstein und Myles Weintraub –, die für die Housing and Development Administration (HDA) tätig waren. Die Schwierigkeiten bei der Bereitstellung von Mitteln und der Gewinnung eines Kreises von Förderern zwangen die TPA, das Bebauungsprojekt der New York State Urban Development Corporation (UDC) zu übergeben, aber sie und andere Organisationen konnten sich eine beratende Funktion und das Recht sichern, die Architekten zu bestimmen.

Das Gelände für Twin Parks Northeast ist ungefähr L-förmig und umfaßt drei Stadtblocks in einem unregelmäßigen Straßennetz, das ein doppelt orthogonales System für die Gebäude erforderte, damit diese sich einfügen. Richard Meier sah für jeden der drei Stadtblocks ein Gebäude vor. Ihre Formen sind so gewählt, daß sie sich gewissermaßen zwischen die vorhandenen Mietshäuser drängen, zu diesen und zum Straßennetz wie auch untereinander in Beziehung stehen und als Gruppe eine gewisse Kontinuität der Form erkennen lassen (Abb. 3). Die Grote Street, die früher den südlichen Block vom Rest des Geländes trennte, wurde mit einer großen Plaza versperrt, die als Forum, als öffentlicher Platz, für die Umgebung gedacht ist (Abb. 1, 2, 4). Da die Straße die Grenze zwischen den Italo-Amerikanern und den Farbigen des Viertels bildet, verwandelte sich der Platz an ein paar warmen Sommerabenden in ein Schlachtfeld für Jugendliche. Gerade auch diese gelegentlichen Schlägereien zeigen, daß der Platz seine Aufgabe als Treffpunkt erfüllt. Eine Mißdeutung von Oscar Newmans *Defensible Space* in Gestalt eines Festungsentwurfs wäre dagegen nur ein Schritt zurück zum Ghetto gewesen. Wie Kenneth Frampton darlegte[9], stellte Meier sein ›Modell‹ auf die Grundlage der überkommenen Tradition der Architektur des 19. und 20. Jahrhunderts. Die gestuften Einzelblocks aus Le Corbusiers Cité Radieuse als Antistraßenelement mischen sich paradoxerweise mit den romantischen Stadtsequenzen, wie Camillo Sitte sie analysierte und vorschlug – zweifellos in dem Versuch, sich in den be-

stehenden nachbarschaftlichen Zusammenhang einzufügen. Mit Ausnahme der diagonal entgegengesetzten Enden, die mit sechzehngeschossigen Türmen betont werden, halten sich die Gebäude höhenmäßig im Rahmen des in der Gegend Üblichen – ›ganz ähnlich wie die georgianische Reihenhauszeile in England‹, kommentiert Frampton, ›nämlich durch Modulation eines Gefüges verwandter Teile, die sich auf eine größere Einheit beziehen‹. Unter dem Gesichtspunkt urbaner Gruppierung und Einpassung hat Meier zweifellos eine brillante Lösung erzielt, nicht nur mit dem gegenseitigen Bezug von allem, sondern auch mit der Verwendung schwieriger Elemente wie den abgewinkelten, eckenbildenden Blocks, die die meisten Architekten zu vermeiden suchen.

Ein weiterer bemerkenswerter Zug von Twin Parks Northeast sind die an das 19. Jahrhundert erinnernden Fabrikfassaden, hinter denen sich alle Wohnungen verbergen (Abb. 5). Die pappkartonmäßige Wirkung verleiht den drei Gebäuden trotz der unterschiedlichen Volumen eine außergewöhnliche Einheitlichkeit. Der regelmäßige Rhythmus der horizontalen übergroßen Flügelfenster zeigt keinerlei Monotonie, und zwar durch zwei geschickte Details: Zum einen wurde beim Wohnzimmerfenster ein Flügel weggelassen und statt dessen eine getrennte kleinere Öffnung vorgesehen, die bei Bedarf eine Klimaanlage aufnehmen kann (Abb. 9); die Öffnung ist jedoch so ausgebildet, daß diese ›Unregelmäßigkeit‹ auf den ersten Blick nicht auffällt. Zum anderen wurde im oberen Fensterbereich ein nach außen aufgehender Flügel mit Milchglas angeordnet, der Licht und Sonne spiegelt, so daß ein unregelmäßiges, stets sich wandelndes Lichtmuster auf den Gebäudefronten entsteht. Wenn dieser Flügel geöffnet ist, erkennt man ein weiteres überraschendes Detail: ein schmales Band von Schiebefenstern zur nächtlichen Belüftung.

Die mit Backstein verkleideten Fassaden reichen bis auf den Boden und bilden dort dicke Pfeiler, hinter denen offene Vorhallen liegen, die die angrenzenden Straßen mit der Plaza und den anderen Höfen verbinden (Abb. 6).

5. The south side of the block south of the 'plaza'.
6,7. Open porches connect the adjoining streets with the 'plaza' and the other courts.
8. The interior of a dwelling.
9. House entrance.
10. Ground-plan detail.

5. Südseite des südlich der Plaza liegenden Blocks.
6,7. Offene Vorhallen verbinden die Straßen mit der Plaza und den anderen Höfen.
8. Inneres einer Wohnung.
9. Hauseingang.
10. Grundrißausschnitt.

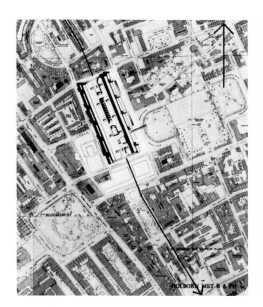

**Foundling Estate, Bloomsbury, London.
1968–72 (first phase)**
Architects: P. Hodgkinson and Sir Leslie Martin

When one emerges from the lift at the Russell Square underground station in Bernard Street, the blank southern end-walls of the Foundling Estate are immediately discernible slightly to the right of the exit. The Foundling Estate is a building that will impel any architect out of curiosity to stop, look, and think. The advantages of the staggered lean-to section are obvious: the open terraces and human scale give a sense of spaciousness at street level that fits happily with the neighbouring buildings; there is the added advantage that the human scale also softens the introduction of taller buildings.

In this case, however, these advantages are partly outweighed by various significant shortcomings.

The main item of our criticism is the space underneath the 'arches' of the double lean-to (ill. 7). This space, with galleries giving access to the dwellings on either side, is monumental, empty and unpleasant. True, this covered 'street' is sheltered from the rain, but not from wind and dust, and above all it is a lonely, even frightening place, where one is unlikely to make contact with other human beings. One feels the architect has not realized that Jane Jacobs' observations[10] are also applicable to these urban structures. There is also a total absence of the minor human scale of touch and vision in the detailing at hand and eye

level. It is a failing that classical, or neo-classical buildings can seldom, if ever, be accused of. The galleries are too narrow (1 metre), too long (60-metre sections giving a total of 200 metres), with only six front doors to each section, providing the perfect setting for an easy 'mugging'. This rather pompous monumentality is even more obvious in the handling of the axial entrance, in the grand beaux-arts manner, from the Brunswick Square Gardens to the east (ill. 4). This excessive stepped entrance reminds one of Mussolini's E.U.R. cultural buildings in Rome. This entrance leads up on to an enormous concrete platform between the two parallel 'lean-to' terraces (ill. 3), which seems to be totally out of scale through under-use, rather like the wind-swept empty platforms around

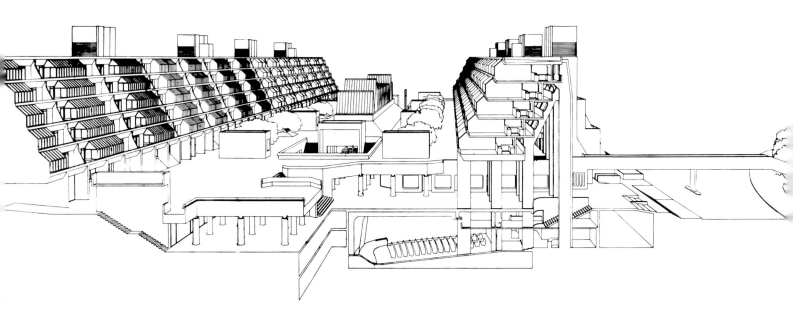

the South Bank Arts Centre. Much of the construction does not seem to be doing anything in particular. It is a useless street architecture stripped of a sense of humour, in quality much inferior to comparable Swiss constructions such as Halen.

While I was there a team of photographers were busy taking 'architectural' photographs. The building photographs well, since the sculptured form is handled with obvious skill and discipline. The funny little 'greenhouses' on the terraces look as though they have been put together by a tired clerk-of-works, but they may be taken as a patronizing gesture towards 'ordinary' architecture, the equivalent of 'arte povera' (ill. 8). The terraces themselves are carelessly designed, too narrow (1.50 metres wide with the pavement width sliced off by the inclined balcony wall to only 1.20 metres), and lack privacy, giving easy views over the neighbours below and even to a slight extent to the neighbour next door (ills. 9, 12).

As I was leaving the building along Coram Street I turned to take a last look as the afternoon sun covered the building, and I realized that the architect had fallen into another of those architectural errors of form. The inner lean-to part of the building rises three stories above the Marchmont Street façade to expose its inside galleries and entrances to the warm afternoon sun while the terraces face the cold north-east. The architect had fallen foul of symmetry, and apart from condemning the poor people living there to turn away from the after-dinner sun, he had missed a real opportunity to link the design to the rhythms of the sky. The same criticism can also be made of the façade facing south into Bernard Street. Perhaps the architect was too concerned about building a prototype to realize that the site was in the middle of a city in a place with all its own particular problems?

1. Site plan.
2. Model of the whole complex.
3. Perspective view of the central area.
4. In the grand beaux-arts manner, the axial entrance from the east reminds one of Mussolini's E.U.R. cultural buildings in Rome.
5. The east side of the complex.
6. The south side of the complex.

1. Lageplan.
2. Modell der Gesamtanlage.
3. Perspektive der Mittelzone.
4. Der in großartiger Beaux-Arts-Manier gestaltete axiale Zugang im Osten erinnert an Mussolinis E.U.R.-Kulturbauten in Rom.
5. Ostseite der Anlage.
6. Südseite der Anlage.

**Foundling Estate, Bloomsbury, London.
Erster Bauabschnitt. 1968-72**
Architekten: P. Hodgkinson und Sir Leslie
Martin

Wenn man an der U-Bahnstation Russell
Square auf der Bernard Street aus dem Aufzug
kommt, fallen einem etwas rechts vom Ausgang sofort die glatten, südlichen Abschluß-
wände des Foundling-Komplexes ins Auge.
Der Komplex weckt die Neugier und wird jeden Architekten zwingen, kurz innezuhalten,
zu schauen und seinen Denkapparat in Bewegung zu setzen. Die Vorzüge der überhängen-
den Schräge sind offensichtlich: offene Terrassen, menschlicher Maßstab mit ausgepräg-
ter Geräumigkeit auf Straßenebene, gute Einpassung in die vorhandene Bebauung mit dem
zusätzlichen Vorteil weicher Übergänge zwischen Gebäuden verschiedener Höhe. Allerdings werden in diesem Fall die beschriebenen Vorzüge durch verschiedene gravierende
Mängel teilweise wieder zunichte gemacht.
Die erste Stelle der Negativbilanz nimmt der
Raum unter den ›Bögen‹ der beiden Schrägen
ein (Abb. 7). Dieser Raum, dessen Galerien
Zugang zu den beiderseits liegenden Wohnungen verschaffen, ist monumental, leer und
unbehaglich. Die überdachte ›Straße‹ ist zwar
vor Regen geschützt, aber nicht vor Wind und
Staub. Es ist ein einsamer, ja furchterregender
Ort mit höchstens gelegentlichem mensch-
lichem Kontakt. Wahrscheinlich war sich der
Architekt nicht bewußt, daß Jane Jacobs Be-
obachtungen[10] auch für solche innerstädtischen Anlagen gelten. Ebenso gibt es im Nah-
bereich des Menschen keinerlei Details, die
zum Berühren oder näheren Hinsehen ein-
laden. Diesen Fehler wird man bei klassischen
oder neoklassischen Bauten so gut wie nie
finden. Die Galerien sind zu schmal (1,00 m)
und zu lang (Abschnitte von 60 m auf eine Ge-
samtlänge von 200 m), außerdem liegen an
jedem Abschnitt nur sechs Wohnungstüren,
so daß ein perfekter Rahmen für Raubüber-
fälle gegeben ist.
Die ziemlich pompöse Monumentalität zeigt
sich noch deutlicher in dem in großartiger
Beaux-Arts-Manier gestalteten axialen Zugang von den Brunswick Square Gardens im
Osten (Abb. 4). Der überzogene Aufgang, der
an Mussolinis E.U.R.-Kulturbauten in Rom erinnert, endet auf der riesigen Betonplattform
zwischen den beiden parallelen Doppelter-
rassen (Abb. 3). Diesem Platz fehlt es durch
seine Verlassenheit an jeglicher Maßstäblichkeit, darin den windigen, leeren Plattformen
um das South Bank Arts Centre gleichend.
Viele Bauteile scheinen keine besondere
Daseinsberechtigung zu haben. Es ist eine
ziemlich nutzlose Straßenarchitektur ohne
jeden Humor, in der Qualität weit unter ähnlichen Schweizer Anlagen wie etwa Halen.
Solange ich mich hier aufhielt, war ein Foto-
grafenteam eifrig damit beschäftigt, ›architektonische‹ Bilder aufzunehmen. Das Bauwerk
läßt sich gut fotografieren, da die skulpturale

7. The covered 'street' is a lonely, even
frightening place.
8. The little 'greenhouses' on the terraces
look as though they have been put together
by a tired clerk-of-works.
9,10. One of the dwellings.
11. Ground plan detail with section.
12. Perspective view of a dwelling.

7. Die überdachte ›Straße‹ ist ein einsamer,
ja furchterregender Ort.
8. Die kleinen ›Gewächshäuser‹ auf den
Terrassen sehen aus, als stammten sie von
einem müden Bauleiter.
9,10. Eine der Wohnungen.
11. Grundrißausschnitt mit Schnitt.
12. Perspektive einer Wohnung.

Form mit offenkundiger Geschicklichkeit und
Disziplin gehandhabt ist. Die seltsamen kleinen ›Gewächshäuser‹ auf den Terrassen jedoch sehen aus, als stammten sie von einem
müden Bauleiter; sie können aber auch als
gönnerhafte Geste gegenüber der ›gewöhnlichen‹ Architektur, dem Äquivalent der
›arte povera‹, aufgefaßt werden (Abb. 8). Die
Terrassen selbst sind ohne Sorgfalt entworfen.
Sie sind zu schmal (1,50 m, wobei die Fuß-
bodentiefe durch die schrägen Balkonwände
auf nur 1,20 m verkürzt wird), und es fehlt an
Intimität, weil man leicht die Terrassen der
Nachbarn unterhalb und sogar auf gleicher
Höhe einsehen kann (Abb. 9, 12).

Als ich mich auf der Coram Street von dem
Komplex entfernte, wandte ich mich um zu
einem letzten Blick auf das von der Nachmittagssonne beschienene Gebäude. Da sah ich,
daß der Architekt einem weiteren jener architektonischen Irrtümer der Form zum Opfer ge-
fallen war. Die innere Schräge erhebt sich drei
Stockwerke über die äußere Fassade an der
Marchmont Street, so daß ihre Laubengänge
und Eingänge von der warmen Nachmittagssonne beschienen werden, während die Terrassen dem kühlen Nordosten zugewandt
sind. Der Architekt war hier auf die Symmetrie
hereingefallen. Abgesehen davon, daß er die
armen Bewohner dazu verurteilte, nicht in den
Genuß der Nachmittagssonne zu kommen,
versäumte er eine echte Gelegenheit, das Kli-
ma zu einer Entwurfsdeterminanten zu
machen. Die gleiche Kritik gilt für die Fassade,
die nach Süden zur Bernard Street hinausgeht.
Vielleicht war der Architekt so sehr bemüht,
einen Prototyp zu schaffen, daß er die Lage
des Bauplatzes in Stadtmitte mit allen sich daraus ergebenden Problemen übersah.

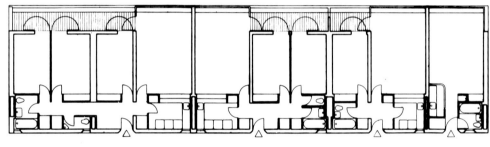

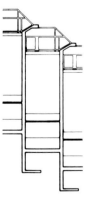

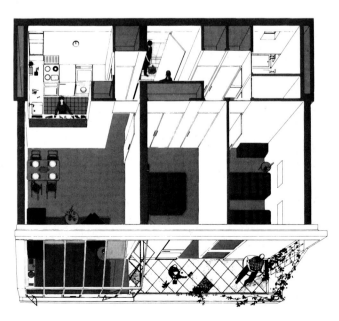

Galgebakken, Herstederne, Denmark.
1969–74
Architects: J.P. Storgård, J. Ørum-Nielsen, H. Marcussen and A. Ørum-Nielsen

It is in Denmark that the words community and housing take on a different significance from that of other countries. Being a small flat country it lies open to attack from a hostile climate or an unfriendly neighbour. This has welded the nation together into one great family or clan, in which each man respects the rights and responsibilities of others. Like the Swiss, their national flag is a symbol of their freedom and is to be found flying nearly everywhere. The government and the ministers of this small socialist welfare state are as accessible as members of a parish council. This enables everyone to feel the reality of participation in community affairs, opinions are listened to and action is possible. So when housing groups are designed and built with community facilities in mind, and with the intention of allowing for spontaneous group activities, it is not for an Utopian socialist all-together world in the imagination of the architect, but for a reality that demands an architectural response.

There were two essential stipulations in the competition programme for Galgebakken:

– the development should be low-compact,
– the development should offer possibilities for social contact among the residents.

The first stipulation coincided with the architects' opinion that each individual dwelling should be in contact with the ground. As for social contacts they decided that 'the family dwelling could be roughly divided into two main sections: an outward pointed entrance section which can accept a certain amount of exposure (hall, playroom, dining-area) and a completely inward pointed or private section (bedrooms, living-room)'.

The fact that the dwellings' 'extroverted' sections faced each other enabled a number of families to maintain reasonable contact. This entailed a shared entrance and front area which is called the 'dwelling lane' (ill. 3). This partially shared dwelling should be related in size to the activities and needs of the residents, the larger the neighbourhood the greater the possibilities for various activities. So the architects arranged the entire housing development around an integrated system of neighbourly co-operation, emphasized firstly by the dwelling lane containing the entrances, and secondly by the area lane (ill. 2) which groups the dwelling lanes together into a larger neighbourhood unit and connects each area to the

communal main street, which leads to the main square where the 'village shop', community centre and other services are located. Both the area lanes and main street are wide enough to allow the residents to erect new buildings to house communal workshops, playrooms, clubrooms, saunas, etc. The 'mother' village of Herstedvester can be reached directly across the green. Motor traffic and parking have been kept to the perimeter, with communal parking places, all within 80 metres of the majority of the dwellings.

Most of the dwellings are designed in the shape of an unequal, truncated cross (ill. 1). The grouping of the dwellings has been so arranged that every two or four families can, if they like, share their own private court (ill. 4). The courts can even be covered (ill. 5). Just as more community life is possible, so more independence within the same family is possible, for elder children, or older relations, can have their own independent dwellings with separate entrances in one of the side arms.

1. Aerial view of the complex.
2. View along an area lane.
3. View along a 'dwelling lane'.

1. Luftansicht der Anlage.
2. Blick durch eine Bereichsstraße.
3. Blick durch eine ›Wohnstraße‹.

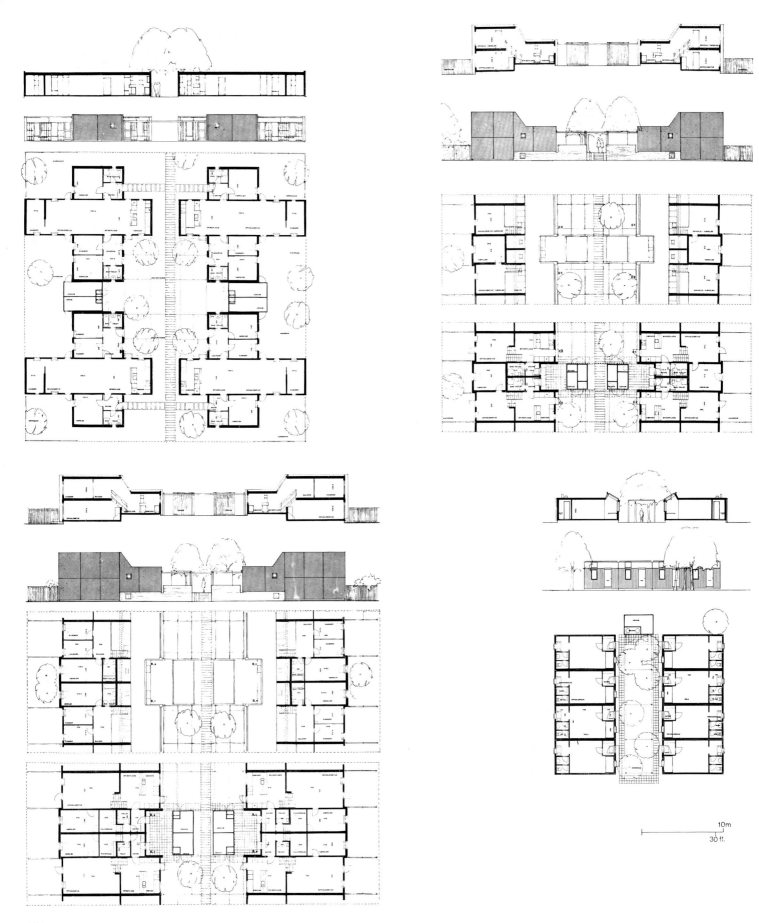

10m
30 ft.

4. Plans of the different dwellings.
5. View of a court.

4. Pläne der verschiedenen Haustypen.
5. Blick in einen Hof.

Galgebakken, Herstederne, Dänemark. 1969-74

Architekten: J.P. Storgård, J. Ørum-Nielsen, H. Marcussen und A. Ørum-Nielsen

In Dänemark haben die Begriffe Gemeinschaft und Wohnbau eine andere Bedeutung als in sonstigen Ländern. Dänemark als kleines, flaches Land ist ungeschützt vor den Angriffen eines feindlichen Klimas oder Nachbarstaats. Das hat das Volk zu einer Großfamilie oder einem Clan zusammengeschweißt, und jeder achtet die Rechte und Pflichten des anderen. Wie bei den Schweizern ist die Landesfahne Symbol der Freiheit; sie flattert denn auch so gut wie überall. Die Regierung und die Minister dieses kleinen sozialen Wohlfahrtsstaates sind so zugänglich wie Kirchengemeinderäte, was jedem das Gefühl gibt, auf gemeinschaftliche Angelegenheiten tatsächlich Einfluß nehmen zu können; Meinungen werden angehört, Aktionen sind möglich. Wenn daher Wohnanlagen im Blick auf Gemeinschaftseinrichtungen und mit der Absicht, spontane Gruppenaktivitäten zu ermöglichen, entworfen und gebaut werden, so nicht für eine utopische, sozialistische, alle einende Welt in der Phantasie des Architekten, sondern für eine Realität, die eine bauliche Entsprechung verlangt.

Das Wettbewerbsprogramm für Galgebakken enthielt zwei grundlegende Forderungen:
– Die Anlage mußte niedrig und kompakt sein.
– Die Anlage mußte Möglichkeiten für sozialen Kontakt unter den Bewohnern bieten.
Die erste Forderung entsprach der Ansicht der Architekten, daß jede Einzelwohnung mit der Erde verbunden sein sollte. Hinsichtlich der sozialen Kontakte beschlossen sie, ›die Familienwohnung grob in zwei Hauptteile aufzugliedern: einen nach außen gerichteten Zugangsbereich, der ein gewisses Maß an Öffentlichkeit verträgt (Halle, Spielzimmer, Eßplatz), und einen völlig nach innen gerichteten privaten Bereich (Schlafzimmer, Wohnzimmer)‹. Durch die nach außen gerichteten, einander gegenüberliegenden Teile der Wohnungen können jeweils eine Reihe von Familien den gewünschten gegenseitigen Kontakt schließen. Daraus ergab sich ein gemeinsamer Zugangs- und Frontbereich, der ›Wohnstraße‹ genannt wird (Abb. 3). Die nachbarschaftliche Beziehung soll an Umfang natürlich den Aktivitäten und Bedürfnissen der Bewohner entsprechen; je größer die nachbarschaftliche Gruppe, um so mehr Möglichkeiten ergeben sich für verschiedenartige Aktivitäten. Dessen eingedenk wurde die gesamte Wohnbebauung auf ein integriertes System nachbarschaftlichen Zusammenlebens bezogen, be-

tont zum einen durch die Wohnstraße mit den Eingängen, zum anderen durch die Bereichsstraße (Abb. 2), die die Wohnstraßen zu einer größeren nachbarschaftlichen Einheit zusammenfügt und alle Bezirke mit der gemeinsamen Hauptstraße verbindet. Diese führt zum Hauptplatz, an dem sich der ›Dorfladen‹, das Gemeinschaftszentrum und andere Einrichtungen befinden. Die Bereichsstraßen und die Hauptstraße sind so breit, daß die Bewohner hier Gebäude für gemeinschaftliche Werkstätten, Spielzimmer, Clubräume, Sauna usw. errichten können. Zum ›Mutterdorf‹ Herstedvester gibt es eine über freies Feld führende direkte Verbindung. Der motorisierte Verkehr bleibt am äußeren Umkreis; dort liegen, nicht weiter als 80 m von den meisten Wohnhäusern entfernt, die gemeinsamen Parkplätze.
Die meisten Wohnhäuser haben die Form eines ungleichen, gekappten Kreuzes (Abb.1). Die Gruppierung erfolgte in der Weise, daß immer zwei oder vier Familien nach Wunsch ihre Privathöfe zusammenschließen können (Abb. 4). Die Höfe lassen sich sogar überdachen (Abb. 5). Ebenso wie mehr Gemeinschaftsleben ermöglicht wird, ist auch an größere Unabhängigkeit innerhalb der Familie gedacht, denn große Kinder oder ältere Verwandte können einen der Seitenarme als eigene Wohnung mit separatem Eingang benutzen.

Lillington Gardens, London. 1961–72
Architects: Darbourne & Darke

The myths and realities that surround the Lillington Gardens housing scheme, the result of an open national competition in 1960/61, have made this comprehensive urban redevelopment in the heart of London between Chelsea and Westminster just south of Victoria Station dear to the hearts of many architects and town planners. The buildings have been singled out by both government and professional circles for special praise and awards, and even now the press continues to eulogize.

The following is a comment from the 1970 RIBA Architecture Award jury's report:

'The layout has a pleasant domestic and informal scale – a most impressive achievement with the need to squeeze so many people into the site. The external modelling of the buildings is handled with great vigour and charm, especially in the lower buildings . . .'

The features that make Lillington Gardens exceptional are as follows: The 12-acre (4.856 hec.) site was converted into a super-block roughly 300m x 125m, with a more-or-less continuous wall of 5- or 6-storey buildings that enclose a series of connecting parks within, echoing the neighbouring street system of squares (ill. 1). The buildings have also been kept low enough so as not to break the scale of the existing terraces; the broken volumes assist in reducing the scale and height of the buildings (ills. 3, 4). Red brick as the basic building material was chosen to match G.E. Street's St James-the-Less church built in 1859 and now in the centre of the super-block (ill. 6). Here we have red brick used to identify the

building with Victorian culture rather than with the Victorian social image at Preston by Stirling and Gowan. The redevelopment is 'comprehensive' in that it includes a hostel for 90 old people with 44 associated old people's flatlets, car parking for 70 per cent of the dwellings, 3 taverns, a laundry, shops, 2 doctors' surgeries, and a public library and a public meeting hall. There is also the existing church, and a new school is planned to go next to it.

The myths that make Lillington Gardens an exceptional architectural feat are to be found in the sacrifices to good design that have been made to achieve the lauded effects. Economics have been carelessly thrown overboard for a warped aesthetic of crumpled façades (ill. 2) and disordered dwellings that sometimes fail to fit a recognizable structural plan (in buildings 6 and 9). There are dwellings that have the kitchen one-and-a-half floors away from the access street, and on the way you have to pass the bedrooms, bathrooms and then cut right across the living-room (in building 5). The wide 'roof-street' leads to cramped accesses to the front doors, sometimes three sharing the same floormat half a flight of steps away, thus both discouraging front-door gossip and infringing the privacy of callers (buildings 1, 3 and 5). Many living-rooms have no sun at all, facing north in order to satisfy the architects desire that everyone should live looking into the community garden. After all, surely facing south over the real street is a valid as well as far more interesting experience. An even more alarming failure is the connection of the roof-streets with the real ones down below: there are sordid windy porches on the ground floor and blind lifts that ferry people to the upper streets as if

they were crossing the Acheron. Ramps, moving-staircases, open-cage lifts, or the like, would have been far better means of providing access to these otherwise isolated upper 'streets'.

In the third phase, economics and experience show through in a far more satisfactory architectural design. Even sociologically they may be better, since 36 per cent of the dwellings have gardens as opposed to only 5 per cent in the first phase. The critics of Architectural Design find the last phase dull, which tells us more about the critics than about architecture. But the simplicity and scale of these back-to-back dwellings is far more in keeping with the Georgian squares of London than the more 'brutal' and primitive attempts of the first and second phases. These dwellings are also perhaps more akin to the sensitivity of G.E. Street.

Finally, apart from the more orderly third phase (in spite of the still confusing bits and pieces of odd 'landscaping'), the sequence of moving from one garden square into the next again shows a hit-and-miss picturesque anti-plan which disorientates one even more than Chesterton's 'rolling English road'. This is disturbing since it shows a lack of understanding of the essence of city-planning – it is as though the authors had mis-read Camillo Sitte. John Darborne said they wanted 'a feeling of one thing opening out on to another rather than a huge easily assimilated rectangular area'[11]. However, the result in the end may be closer to the comment in the Illustrated London News at the time that when Street's church was built it was described as 'rising . . .as a lily among weeds'.

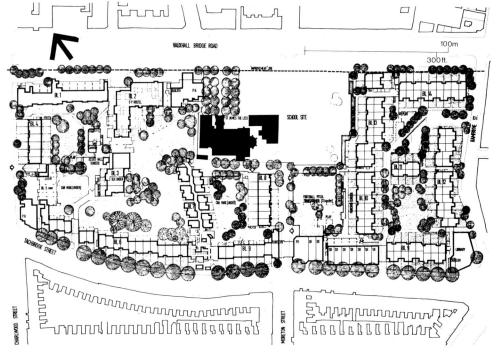

1. Site plan.
2. View of the group from Vauxhall Bridge Road.
3. View along Tachbrook Street from the south-east.
4. View along Tachbrook Street from the north.

1. Lageplan.
2. Blick über die Vauxhall Bridge Road auf die Gruppe.
3. Blick in die Tachbrook Street von Südosten.
4. Blick in die Tachbrook Street von Norden.

Lillington Gardens, London. 1961-72
Architekten: Darbourne & Darke

Die Mythen und Tatsachen um die Wohnanlage Lillington Gardens, Ergebnis eines offenen Wettbewerbs von 1960/61, ließen dieses umfassende Sanierungsprojekt mitten in London, zwischen Chelsea und Westminster, knapp südlich der Victoria Station, vielen Architekten und Stadtplanern ans Herz wachsen. Die Gebäude wurden von der Regierung wie auch in Fachkreisen mit Lobeshymnen und Preisen überhäuft, und auch heute noch ist die Presse voll von Elogen.

In dem Bericht der Jury für den 1970 vergebenen R.I.B.A.-Architekturpreis steht zu lesen: ›Die Anlage hält sich in einem angenehmen, häuslichen und zwanglosen Maßstab – eine höchst eindrucksvolle Leistung angesichts der Notwendigkeit, so viele Menschen unterzubringen. Die äußere Gestaltung der Gebäude zeugt von großer Kraft und Anmut, besonders bei den niedrigen Gebäuden‹.

Die Tatsachen, die Lillington Gardens außergewöhnlich erscheinen lassen, können wie folgt zusammengefaßt werden: Der 4,86 ha große Bauplatz wurde mit einem ungefähr 300x125 m großen Superblock überzogen; eine mehr oder weniger kontinuierliche Mauer von 5- oder 6geschossigen Gebäuden umschließt eine Reihe zusammenhängender Grünanlagen, die auf das umgebende Straßen- und Platzsystem Bezug nehmen (Abb. 1). Die Gebäude wurden so niedrig gehalten, daß kein Bruch gegenüber den benachbarten Hauszeilen entsteht; auch die Brechung der Volumen dient dem Zweck, die Gebäude in Maßstab und Höhe der Umgebung anzupassen (Abb. 3, 4). Als vorherrschendes Baumaterial finden wir wie bei der Kirche St. James-the-Less, die G.E. Street im Jahr 1859 erbaute und die heute den Mittelpunkt der Anlage bildet (Abb. 6), roten Ziegel; der rote Ziegel wurde hier eingesetzt, um die Identifikation

5. Plans of different buildings.
6. View towards the church of St James-the-Less.

5. Pläne verschiedener Gebäude.
6. Blick gegen die Kirche St. James-the-Less.

BL. 1 & 3

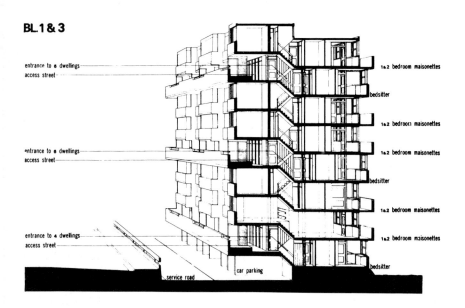

entrance to 6 dwellings
access street

1 & 2 bedroom maisonettes

bedsitter

1 & 2 bedroom maisonettes

entrance to 6 dwellings
access street

1 & 2 bedroom maisonettes

1 & 2 bedroom maisonettes

bedsitter

entrance to 4 dwellings
access street

1 & 2 bedroom maisonettes

bedsitter

service road | car parking

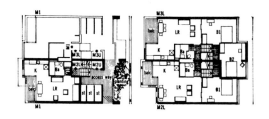

BL. 4 & 8

bedsitter

access walk & patios

entrance court

4 bedroom house | garden

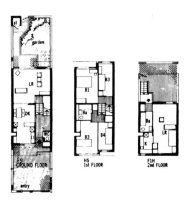

BL. 6 & 9

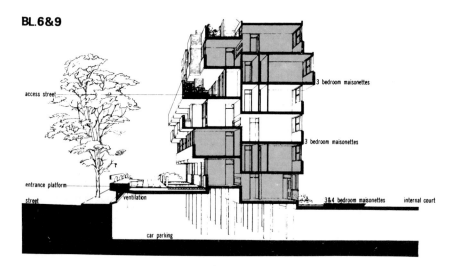

access street

3 bedroom maisonettes

3 bedroom maisonettes

entrance platform
street

ventilation

3 & 4 bedroom maisonettes | internal court

car parking

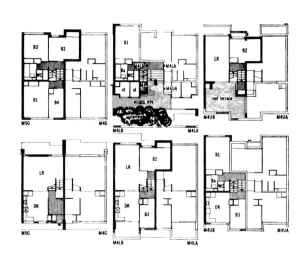

mit der viktorianischen Kultur herbeizuführen, weniger mit der viktorianischen Sozialvorstellung wie in Preston (Stirling und Gowan). Die Sanierung ist insofern ›umfassend‹, als sie ein Heim für 90 ältere Menschen sowie 44 dazugehörige Kleinstwohnungen für Ältere enthält, außerdem Wageneinstellplätze für 70 % der Wohnungen, drei Restaurants, eine Wäscherei, Läden, zwei Arztpraxen, eine öffentliche Bibliothek und eine öffentliche Versammlungshalle; außerdem gibt es die bereits genannte Kirche, und daneben ist eine neue Schule geplant.

Die Mythen, die Lillington Gardens den Charakter der außergewöhnlichen baulichen Leistung verleihen, ranken sich um die Abstriche vom guten Entwurf, die nötig waren, um die gepriesenen Wirkungen hervorzubringen: Die Wirtschaftlichkeit wurde skrupellos über Bord geworfen zugunsten einer verschrobenen Ästhetik aufgelöster Fassaden (Abb. 2) und verwirrender Grundrisse, die gelegentlich nicht einmal eine erkennbare Ordnung aufweisen (in den Gebäuden 6 und 9). In einigen Wohnungen liegt die Küche eineinhalb Geschosse von der Zugangsstraße entfernt, der Weg dorthin führt an den Schlafzimmern und Badezimmern vorbei sowie quer durchs Wohnzimmer (in Gebäude 5). Die breite ›Deckstraße‹ führt zu Engpässen an den Wohnungstüren; manchmal teilen sich drei Türen,

nur eine halbe Treppe auseinander, die gleiche Fußmatte; dies ermutigt nicht gerade zum behaglichen Schwatz unter der Wohnungstür und führt dazu, daß man sich als Besucher beobachtet fühlt (in den Gebäuden 1, 3, 5). Viele Wohnzimmer sind überhaupt nicht besonnt, weil sie nach Norden liegen müssen, damit der Wunsch der Architekten, daß jedermann aus dem Wohnzimmer in den gemeinschaftlichen Garten blickt, erfüllt wird, obwohl doch der Blick nach Süden auf die echte Straße auch ein wertvolles – und viel interessanteres – Erlebnis ist. Ein noch erschreckenderer Fehlschlag ist die Verbindung der Deckstraßen mit den wirklichen Straßen unten. Die Vorhallen im Erdgeschoß sind schmutzig und windig, und geschlossene Aufzüge befördern die Menschen auf die oberen Straßen wie bei der Fahrt über den Acheron. Mit Rampen, Rolltreppen, offenen Aufzügen oder ähnlichen Beförderungssystemen hätte man eine wesentlich günstigere Verbindung zu diesen jetzt isolierten oberen ›Straßen‹ schaffen können.

Im dritten Bauabschnitt zeigt sich die Lehre aus Wirtschaftlichkeit und Erfahrung in einer weitaus befriedigenderen Lösung. Sogar soziologisch dürfte der dritte Abschnitt besser sein, denn 36 % der Wohnungen haben einen Garten, während es im ersten Abschnitt nur 5 % waren. Die Kritiker der Zeitschrift *Architectural Design* finden diesen letzten Abschnitt

langweilig. Das offenbart uns mehr über die Kritiker als über die Architektur. Die Einfachheit und der Maßstab dieser Rücken an Rükken angeordneten Wohnungen paßt viel besser zu den georgianischen Plätzen Londons als die ›brutaleren‹ und primitiveren Versuche im ersten und zweiten Abschnitt. Vielleicht nähert sich der dritte Abschnitt auch mehr der Ausdrucksweise von G.E. Street.

Obwohl der dritte Abschnitt eine größere Ordnung zeigt, schimmert auch hier immer wieder eine seltsame ›Landschaftsgestaltung‹ durch. Der Zug der Bewegung von einem Gartenplatz zum nächsten zeugt wiederum von einem dem Zufall unterworfenen, pittoresken Anti-Plan, der labyrinthischer wirkt als Chestertons ›rolling English road‹. Dies ist erschreckend, denn es zeugt von Mangel an Verständnis für das Wesen der Stadtplanung. Es ist gerade so, als hätten die Urheber Camillo Sitte mißverstanden. John Darborne sagte, es sei der Wille der Architekten gewesen, ›ein Gefühl zu schaffen, als laufe eines ins andere über, und nicht den Eindruck eines riesigen, leicht überschaubaren rechteckigen Bereichs‹.[11] Es scheint jedoch, daß das Ganze letzten Endes dem Kommentar in der *Illustrated London News* näherkommt, der erschien, als Streets Kirche erbaut wurde, und wo es hieß, daß sie sich ›wie eine Lilie im Unkraut erhebe‹.

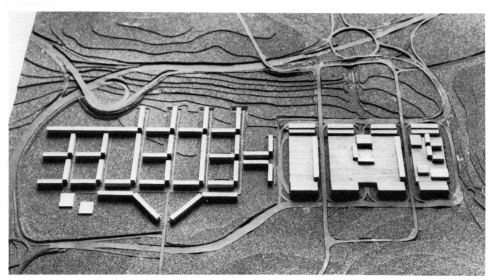

Southgate, Runcorn New Town. Since 1967
Architects: James Stirling and Michael Wilford

One of the nicest things about this housing group is its urbanity. It may not be *the* answer to building large groups of public housing, but at least it breaks with the tiresome neo-romantic haphazard dullness of ever-repetitive 'surprises' that English architects and planners have been playing with ever since Lutyens, the Garden City movement, and Muthesius' report on the English tradition of domestic architecture. Everyone, except Stirling, and perhaps the Smithsons, seems to have forgotten England's neo-classical tradition with its beautiful, humanly scaled streets, squares and crescents. Not only England, but also Wales, Ireland and above all Scotland, belong to this extraordinary domestic urban heritage.

The five-storey L-shaped terrace housing forms a succession of enclosures (ill. 1) based on the size of the neo-classical squares that can be seen in Bath, Edinburgh or London. Looking across from the windows of one house to the terraces of the houses opposite one realizes immediately that the distance is just sufficient to make privacy a reality (ills. 2, 3). The repetitive geometry of the whole gives a restful air, it is an order that is not overpowering. The giant megastructure of the access façade gives one the feeling of being a member of the crew of an enormous battleship (ill. 5), which is in one way what community architecture should be about. This massive urban scale certainly marries the building to the scale of the shopping centre opposite. The building is in fact very closely related to the centre, with its second-floor walkway designed to coincide with the main shopping level (ill. 6), thus creating a comprehensive pedestrian deck right through the neighbourhood with the express purpose of being the most convenient level to walk about on, to go shopping or to meet others doing likewise. Cars are kept to their proper level, together with children, in the squares below, which are thoughtfully provided with approach ramps for prams and bicycles. At the junction of each square, where the walkways and roads cross-over, the buildings do not (ill. 7). Stirling explains that he deliberately left them out so that the old pub or corner shop could be added later if necessary. In actual fact two are now occupied with a church hall and a laundry.

On the ground floor of the buildings look-up garages face the street, while the living-rooms and kitchens of the larger of the two duplexes on the other side face the square. The entrance to these dwellings under the staircase is extraordinarily sordid – one of the penalties of living on the ground floor. The first floor contains the bedrooms of the ground-floor dwellings. On the second floor we meet the living-rooms and kitchens of smaller duplexes as well as a gallery, which appears at first to be quite Utopian since there is already a staircase access for every pair of dwellings. There is

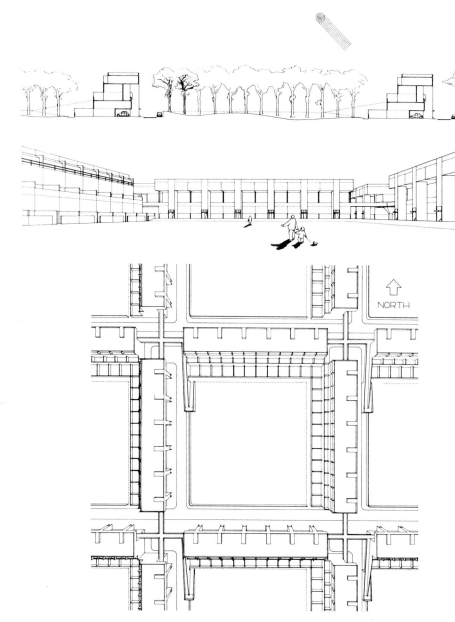

NORTH

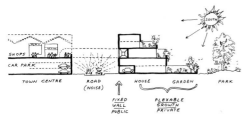

something obsessive about the way English architects always introduce these pedestrian decks as though the whole of England was expecting an imminent flood. Or is it thought that only when people have their feet off the ground will they suddenly become matey-like fellow-survivors who have not been killed crossing the road where a car or van passes every twenty minutes or so? Since the buildings were empty when I saw them perhaps my criticism is a little hasty; this is a question I should like to check up on some day. But what is a pity is that the ground-floor people are so segregated from this social concourse. The inner façade of the two-storey-high walkway is made up of delicately designed yellow-and-blue plastic panels that are pleasant to touch and impossible to write on (ill. 9). The third floor contains the bedrooms and bathrooms of the second-floor flats. The fourth floor contains apartments for the elderly or childless, who according to English custom apparently have more time

and energy to walk up four flights of stairs. Nevertheless the peace that the absence of children brings is probably worth it.

Architecturally, the terraced façade (ill. 10) is much weaker than that of the gallery access. This is probably due to the oversimplified detailing and rather ugly proportions of the metal windows giving on to the terrace (ill. 13). A special feature are the circular bedroom windows. They give one the strange sensation, from the room inside, of being in an attic, always an attractive cosy protective kind of atmosphere. From the outside they seem rather obsessive.

The main architectural lesson to be learnt from Southgate is the recovery for domestic building of its urban heritage. Towns and cities need no longer be everlasting suburbs. One thinks and writes of Southgate as a single building rather than a collection of dwellings. It is a place which promises to bring back a noble dignity to the role of urban living.

1. Model.
2,3,4. The terrace housing forms a succession of enclosures based on the size of the neo-classical squares that can be seen in Bath, Edinburgh or London.
5. The buildings remind one in shape of big battleships.
6. Early sketch.
7. Corner of a square.
8. Elevated footway.

1. Modell.
2,3,4. Die Terrassenhäuser bilden eine Folge von Räumen, die in ihrer Größe den neo-klassischen Plätzen, wie man sie in Bath, Edinburgh oder London findet, entsprechen.
5. Die Gebäude erinnern in ihrer Form an große Schlachtschiffe.
6. Frühe Skizze.
7. Platzecke.
8. Fußgängerstraße.

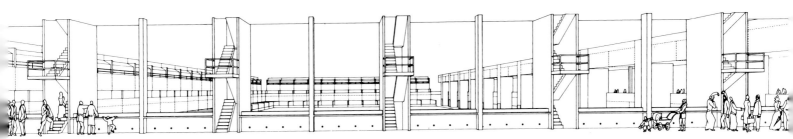

Etwas vom Schönsten an dieser Siedlung ist ihre Urbanität. Vielleicht stellt sie nicht *die* Lösung für den Bau großer Wohnhauskomplexe dar, aber sie bricht wenigstens mit der ermüdenden, neoromantischen, zufälligen Langweiligkeit der stets sich wiederholenden ›Überraschungen‹, mit denen englische Architekten und Planer seit Lutyens, der Gartenstadtbewegung und Muthesius' Bericht über die englische Tradition der Wohnhausarchitektur spielen. Alle mit Ausnahme von Stirling und vielleicht den Smithsons scheinen die englische neoklassische Tradition mit den auf menschliches Maß gebrachten Straßen, Plätzen und Crescents vergessen zu haben. Nicht nur England, sondern auch Wales und Irland, vor allem aber Schottland haben teil an diesem städtebaulichen Erbe.

Die fünfgeschossigen L-förmigen Terrassenhäuser bilden eine Folge von umschlossenen Räumen (Abb. 1), die in ihrer Größe den neoklassischen Plätzen entsprechen, wie sie sich in Bath, Edinburgh oder London finden. Wenn man von den Fenstern des einen Hauses auf die Terrassen des gegenüberliegenden Hauses blickt, wird man sofort gewahr, daß die Entfernung genau ausreicht, um private Abgeschlossenheit zur Realität werden zu lassen (Abb. 2, 3). Die sich wiederholende Geometrie des Ganzen wirkt erholsam, die Ordnung überwältigt nicht. Angesichts der riesigen Megakonstruktion der Zugangsseite hat man das Gefühl, zur Mannschaft eines großen Schlachtschiffes zu gehören (Abb. 5) – in gewisser Beziehung ist dies das, was eine Architektur für die Gemeinschaft immer bieten sollte. Mit seinem massiven städtischen Maßstab ist der Komplex zweifellos ein ebenbürtiger Partner des gegenüberliegenden Einkaufszentrums. Er ist mit diesem so verbunden: Seine Fußgängerstraßen im zweiten Geschoß ließ man direkt in die Haupteinkaufsebene übergehen (Abb. 6); so entstand ein durchgehendes Fußgängerdeck quer durch die gesamte Nachbarschaft mit dem klaren Zweck, als bequemste Ebene zum Spazierengehen, zum Einkaufen und zum Zusammentreffen mit denen, die den gleichen Beschäftigungen nachgehen, zu dienen. Die Autos sind auf ihre eigene Ebene verwiesen. Kinder spielen auf den unten liegenden Plätzen, deren Zugänge wohlüberlegt als Rampen für Kinderwagen und Fahrräder ausgebildet sind. In den Platzecken kreuzen sich die Fußwege und Straßen, die Gebäude jedoch nicht (Abb. 7). Stirling sagt dazu, er habe diese Stellen absichtlich frei gelassen, damit man später gegebenenfalls die alte ›Kneipe‹ oder den Laden an der Ecke hinzufügen könne. Zwei Ecken sind heute schon von einem Gemeindesaal und einer Wäscherei besetzt.
Im Erdgeschoß der Gebäude liegen zur Straße hin verschließbare Garagen und zum Platz hin

die Wohnräume und Küchen der größeren der
beiden angebotenen Maisonettetypen. Der
Zugang zu diesen Wohnungen unter dem
Treppenhaus ist entsetzlich düster – offenbar
als Strafe für das Wohnen im Erdgeschoß. Der
erste Stock enthält die Schlafräume der Erdgeschoßwohnungen. Im zweiten Geschoß finden wir die Wohnräume und Küchen der
kleineren Maisonettes sowie eine Galerie, die
auf den ersten Blick völlig überflüssig wirkt,
da ja schon ein Treppenzugang für jedes Woh-
nungspaar vorhanden ist. Man muß bei den
englischen Architekten aus ihrer Manie, stets
und ständig diese Fußgängerdecks einzu-
bauen, als erwarte ganz England eine unmittelbar drohende Sintflut, auf eine Art Zwangsvor-
stellung schließen. Oder glaubt man denn, daß
die Leute nur dann, wenn sie ihre Füße nicht
auf Bodenebene haben, plötzlich das Gefühl
kameradschaftlich verbundener Überleben-
der entwickeln, die beim Überqueren der
Straße, auf der ungefähr alle 20 Minuten ein
PKW oder ein Lastwagen fährt, nicht über-
fahren wurden? Da die Gebäude noch nicht
bezogen waren, als ich sie besichtigte, ist meine
Kritik vielleicht etwas verfrüht; aber dieser
Frage würde ich später einmal sehr gern nachgehen. Wirklich schade ist, daß die Erdge-
schoßbewohner von diesem gesellschaftlichen Umgang ausgeschlossen sind. Die innere Fassade des zwei Stock hohen Lauben-
gangs ist mit hübschen gelben und blauen
Kunststoffpaneelen verkleidet; sie fühlen sich
gut an und können nicht bekritzelt werden
(Abb. 9). Im dritten Geschoß befinden sich die
Schlafräume der kleineren Maisonettes. Das
vierte Geschoß umfaßt Wohnungen für ältere
oder kinderlose Menschen, die nach engli-
scher Auffassung offenbar mehr Zeit und
Energie haben und ohne weiteres vier Treppen hinaufsteigen können. Wahrscheinlich
finden sie es aber auch der Mühe wert, weil
über ihnen Ruhe herrscht und keine Kinder
herumhüpfen.

Architektonisch ist die terrassierte Fassade
(Abb. 10) viel schwächer als die auf der Seite
des Galeriezugangs. Dies rührt wahrscheinlich von den übervereinfachten und ziemlich
häßlich proportionierten Metallfenstern hinter
den Terrassen her (Abb. 13). Eine Besonder-
heit sind die runden Schlafraumfenster. Nach
innen vermitteln sie den Eindruck einer Dach-
kammer, also einer reizvollen, gemütlichen,
geschützten Atmosphäre. Von außen wirken
sie allerdings ziemlich zwanghaft.

Die wichtigste bauliche Lektion von Southgate
liegt in der Wiederaufnahme des städtebaulichen Erbes im Wohnhausbau. Städte und
Großstädte müssen nicht länger endlose Vor-
orte sein. Man denkt und spricht von Southgate wie von einem einzigen Bauwerk und
nicht wie von einer Ansammlung von Wohnhäusern. Die Anlage verspricht, die Würde
des Lebens in der Stadt wiederherzustellen.

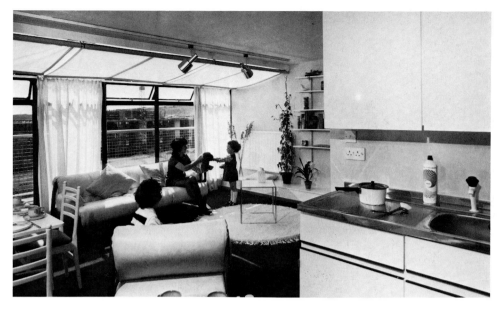

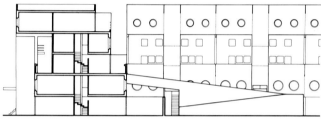

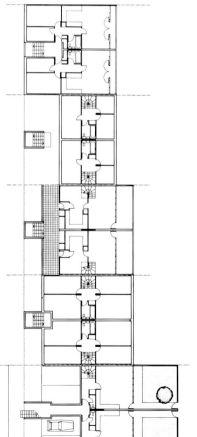

9. Street side of a building.
10. Garden side of a building.
11. Living-room in a ground-floor dwelling.
12. Plans of a bay.
13. Garden court of a ground-floor dwelling.

9. Straßenseite eines Gebäudes.
10. Gartenseite eines Gebäudes.
11. Aufenthaltsraum einer Erdgeschoßwohnung.
12. Pläne einer Bauachse.
13. Gartenhof einer Erdgeschoßwohnung.

La Grande Borne, Grigny, France. 1964–71
Architect: Emile Aillaud

France took the Athens Charter seriously. It also took industrialized building seriously. The result, as anyone can see, was tens of thousands of dwellings upon dwellings ('les grands ensembles') looking almost exactly the same. So much so, that amongst other European architects a reference to the 'French style' became synonymous for poor taste and ugliness. Now the French government and others are beginning to look critically at what has been done and perhaps things will change. One cry of protest has been made, in what is perhaps the best of ways, with a great sense of humour, by the architect Emile Aillaud and the painter F. Riéti. With not a little mischief they have played a child's game with the industrialized system, showing how with wit, imagination, culture and a good understanding of human nature fun can still be had out of life, living in homes. Their ingenuity has made 'La Grande Borne', a 90-hectare site with an overall density of 40 dwellings a hectare, somewhat like a great permanent exhibition. Its visual impact is unforgettable. If one doesn't tire of the humour, it must be a pleasant place to live in. Like all exhibitions it does have an air of arbitrariness and superficiality, but that is the price of protest.

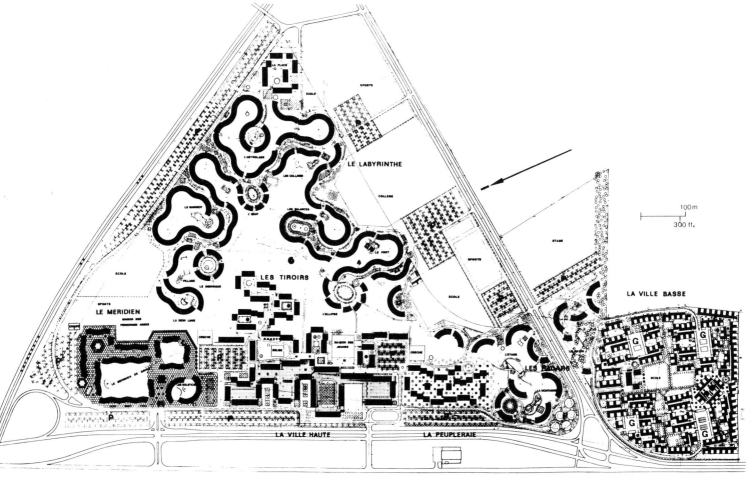

The main part of the site, triangular in shape, 1 kilometre each side, is surrounded by busy main roads and the Autoroute du Sud. At first the architect intended to design only two-storey houses so that people could enter their homes direct from the street, but the result was felt to be inadequate for a development of this size; it was after all really a new town. So it was decided to make the buildings higher and to create neighbourhoods each with a distinctive character. Car parking is kept to the perimeter, and trees are planted thickly (two for every five cars), which helps to create a visual and acoustic sound barrier against the surrounding motorways. Some fingers of parking penetrate the development to ensure that the maximum distance to a dwelling does not exceed 150 metres. Service roads allow essential traffic to nearly all the entrances.

Submitting absolutely to the discipline of industrial building, for that was essential to Aillaud's protest, only three dwelling types were used and three window openings in the seven different neighbourhoods that were evolved. Three of the neighbourhoods were composed using curved components and faced with glazed mosaic (Le Labyrinthe, Le Méridien, Les Radars), three using straight components and faced with strongly coloured tile (La Peupleraie, Les Tiroirs, La Ville Haute) and finally the seventh neighbourhood, outside the triangle, was composed using single-storey L-shaped patio houses (La Ville Basse).

The message of 'La Grande Borne' is clear, there is room for imagination in these large estates, size is no impediment to character and a sense of place which can help a community to identify itself. One of the secrets is not so much the lighthearted urban compositions but the acknowledgment that money must also be spent on the rich variety of pavements, on tree-planting and on other street and garden 'furniture'. Place too (for mental health) is just as important as sun (for physical health). The shapes of 'La Grande Borne' are exotic, nobody would like to see too many of them, but they do swing the balance away from the unimaginative 'grands ensembles'. Monotony too, it should be remembered, need not be dull if properly handled; Cameron's Leningrad, Adams' Edinburgh, or even Berlage's Amsterdam are amongst some of our more recent historical examples that prove the point. Uniformity itself is not necessarily a negative factor.

1. Aerial view.
2. Site plan.
3,4 Detailed views.

1. Luftansicht.
2. Lageplan.
3,4 Detailansichten

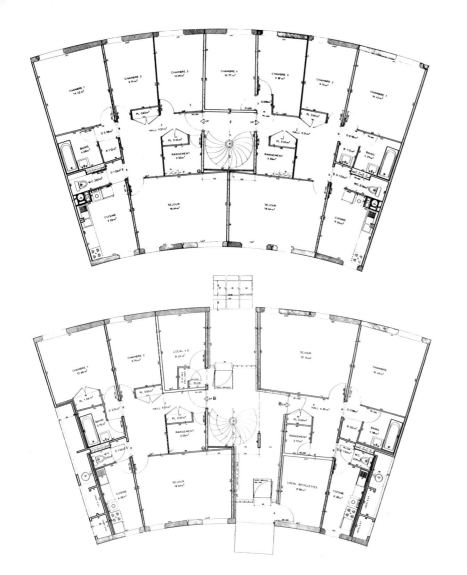

Frankreich nahm die Charta von Athen ernst. Es nahm auch das industrialisierte Bauen ernst. Das Ergebnis waren – wie sich jedermann überzeugen kann – Zehntausende von Wohnungen (die grands ensembles), die fast alle gleich aussehen, und zwar so sehr, daß bei den Architekten in anderen europäischen Ländern der Begriff ›französischer Stil‹ heute mit schlechtem Geschmack und Häßlichkeit gleichgesetzt wird. Jetzt fangen aber die französische Regierung und andere an, die Dinge kritisch zu betrachten, und vielleicht ergibt sich eine Änderung. Einer der Protestrufe kam von dem Architekten Emile Aillaud und dem Maler F. Riéti, und dies in der wahrscheinlich besten Art, nämlich mit viel Humor. Zweifellos liegt ein gewisses boshaftes Vergnügen in ihrem Spiel mit dem industrialisierten Bauen, mit dem sie zeigen, wie man mit Witz, Phantasie, Kultur und Verständnis für die menschliche Natur den Wohnungsbau so gestalten kann, daß er Lebensfreude vermittelt. ›La Grande Borne‹, eine 90 ha große Siedlung mit einer Gesamtdichte von 40 Wohnungen je Hektar, ist so etwas wie eine große ständige Ausstellung geworden. Der optische Eindruck ist unvergeßlich. Für den, dem der Humor nicht langweilig wird, muß es dort hübsch zu wohnen sein. Wie alle Ausstellungen hat auch diese Siedlung einen Zug von Willkür und Oberflächlichkeit, aber das war der Preis für den Protest.

Der Hauptbereich in Form eines Dreiecks mit 1 km Seitenlänge ist von belebten Hauptstraßen und der ›Autoroute du Sud‹ umgeben. Zuerst hatte der Architekt nur zweigeschossige Häuser vorgesehen, damit alle Wohnungen unmittelbar von der Straße aus zu-

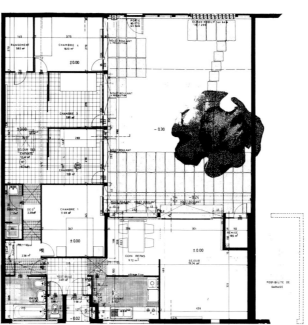

gänglich wären, doch dieser Entwurf schien für eine Bebauung dieser Größe, die in Wirklichkeit eine neue Stadt ist, nicht angemessen. So beschloß man, die Stockwerkszahl zu erhöhen und nachbarschaftliche Gruppen mit Eigencharakter zu schaffen. Die Parkplätze befinden sich am äußeren Rand und sind dicht mit Bäumen bepflanzt (zwei Bäume auf fünf Autos); so entstand eine optische und akustische Abschirmung gegen die umgebenden Autostraßen. Einige Parkplatzausläufer reichen in die Siedlung hinein, damit keine Wohnung mehr als 150 m von ihrem Parkplatz entfernt ist. Versorgungsstraßen bieten Zufahrt zu fast allen Eingängen.

Die Disziplin des industriellen Bauens einzuhalten, war für den Protest wesentlich. So wurden für die sieben nachbarschaftlichen Gruppen nur drei Wohnungstypen und drei Fensteröffnungen festgelegt. Drei Gruppen bestehen aus geschwungenen Gebäuden mit Fassaden aus glasiertem Mosaik (Le Labyrinthe, Le Méridien, Les Radars), weitere drei Gruppen aus geraden Gebäuden mit Fassaden aus buntfarbigen Fliesen (La Peupleraie, Les Tiroirs, La Ville Haute). Die siebte, außerhalb des Dreiecks liegende Gruppe setzt sich aus eingeschossigen L-förmigen Patio-Häusern zusammen.

Was uns ›La Grande Borne‹ zu sagen hat, ist klar: Solche Großbebauungen schließen Phantasie nicht aus; die Größe ist kein Hindernis für Eigencharakter und ein Ortsgefühl, das einer Gemeinschaft zur Identifikation verhelfen kann. Nicht so sehr die mit leichter Hand hingeworfene städtebauliche Komposition birgt das Geheimnis, sondern vielmehr die Einsicht, daß man auch für Pflasterungen, Bepflanzungen und andere ›Ausstattungen‹ von Straßen und Gärten Geld ausgeben muß. Die Wohnwelt ist für die geistige Gesundheit von ebenso großer Bedeutung wie die Sonne für die körperliche Gesundheit. Die Formen, die ›La Grande Borne‹ aufweist, sind exotisch, und niemand möchte sie zu häufig wiederholt sehen, aber sie lassen das Pendel von den phantasielosen ›grands ensembles‹ weit in die andere Richtung schwingen. Bei richtiger Verwendung braucht die Monotonie nicht langweilig zu sein; als Beweise aus jüngerer Zeit seien dafür Camerons Leningrad, Adams' Edinburgh oder sogar Berlages Amsterdam angeführt. Einförmigkeit an sich ist noch kein negativer Faktor.

5. Ground plan (above left: rounded blocks; below left: straight bocks; below right: patio houses).
6,7 Detailed views.

5. Grundrisse (oben links: geschwungene Blocks; unten links: gerade Blocks; unten rechts: Patio-Häuser).
6,7 Detailansichten.

Märkisches Viertel, West Berlin. 1962–72
Town-plan architects: Hans Müller, Georg Heinrichs and Werner Düttmann

Märkisches Viertel lies to the north of Berlin. Tegel is its natural shopping and civic centre. The site itself is bordered by two railway lines and the famous wall that separates the two Berlins. It was formerly occupied by small houses and allotments, and before planning began social workers and others took stock to see what should be left and what should be taken down, with the pre-determined intention of keeping part of the existing neighbourhood character. This sociological basis of the plan arose from the ambiguity of the sixties, and its confusion between 'closely packed urban images'– town planners smarting from the prairie failures of England's New Towns – and Jane Jacobs' polemic against the ruthless destruction of city soul and life by urban redevelopment. Müller, Heinrichs and Düttmann were culturally and politically conscious of their task. They looked to Germany's leading architects and even a few foreign ones as well, to ensure a high standard of design. They were obviously determined not to fail. A quick analysis of the neighbourhood plan (ill. 2) shows one main avenue that fits naturally into the city road network. The fact that it finishes right up against the wall is more a hopeful political gesture than a result of a self-contained plan. No rigid line defines the new neighbourhood, which is carefully grafted on to the old with fingers of new buildings stretching around the little boxes with their little gardens and backyards (ill. 1). A lineal park swings its way through the buildings, complete with lake and canals. The park is planned to link up with Tegel within the next two or three generations. A compact shopping centre with pedestrian squares and streets (ill. 5), next to some other service facilities, marks off the centre of gravity of the whole affair, heightened visually by the post-office that spans the main avenue (ill. 4). Every building had to be considered together with the space about it, which usually meant curved buildings forming backcloths to gardens and squares. Schools were naturally scattered about the site, and with advanced social thinking, not only were all the buildings to contain flats of various size, but old people's apartments of flatlets were also to be mixed with the families. Graphic artists were employed to ensure an overall colour scheme so that people could recognize where they were. As has already been said, density was not only a necessity but a philosophy. A real town-like hurdy-gurdy was to be produced to imitate the magic of metropolitan urban life (ills. 7, 8). For every square metre of land, 1.5 – 1 square metres of built floor area was to be allowed with a density of 390 inhabitants per hectare.

After looking at the plan, a visit to the neighbourhood confirms the simplicity of the road network: one is not lost, but somehow the roads bear little relationship to the restless

1. Aerial view.
2. General site plan. Key: AW, W housing; K1-K6, K9 shops; K7 workshops; K8 restaurant; K10 service station; K11 heating plant; S1-S7, S28, S29, S31, S33, S36 schools; S8-S13, S16, S21, S25, S30, S34 nursery schools; S15, S32 sports grounds; S18-S20, S27 parish centres; GE business area; GI industrial area.
3. Dwelling-group W3a (architect: Oswald Mathias Ungers).
4. View of the post office.
5. View of the main shopping-centre.

1. Luftaufnahme.
2. Gesamtlageplan. Legende: AW, W Wohngebäude; K1-K6, K9 Läden; K7 Handwerkerhof; K8 Restaurant; K10 Tankstelle; K11 Heizwerk; S1-S7, S28, S29, S31, S33, S36 Schulen; S8-S13, S16, S21, S25, S30, S34 Kindergärten; S15, S32 Sportanlagen; S18-S20, S27 kirchliche Gemeindezentren; GE Gewerbegebiet; GI Industriegebiet.
3. Gebäudegruppe W3a (Architekt: Oswald Mathias Ungers).
4. Blick auf das Postamt.
5. Blick auf das Hauptgeschäftszentrum.

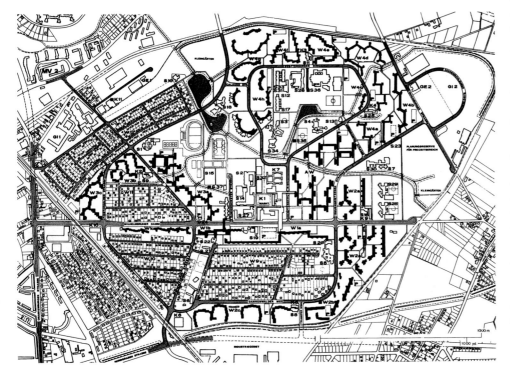

buildings that twist and turn and jump up and down like clowns in a circus. But unlike Charlie Rivel there is little to laugh at. The huge high flats all go through their acts with a precision that defies reason and humanity. Märkisches Viertel is like an enormous continuation of the 1957 Hansaviertel Interbau, like a symbol of the diversity of modern technology that pretends to be free and spontaneous. The sociologists and critics are quick to say that it works better than other developments, but it is hardly a place where one would want to live. What went wrong when all the apparent precautions were taken? Märkisches Viertel aimed high and built high. But the result is a loose emptiness that degenerates into ugliness, and is made worse by the fact that it represents the failure of a noble attempt. There is much to learn in Märkisches Viertel.

The sources of ugliness are buildings that float away from the street, still too low a density and too-high buildings too far apart, and lack of money for quality finishings. Above all, however, the design fails because of the lack of an imaginative geometrical spatial organization that could have given the neighbourhood a proud sense of grandeur and beauty. A collection of good ideas is no substitute for a Cerdà, a Soria, or Baron Haussmann, or a town plan such as at Rotterdam, Bath, Karlsruhe or Philadelphia. The one and only failure of Märkisches Viertel is architectural. Good, honest professionalism is no substitute for genial poetic creation, and 50,000 people need beauty for their dignity. But neither Berlin nor the epoch we live in is prepared to give it. Time, economy, and consumer ideals tangle the path with weeds so thick that not even the artist believes in himself anymore. Until the schools teach the value of beauty, until the trade unions fight for the workers' right to it, architecture will fail to provide it because it was never asked.

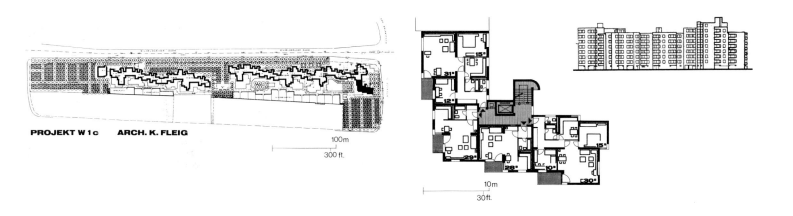

PROJEKT W 1 c   ARCH. K. FLEIG

100m
300 ft.

10m
30 ft.

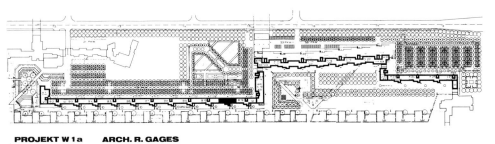

PROJEKT W 1 a   ARCH. R. GAGES

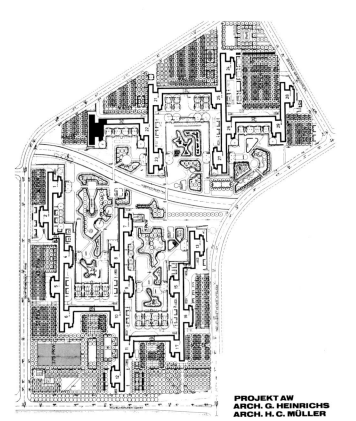

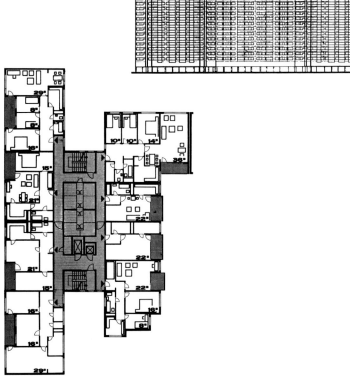

**PROJEKT AW
ARCH. G. HEINRICHS
ARCH. H. C. MÜLLER**

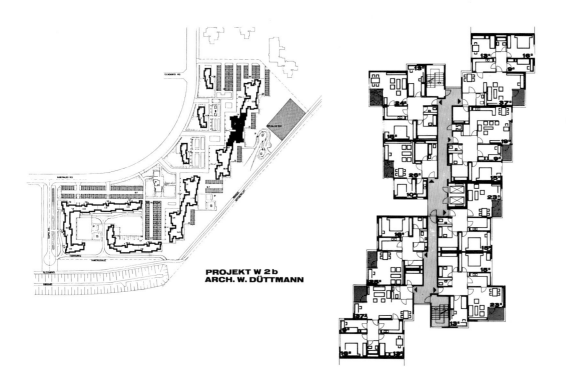

PROJEKT W 2 b
ARCH. W. DÜTTMANN

6. Plans of different dwelling-groups (site plan, ground-plan, detail, sectional detail; the project numbers refer to the general site plan on page 146).

6. Pläne verschiedener Wohnhausgruppen (Lageplan, Teilgrundriß, Teilansicht; die Projektnummern beziehen sich auf den Gesamtlageplan auf S. 146).

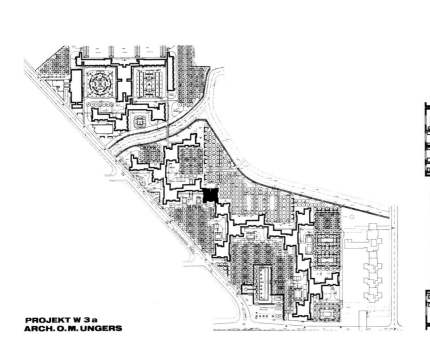

PROJEKT W 3 a
ARCH. O. M. UNGERS

7,8. Dwelling-group W2a (architect:
Ernst Gisel).
9,10. Threshold areas.

7,8. Gebäudegruppe W2a (Architekt:
Ernst Gisel).
9,10. Schwellenzonen.

Märkisches Viertel, Berlin. 1962-72
Stadtplaner: Hans Müller, Georg Heinrichs und Werner Düttmann

Das Märkische Viertel liegt im Norden Berlins. Tegel ist sein natürliches Einkaufs- und Stadtzentrum. Das Gelände wird von zwei Eisenbahnlinien und der Berliner Mauer begrenzt. Früher fand man dort nur kleine Häuser und Schrebergärten, und ehe die Planung begann, machte man eine Bestandsaufnahme, um festzustellen, was beibehalten und was abgerissen werden sollte, wobei man die Absicht hatte, den bestehenden nachbarschaftlichen Charakter wenigstens teilweise zu wahren. Die soziologische Basis des Plans entstammte der Ambiguität der sechziger Jahre zwischen ›urbaner Verdichtung‹ (die Stadtplaner bereuten die Prärie-Mißerfolge der neuen Städte Englands) und rücksichtsloser, lebenzerstörender Stadtsanierung, gegen die sich besonders Jane Jacobs wandte. Müller, Heinrichs und Düttmann waren sich ihrer kulturellen und politischen Aufgabe durchaus bewußt. Um einen hohen Entwurfsstandard zu gewährleisten, zogen sie die führenden deutschen und auch einige ausländische Architekten heran. Sie waren nicht gesonnen, einen Fehlschlag zu riskieren. Ein erster Blick auf den Übersichtsplan (Abb. 2) zeigt eine Hauptachse, die sich natürlich in das städtische Straßensystem einfügt. Daß sie auf die Mauer zuläuft, ist mehr eine politische Geste der Hoffnung als das Ergebnis eines in sich schlüssigen Plans. Das neue Viertel ist nicht von einer starren Linie begrenzt; es ist vielmehr sorgsam auf das bestehende Gefüge aufgepropft (Abb. 1). Wie Finger erstrecken sich neue Gebäude um die Häuschen mit ihren Gärtchen. In die Anlage eingebettet ist ein kleiner Park mit Seen und Kanälen; er soll innerhalb der nächsten zwei oder drei Generationen bis Tegel weitergeführt werden. Ein kompaktes Einkaufszentrum mit Fußgängerplätzen und -straßen (Abb. 5) bildet zusammen mit einigen weiteren Dienstleistungseinrichtungen den Schwerpunkt des Ganzen, optisch herausgehoben durch das die Hauptachse überspannende Postamt (Abb. 4). Jedes Gebäude war mit dem umgebenden Raum zusammen zu sehen; das bedeutet meist, daß gekröpfte Bauten den Hintergrund für Grünanlagen und Plätze abgeben. Schulen wurden im ganzen Viertel verteilt. Einem fortgeschrittenen Sozialdenken zufolge mußten nicht nur alle Gebäude mit Wohnungen in verschiedenen Größen ausgestattet, sondern auch Ein- oder Mehrzimmerwohnungen für ältere Menschen zwischen den Familienwohnungen angeordnet werden. Künstler wurden beauftragt, einen Farbenplan zu entwickeln, damit sich die Menschen zurechtfinden können. Wie bereits erwähnt, war Dichte nicht nur eine Notwendigkeit, sondern auch eine Philosophie. Es wurde ein echtes Stadtbild angestrebt, um den Zauber des Großstadtlebens einzufangen (Abb. 7, 8). Pro Quadratmeter Gelände wurde eine bebaute Fläche von 1,5 bis 1,2 m^2 vorgesehen bei einer Dichte von 390 Personen je Hektar.

Wie beim Blick auf den Übersichtsplan, so springt auch bei einem Besuch im Märkischen Viertel die Einfachheit des Straßennetzes ins Auge; man verirrt sich zwar nicht, aber irgendwie sind die Straßen kaum auf die ruhelosen Gebäude bezogen, die sich drehen und wenden und auf- und niederspringen wie Clowns im Zirkus. Doch anders als bei Charlie Rivel gibt es hier kaum etwas zu lachen. Die großen, hohen Bauten spielen ihre Rolle mit einer Präzision, die der Vernunft und Menschlichkeit zuwiderläuft. Das Märkische Viertel erscheint wie eine riesige Fortsetzung der Interbau von 1957, wie ein Symbol für die Vielseitigkeit moderner Technologie, die angeblich frei und spontan ist. Soziologen und Kritiker bringen vor, es bewähre sich besser als andere Siedlungen, und doch ist es kaum der Ort, an dem man wohnen möchte. Was ging schief, nachdem doch offenbar alle Vorsichtsmaßnahmen ergriffen worden waren?

Das Märkische Viertel steckte sich ein hohes Ziel und baute hoch. Das Ergebnis aber zeigt eine gewisse Leere, eine sich auf die Seele schlagende Häßlichkeit; dies ist um so betrüblicher, als es sich hier um den Fehlschlag eines großmütigen Versuchs handelt. Am Märkischen Viertel kann man vieles lernen.

Ursachen der Häßlichkeit sind das Zurückweichen der Gebäude von der Straße, die zu geringe Dichte bei zu weit auseinanderstehenden, zu hohen Gebäuden und das fehlende Geld für eine qualitätsmäßig einwandfreie Bauausführung, vor allem aber ein Mangel an imaginativer geometrischer Organisation der Gesamtanlage, die das stolze Gefühl der Größe und Schönheit nicht aufkommen läßt. Eine Ansammlung guter Ideen ist kein Ersatz für einen Cerdà, einen Soria oder einen Baron Haussmann, ebensowenig für Stadtpläne wie die von Rotterdam, Bath, Karlsruhe oder Philadelphia. Der Mißerfolg des Märkischen Viertels beruht einzig und allein auf der Architektur. Berufliche Könnerschaft ist kein Ersatz für geniales, poetisches Schaffensvermögen, und die 50 000 Menschen, die dort wohnen sollen, brauchen Schönheit für ein würdevolles Dasein. Doch weder Berlin noch die Zeit, in der wir leben, kann sie ihnen geben. Zeit, Kosten und Verbrauchervorstellungen bilden ein Dickicht auf dem Weg, und nicht einmal der Künstler vermag mehr an sich selbst zu glauben. Wenn nicht die Schulen den Wert der Schönheit lehren, wenn nicht die Gewerkschaften um das Anrecht der Arbeiter auf Schönheit kämpfen, wird die Architektur sie nicht bieten können, weil nie nach ihr gefragt wurde.

Thamesmead, London. Since 1966

Architects: Greater London Council, Department of Architecture and Civic Design

Thamesmead is neither a New Town nor a large estate, but a new district within an existing urban fabric. It thus has the benefits of existing transport connections and a physical built containment that is larger than the area itself. The other obvious advantage of Thamesmead, which the planners, architects and others involved have been quick to seize, is the meandering presence of the River Thames to the North. The immense scale of this flat cold windswept landscape with its flood dykes and banks has inspired the imagination of the whole development. The town centre with its large yacht basin will be a regional primary attraction that will draw in a transient population from the rest of London – just as Hyde Park, Hampstead Heath or the Earls Court exhibitions do in other districts. From this yacht basin canals will connect with other lakes that will play in with the nautical air that the whole development must, because of its location, breathe.

The main feature of the town is an immense, high-density lineal terrace about three miles long, which branches into two one-mile spurs to the east (ill. 2). At the centre, near the branch, and at rightangles to this terrace and the river, is the half-mile-long town-centre that from the model reminds one of Cumbernauld. The terrace both encloses various urban spaces with low-rise high-density housing neighbourhoods (between 1,500 and 2,000 dwellings), and visually connects these places with the next and so on, until either the centre or the existing communities of Woolwich or Abbey Wood are reached.

The site is intruded upon by the cross-Thames motorway that will eventually connect the Port of London with the south-east-region airports. This motorway will have an interchange with an east-west 'spine' road that will connect it with Woolwich and Erith as well as the Thamesmead centre. These major roads run independently of the interior roads of the new town, which connect with the existing neighbourhood network such as the north-south Harrow Manor Way from Abbey Wood station, and the east-west Eynsham Drive which runs into Yarnton Way, cutting through the middle of the housing communities that have actually been built (stages I and II).

Rail transport runs across the south, almost touching the extreme ends of the lineal terraces; Plumstead and Abbey Wood are the stations for commuters to the City and West End.

That 35 per cent of the housing will be privately developed for speculation, under some control of the public authorities, is an interesting practical move by which the growth of a varied community is hoped to be encouraged. It is interesting to note that the experience to date indicates an occupancy rate of only 0.55 – 0.7 persons per habitable room in the private sector. This means that the density of the private sector is lower than that at first planned for, which, if the ratio of 35 per cent is to be maintained, has forced the original target population of 60,000 to be cut to somewhere around 45,000. To maintain the densities required to support the costly urban infrastructure the ratio of 5 acres of open space per 1,000 population has had to be cut to 4 acres. The quality of the open spaces, with boating lakes and the Thames to the north and Abbey Woods park to the south, is thought to compensate for this. The construction time schedule, regulated by the heavy engineering works necessary for flood protection and the Thames tunnel motorway connection, is for the housing to be completed within 16 years. The acute labour shortage led to the decision to use an industrialized system of prefabrication. The lowest tender using the French Balency system (heavy precast walls, in-situ floor slabs) was accepted and the capital costs of the site factory will be absorbed in the first 4,000 dwellings. The cheap site costs have been offset by the difficult foundation problems (piles have been used throughout) and drainage (the site is below high-tide level). Because of the low level of the site the local bye-laws forbade habitable rooms on the ground floor. This also added to the construction costs.

The image of the urban street has been the basic architectural concept of Thamesmead –

one should perhaps say the image of the high street with all the other alleys, squares and precincts leading off it. As in Le Corbusier's 'Project Shrapnel' for Algiers, and Quaroni's winning design for St Giuliano near Venice, the bending building-street is used on the model with great effect (ill. 1). The architects claim that these 'walls' shield the lower housing and public spaces from the east winds that blow in from the North Sea. The argument about wind barriers loses credibility when one visits the first group of dwellings (stage I ill. 3) for the building street lies to the west of the lower buildings. Why, one asks moreover, did they build tower blocks along Yarnton Way and Hartslock Drive that are inconsistent with the original idea and are also a rather violent break in scale with the rest of the buildings (ill. 5). The lineal street building itself got off to a bad start with its romantic break-up of the volume – hankering after traditional effects of growth that Habraken calls 'apeing spontaneity with impulsive imaginative guesses'. Fortunately, economics and production methods have turned the north-south terraces of the stage II area into what must be one of the finest examples of town architecture at the right scale since Nash. The great artificial earth 'mole' that faces this terrace sets off the whole architectural effect wonderfully, while the pedestrian is kept a reasonable distance away and at such a height that he seems to look down into the buildings. The terraces are

broken at either 50-metre or 60-metre intervals, which helps to assimilate the whole visually and prevents simple monotony.

The three-storey housing groups built around common patios are strongly designed and allow the occupiers to add on their own popular decorative bits and pieces as well as the washing on the line.

The small shopping area just south of the lake (South Mere) is a real bit of repulsive suburban jerry-building (ill. 8). It is incredible that such an opportunity to design a place well should be lost, given the generally high level of design everywhere else. The proportion of the paved platform in relation to the height of the shops is completely wrong and there is no protection from the wind that blows in from the nearby lake. The health centre over the lake is also depressingly naive.

Generally, however, one has the feeling as one walks around the courts, along the pedestrian deck, and even more so along the 'mole' that divides stage I from stage II, that Thamesmead has character, personality, and, such are its connections with the rest of London, history too.

1. General site plan.
2. Model.

1. Gesamtlageplan.
2. Modell.

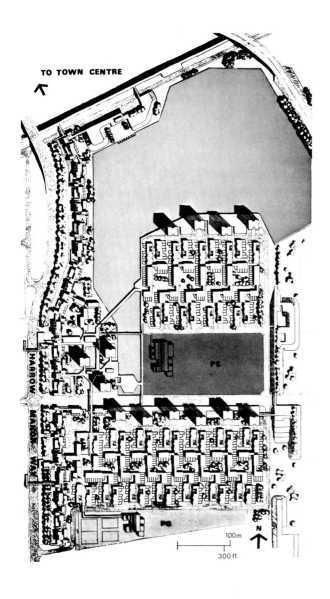

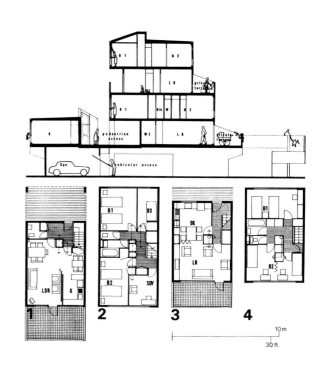

3. Site plan of stage 1.
4. Plans of different house types in stage 1 (three-storey row houses and street building).

3. Lageplan des 1. Bauabschnitts.
4. Pläne verschiedener Haustypen des
1. Bauabschnitts (dreigeschossige Reihen-häuser und lineares Straßengebäude).

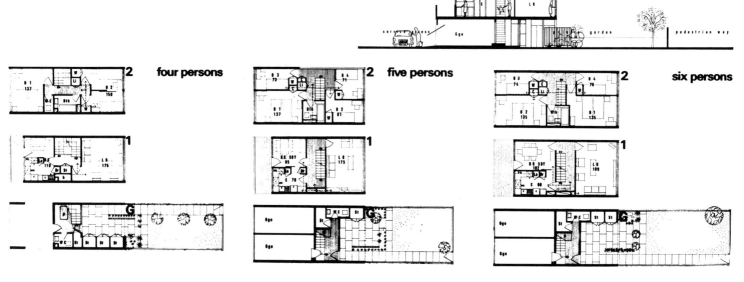

four persons

five persons

six persons

Thamesmead, London. Seit 1966
Architekten: Greater London Council, Department of Architecture and Civic Design

Thamesmead ist weder eine neue Stadt noch eine Großsiedlung, sondern ein neues Viertel innerhalb eines bestehenden Stadtgefüges und genießt somit die Vorzüge der vorhandenen Verkehrsverbindungen und eines größeren baulichen Zusammenhangs. Der weitere offenkundige Vorteil von Thamesmead, den Planer, Architekten und andere Beteiligte rasch erkannten, ist die Themse, die sich im Norden vorbeiwindet. Der ungeheure Maßstab der flachen, kalten, windigen Landschaft mit ihren Flutdämmen und Uferbänken gab dem Entwurf sein unverwechselbares Gepräge. Das Stadtzentrum mit dem großen Jachthafen gilt als lokale Attraktion erster Ordnung, die viele Besucher aus ganz London anziehen wird, ähnlich wie der Hyde Park, Hampstead Heath oder die Earls-Court-Ausstellungen in anderen Stadtbezirken. Von diesem Jachthafen verlaufen Kanäle zu zurückliegenden Seen, so daß die ganze Anlage das nautische Flair erhält, das sie wegen ihrer Lage haben muß.
Hauptmerkmal des Viertels ist eine hochverdichtete lineare Terrasse mit einer Länge von etwa 5 km, die sich nach Osten in zwei 1,5 km lange Ausläufer verzweigt (Abb. 2). In der Mitte, nahe bei der Verzweigung und im rechten Winkel zu dieser Terrasse und zum Fluß, befindet sich das 800 m lange Stadtzentrum, das im Modell an Cumbernauld erinnert. Die Terrasse umschließt verschiedene Stadträume mit niedrigen, sehr dichten Nachbarschaften (zwischen 1500 und 2000 Wohnungen) und stellt zugleich die optische Verbindung zwischen diesen Räumen, dem Zentrum sowie den bestehenden Bezirken Woolwich und Abbey Wood her.
Das Gelände wird durchschnitten von der die Themse unterquerenden Schnellstraße, die später den Londoner Hafen mit den Flughäfen der südöstlichen Region verbinden wird. Diese verknotet sich mit einer in Ost-West-Richtung verlaufenden Straße, die die Verbindung zu Woolwich und Erith wie auch zum Zentrum von Thamesmead bildet. Die beiden Hauptstraßen verlaufen unabhängig von den internen Straßen der neuen Stadt, die an das bestehende umliegende Straßennetz angeschlossen werden, so an den in Nord-Süd-Richtung verlaufenden, vom Bahnhof von Abbey Wood herkommenden Harrow Manor Way und an den ost-westlichen Eynsham Drive, der in den Yarnton Way mündet; dieser wiederum durchquert die schon erbauten Wohnhauskomplexe (Abschnitte I und II).
Der Schienenverkehr läuft im Süden quer vorbei und berührt mit den Bahnhöfen von Plumstead und Abbey Wood, die dem Pendlerverkehr zur City und zum West End dienen, beinahe die äußersten Enden der Terrassen.
35 % der Wohnungen werden unter geringer Kontrolle der Behörden von privaten Bauherren für den freien Wohnungsmarkt errichtet; dies ist ein interessanter Versuch, das Wachstum eines gemischten Gemeinwesens zu fördern. Nach bisheriger Erfahrung beträgt die Belegung im privaten Sektor nur 0,55 bis 0,7 Personen pro bewohnbarem Raum und im öffentlichen Sektor 1 Person pro bewohnbarem Raum. Die Wohndichte im privaten Sektor ist also geringer als geplant, und wenn der Satz von 35 % beibehalten werden soll, wird sich die ursprünglich anvisierte Gesamteinwohnerzahl von 60 000 auf 40 000 reduzieren. Um die für die kostspielige städtische Infrastruktur notwendigen Dichten zu halten, muß daher das Freilandangebot je 1 000 Einwohner von 2 ha auf 1,6 ha gesenkt werden. Man glaubt, daß dies durch die Qualität des Freiraums – Seen mit Bootsbetrieb, die Themse im Norden, der Park Abbey Woods im Süden – ausgeglichen wird.
Der Zeitplan mußte die umfangreichen, zur Absicherung gegen Überschwemmungen notwendigen Bauarbeiten und den Straßentunnel unter der Themse berücksichtigen und sieht die Fertigstellung des Viertels innerhalb von 16 Jahren vor. Der akute Mangel an Arbeitskräften führte zu dem Entschluß, ein industrialisiertes Vorfertigungssystem zu verwenden. Gewählt wurde das im Angebot günstigste französische Balency-System, das mit schweren vorgefertigten Wänden und Ortbetondecken arbeitet. Die Kapitalkosten der Bauplatzfabrik wurden den ersten 4000 Wohnungen zugeschlagen. Der Bauplatz war zwar billig, aber die schwierigen Probleme der Gründung (es mußte durchweg unterpfählt werden) und der Drainage (das Gelände liegt unter Flutniveau) machten diesen Vorteil wieder zunichte. Wegen des niedrigen Niveaus des Geländes durften im Erdgeschoß keine bewohnten Räume vorgesehen werden. Auch dadurch erhöhten sich die Baukosten.
Der Ausgangspunkt für das architektonische Grundkonzept von Thamesmead war die Idee der städtischen Straße oder vielmehr der städtischen Hauptstraße, auf die alle Wege, Plätze und Bereiche bezogen sind. Wie bei Le Corbusiers ›Shrapnel-Projekt‹ für Algier und bei Quaronis preisgekröntem Entwurf für San Giuliano bei Venedig macht die gebogene Gebäudestraße im Modell einen guten Eindruck (Abb. 1). Die Urheber behaupten, diese ›Wände‹ schützten die niedrigeren Bauten und öffentlichen Plätze vor den Ostwinden der Nordsee. Das Argument der Windbarriere verliert jedoch an Glaubwürdigkeit, wenn man die erste Gebäudegruppe (Abschnitt I; Abb. 3) besichtigt, denn die Gebäudestraße liegt hier westlich von den niedrigeren Gebäuden. Außerdem muß man sich fragen, warum am Yarnton Way und Hartslock Drive Turmblocks gebaut wurden, die sich nicht mit der Gesamtkonzeption vereinbaren lassen und die darüber hinaus einen maßstäblichen Bruch gegenüber den übrigen Gebäuden darstellen (Abb. 5). Das lineare Straßengebäude selbst machte einen schlechten Anfang mit dem romantischen Aufbrechen des Volumens (Abb. 6). Man spürt die Sehnsucht nach traditionellen Wachstumseffekten, die Habraken ›ein Nachäffen der Spontaneität mit impulsiven, phantasiereichen Mutmaßungen‹ nennt. Glücklicherweise bewirkten wirtschaftliche und produktionstechnische Bedingungen, daß die Nord-Süd-Terrassen in Abschnitt II zu einem der besten Beispiele für den richtigen Maßstab der Stadtarchitektur seit Nash wurden (Abb. 7). Die gegenüberliegende große künstliche Erd-›Mole‹ bildet einen hervorragenden Kontrast zu dem ganzen städtebaulichen Ereignis; der Fußgänger wird in genügender Entfernung gehalten und befindet sich auf so großer Höhe, daß er auf die Gebäude hinunterzublicken scheint. Die Terrassen sind in Abständen von 50 oder 60 m unterbrochen, so daß das Ganze überschaubar wird und keine Monotonie auftritt.
Die dreigeschossigen Häusergruppen, die um gemeinsame Patios angeordnet sind, haben kraftvolle Formen, die ohne weiteres dies und jenes an den landläufigen Zutaten der Bewohner sowie auch die Wäsche auf der Leine vertragen.
Der kleine Einkaufsbereich südlich des Sees (South Mere) ist ein Stück abstoßender vorstädtischer Bruchbudenarchitektur (Abb. 8). Es ist kaum zu glauben, daß eine derartige Gelegenheit zur Gestaltung eines Platzes bei dem sonst überall hohen Entwurfsniveau versäumt wurde. Die Proportionen zwischen der gepflasterten Plattform und der Ladenhöhe sind völlig mißglückt, und es gibt keinen Schutz vor dem Wind, der von dem nahen See herüberweht. Das Gesundheitszentrum am anderen Ufer des Sees ist ebenfalls bedrückend naiv.
Wenn man aber in den Höfen, auf dem Fußgängerdeck und besonders auf der ›Mole‹, der Trennung zwischen den Abschnitten I und II, herumwandert, gewinnt man ganz allgemein den Eindruck, daß Thamesmead Charakter, Persönlichkeit und wegen seines Zusammenhangs mit London sogar Geschichte besitzt.

5. Blick auf die vier nördlichen Turmblocks
des 1. Bauabschnitts.
6. Blick über den Harrow Manor Way auf den
1. Bauabschnitt.
7. Blick entlang der Westseite des Straßen-
gebäudes im 1. Bauabschnitt.
8. Das Ladenzentrum des 1. Bauabschnitts.

Notes

[1] Masahiro Ono in *The Japan Architect* (Tokyo), 161 (February 1970), p. 37.

[2] N.J. Habraken, *Supports: An Alternative to Mass Housing,* London 1972.

[3] See Ruskin's *Unto this Last* (1862).

[4] *Wordsworth – Poetry and Prose,* selected by W.M. Merchant, London 1969.

[5] Lodovico Meneghetti in *Casabella* (Milan), 364 (April 1972), p. 21.

[6] Shozo Uchii, 'Sakura-dai Village, a new kind of living environment', *The Japan Architect* (Tokyo), 154 (July 1969), p. 89.

[7] Leslie B. Ginsburg, 'Summing up', *The Architectural Review* (London), 920 (October 1973), pp. 263–266.

[8] Peter Eisenman in *Architectural Design* (London), September 1972, pp. 557, 558.

[9] Kenneth Frampton, 'Twin Parks as Typology', *The Architectural Forum* (New York), 138, no. 5 (June 1973), pp. 56–60.

[10] Jane Jacobs, *The Death and Life of Great American Cities,* New York 1961.

[11] Cited in: Judith Chisholm, 'People v. Architects', *The Architect* (London), February 1972, pp. 48, 49.

Anmerkungen

[1] Masahiro Ono in *The Japan Architect* (Tokio), 161 (Februar 1970), S. 37.

[2] N. J. Habraken, *Supports: An Alternative to Mass Housing,* London 1972.

[3] Siehe Ruskins *Unto this Last* (1862).

[4] *Wordsworth – Poetry and Prose,* ausgewählt von W. M. Merchant, London 1969.

[5] Lodovico Meneghetti in *Casabella* (Mailand), 364 (April 1972), S. 21.

[6] Shozo Uchii, 'Sakura-dai Village, a new kind of living environment', *The Japan Architect* (Tokio), 154 (Juli 1969), S. 89.

[7] Leslie B. Ginsburg, 'Summing up', *The Architectural Review* (London), 920 (Oktober 1973), S. 263-266.

[8] Peter Eisenman in *Architectural Design* (London), September 1972, S. 557, 558.

[9] Kenneth Frampton, 'Twin Parks as Typology', *The Architectural Forum* (New York), 138, Nr. 5 (Juni 1973), S. 56-60.

[10] Jane Jacobs, *The Death and Life of Great American Cities,* New York 1961. (Deutsch: *Tod und Leben großer amerikanischer Städte,* Berlin, Frankfurt/M. und Wien 1963.)

[11] Zitiert in: Judith Chisholm, 'People v. Architects'. *The Architect* (London), Februar 1972, S. 48, 49.

Photo Credits/Fotonachweis

Numerals in brackets indicate illustration numbers
Die Zahlen in den Klammern verweisen auf Abbildungsnummern

Reyner Banham, *Theory and Design in the First Machine Age* 15 (43)
Leonardo Benevolo, *Storia dell'architettura moderna* 14 (36, 37, 38), 15 (39, 40), 16 (44, 45, 52), 22 (78, 80, 81, 82)
Boesiger/Girsberger, *Le Corbusier 1910–60* 18 (53, 54, 55, 56)
Hansmartin Bruckmann/David L. Lewis, *Neuer Wohnbau in England* 22 (83), 23 (88)
Trevor Dannatt, *Modern Architecture in Britain* 19 (59), 21 (76, 77)
Arthur Drexler, *The Drawings of Frank Lloyd Wright* 24 (90)
Karl Fleig, *Alvar Aalto* 25 (94)
S. Giedion, *Walter Gropius – Mensch und Werk* 19 (60)
Hans G. Helms/Jörn Janssen, *Kapitalistischer Städtebau* 17 (50)
The Japan Architect 30 (1), 31 (2,3), 32 (5, 6), 33 (7), 90 (1, 3), 91 (4, 5), 92 (7), 93 (10)
Ludwig Münz/Gustav Künstler, *Der Architekt Adolf Loos* 16 (46, 47)
Lewis Mumford, *The Culture of Cities* 21 (74)
Peter Pfankuch, *Hans Scharoun – Bauten, Entwürfe, Texte* 20 (66)
Rolf Rave/Hans-Joachim Knöfel, *Bauen seit 1900 in Berlin* 20 (69)
J. N. Tarn, *Working-class Housing in 19th-century Britain* 9 (7, 8, 9), 10 (10, 11, 12), 12 (22, 23)

Aerodan Luftfoto 130 (1)
Dorothy Alexander 122 (1), 123 (4)
Reiner Blunck 28 (5)
Rudolf Branko Senjor 34 (1), 35 (2), 37 (4, 5)
Brecht-Einzig Limited 127 (4, 5, 6), 128 (7, 8), 129 (9, 10), 135 (2, 3, 4), 137 (6), 140 (9, 10)
Balthasar Burkhard 58 (1, 2), 61 (12, 13)
F. Catalá Roca 42 (1, 2), 43 (3), 44 (4), 45 (5, 6, 7), 50 (1, 2, 3), 53 (6, 7, 8), 114 (1), 117 (9)
Reinhard Friedrich 146 (1)
Photoatelier Gerlach 17 (49, 51)
Ghizzoni di Scotti 15 (42)
Greater London Council 153 (2), 156 (5, 6)
Hedrich-Blessing 24 (89)
IPS 12 (28)
Roger Kaysel 63 (4)
E. Kossakowski 143 (3)
Carlo Leidi 41 (8)
Sandra Lousada 107 (3, 4, 5), 109 (8)
Donald Luckenbill 99 (2)
Mann Brothers 126 (2)
Norman McGrath 47 (2, 3), 49 (7)
Thilo Mechau 26 (1), 27 (3), 29 (7)
John Mills 141 (11, 12)
Joseph W. Molitor 101 (7)
David Moore 78 (1), 79 (2), 80 (4), 81 (5)
Jerry Morgenroth 49 (7)
Numay 84 (3)

Van Ojen 14 (35)
Publifoto 24 (92)
Deidi von Schaewen 115 (4)
Terrence Shaw 103 (2)
Ron Shuller 46 (1)
Hans Sibbelee 13 (31, 32)
Helmut Stahl 119 (3)
Ezra Stoller 122 (2), 124 (7)
Strüwing 21 (72), 23 (87), 110 (1), 111 (3, 5), 113 (8)
Wilfried Täubner 118 (1)
Gerhard Ullmann 20 (67, 68), 25 (93), 147 (3, 4, 5), 150 (7, 8), 151 (9, 10)